REMAR SUTTON'S
BODY
WORRY

Also by Remar Sutton
DON'T GET TAKEN EVERY TIME

REMAR SUTTON'S

BODY
WORRY

BY REMAR SUTTON

VIKING

VIKING
Viking Penguin Inc., 40 West 23rd Street,
New York, New York 10010, U.S.A.
Penguin Books Ltd, Harmondsworth,
Middlesex, England
Penguin Books Australia Ltd, Ringwood,
Victoria, Australia
Penguin Books Canada Limited, 2801 John Street,
Markham, Ontario, Canada L3R 1B4
Penguin Books (N.Z.) Ltd, 182–190 Wairau Road,
Auckland 10, New Zealand

First published in 1987 by Viking Penguin Inc.
Published simultaneously in Canada

All photographs, unless otherwise indicated,
are by Will and Deni McIntyre.
Copyright © Will and Deni McIntyre, 1987.

LIBRARY OF CONGRESS CATALOGING IN PUBLICATION DATA
Sutton, Remar.
Remar Sutton's body worry.
Includes index.
1. Health.   2. Physical fitness.   3. Body image.
I. Title.   II. Title: Body worry.
RA776.S945   1987   613.2   86-40353
ISBN 0-670-81653-1

Printed by
R. R. Donnelley & Sons, Harrisonburg, Virginia
Set in Aster
Designed by Beth Tondreau

To 603 and G.A.P.
To M.A. and M.M.
And to N.L.

A C K N O W L E D G M E N T S

Before I started my remake, I knew as much about hunkdom, health and fitness as I know about the moon. And I am not an astronomer.

Hundreds of people, therefore, needed to educate me, if my experience was to be valuable for others. I can't name them all here, but would like particularly to thank these.

Christopher Scott and Dr. Mary Abbott Waite are my two fellow members of the Body Worry Team. Chris Scott's knowledge and research skills in the medical and physiology fields are the reason this book is, I hope, an unusually complete layman's guide. Dr. Waite, my friend, personal editorial adviser, and partner in most endeavors, researched, organized and edited the enormous amounts of information in the narrative and discussion portions of this book. Mary Abbott makes writing a joy for me. *Body Worry* would not be a book without these two people, and I am thankful for them and look forward to working with them on other books.

Margaret Mason, then the Style Plus editor at the *Washington Post*, believed in my year before anyone else in the media found it interesting. The power of that paper, and therefore the impact of her decision, have in many ways changed my life. Since Margaret has retired, Peggy Hackman and the rest of the Style Plus staff have been as helpful to me.

As has Tracy Brown, my editor at Viking Penguin. Tracy has fought many battles for me.

Thomas P. Rosandich, Ph.D., president and founder of the United States Sports Academy, advised me on the structure and make-up of my Body Worry Committee. Tom's enthusiasm for my idea kept my enthusiasm high when others weren't so encouraging. His contacts, and the help of the Academy, were invaluable.

Dr. Kenneth Cooper, president and founder of the Aerobics Center in Dallas, has provided me constant advice, testing and access to his medical and sports associates throughout the year. Dr. Arno Jensen, Pamela Neff, Georgia Kostas, and Kia Vaandrager all worked with the Body Worry Team virtually weekly. Dr. Cooper, Dr. Jensen, and Georgia Kostas, M.P.H., R.D., L.D., director of the Aerobics Center nutrition program, also spent hours reviewing this manuscript, and all improved it. Kia Vaandrager, her daughter Kiki, and her husband, Dr. Johan Vaandrager, have gathered more research papers and answered more of Christopher Scott's questions than I think *they* want to know!

Gideon Ariel, Ph.D., LaVon Johnson, Ph.D., and Robert Stauffer, Ph.D., all worked with me, thanks to Tom Rosandich. Gideon Ariel has advised me on my weight lifting goals and techniques, and has also been a valuable source on many matters. Spending a weekend with him is like spending the weekend with a rocket—brilliant! Von Johnson, at that time Chairman of the Department of Fitness Management at the Sports Academy, both recommended Christopher Scott as my physiologist and planned portions of my year's physical regimen. Bob Stauffer, a fellow of the American College of Sports Medicine, introduced me to Dr. Kenneth Cooper. During the entire project, Bob has guided me down the middle road in research, exercise, and hunkdom. The soundness of his advice is very evident in this book.

ACKNOWLEDGMENTS

Dr. Robert Bell, at the very beginning of my planning, encouraged me to make my year a search for health and then hunkdom. I didn't want to listen to him at first, but I owe him thanks for his insistence. Bob's testing, advice, and suggestions on this manuscript were all important to me.

David Heber, M.D., Ph.D., Chief of the Division of Clinical Nutrition at UCLA's School of Medicine, answered many questions for both Chris and me. Dr. Art Leon at the University of Minnesota shared his considerable epidemiological knowledge with Chris; Michael Pollock, Ph.D., an internationally noted exercise physiologist, talked with us several times from his offices at the University of Florida. Dr. Herbert deVries, a noted authority on exercise and aging, advised us on our comments and opinions on those topics.

Eric Goldstein, Ph.D., shared with us his insights on stress. He is a stress management specialist in Miami. Dr. Frank M. Kamer raised my opinion of plastic surgeons. When I visited his very upscale practice in Beverly Hills, he recommended against surgery for me. How long since a doctor has sent you away?

William T. Jarvis, Ph.D., taught me a lot about quacks. He is President of the National Council Against Health Fraud, and a Professor of Health Education at Loma Linda University. Dick Clark, Clinical Director of the Hyperbaric Center at Richland Memorial Hospital, gave me a first-hand education in hyperbaric medicine, and I am thankful for him.

David Prowse, both in London and in the Bahamas, has taken a great interest in my year. His advice on weight lifting techniques and strength-building exercises has contributed a lot toward my remake.

Former Mr. Universe Tony Pearson not only helped me with my weight lifting routine, he allowed me the great fantasy of kicking sand vaguely in his direction at muscle beach, as did Champ McGregor and Debra Walker. Mike Christian, Mr. Universe 1985, brought me back to earth when he showed me his routine *and* his right bicep. Do not compare right biceps with him.

Russell Burd, my trainer, has done the most to actually change my body. Russ had the terrible chore of getting me to the gym six days a week, for months on end. His patience and skill as a trainer in working with me made these days nearly pleasurable. Russ and Kim, his wife, are now back in Perkiomenville, Pennsylvania, and I look forward to the day they open their own gym. I would like to work out there.

Until that time, I work out most often with Bill and Marilynn Carle at the Grand Bahama YMCA. Neither Bill nor Marilynn, owners and managers of the gym, has ever laughed at my weight lifting efforts, and that in itself endears them to me. Dr. John Clement, my island doctor, both doctored my weight lifting ills and my spirits. He makes a great neighbor. Doc was even a part of the Body Worry aerobics class. Lauren Hunt-Manning, now living in Taiwan, ran that class for me, and all of us alumni would like her back: Warren Manning, Gerry Matt, Judy Graham, Bill Nelson, Joan Munnings, Pam Ferguson, Keith Thompson, Sarah Lihou, Kim and Russell Burd, plus Ricky and Doc. Thanks to you all for participating.

John Englander, president of The Underwater Explorer's Society, didn't ever exercise with us, but he did keep my brain working. He has been a good sounding board for me during the year, and also spent many hours reading this manuscript for accuracy. Will and Deni McIntyre *did* exercise with us, and did about everything else with me, too, as they took over 18,000 photographs of me during the months.

Hunkdom and health don't mean much without the right people to share them. My right people include my family: Mom, brother George and his family, Bunny and Buck, Peggy, and all the cousins and friends in Swainsboro and Marietta.

Chris Scott wouldn't have made it through the year without the help of Debbie and Bob Spusta, John Sheetz, Tom Sekeres, Keith Markolf, Michele Coyne, and Jonathan Scott, Chris's identical twin brother. I do not think the world is ready for two.

Dean Huthmacher and Phil Frieder at American Computer and Communications in Riverdale, Georgia kept my three computers humming across the Bahamian waters, for which I thank them heartily.

I wouldn't have made it through the year without all of the people listed in these pages, and thank them all from the top to the bottom of my healthy and semi-hunky body.

Because in many instances I have provided my own interpretation of others' works and thoughts, I, of course, am solely responsible should those interpretations or any fact be in error. Since I'm pretty strong now, though, I wouldn't pick a fight with me. Muscles and health.

C O N T E N T S

CONTENTS

REMAR SUTTON'S

BODY
WORRY

CHAPTER

I

RAW MATERIAL

I

Week 1
Grand Bahama Island

I can look out the window and see the ocean, a calm one, and a shimmering red Bahamian sun breaking through scarlet clouds scattered low along the horizon, like in the movies. A very nice day to start, I think.

I am a forty-five-year-old man without muscles, bald, twenty-seven pounds overweight, no longer involved in much physical activity, somewhat self-conscious about my looks, and even more self-conscious about the thought of trying to improve them within smirking range of those god types who were born fit, don't sweat, and seem to be everywhere I am when vanity prods me to the thought of exercise.

In June 1985, I decided it would be nice to chuck it all and spend a year devoted solely to making myself handsome. By November, even my publisher seemed to be intrigued with the idea. What could you do to a middle-aged body in a year? By December, we had come to terms—a milestone, I might add. It takes a lot of money and discipline to chuck it all, hire a full-

1

time trainer, move to an island, recruit a fancy committee of medical, strength, and fitness experts, build lots of muscles, turn a watermelon belly into a sexy, flat stomach, perhaps add hair, maybe even have a face-lift, and in the process report on the good and bad things out there in the fitness and male hunkiness world. I was game, though.

I planned a partial nod to health during the year, but the plans that really interested me centered around looks. I wanted to see some muscles on my body and some lust in the eyes of a tropical beauty or two much more than I wanted to feel healthier. I felt fine, anyway. Most people are a little overweight and get a little tired and a lot of people used to smoke and still drink regularly. Besides, I used to jog forty miles a week until 1981.

About the time I was packing my full-length mirror for the trip to the islands, the results from my physical exams began to come in. The first doctor to call was a friend, Dr. Bob Bell, and I knew him well enough to know that a cough and slight stutter before he speaks means that bad news is coming. It did.

"Remar, I'm afraid you're not as well as you think." He paused. I remember the pause very well and don't know how to describe its feeling other than lonely. "I'm afraid you have some heart disease."

What was this man talking about? I wanted to be a hunk, not worry about my health. Even before I could try to hide from his words, Dr. Bell emphasized them with specifics. The thallium stress test and first-pass radionuclide angiogram showed that I have mild coronary heart disease: mild left ventricular dysfunction. Reduced left ventricular ejection fraction; drop in the stroke volume; abnormality on the front and back walls of the left ventricle. The possible causes? Probably the result of too little exercise, too many cigarettes, and those extra pounds. Another test showed that I have a small pulmonary dysfunction. The cigarettes I enjoyed for so long, of course. A final test showed that one of my liver functions is abnormal.

None of these unpleasant bits of information, incidentally, would show up during the normal yearly physical you may undergo, even if you have a stress EKG and standard bloodwork.

2

I had three stress EKGs, and they were all normal. I hope that's an unnerving thought for you but I am not complaining here. At least I know what is wrong with me. According to my good adviser Dr. Kenneth Cooper, the man who started America jogging, forty percent of people with coronary heart disease have only one symptom of that disease: death from a heart attack.

Well, if all of this wasn't enough to temporarily still my yearnings for a high lust factor, two other members of my medical team rated me in the high-risk category for heart attack, even though I don't have high blood pressure, exercise more than the majority of people, and haven't been a smoker in over a year. The extra pounds and lack of meaningful exercise and my diet, too, are the culprits in their minds.

Dr. Von Johnson, Chairman of the Department of Fitness Management at the United States Sports Academy, tested my oxygen consumption per kilogram of weight, a measure of cardiovascular fitness. He did not comment on the results, but simply handed me a chart entitled "Risk Category" with my name at the top and a red circle around the fifth line from the bottom, the one labeled "very high."

Finally, Dr. Cooper, who had put me on another treadmill and poked and pried some more, said if I didn't change my ways, I could look forward to bypass surgery, developing angina pectoris, heart attack, or sudden death. Sudden death. I don't know why that sounded worse than death alone, but it did. Does sudden death mean there's no time for regrets? Does it hurt?

I dream a lot when things bother me, and my dream that night was of a very well-built Remar Sutton, dressed to show my muscles, laid out in a coffin.

I still want beauties to swoon when they glimpse the new me. But my year is going to be a more balanced one now. I have to make my insides as healthy as my outside will be hunky, a thought with some urgency in it. I want to understand more about my decline in health, too. In 1983, my hometown doctor rated me as a nearly "ideal" health profile. What happened?

Can you lose your health in two years? If you can, that's a damn scary thought for a lot of people.

It's 7:30 A.M. now. Before noon I'll have stretched for thirty minutes, walked for a good distance along a palm-fringed beach lined with half-naked people (most of them overweight), biked, and lifted weights for the first time in my life. By sunset I will have talked to a few of the doctors who are worrying over me more than I like, eaten fresh conch salad, drunk papaya juice, and probably flipped through a copy of a muscle magazine. I'm clipping pictures of sample muscles, sort of a hit list for the new surface me.

Doc Clement, my local doctor, lives across the backyard, even closer to the ocean. He checks on me nearly every day, more out of curiosity than concern, I believe.

I am not at all sure what is going to happen to me this year, but I do know it will not be a boring time. More later.

Muscles and health.

In January l986, when I wrote the above letter to a group of friends and media contacts, I had no idea of the interest my story (or my letters) would generate around the country. Letter writing runs in my family, and I simply hoped the recipients would enjoy a personal and very informal blow-by-blow account of my trials and triumphs, assuming there would be triumphs, just as I over the years had enjoyed many of their personal experiences via mail.

It perked me up quite a bit, therefore, when Margaret Mason from the *Washington Post* called and asked to run my letters as a bimonthly column. United Features Syndicate didn't exactly make me feel bad, either, when they asked to run versions of the letters in papers around the country. Because the letters have been so popular, I have used portions of them as the basis for many of the narrative sections of this book. Most of the time, the letters have been rewritten and expanded, and I think you will enjoy these more detailed versions.

Behind each narrative section are the really important parts of this book, the discussion portions. All of this material is new, and I think, the truly interesting part of the book. Apparently, I'm not the only one, for as I was writing it, this unusual family, how shall I say it? . . . "appeared"—Phil, Norma, and the kids. I don't know any way to describe Norma and Phil other than to say they're real nice folks but probably not the type you would want to sit by at your twenty-fifth high school reunion. Phil certainly sat down by my typewriter, however, and kept butting in, adding his body worry questions to mine. To my surprise, his persistent curiosity turned out to be a big plus as I explored myriad facts and issues of interest to body worriers.

If you exercise regularly, are careful about what you eat, don't abuse drugs (including alcohol and cigarettes), can still fit into your high school clothes, and are happy about your looks, please take this book back and buy something you need. Like a book on Tantric Yoga or something.

Remar Sutton's Body Worry is not for those who already lead the clean and godly life, those health nuts who are always trying to learn a new sport or sport a new diet. It's really a primer about health and fitness in general, revolving around the story of my own year-long quest for hunkdom.

I had originally planned for the book to be simply my story. But since I've never really thought about health and fitness much, and am essentially unschooled in even the basics of those things, I gathered up a couple of dozen specialists to help educate me, to answer the simplest questions. For instance, what is health? What is fitness? Why is fat bad, if it is? Why are seemingly all the things that taste good bad for you? To my surprise, a lot of the simple questions hadn't been answered in layman's terms. I've incorporated them, and hope you find them interesting.

I also originally planned to find shortcuts to health and fitness. Since I hate a fat stomach, and had one that qualified for the *Guinness Book of World Records*, I wanted to buy one of those machines that supposedly melt the fat away with electrical currents. And I thought about getting the machine that looks like a barrel-shaped abacus and supposedly just rolls the fat off you.

Not really to my surprise, I found out those things were junk, as were an awful lot of the products, books, and methodologies in health and fitness. The only quick fix out there was the fast injection of money into the pockets of those who take us for suckers. I decided to write about those things, too.

And then I began to learn about the myths in health. For instance, did you know some people think all that exercise may not add a day to your life? I nearly quit my year when I heard that. And I'm sure you think exercise, when you finally get around to it, will make up for bad eating patterns. You know, walk a mile and work that greasy piece of fried chicken and that biscuit soppy with butter out of your system. Lots of people have died because they believed that myth.

And finally I started learning things which seemed interesting by themselves. Do you know someone with thin arms and legs but a large belly? That person, particularly if he is bald, is statistically much more likely to have a heart attack than a more symmetrically shaped person.[1] And I do hope you notice what *my* shape was at the start of this year.

We are, therefore, going to look at myths, scams, and interesting questions, and, before you reach the end of this, I think you will at least know what's good for you, whether you do it or not. And I've always been one to like good intentions, anyway.

And speaking of good intentions, I have always meant to be a better-looking person. My looks—or more specifically, my insecurities about my looks—have probably ruled my life more than I want to admit. Portions of this book therefore deal with surface things, things which may seem shallow. They are not. Most of us are motivated by concerns about our outsides rather than the running of our engine and the things associated with it. I still feel that way, even though heart disease has entered my consciousness.

As I said, I'm not a scientist or a doctor, and I still don't read the AMA journal or jogging magazines. I can't stand complicated explanations of simple things, or the word "because." I don't like all doctors and think many of them care more about money than their patients. I resist evangelists in anything. I still don't love exercise, even after nearly a year of work and dramatic changes in my health brought on by exercise, and I still wish there was a health and fitness pill.

I also like to distill information, and at times that means you will be reading my interpretation of some very complicated and controversial issues and definitions. Since very little is black and white in health and fitness, I have relied on the opinions of a lot of doctors and scientists as well as extensive research by Christopher Scott, my exercise physiologist, to help mold that interpretation. In the back of the book you'll find sources for all of my thoughts, most of them noted in the text. And finally, I at least come to you from a nonbiased and essentially ignorant point of view.

Won't all that do?

But enough of this. Let's begin.

So, *what is health, anyway?*

Being without pain mentally or physically, having an engine and supporting parts which don't labor under any unnecessary burdens, and possessing habits which protect you mentally and physically from the attack of disease and age.

What *is fitness?*

A state of training in which your body performs tasks efficiently, without undue fatigue. Because it is a trained response, fitness decreases with inactivity.

Can *you be physically fit—a jock—and not be healthy?*

Physical fitness has to do with your ability to do things. For instance, to run hard and fast or to be strong and flexible. Health has to do with the state of your engine and its supporting systems, as I said earlier. Your health is impacted by the things that come into your body. Food. Liquids. Things in the air. You can change your health, and probably the likelihood of having many diseases, without doing any exercise. Simply changing your intake habits can improve your health. Health is also impacted by heredity. Health and fitness, therefore, don't necessarily go hand in hand. If you have a choice between being physically fit and healthy, choose the latter. Now, with all that said, most people who are physically fit are healthy, and most people who are healthy are physically fit. But don't assume one brings the other.[2]

Does *heredity predispose us to physical well-being or the lack of it?*

It does in many ways. For instance, many diseases appear to haunt families; aging itself seems to be passed through genes, and lots of people are from long-lived backgrounds. The tendency to heart attacks definitely seems to be genetically passed on.[3]

If *I've inherited bad genes in the health sense, what's the sense in trying?*

If you know your particular danger areas in health—for instance, a history of high blood pressure or family tendencies to cancer or heart attack, you can learn to stop damage before it begins in many instances. If you can't stop it, you can modify it. What kills people normally isn't simply a disease itself, for instance, but a disease gone wild.

How *ow much of my shape itself is determined by heredity? (Which is a sneaky way of asking, "Can my wife Norma blame her fat on bad genes?")*

The American Medical Association recently reported on the largest study done to date on obesity and identical twins. If it's right, about 80 percent of body composition is determined by heredity.[4] For some people, fat may not be due solely to that extra piece of chocolate or one more six-pack of beer. But a genetic tendency to obesity does not mean Norma is doomed to fat. It may mean she has to control her fat problem differently, and we'll talk about that later.

S *peaking of fat, is a little fat all that bad?*

Probably not from a health point of view, but the problem is in the definition of "little." Too much fat places a strain on the heart and joints simply from its weight, probably causes increased cholesterol (a fat itself) in our blood, and may lead to "adult onset" diabetes. It also may lead to high blood pressure, arthritis, gall bladder disease, increased blood lipids, increased risk from surgery, impaired heart function, lung problems, and, that most familiar demon of all, psychological distress from looking blimpish.[5]

S *o how much fat is too much fat?*

Five percent above your age group's norm would be considered dangerous.[6] For instance, for me, 16 percent of my weight in fat would be ideal, and 20 percent would be considered normal.

When the sickening "before" cover picture for this book was taken, my fat level was *30 percent*. In the "after" picture I'm 15 percent.

How *is a body fat percentage determined?*

You are composed of bone, lean tissues such as organs and muscles, and fat. Bathroom scales may be good for tracking the changes in your weight, but they can't measure fat itself, obviously. Doctors do that several ways, including underwater weighing and skinfold tests which I'll describe more fully in Chapter 3. But there are a couple of tests you can do at home that are highly accurate. Also, free is nice:

1. Take off your clothes, all of them. Grab a pinch of skin on your love handles, and don't be dainty. You will feel the fat, unconnected to your skin. If your pinch is more than an inch thick, you probably need to read on. Incidentally, you can do this to your spouse, too, if it'll make you feel better. Pinch her on her hips, legs, or back of the upper arm, where women put on most of their fat.
2. Stand in front of a mirror and look at yourself. Don't hold it in. Rolls of fat and a memory of a far thinner body when you were younger are good indications of too much *dolce vita*. If your stomach is larger than your chest, you may have a real problem. Did you know actuarial tables deduct two years of life for every inch a man's stomach is larger than his chest?[7]

A*re you saying even five pounds overweight can be a bad thing?*

Dr. Cooper, president of the Aerobics Research Center, certainly thinks so. On his desk sits a brand new teaching model of five pounds of fat. How big would you guess the model is? A cupful? The size of a bag of sugar? The model, an exact replica, is eighteen inches long and approximately the height and width of a loaf of bread. From its size most people think it weighs fifteen pounds.

W*ell, I may be a little overweight, but I'm in shape. I mean, I cut the grass each week, play ball at the exalted lodge, and run like hell at work. Doesn't that count in fitness?*

The only real fitness that counts is fitness that helps your cardiovascular system do the best job your particular system can do. And the cardiovascular system is hard to exercise. Most doctors believe that any conditioning effect requires at least twenty minutes of sustained exercise that substantially raises the level of your heart's work at least three times each week. That's called aerobic exercise, and only takes place when you are working very large muscle groups (such as legs when you jog, or legs and arms when you swim) for long periods of time.[8] Stop-and-go activities don't count aerobically, and simple exercise, such as pushing the lawn mower, doesn't count, either. Any movement more than your normal daily movements is good in building endurance and stamina, but it will not really help your engine and its support systems.

B*ut I thought you said exercise may not make me live longer.*

It may not, but the *factors associated with the LACK of exercise— overweight, bad intake habits—can definitely kill you.*[9] And exercise will definitely improve the quality of your life, however long that may be. "Quality of life" has nearly become a trite, buzz expression in health and fitness, but is really all that counts. I want to feel good as long as I'm conscious, don't you? And when things go wrong, when that probably inevitable heart attack happens to me, for instance, I want to know that I've made my engine and its support systems as strong as possible to lessen damage. And exercise makes many things strong. Just to give you some hope: the heart, a muscle, responds quickly to it; bones, which grow brittle with age, actually gain more calcium and become strong because of it; soft saggy skin tightens; the lungs provide more oxygen; and the blood actually changes.

B*ut you don't know how I've abused my body, and for how long. Can all this health stuff rebuild burned bridges?*

No one can be as bad to his body as I have been. I smoked three packs of cigarettes a day for fifteen years, did the right type of exercise for only two of the past twenty-five years (and overdid it then), and ate foods that would make any sensible person gag or die of fright. I am a type "A"—high-strung, intense. I could drink Hemingway under the table, and tried to best his types for years. But my insides and outsides have totally changed in a matter of months without radical changes in my life. Too late is only when you're dead.

Well, anyway, let's get on with the story.

Week 2

<u>*Grand Bahama Island*</u>

Grand Bahama Island is located about fifty miles off the coast of Palm Beach, Florida, in the Gulf Stream, in Columbus's path to the New World (some say he stopped in the Bahamas first), and in the path of pirates and bootleggers at various times during the last five hundred years. Back in the early days of the Spanish explorers, the island was occupied by Lucayan Indians, but later the European colonists of Hispaniola and Cuba decided all those heathen Indians needed saving and carted virtually the entire population of our island off to work in their mines and plantations and to find God.

Pirates used to hang around here because the waters are deceptively shallow and booty-laden boats sank as regularly as the tides rise and fall. I don't feel sorry for any of the captains of those booty-laden ships, either, for maps as early as the sixteenth century labeled our waters the *"Gran bajamar,"* the great shallows. Even now treasure finds refuge in those shallows. In 1964, within sight of the Lucayan Beach Hotel, four divers stubbed their flippers on a cache of gold coins and jewels worth over two million dollars.

Former slaves—both freed and escaped—liked the island for the same reason we do now: the weather's great, the ocean is warm and air clear; the shallows themselves, composed of living, vibrant coral reefs, are home to thousands of types of fish, and the supply of fresh water seems endless. Grand Bahama is a limestone island, a porous island. Under our surface layer of palms and pine trees and deserted white beaches is an enormous cave system. When it rains, the waters filter through the limestone and fill the caves. Some of the caves open in the island's interior, and one of the most dramatic ones, Ben's Cave, is part of the Bahamas National Trust. Walk down a spiral staircase and you can see bats hanging from the ceiling and the entrance to deep black holes that run for miles.

These holes eventually end up joining other cave systems in the ocean, and when you fly over Grand Bahama, you can see their ocean openings: dark-blue dots on an aquamarine sea. Island lore says these particular holes are the nostrils and mouth of a monster called Luska. Luska lives under the island. He (or she—the sex of this monster is as of now undetermined) sucks in when hungry, and *watch out!* if you're around that hole. Children have disappeared. Luska blows out, too, making the water boil. Hence, the name Boiling Holes. Scientists say this blowing and sucking has to do with the tides, but I prefer this more likely version.

The bootleggers were aware of these holes, too, and filled their barrels with our pure water just about as regularly as they offloaded bootleg liquor down on the island's west end. From big, slow boats it was stored in warehouses until sleek mahogany speedboats picked it up for the night run to the Florida coast. One or two of the warehouses which housed that good Canadian still sit in the village of West End, an exotic community about twenty buildings long, and outside the most run-down, you can occasionally find a man who will tell you Joseph P. Kennedy's yacht used to anchor right offshore a good bit each year. Maybe he liked our fishing.

I use the word "our" in referring to Grand Bahama, because I have vacationed here regularly for the past seven years, and am fond of both the island and its people. My friends here are both native and expatriate, and all of them have seen my weight go up and probably my health go down with the regularity with which I used to drink island rum. Ollie Ferguson, a Bahamian, has always been very diplomatic about my shape. "Well! You're looking, uh, like a fullback these days, Remar." Judy Graham, in her forties and with the energy of a high-tide boiling hole, was just as nice, but got the message over to me, anyway. "Do you need help in zipping your wet suit?" she said once as we prepared to scuba dive.

When I decided to remake myself, therefore, the site for the effort was a given. All I needed was a house, which I found on Seagrape Lane, and a plan, which God knows everyone wants to give me. Also I need more energy, a thought which fills me after about one hour of my normal day.

After stretching and jogging, I bike five miles to the YMCA with my trainer. Right out of an ad for Soloflex, Russell Burd is a young gymnast from Perkiomenville, Pennsylvania. Put my brain in his body and I'll be happy. Russ spent two months meeting with the doctors who are planning the new me, and moved here to the island with his equally dramatic fiancée, Kim, to implement my Master Body Plan. Quiet, calm, and patient, Russ doesn't make me feel like a fool when I do foolish things. On our first bike trip to the gym, for instance, we stopped by a sporting goods shop to buy some gym shorts. Against the back wall of the store was a set of chrome hand weights. I thought they looked handsome, even serious, and quickly pointed them out to Russ as I reached for a credit card. "Boy, I really like these," I said as I waved to the brawny Bahamian behind the counter, "Let's get them for the house." Russ gave a fleeting glance to the Bahamian. The man had not seen or heard me, thankfully. "We call those 'La Femme Spa' weights, Remar," Russ said quietly. Shiny weights are not in vogue in serious gyms, I've since learned. My hands now touch only the most rusted ones.

Our weight room is filled with them, too. The Grand Bahama YMCA, a modest place, leases the gym to Bill and Marilynn Carle, both Bahamian weight lifting champions. Marilynn recently won the Miss Southeastern United States title, too. With a waist about like my arm, arms like my waist, and a pair of legs only a giant rabbit could emulate, she isn't the type of woman I would pick a fight with; she is very feminine and bright, though, qualities that surprised me. Bill, her husband, is an equally humbling sight for neophytes. Arms like the trunk of an old oak.

Each day, the faithful and the hopeful gather here. But in the mornings, when we usually arrive, only the enormously well-developed seem to occupy the large white-walled, blue-carpeted room. Bill is usually putting Marilynn through her workout in the front part, his voice deep and loud, pushing, taunting her. Other voices mix with his, drifting from behind the partition which divides the gym. One of those voices invariably belongs to the 1985 World Games posing champion. Henry Charlton is referred to as a "big boy" in the parlance of lifting circles, though he is relatively small-statured. He has developed a posing routine which is now his ticket to weight lifting competitions all over the world. It's akin to watching the movement of a person under a strobe light, and in London last year it brought down the house. As Henry began to twitch, the audience "went crazy, hooting and hollering," he says calmly. At the memory, he flexes involuntarily and watches his muscles jump in one of the thirty mirrors which line the walls. Except for the glass section which allows lesser mortals standing in the hall to watch, mirrors line the walls.

My first view of the gym was from the hall, too, and the sight of all that rust and sweating muscle and the sound of all that power vibrating the glass partition poured insecurities and fears on me like a lumberjack pours syrup on hotcakes. Though I am six-one, my self-image has always pretty much been that of a nonmuscular, rather frail-looking, nonathletic, recently fat wimp, and at that terrible moment, my image seemed like reality. My bike was wrong, too. Lollipop red with shiny new chrome accents, it was the La Femme Spa of gym bikes, pretty in the midst of black, fenderless, and, yes, rusted bikes.

I had never walked into a weight room before with the intent of lifting weights or consciously looking at muscles, never been embarrassed by a bicycle, and certainly never prayed as fervently that I wouldn't be noticed as I did that first day. An unanswered prayer. The big boys looked at me. I fully expected to see Henry Charlton, the posing champ, lose his composure at the sight and roll from the bench in uncontrollable laughter. He gave me the most inconsequential nod instead, the reaction of the others, too. I was to learn that serious lifters don't go out of their way to greet novice lifters, but they don't laugh at them, either, a respectful pecking order on both sides. Henry said nothing of consequence to me until the second week, incidentally, but when he spoke, I listened and wanted dearly to believe: "Legs you got, and you're gonna have a good chest, too," he said, his eyes seemingly ignoring the twenty-odd pounds of fat on my belly. Henry is a man of vision, maybe a man of blurred vision, but I think he sees real well.

We are in the weight room for about two hours each day, but our actual lifting time is no more than ninety minutes. On Mondays and Thursdays we work only shoulders and back. Tuesdays and Fridays are for arms, and Wednesdays are for legs. It will take a few weeks, Bill Carle says, for my body to adjust to the type of straining and pain weight lifting brings, but both sensations are bearable and at times pleasant. So far. Some of the pain, such as that brought on by leg lifts, is high-pitched and vicious in its intensity and slightly delayed, a flood hitting you an instant after the last push. The relief which follows the pain puts the relief which accompanies a desperately needed leak to shame.

It will be worth it, however, if the muscles come. I obviously can't see them yet. All of me is hidden under fat. The experts say I already have some under there which will begin to show within the month. My new muscles will supposedly begin to

17

show within three or four months. Since I've been waiting all my life, that doesn't seem too long.

Eating and Weight Loss. I have been putting on my fat quietly for about five years, drops of sand steadily piling. The insidiousness of the change made it even worse, of course, for I was never bothered by the gains. Except when I changed closets each season. In 1981, my winter thirty-threes seemed tight. In 1982, spring thirty-fours just wouldn't fasten. Thirty-sixes felt nice in 1983, tight in 1984, and caused a hernia and a move up to thirty-eights in the spring of 1985.

I attributed the tightness to heat shrinkage in my closets at first (they just didn't make clothes like they used to) but finally faced a version of reality in June 1985. June was the month I first thought about redoing myself and I instantly took the thought as an excuse to worry even less about my weight and shape. I needed fat. My thirty-eight-inch stomach didn't seem big enough to deserve its own book yet, and, more importantly, I theorized that muscle was simply rearranged fat. A little weight lifting would in essence tie a string around the two ends of a blob of fat, thereby shaping it, much like a balloon filled with water can be shaped with a knot or two. Ergo . . . more fat meant more muscle.

My theory, fortunately, didn't carry much weight with the doctors who advise me. My excess twenty-seven pounds of free-flowing, greasy-smelling fat, just like the fat I hope you pull from a chicken before cooking, had already jeopardized my health, a jeopardy multiplying geometrically, not arithmetically, with each new pound.

I therefore undertook my new eating patterns with the utmost seriousness. Nothing less than pure would touch my lips. For two days, even the juice we drank was extracted seconds before we drank it with our new ninety-dollar juicer. Liquefied apple, banana, plum, peach, and sapodilla fruit was delicious and supposedly teeming with living vitamins and other terribly healthy organisms; each four-ounce drink took only a minute to make, too. Unfortunately, we figured each four-ounce drink cost about three dollars in fruit, and it took twenty minutes to clean the juicer each time we wanted a four-ounce-three-dollar drink, something I tired of quickly, so I traded the juicer to a fisherman friend for thirty lobster tails (about a hundred and twenty dollars' worth), started buying juice at the grocery store, feel just as healthy, and eat a lot better.

In addition to lobster, fish, and lots of chicken, our diet consists of many vegetables lightly steamed or raw and lots of fruit. We eat pasta at least twice a week, steak probably once a week, and wheat pancakes smothered in a heated sauce of fresh orange juice, crushed bananas, and cinnamon on Sunday. Conch salad, low in fat and calories, is in the fridge at all times for snacking. Every single thing I eat or drink is logged in our computer with a code which identifies the item, quantity, and time consumed. I attribute my weight loss solely to the fact that it's a damn lot of trouble to write down everything you eat or drink, so I eat and drink less. Try it sometime.

My island friends are tremendously supportive of all my efforts, both exercise- and food-wise. They honk and cheer when passing me as I jog or bike. If I'm asked to dinner, all sinful things are kept hidden away as securely as bottles of booze from an alcoholic. I accidently found a chocolate cake in one friend's closet, though, and did take one bite. I tried to make the hole look rat-ish.

R*emar, you spend more time being good than I'll probably ever spend. I want to know if a little exercise—all I'll ever do—is better than no exercise at all.*

Cardiovascular fitness requires an absolute minimum of twenty sustained minutes three times a week. Period. But if you absolutely refuse to think about cardiovascular/aerobic fitness, do something anyway.

Recent research on physical activity and longevity suggests that an active lifestyle will help you keep what you've got and may keep you living longer (more on that later).[1] Any activity or exercise is an improvement over sitting still. A long walk three times a week will at least build stamina. Walking up one flight of stairs at work is better than riding, and you never know who you'll meet on that stairwell. But your engine and its supporting systems won't adapt and strengthen themselves if you don't push them long enough to make them change for the better. This threshold, sorry to say, is twenty minutes three times a week.[2]

But remember, particularly if you've been a couch potato, that consistency is the key. You cannot safely go without exercise for even a few days and then try to make up for your sins by overdoing. A lot of people injure themselves, even die of heart attacks, doing that. So if you've laid off for a week or a lifetime, start moderately and work up.

O*kay. Let's say I'm overweight, depressed, high in cholesterol, and thinking about living a long time. Specifically, what can exercise do in each of these areas?*

Life span. A very interesting study of Harvard alumni indicates that persons with active lifestyles *do* live longer than those of us who seek the tranquillity of minimal movement.[3] Exercise is part of an active lifestyle. Painting the house is an active lifestyle. Pulling a Tom Sawyer is not.

Changing your lifestyle, something my year was all about, isn't as hard as you think, either. And do remember that feeling better is more important than living longer.

Lowering cholesterol. Cholesterols are chemical compounds in the blood. Most doctors believe high levels of the wrong types definitely increase the incidence of heart disease, most particularly the development of atherosclerosis (a narrowing of the arteries). Exercise can increase your good cholesterols.

Losing weight. Run a marathon, 26.2 miles, and you won't even lose a pound of fat. Why not? A marathoner burns only about 2,400 calories during the race,[4] and a pound of fat has 3,500 calories. The six- and seven-pound weight losses many marathoners experience is caused primarily by temporary fluid loss. So if you're close to thirty pounds overweight like I was, you would need to run over a thousand miles to lose your fat. I'd rather be fat. But exercise helps you lose weight in more ways than the simple burning of calories. As we'll see later, exercise can lower your appetite, make your body more efficient in burning fat, and simply make you look healthier. Looking better makes diet changes more worthwhile.

I *don't want to exercise because all those muscles will turn to fat when I get bored and quit.*

First, big muscles don't have to come with exercise, even though they can. I'm busting my butt for big muscles. Second, muscle can't turn to fat. Big muscles do atrophy when they're not used and lose their tone. Big athletes who decrease their exercise programs without decreasing their caloric intake do get fat, too. Too much fuel for too little work. That's exactly what happens to lazy amateurs, too, who use weight lifting as an excuse to overeat and then blame the fat on flabby muscle. It can't happen—fat is fat.

D*o diets really work?*

No. Diets for most people mean being *deprived*, and no one other than the occasional weird monk can deprive himself for all of his conscious life. That's why serious weight-loss researchers say that being overweight is not the *problem* with anyone—it is the *symptom* of the problem.[5] As with most problems, treating the symptom solves nothing, and usually just creates more problems. Lasting weight loss happens only when your long-term consumption of calories is balanced with your long-term consumption of food.

Do you mean to say all those diet books my wife Norma bought that promise quick weight loss aren't going to make her svelte?

Any diet that cuts calories will bring about weight loss. Any diet that dramatically cuts back your caloric intake will bring dramatic weight loss. But diets that promise weight losses of more than two pounds a week can be dangerous and are certainly taking off more than fat. For example, rapid loss usually takes water with it and virtually always takes muscle tissue with it. Because muscle tissue burns calories much more actively than fat, any loss of muscle will make it harder for you, excuse me, Norma, to lose weight the next diet book around.[6] Some of the dangers posed by too-rapid weight loss include dehydration, nausea, dizziness, and impaired kidney function.

Why are there so many diet books?

Because people like to make money.

But, if it's in a bookstore and promoted like mad on television, and associated with or written by some doctor, doesn't it have to be legitimate?

There are no moral or legal restraints in the diet business. Anyone can think up a new diet, and virtually any publishing house will publish it if it's radical or new-sounding enough. Money is the motivation, not good information.

Even the best sellers?

Some of them, the quack diets, kill people. Virtually all of the fad diets will leave Norma discouraged and even more overweight. Most diet books are like a math book that says four plus four equals nine. Most of us don't understand the math of weight loss and we therefore don't see the obvious mistakes.

The only way to get Norma svelte again is this: you must convince her to slightly modify her eating habits for the rest of her life. An article in the *Journal of Addictive Behavior* says it best: successful weight loss only happened when people like Norma *"recognized their own responsibility for their body size. They felt a strong need to take charge of their own weight loss plan"* [emphasis added].[7] Real weight loss, like real health changes, only take place with lifestyle changes. Those changes do not have to be radical.

So how can Norma recognize a fad diet?

They promise dramatic results; their authors have discovered a "secret"; they present one-food solutions; they claim persecution from medical and scientific authorities; they misrepresent basic information; they use scare tactics.[8]

An average man will burn nearly 2,500 calories in a day if he simply sits in a chair. Burning calories isn't magic and dieting doesn't require a quack's book.

What is a calorie, incidentally?

It's an amount of food energy measured in heat. One calorie is the amount of energy it takes to raise the temperature of one liter of water one degree Celsius. If you eat a 900-calorie meal, for example, you've just eaten enough energy to raise the temperature of 900 liters of water one degree. This is a handy way to calculate how much food we eat because we are engines burning food to release energy to keep us alive.

How *do researchers actually know how many calories are in something?*

They burn it. The item, such as a chocolate fudge sundae with crushed nuts, fresh cream, and a cherry on top, is actually ignited in something called a "Bomb Calorimeter." The heat released by that tragedy is measured.

How *many extra calories do I have to eat to gain a pound of fat?*

3,500. And, logically enough, fat has a lot of calories itself. More than twice as many as carbohydrates and proteins per measure. So it doesn't matter whether you're a connoisseur of greasy pork barbecue or well-aged, well-marbled prime beef; the more fat you eat, the faster you grow fat. To say nothing about what you do to your arteries, but more about that later.

How *do I really know how much food to eat to keep my weight stable?*

Doctors can measure this with complex tests, but if your clothes seem tighter each year, as mine did, you're eating too much.

So *what weight should anyone want to be? Isn't fat inevitable with age?*

"Creeping fat" is real. As we grow older, our lean body mass— the muscle, essentially—is replaced somewhat by fat. But you can dramatically retard that process. Exercise and good eating patterns can make you nearly as lean as an eighteen-year-old quarterback. It will take away that softness in your flesh.

Do *you really mean I should look like I used to in high school?*

The healthy state for any body is lean. If you were lean in high school, muscular in high school, there's absolutely no physiological reason you can't be that way now and forever. If you've never been lean and muscular, like me, you can still be that way.

Let's *get back to exercise, then. No living person is going to see the real state of my body, if I can help it, other than Norma, and her eyes are going these days. Can I start all this changing and exercising alone? Do I need a gym?*

You don't have to have a gym or a partner, but it helps. Partners can monitor each other's effort and simply be there to help and to share the misery. Gyms of some sort can actually be fun, once you realize other people are as bad off as you may be. Gyms provide lots of toys, too, and supposedly provide good supervision. But many are in business only to sell memberships, and their tactics make the car business pale in comparison, and I should know.

How *can I choose the right gym?*

They're all different, so don't choose one quickly, don't fall prey to a pressure sell, and don't fall simply for high-tech looks. First, decide what your goal is: aerobic fitness, social contact, or muscle work. Serious weight lifting gyms, for instance, aren't good places to meet a date for the night. When you do meet ladies there, they can break your arm if you cross them. Second, visit the gym during the time you'll normally be working out there. If the gym is too crowded for your particular activity, choose another one.

If you decide to go to a real gym, the lingo there can be pretty foreign; here are few terms to roll off your tongue casually, if you're game:

• *Z-Bar*   (also called a curl bar)—It weighs about twenty pounds, and is angled in the middle to relieve pressure from the wrists.

• *Nickels*   Five-pound weights.

• *Dimes (biscuits)*   Ten-pound weights.

• *Quarters*   Twenty-five-pound weights.

• *Ripped*   What I'm going to look like at the end of this year: having well-defined muscles.

• *Pumped*   Muscles filled with blood from hard exercise.

• *Bodybuilder*   A lifter interested primarily in esthetic changes.

• *Power Lifter or Olympic Lifter*   A lifter interested primarily in strength changes.

• *Big Boy*   Larger, stronger, or better proportioned than the average person. I'm going to be one of these guys, too.

• *Pencil Neck*   Opposite of a big boy, and a term I'm trying to forget.

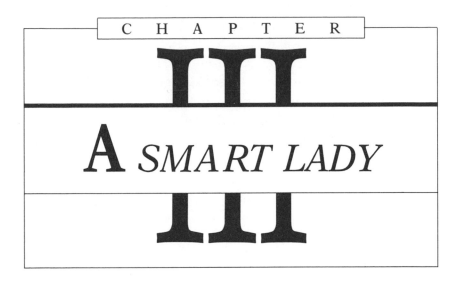

CHAPTER III

A SMART LADY

Week 4

Grand Bahama Island

One month of my remake is over and I'm still alive after 204 bicycling miles, fifteen days of jog-walking, my first injury, and no booze (do you know how scary that thought was at first?). I'm also seventeen pounds lighter and six inches smaller around the waist. I lifted weight six days a week, too. How much total weight do you think a nonmuscular first-time lifter can lift his first month? Would 10,000 pounds impress you? 75,000 pounds? Neither should. For you are reading about a man who lifted 385,000 pounds.

The greatest thrill of the month? When Kathy, a friend's very beautiful, blond, and athletic steady, said, "My God, Remar, you look good." I think she said it with an exclamation point, but I'm trying to be conservative here. I don't think I detected the least bit of swoon or a *soupçon* of lust in this perceptive lady's words or demeanor, unfortunately, but there was a lot of surprise there, and I'm real patient.

Just a few minutes ago, something nearly as exciting hap-

27

pened. After finishing my thirty-minute, twenty-two-position stretching routine, I, on impulse, decided to try a push-up. I did three. With perfect form. Though that may not sound impressive for a man who in one month lifted 385,000 pounds, the accomplishment was as sweet to me as the small piece of chocolate pie we had for dessert Sunday, the day we pretty much forget our normal eating routine, for I have never been able to do push-ups.

Many of the small gains mean a lot to me. One month ago standing up quickly and walking to the beach path, only fifty feet away, tired me; scared me, too, since the reality of heart disease had entered my consciousness. I jog-walk two miles now, jogging until I'm breathing hard, then walking until my breathing calms, then jogging again. The first day, I shuffled along for twenty seconds before stopping. This morning, I went five minutes, passing an old lady and a slow-moving dog.

I had one real scare in the gym, or rather I scared the hell out of Russ once. I was doing curls with a forty-pound Z-bar, my third set. After twenty repetitions, my form became sloppy. On the twenty-first repetition, rather than keeping my back straight and my knees slightly bent (which keeps the weight on the legs), I stood straight, then shifted my back to one side. That instantly pulled my back and I turned white, started to drop the bar, and nearly fell backward. Russ, who stands facing me during exercises like this, caught the bar, but was positive I was having a heart attack. The look on his face even scared me.

Funny pains do affect me a little more, now that I think about it. When I'm walk-jogging, I am at times conscious of my heartbeat. When it occasionally skips a beat, as all hearts do, I wonder if the skipping will become more frequent and then become pain and then really become a heart attack. The first time it skipped, I thought of my grandparents. I used to look forward to my summer stays with them because they, like all good grandparents, let my brother and me get away with things. Grandmom let me drive their white 1950 Ford station wagon, handsome wood paneling down the side, the day they bought it. As a ten-year-old driver, my skills weren't too good, and when I backed into the corner of the garage, she did not yell. Granddad didn't yell, either, he simply said I needed more driving lessons and took me out himself. I remember driving by some summer friends of mine, and holding my head high enough, it seemed, to touch a good homemade kite in the Swainsboro sky.

But on my fifteenth birthday my grandad did yell, a sound that still haunts me over thirty years later. On that morning, my grandparents had arrived in Marietta, Georgia, with a new pet for my brother and me, a 300-pound sow quickly nicknamed Petunia the Pig. The pig was to join our growing menagerie of country pets—dogs named Rumpus and Mickey, horses named Trigger (of course), Toni and Red, and a large, gray field rabbit named Humphries. Grandfather worked hard to unload and pen our new pet, trained on command to roll over on her back and "oink," and seemed tickled with his gift.

I was asleep that night when I heard the first yelling, a gasping for air when the heart attack struck him. I had never been that scared before, because I had never seen a person facing death, and did not know that anything could hurt that much. Do you know what really bothered me about that night? There was nothing I could do, there was nothing my grandmother could do but watch the pain. Though my grandfather survived that attack, it was the first time I had ever thought seriously about heart attack. His death from a second attack was one of the few other times I thought about heart disease until this year.

Here on the island, when I become a little discouraged and a lot worn-out from all the work it's taking to remake myself, I think about that night, and the feelings of mortality it brought me. Living is not just a gift. It is earned, too.

And, God knows, I am earning it. My first month's gains in both strength and endurance were more than even my most wishful supporters had thought possible; my looks are improving, and none of my clothes fit me any more (the first time in years that problem has made me smile). And, most important of all, I feel so damn good about myself. Do you know how nice that feels?

If it's earned, when does the work begin to pay off?

Changes on the inside.   Even if you spent a lifetime abusing your insides with bad food, smoking, and a sedentary and/or sinful lifestyle, you can make things better relatively quickly. Cardiovascular changes begin to take place in three to five weeks, cholesterol and other blood-related factors in as little as three to eight weeks, depending upon the individual.[1]

Strength and stamina.   Changes here can take place quickly, within a week or two, if you are consistent in your exercise program. Anything more than your current activity level will promote change in these areas.

Muscle growth.   Hunkdom comes slowly, very slowly. Change is measured in pieces of inches. If you're over forty, be happy with an inch on your arm in a year. But an inch on your arm combined with several inches off your belly makes for a dramatically different shape. I refer you to the handsome devil on the cover of this book.

Weight loss.   The slower you lose it, as I said, the longer it will be off. Eliminate 200 calories a day, for instance (drink two diet drinks rather than regular drinks) and cut out enough calories to lose twenty pounds, probably permanently, in a year.

That's all very interesting, but what is the very first thing I will notice if I begin to exercise?

A dramatic improvement in energy. Most people notice that within days, along with improvements in their sleeping. But some of the long-term changes are as interesting. Did you know consistent, sustained exercise will eventually increase the number of blood vessels throughout your body? Increase the pumping power of the heart? Make the burning of fat, not that you have much, a much more productive process?[2]

Norma *says she hates exercise, period. Does it ever become fun?*

People who really don't like exercise probably are not ever going to begin giggling about it. But attitudes do change somewhat. Tell her to pick the exercise she likes the most (or hates the least) and stick with it for a few months. In time, it will become habit, just like taking out the garbage.

Okay, *muscles may not come easy but you seem able to lose weight easily and that makes a big difference. But not at my house. Norma always quits dieting and quits exercising because her losses or gains seem to stop. I know she's weak-willed, but is she also running into physiological plateaus?*

I have a feeling Norma runs into a lot of things, including plateaus. Weight loss may stop, according to one current theory, because of a protective survival mechanism dating back to caveman days when we humans stored fat like other animals for use in times of famine. This "setpoint" theory says that when weight loss such as that caused by fasting or near fasting threatens the body's encoded minimum fat requirements, it lowers metabolism, cutting back on the calories normally needed for proper function.[3] In other words, the body simply stops burning as many calories, and you hit a plateau. Of course, Norma's problem is that midnight snack of chocolate cake you don't know about. She hides it in her wig box, the one that held her platinum beehive for the senior prom, remember?

You will reach plateaus in your strength and muscle-building programs, too. Your body simply adapts to your new level of activity. Increase the level again or change the activities themselves to keep your progress going.

What about fasting as the answer? Will it help me lose weight faster, clean out my body, or do something spiritual to my mind?

Fasting can obviously bring rapid weight loss, but it's virtually never permanent, can cause traumatic loss of lean tissues such as muscle, and eventually harm even organs. It should be undertaken under the care of a doctor only, and most doctors recommend it only for extremely obese persons as a last ditch-effort before surgical intervention.[4] People out there have died from it, too. So, even if it'll clean your body and mind (which it probably won't), don't undertake it lightly.

Well, what if I just eat only one big meal a day?

What you'll probably do is interfere with your body's metabolism if you do this often. The one-meal-a-day diet can also lead to an increased appetite, and a poor blood-fat profile because your system cannot efficiently handle the rapid intake of a large amount of fat.[5] Spreading your calories over the day is the best way to eat.

Shortcuts—fasting or one big meal—don't work.

You had a bunch of tests before beginning your program. But most people aren't going to exercise as radically as you do. Is a physical really necessary before beginning exercise? What can it show?

I didn't really think my physicals were necessary from a safety point of view, and I was very wrong—remember my heart disease. A physical is good even if you are healthy, simply to give doctors measuring points for later changes in your health. But any time you undertake a change in the stress patterns on your body and heart, a physical should be a must. (In Chapter 17, I pass along some guidelines for getting the right one.) Since I was planning a pretty rigorous year, I wanted to know precisely how overweight I was, what my endurance levels were, and how healthy my engine and its systems really were.

N*orma wanted to know how much fat was on her body, too, before she let any doctor see her naked. She took the home pinch and mirror tests you mentioned in Chapter 1, and thinks you're a dolt. How can we get a second opinion?*

Second opinions are always a good thing, and here are some precise methods used by professionals.[6] Norma probably won't like them, either.

1. Underwater weighing is probably the most accurate way. You're dunked in a water tank. Since fat floats and lean tissue sinks, your weight out of water and in (used in the proper formula) gives a good indication of your total fat. You can't, incidentally, put your bathroom scales in the tub for this one, since other lab tests are required for accuracy. Fitness clinics and some health clubs have special weighing rooms, though they are not numerous. Your best bet of finding a place near you is to check with the physical education department of a local college or university or with any preventive or sports medicine clinics.
2. Another popular but probably not as accurate method is the skinfold measurement. Skin calipers measure the amount of fat in predetermined areas.[7] Most health clubs and fitness centers can do this for you, but the results can vary widely, based on the experience of the user.
3. The bioelectrical impedance analyzer is another way.[8] It sends a small unfelt current through your body and measures the greater resistance of current through fat. Analyzers are new and are looked down upon by some doctors and clinics, as are all things new, as being inferior. I don't know who will win that argument, but these machines are probably a lot better than nothing.

You've said you're glad you had all those fancy tests because they showed heart disease. Everybody from my doctor to you to the margarine commercial on TV tries to scare the hell out of us with the words. But nobody explains. Just what is coronary heart disease?

A narrowing process in your coronary arteries, three major arteries attached to the walls of your heart. Arteries carry oxygen-loaded blood from your heart to feed your organs and other cells. Block the coronary arteries and you strangle the heart.

Coronary heart disease kills nearly half the people who die of any cardiovascular disease. It is particularly scary because of its first symptom in 40 percent of us: immediate death. It is also one of the few very deadly diseases for which the risk factors respond quickly to changes in our health patterns, good or bad.[9]

How can I tell if I am a high-risk candidate for coronary heart disease?

If you smoke, have the wrong cholesterol levels, or have high blood pressure, your chances of dying from it are greater. If you, like me, claim a couple of these things, your chances of dying from it are a lot greater. If you claim them all, your risk of death increases geometrically.

Other things you can control probably contribute to coronary heart disease, too: the lack of meaningful exercise, high body fat, diabetes, tension, and stress. And finally, your age, personal history, and heredity will have some impact.[10]

What tests can tell me if I have coronary heart disease?

Doctors don't entirely agree on what tests tell them. But the ones presented here are the best indicators to date of the presence of CHD, and if they err, they do so on the conservative side. By that I mean the side of heart disease. The side which might make you make some changes in your lifestyle.

One test usually indicates a need for the other here, too. If the first seems perfectly okay, the others may not be necessary. Remember, however, that my regular stress tests, the tests you'll find at health clubs and most clinics, indicated no problems, but my extra tests indicated a problem—even though I had no symptoms of heart disease.

EKG Stress Testing.   You are probably familiar with this test. Electrodes, up to fifteen, are attached to your chest. All simply pick up the heart's electrical activity, the activity which makes the heart beat. As you move on the treadmill, the electrodes pick up any changes in your heart's electrical activity as you place it under stress. For instance, missed beats, extra beats. Electrical changes can indicate problems in getting oxygen to your heart.

How *accurate is an EKG?*

Dr. Henry Solomon, a cardiologist from Cornell and author of *The Exercise Myth*, argues that "stress tests are not sensitive enough, specific enough, or reproducible enough for anyone to be sure they're telling you anything at all."[11] At times, he states, they show heart disease when none is present. At times they don't show disease when it's definitely there.

But the problem with EKG stress testing may lie not with the test but with the test administrators. Because many factors are associated with heart disease, not just the presence of an EKG irregularity, physicians monitoring the test need to look at many aspects of a person's physiological response to exercise: heart rate, blood pressure, time of the onset of changes in electrical patterns, and the shape of those patterns; the duration of the electrical wave changes and the like.[12] Again, the right answer here isn't as clear-cut as math. The test administrator's skill will be very important to you.

Stress tests have also become a gimmick. Health clubs perform them. Stress clinics open up weekly. Physicians with an extra room buy stress treadmills as an easy income-producer. My barber's even thinking about installing a few. Some of these people may be administering meaningful tests, but most are not.

Should I go have a test?

If you are over forty-five, have a family history of coronary heart disease, or are in one of the three high-risk groups, the American Heart Association and the American College of Sports Medicine and many other reasonably nonbiased scientific types consider you a "candidate" for an exercise stress test.[13] This very cute word is their way of dancing around a yes-or-no answer.

So what are the real risks to you if you do?

If you pick a quack administrator, you will waste your money and time; if a test shows you have heart disease and you don't, it will scare the hell out of you, probably make you turn to clean and godly living (which is good), and definitely make you see a heart specialist (which isn't bad after forty anyway), but you will have wasted about a thousand dollars in total. If the test shows you don't have heart disease and you do, that can obviously be a problem. To minimize this risk, you must go to a competent testing center or individual. If the test correctly shows you have heart disease, and if you take the right corrective measures, it could save your life.

However—you could die from one, too. But the odds here are astronomically in your favor. At the Cooper Clinic in Dallas sixty-five thousand maximal stress tests have been administered with no fatalities.[14] In a study in Indianapolis, twelve thousand tests have been administered with no fatalities.[15] When the rare death has occurred, it has usually been among high-risk persons.[16] It's absolutely imperative, therefore, that your test (if it's a "maximal" test, where you go until exhaustion) be administered by very experienced personnel and that you be absolutely honest in giving your personal history before the test.

Does a correctly administered stress test do anything other than check for heart disease?

The other things it can show are very important. For instance, it can indicate your physical work capacity—what levels you are capable of working up to at a particular point in time. How much exercise can you tolerate? Don't start a meaningful exercise program without knowing that, especially if you're over forty-five. A stress test is also a good base-line measurement for later changes in your health. Four years from now it might let a doctor see changes in your heart's electrical patterns which could indicate heart disease or other irregularities.

How do you know a good testing place from a bad one?

Generally speaking, go to a place that specializes in cardiovascular testing. Your local fitness spa probably doesn't fit in that category. Remember, interpretation is the key to a meaningful test. A person who administers many stress tests might understand their implications better. Your regular family physician probably doesn't administer them regularly, either, though he may have a treadmill machine.

Also before making an appointment ask the administrators these obvious things: (1) The EKG machine should have at least seven leads, or terminals fastened to your body. Does it? (2) The attendant should monitor your blood pressure at frequent intervals. Will he or she? (3) A physician should definitely be within walking range. Does this center have such an on-staff physician? Some testing centers don't have on-staff physicians, and therefore can't take you to your maximal workout range, where most trouble would probably show up.

What if the test does show a problem?

If the test shows anything, it will probably indicate you simply need other tests. Obviously a good doctor should do the choosing, but you should know the types of tests available.

The **Tomographic Thallium Stress Test** "often provides the earliest information about reduced blood flow to the heart, the cause of most heart attacks," says Dr. Bob Bell, my nuclear medicine adviser. First, you run on a treadmill, then thallium, a radioactive material, is injected into your bloodstream. Images are then taken on film which show blood flow in the heart.

The **Stress Radionuclide Angiogram** determines how the heart works as a pump. You sit on a bicycle with your chest against a camera. Radioactive technetium is injected into your bloodstream, and moving pictures of your heart pumping under stress are made. Quantitative data is also collected—for instance, the volume of blood pumped, the speed of the blood in and out of the heart.

An **Echocardiogram** uses sound waves to determine heart anatomy and function. It is a noninvasive test now being used to evaluate the motion of heart valves and heart walls. Although it is used primarily to depict anatomy, future improvements will probably provide more functional information. (At present this is not used primarily for coronary artery disease detection.)

A **Cardiac Catheterization** is the most accurate test, but it is usually the last resort because it is also the most dangerous. One out of a thousand people die from this test, also called a coronary angiogram, so you don't want to undertake it casually.[17] A catheterization places a catheter, a long, thin, flexible tube, in an artery, and literally pushes it through the body to the heart. A dye is injected into the catheter. The dye lights up the coronary arteries, which give an indication of blood flow in the coronary arteries. This test is very accurate. It tells which arteries are blocked, how much they are blocked, and also can help a good physician determine a course of action.

Catherizations require hospitalization and a very experienced staff, and may cost several thousand dollars. Before undertaking one, you should definitely ask for a second opinion.

I've had my blood pressure taken a hundred times, but those numbers are a mystery. What does it all mean?

Your blood system is obviously a closed system; therefore, the blood exerts pressure at all times on the vessels. Your "blood pressure" is determined by measuring in millimeters of mercury (just like a barometer) the pressure applied to all the interior walls of your arteries. The systolic number, the one on top, is the pressure the vessels are under when the heart pumps. The diastolic, the bottom number, is the pressure when the heart is at rest, between beats.

So what is high blood pressure, then, and how bad is it?

When your systolic and diastolic pressure measurements move up out of statistically normal ranges, you have "high blood pressure" or hypertension. And why is it bad? When your blood pressure is within normal ranges, the pressure itself does no damage to the arteries. However, when that pressure is high enough, over a period of time, it can damage the artery walls and make them less elastic. Arteries must have elasticity to help move your blood properly. High blood pressure also places a strain on the heart. The increased pressure forces the heart to work harder and can eventually lead to congestive heart failure, a general deterioration of the heart's pumping capacity.[18]

A*re there any physical symptoms for high blood pressure?*

There are none specifically, but certain types of people are more likely to have it: those with a family history of it, black males, people who are overweight, and people under stress and tension, perhaps.[19]

W*ill a blood pressure check in my drugstore tell me any-thing?*

If these instruments aren't calibrated regularly, they can be inaccurate. But it's better than nothing. If it does indicate your pressure is a little high, have it checked again professionally. Don't use this "curbside" check as an excuse to delay a doctor's checkup.

E*veryone I know seems to have a little high blood pressure. Everyone seems to put off doing something about it, too, and I don't see them having strokes and heart attacks from it. So, what's the big deal?*

Please don't be casual about this stuff. Some people I've loved very much are dead from it, and each year, more people develop cardiovascular disease, particularly strokes, from it than from anything. Dying is one thing, but being paralyzed and conscious enough to live to regret your carelessness is another.

O*kay, how can it be treated?*

Many degrees of high blood pressure can be safely and reason-ably quickly treated with changes in your eating habits, changes in your weight, and changes in your exercise patterns.[20] If you have high blood pressure, don't put this book down and go jogging, but do see a doctor who understands the importance of exercise. If you're already on medication, for God's sake, don't stop taking it simply because you start exercising. Let your doctor make that decision.

In my wilder days, doctors constantly told me my blood pressure was high. My reaction was to drink a little more and worry a little more. When I began to exercise, my personal blood pressure problem went away, and did not return even when I took on my barrel shape.

What if I already have heart disease? Can clean and godly living and exercise reduce, arrest, or reverse it?

No one will say definitely yes to this, but virtually all researchers and doctors say that aerobic exercise can directly effect or stimulate changes in many of the risk factors which cause heart disease.[21]

Isn't your risk of dying much greater during exercise?

According to a very respected epidemiologist, Dr. Steve Blair, there is a slight, short-term increased risk of sudden death during exercise. But sedentary people are at greater risk overall than people who exercise. In fact, more people die from a heart attack in bed than while exercising.[22] And a recent study reported the risk of death in cardiac rehabilitation programs as only one death in 800,000 hours of exercise.[23] Go do something.

But in time will exercise make me live longer or not?

Some people, such as Dr. Henry Solomon, like to say there is absolutely no proof exercise increases life span, and they've sold an awful lot of books saying that, too. Technically they may be "right" because how could any study, for instance, ever prove a person had lived longer because of anything? Direct evidence here is impossible.

But the evidence is overwhelming that sedentary living increase the risk of CHD;[24] the evidence is building that physically active people have lower mortality rates in general;[25] the evidence is specific and convincing that aerobic exercise can improve the work of the heart and its supporting systems.[26] Cumulative evidence points to longer life for those who exercise correctly.

CHAPTER IV

BODY WORRIERS

Week 6

Grand Bahama Island

George Plimpton called me today, elated and relieved at the rapidly declining state of my stomach. "Why, you're a virtual wisp these days!" he proclaimed.

George was elated because he's a good friend who cares for my health; relieved because, almost single-handedly, he was responsible for creating the last four inches of my former belly. As I tried to sell my idea for a book on redoing my body, George encouraged further deterioration for the sake of the book. "How's the belly today, Bub?" he'd say. "Are we gaining some more weight?" He was concerned about my drinking habits. "Drink cheap scotch, doubles, lots of them," he advised on one call. He took an interest in my exercise program (don't have one) and my sleeping habits (late to bed was recommended).

Plimpton is a participatory journalist of some note, so I, of course, wanted to trust his judgment in these matters as a true chocolate lover wants to trust a chocolate diet plan. Except for George's heart theory. "You know, I was thinking," he said in

August, "a little stroke would be nice. Nothing debilitating, you understand." We both laughed.

We both laughed even when it appeared my publisher was having second thoughts. ("You mean we're belly-up, great Bub?") But the next week, when we met in Florida for a strategy session, when George saw my forty-three inches of freshly wrought flesh, he did not laugh. *"Good Lord,"* he said, "Poor Bubba, what have I done?" Earned an unusual title as the first member of my Body Worry committee, that's what--Chairman of the Debauch.

Normally, I don't think much of committees. They seem to either be for things we already agree on ("Keep America Beautiful"), or things we'll never agree on anyway (tax reform), or things we need to meet on to see if we agree or disagree. On the surface, my committee is no different. Let's face it, my body is a mess—it doesn't take a committee to decide that—and none of my members will ever entirely agree on what it takes to make me whole. *All*, nevertheless, are convinced that two, maybe three, tax-deductible visits here to my tropical island will make everything right.

Similarities to other bodies aside, my group has a real purpose: I want my health back. I want muscles. I want to be able to touch my toes again, and know that whatever exercise I do is the right exercise. I want someone like Kathy to keep telling me I'm looking more handsome these days. And more than anything, I want answers to questions. There the committee excels. Though my experts may not all agree, their opinions in their particular fields are as good as you can get.

Dr. Kenneth Cooper, for instance, doesn't really care about any of my muscles except for my heart. A quiet, slender man with a Texas-dry sense of humor and a great sense of mission when it comes to God, aerobics, and preventive medicine, Dr. Cooper does two things that especially impress me. Though he has sold more books than there are committees and is an international celebrity in the sports and medicine fields, he still practices medicine regularly. Would you be giving proctoscopic exams to middle-aged men when you could be giving autographs and interviews?

Dr. Cooper also admits when he's wrong. Years ago, Cooper believed that exercise alone could overcome poor diet and bad habits such as smoking. He was wrong: runners and sports addicts who ate fatty foods and smoked developed heart disease and died just like the rest of us who do those things. Cooper tells the story often, and I think of it when temptation sends me to the fried food portion of menus.

Cooper is balding, a sign of great intelligence. Some say he is too evangelical when it comes to aerobic fitness. But that's okay. In the past six weeks, over 100,000 Americans have died from some disease of the heart and blood vessels, much of it preventable.[1] That's more than twice the population of Grand Bahama Island. I think of the number during the hard part of my jogs, the first part.

Remember how far I could jog when I began? Less than thirty seconds the first day, about five minutes on the fifteenth day. On the twentieth jogging day, I jogged down Royal Palm past the sea streets—Sea Fan, Sea Horse, Sea Shell, etc.—to the ocean at Silver Point Jetty and then back to my street, Seagrape, twenty minutes without stopping. I was very smug after that, even called Dr. Cooper to casually drop the news, for twenty minutes of jogging three times a week is all the aerobic exercise most people need to remain healthy.

The smugness stuck to me as tightly as the barbed spines of a sea urchin until about eleven-thirty the next morning when I watched Ruth Goldfarb cross the finish line at the Bahamas Princess 10K Race (6.2 miles). Ruth isn't even five feet tall, isn't fast, either, but she still finished in good time. She is eighty-three.

I told Gideon Ariel, another member of my committee, about Ruth, and he immediately asked me if she also did strength training, an expected question from him. Many believe Gideon is the preeminent authority on strength in America. Gideon jogs, swims, and works out every day. He doesn't lift weights in the normal sense but uses instead his own innovative setup, a computer-driven, piston-powered, four-color gizmo which beeps at you, makes you stronger, burps when you try to cheat, and makes weight training infinitely more interesting. The machines are called Ariels and are considered the most advanced around.

Aside from being a strength expert and equipment designing wiz, Gideon is known as the Godfather of Biomechanics, the science that combines the study of physics with the study of human anatomy and movement. Boxers (Muhammad Ali), horses (Spectacular Bid), the U.S. Olympic Committee, and just about everything in between, including bald and plump writers, have been to Gideon's Coto Research Institute to profit from his understanding of the things the eye can't comprehend.

Rosy-cheeked, Gideon looks like a grown-up but well-developed cherub; his smile is mischievous in a comfortable way, and his thoughts move about as fast as the spin of the discus thrower he used to be. He likes to invent things, tinker with things. He is trying hard to make me an athlete and to make me constantly stronger.

Though I test on his machines in Miami, Gideon's strength training routine for me essentially involves free weights, since my gym on the island doesn't have an Ariel machine. Free weights are *great*—but while there are only two Ariel machines to remember (they do just about everything), free weights are like an iron jigsaw puzzle. Our gym set has hundreds of pieces.

At first, I didn't even try to keep things straight or understand the importance of the clipped phrases which make up gym dialect. I used instead a drawn-out but logical-sounding approach when I needed something: "Pardon me, but could you hand me that short, crooked bar over there and two of those medium-sized weights?" People looked at me as if I were from the moon.

As I calmed, the sentences shortened. Today I worked out next to Henry Charlton, the World Games posing champion, and I said it like this, "Hey, man, hand me that Z-bar and some quarters, will ya?" Henry didn't blink an eye as he reached for the bar, but before handing me the twenty-five-pound "quarters," he looked me up and down, then picked up some thirty-fives. "You look like you're ready to pump some heavy iron now," he said.

I'm thinking about adding Henry to my committee.

Remar, you say raising my heart rate is the thing that counts in fitness. If that's the case, why won't watching a porno movie make me aerobically fit? Or smoking?

Aerobic activity requires the movement of large amounts of oxygen in the blood and the absorption of that oxygen by tissues. The absorption of large amounts of oxygen requires the work of large muscle masses, such as your legs. Simply increasing your heartbeat won't increase the absorption of oxygen in areas other than your heart. The ability to pump volumes of oxygenated blood is the key to developing cardiovascular fitness.[2]

Is all exercise aerobic exercise?

Our bodies have essentially two ways to derive energy from its fuels: aerobic metabolism and anaerobic metabolism. Aerobic metabolism refers to a production of energy requiring oxygen, much like a fire requires oxygen to burn. Anaerobic metabolism is a process that releases energy to the body without the presence of oxygen.

These two types of metabolism happen at specific times. Aerobic metabolism is a slow-reacting process. It doesn't react instantly to an immediate increase in energy requirements, such as a sudden sprint in the rain from the car to the store, when your individual cells suddenly gasp for breath. At that point, sugar in the cells begins to break down and form lactic acid, releasing energy—anaerobic metabolism.[3]

Lactic acid is a by-product of metabolism. During intense activity, the acid builds up in our cells. When lactic acid production is greater than the body's ability to remove it, your blood becomes acidic. Your muscles don't work as well when the blood is more acidic, and you fatigue quickly.

Anaerobic exercise, generally speaking, is a more traumatic exercise for your body. Just like drag car racing wears engines more than everyday driving. Most people can't continue exercising at an anaerobic pace, either. Instead your engine and its supports systems need long-term, lower intensity demands on them to provide the most cardiovascular benefits. For safety and practical reasons, anaerobic exercise isn't appropriate for most people.

What are the aerobic exercises?

Running, jogging, brisk walking, rowing, swimming, race-walking, skiing, biking, and any other movement that uses large muscle groups continuously and for sustained periods of time.

Are some aerobic exercises more efficient than others?

Some aerobic exercises provide your body a better total workout. For instance, cross country skiing. But twenty minutes of aerobic work at the right level is twenty minutes, regardless of the sport or machine. You can't cheat the twenty minutes, that's the point.

So are you saying walking briskly is as good as running at a fast pace?

Yes. Especially if you're out of shape. If your goals, for instance, are weight loss and stamina increase, low-intensity, long-duration exercises are particularly good. Fat really doesn't even burn itself up much faster during exercise until you cross the twenty-minute barrier.[4]

Norma wants me to go to an aerobics class and jump up and down like Richard Simmons. Aren't the men who do that a little "funny"?

Constant movement of your major muscle groups like this is aerobically like running a race, and a lot more fun at times, as you'll find out later when you read about our island class. Go with Norma.

How *safe is aerobic dancing?*

A lot of people do injure themselves with regular aerobic dancing, mostly injuries related to the pounding of your feet and the movement of your back. If you're really out of shape, find a place that teaches low-impact (or soft) aerobics. Low-impact aerobics are designed to provide the same cardiovascular benefits with minimized trauma. You keep one foot on the ground to reduce the impact, but still get your heart rate up through exaggerated movements such as high steps, lunges, and vigorous arm motion.

Whichever you chose, high- or low-impact, do start out in a class that fits your fitness and ability level.

If *I'm out of shape, can I build endurance and strength at home before I put my act on the road?*

Push-ups, even partial ones with your knees on the floor, will definitely help build your strength. Running in place or stepping up and down on something like a box can quickly build your stamina. Things you can do at home can do as much for you as most machines and clubs (and cost you a lot less, too), but gyms and the like can provide you company, which is good for misery, as we know.

I'll *do the aerobics if it's good for me, I guess, but weight training appeals to me more. What can it do for me?*

For most of my life, I've wanted to be comfortable in weight rooms but was sure people like Bill and Marilynn Carle, god-type bodies, would laugh at me if I went there.

For most of my life, I also thought weight lifting was for the narcissistic or worse—guys and women who put the size of muscles above their health. Part of that, I think, is true: serious weight lifters at times jeopardize their health for their looks.

But weight training (the term generally used for people who aren't competing) has health values, physically and mentally, if you are a person who undertakes it with some sense of proportion. Weight training (or any good resistance training) is the only thing that will take the softness from your flesh. Jogging, for instance, will not create a washboard stomach. Aerobics won't take the softness from your arms. The right weight program will, and, more importantly, it will make you feel so damn good about your body if you stick with it. Change comes so very slowly here, but that in itself makes the change meaningful. After what I've been through to have a flat stomach, no fat will ever live there again.

Well, *if I weight train, can I skip aerobic exercising altogether?*

You can't skip it at all, for weight lifting is not aerobic, regardless of what some weight lifting advocates say. When aerobic gains are made as a result of lifting, they're nearly inconsequential.

"Circuit training," a type of weight training involving moderately heavy weight and many repetitions with little or no rest between exercises, is pushed by many gyms as a way to be aerobically fit and get the benefits of lifting at the same time. Most studies show improvement in aerobic capacity doesn't happen significantly, though.[5] Separate your activities. Or, perhaps, do something aerobic such as running in place or cycling between lifting exercises—Rambo-level training!

Won't weight lifting give me high blood pressure? Maybe damage my heart or something?

Lifting does little to improve the heart's function, but it doesn't hinder it, either. It definitely doesn't cause high blood pressure, but it raises your blood pressure when you're doing it, which isn't bad if you're healthy and normally pressured, but can be very bad if you already have high blood pressure.[6]

Some cardiac rehabilitation centers, incidentally, are beginning to use light to moderate weight training for rehabilitation in very supervised settings.[7] If you have any type of heart or high blood pressure, talk to an experienced doctor before undertaking a program.

Won't weight lifting make me less flexible?

No. A lot of flexibility can be hereditary, but most physiologists believe the proper weight training can increase your range of motion.[8] I personally am bored with too much stretching.

Should I start out lifting with free weights or with machines?

Free weights require more balancing skills than machines, since the weight isn't guided by anything but your skills. Machine weights usually move along some form of controlled track. It's hard to drop them on yourself unless your klutz factor is very high. Machines also give you a faster workout, because changing weights is usually done with a pin rather than actually moving and rearranging weights.

Manufacturers of machines will also tell you their products are more efficient in building muscles and strength because they vary the resistance to make you work harder where you're stronger. The pitch is appealing, but no one has proved it's true.

I learned how to lift with free weights, so my opinion may be biased (disagree with me and I'll punch you out), but I like free weights better. Lifting a hundred pounds on a machine just isn't as satisfying as attacking that hundred pounds by yourself. Doing a bench press with a free weight also uses more muscles than doing a press on a machine: a machine press essentially uses up and down muscles. A free press uses up and down muscles plus front and back and left and right muscles because you must balance the weight. Got that? There's a lot of healthy tension with free weights.

N*orma tells me she has "weak flesh"—there's no hope for her sagging flesh. Is she right?*

Flesh on your arm or leg or neck sags from several things, including the effects of gravity, the aging process itself, and, most important, from the loss of muscle tone. Muscle tone really means muscle is always in a state of partial contraction. Quit using a muscle, and it loses that tone. Start using a muscle again, and lots of the sagging will eventually go away.

I *want muscles. Norma wants tone. Do we do different things?*

It takes strength, and therefore more tissue, to be able to lift steadily increasing amounts of weights. It takes endurance, and therefore more stored fuel, to keep lifting a weight for a large number of repetitions. To build or keep your muscle balance (tone) follow a weight lifting program which emphasizes moderate weight and large numbers of repetitions. To become a hunk, build your weight program around steadily increasing resistance. Tone, incidentally, obviously comes with increased muscle size also, but muscle size isn't a necessity for tone.

Can weight training do anything to protect me from heart disease?

Weight training can make you look good, strengthen your bones, obviously strengthen and enlarge certain muscles, improve your mental attitude, give you more energy reserves for such fun things as cutting the grass or going shopping with Norma, but . . . weight training's beneficial impact on your engine and its support systems is minimal.[9] Don't substitute weight work for cardiovascular work.

TROUBLE

Week 8

<u>*Grand Bahama Island*</u>

I am approaching slim and healthy with great speed, it seems, but some cracks are beginning to appear in my smile.

My right shoulder (specifically, the rotator cuff) isn't taking well to weight lifting; that's the first problem. I haven't been able to work it at all for a week. And then an acquaintance, I think without meaning to, belittled both my progress and my effort. And then the real world came to visit my island and hasn't left yet. My phone rings too much, my budget isn't working, and my typewriter won't talk to me.

But my shoulder scares me the most. Right now, I worry about it more than my health, a stupid thing to say but the truth, for it is part of the very beginning of my story. I have wanted muscular shoulders and arms—really wanted a whole new body—longer than I want to admit. The thought was never overpowering, but it nagged.

The nagging started with a patch I had my mother sew on a shirt when I was in the first grade. It was a large red "S" purchased at Dupree's Five and Ten. I collected Superman trinkets and comic books avidly until that patch. I don't think it was the beauty of muscles which attracted me to the Man of Steel, but rather the fact that he was strong and invulnerable to bullies; I had felt frail and, worse, had recently drawn the attention of a bully named Lawton.

Lawton didn't beat me up much, but he threatened to all the time, occasionally using his right center knuckle to raise a frog on my arm and constantly standing too close to me, reminding me that he could invade my territory at will. If a very young person can feel adult impotence, I felt it then.

The feeling was especially strong the first day I wore my Superman "S." I ran to the small wooded area where Lawton and his friends held their secret meetings, hoping that they would accept me, knowing that belonging to the group would protect me. But the boys were not impressed with my shirt. Lawton laughed first, and then he punched me once in the stomach, at the very bottom of the "S." I buried the shirt that day and gave my comics and trinkets to a kid much smaller than I.

After that I decided that muscles and strength were not as important as personality. I smiled a lot. Boy, could a smile and a few well-chosen words make things happen. By the third grade I was a glib, friendly, very gregarious young boy, and by the end of that year I had been elected to my first class office. Vice-president of Mrs. Dasher's homeroom may not be very important to the outside world, but to me it was a heady, powerful moment. My body said very few negative things to me for several years.

Ah, but puberty arrived on a dark horse, or more precisely, in the person of Lawton again. Lawton (to this day I think out of spite) asked my first great love, Felicia, to attend the seventh grade dance with him. When I had asked her, Felicia had unconsciously glanced up and down my body and begged off. She looked at Lawton's body, too, slowly, then said yes. When neither of them acknowledged me, my arms felt especially frail.

Looking back, I think that incident was pretty much an epiphany for me in the negative sense. I first went to a doctor who told me that I had not been born with the right body for large muscles. I tried to accept those life-changing words right then (the doctor's office, his words, even the color of his tie under the white jacket are as vivid to me now as the pain in my shoulder). I began several lifelong habits. I learned to dress to be comfortable with my arms and shoulders. Long-sleeved shirts rolled up just right gave an impression that muscles might be hiding under the folds. Short-sleeved shirts, when they had to be worn, couldn't have elastic in the cuffs.

I avoided sports which required me to perform in front of others and became a water skier and scuba diver and, on one, uh, hair-raising occasion, a sky diver—things which were a little exotic and conversationally interesting.

But I never, never could really put away my dream of shoulders and arms. Last year, when those who know muscles said I really could have honest-to-God muscles, my heart skipped a beat, like the flutters brought on by my crush on Felicia thirty years ago. Last week, when one of my doctors said matter-of-factly my dream could end with too many shoulder injuries, it skipped again, an unpleasant lurch which seemed prolonged and dangerous.

Now, intellectually, I know the shape of my body isn't important. I am happy my life has been guided more by the meatiness of the mind than the shallowness of muscle tissues. I know how very trite it is to be bothered by surface things. And, hurt shoulder or not, I'm living an exotic year. But I'm still very capable of a trite and shallow thought or two. As I sat glumly nursing my shoulder after visiting the doctor, a friend tried to perk me up by admiring the many pluses in my life. To his kindness, I snapped, "And I suppose you're going to tell me I have a nice personality, too."

The following day things got worse. An acquaintance who'd recently returned to Grand Bahama stopped me outside UNEXSO, the Underwater Explorers Society, with a "My God, Remar, you look awful! Stringy." The word took me back years. She continued, "You know, you should take up weight lifting." This to a man who had lifted over half a million pounds in the last two months. I had a fleeting image of what it would be like to trip her accidentally into the sharp spikes of the giant century plant by the front door, but simply nodded. "Yes, that would be a good idea. Nice to have you back," I lied as I walked on, rubbing my hurt shoulder.

It's a mile from UNEXSO to my house, a pleasant walk even when things aren't going well, past tennis courts, three ocean-side hotels separated by large open spaces, and dozens of large mushroom-shaped banyan trees.

I stopped under the banyan before the Holiday Inn and purchased a Styrofoam cup of conch salad from the small native stand there. The tree virtually surrounds the stand, roots touching its roof and sides, attaching there in places, but Bertha, the proprietress, doesn't seem concerned about the creeping roots. Good island psychiatrist that she is, Bertha sensed my mood. "Give it away," she said when I told her about my slight depression. I blinked. She was right. If exercise even when it brings a little injury is good and if diet even when it makes you look "stringy" is healthy, decent people like me should share their blessings. Right then, under the banyan tree, I decided to form my own exercise class.

I called Lauren Hunt-Manning. Laurie and her husband are both instructors at UNEXSO; she is also a certified aerobics fitness specialist. During the past ten years, the Mannings have lived, exercised, and scuba dived from the Great Barrier Reef of Australia to the Taiwan Straits, the Gulf of Siam, the island of Barbados, New Guinea, and finally back to Grand Bahama. Laurie is slightly built, a wisp, and blond. For a while there, she dyed a small shock of her hair pink. Coupled with her smile, the effect was fun and indicative of independence rather than punk.

Laurie looked me straight in the eyes without blinking when I asked her to form an aerobics class at my house. She spoke quickly, "Why do you want a class, Remar?"

"Well, I thought it would be good for my book, you know," I said, "understanding the dynamics of exercise physiology and all that."

She smiled, and continued as if her words were part of my sentence, "You mean the principle of misery loves company, eh?" Bingo.

We met for the first time last night, a get-acquainted session. Five other scuba instructors have joined, all under thirty. Three ladies over forty have joined, too. None of them appear overweight to me, but all say they feel that way. Doc Clement has agreed to participate and serve as our official medical attendant. Dr. Clement's wife seems to be very glad he's participating, too. "She's been pushing me to do something about this," he says as he smiles broadly and rubs his stomach. Doc is tall, chisel-chinned, and enormously jolly in a clipped, British way. In my opinion, he has way too much hair for a man over forty, but he will not share it.

Everyone in the group says they want to slim down and firm up; everyone says they want more energy. Those under thirty seem to want more energy to party. Those of us over forty want more energy to function. The men, at first, were hesitant to discuss specific body goals, but when I told the group about my desire for muscles enough to bring swoons from the opposite sex, all of the men in unison said, "Yeah, *that's it.*" Keith, considerably overweight, was the most honest and most touching. "I want to feel better about myself," he said quietly.

The men are also a little nervous about the thought of aerobic dancing itself, of doing those "funny Richard Simmons movements" I mentioned earlier. I laughed when he said it, for Laurie had already shown me how much work those funny movements really are.

I also told them about my cousin Wayne's friends at the Daniels Creek Hunting Club, down in the pine woods of South Georgia. Dressed in beat-up boots and beat-up clothes, driving a truck even more beat-up, and probably fortified with some good whiskey, lots of beer, and a chew or two of tobacco, the boys arrive at their leased 6,000 acres at about five in the morning during hunting season.

The guys spend about five hours there, usually bag some game, then drive back to downtown Swainsboro (population 8,000 on

Saturdays) just in time for their aerobic dancing class. Kenny Loggins provides the beat and a black man leads the class.

Now, if Chuck Yeager or my cousin's friends had been the first people to adopt and promote aerobic dancing, probably a lot more men would be doing it now. It *is* fun, especially with people who are as rotten at dance as I am, and God knows it is work. I lasted about four minutes of the first forty-minute class before finding an excuse to make a very long phone call. But Simmons is the person many men associate with aerobic dancing, and, unfortunately, he doesn't fit the physical image we dream of having, the Yeager image. He's short, fuzzy-haired, and wildly enthusiastic. Before you raise an objection to aerobic dancing as an unmanly pursuit, however, I suggest you try it nonstop for even ten minutes. You won't be able to raise your hand to swat a fly.

Our class meets three times a week for an hour. My living room, with furniture pushed against the walls, serves as our stretching and limbering-up room. I, like most of the men, am as limber as a rock. After about twenty minutes of warm-up movements to music, we move to my backyard and dance among the palm trees, to fast music. Laurie demonstrates the motions, but I can't follow them too well yet. I try, but everything comes out like some funny version of the Twist.

But my cousin and his friends would not laugh at me, especially Gary Curry. Gary belongs to *two* hunting clubs, a big deal in South Georgia, and is a darn good shot, too, a bigger deal. But he's most proud of the sixty pounds of fat and twenty points of blood pressure Richard Simmon's funny movements have taken from him. On second thought, Gary Curry really does have the last laugh, doesn't he?

Meanwhile, my injured shoulder still continues to slow the weight lifting. If it hasn't improved in another week, the shoulder doctor is sending me to the States to a specialist. If it's better, I'll be working shoulders that day in the gym. The difference between "stringy" and "hunky" in inches is very small— perhaps three more inches on the biceps and a couple of inches over the shoulder. I am beginning to realize how far those distances may be.

T*oo bad about your shoulder, Remar, but you know what they say: "No pain, no gain."*

I think Cher is good-looking enough to eat, so when I first heard her say, "No pain, no gain," about the time I started to redo myself, I didn't doubt the wisdom of her words. Nothing bad could be uttered by a body that charged with sex. I, however, don't like pain and was, therefore, happy to learn that Cher was wrong. Real pain doesn't and shouldn't come with proper exercise.

Stress, on the other hand, is what exercise is about. The proper stress causes beneficial change. Sometimes after the proper stress, you will feel soreness, too, usually from the buildup of fluids in an area.[1] Soreness happens when your body isn't used to stress, and generally isn't bad for you. Pain on the other hand—an instant feeling that something isn't right—should not happen. If it does, slow down or stop exercising, depending on the severity of the pain. If it continues, seek medical help.

The healthy soreness you feel a day or two after first jogging or weight lifting will go away quickly as your body adjusts to the new stresses you're putting on it.

N*o body has ever needed muscles like my body needs muscles. If I work out twice as hard, will I hunkify twice as fast?*

I used to think that. For a while, I worked out much more than any of my doctors or weight coaches recommended. That's when my real injuries started, too.

Think of weight training—really, any exercise—as a prescription from your doctor. It generally isn't safe to take twice the dosage. Exercise twice as much and your injuries will increase nearly geometrically and, more importantly, your improvements may come slower. My strength and muscle gains have been much more dramatic since I started cutting back on my lifting.

That's the best news I can give you, too. No one has to devote his life to exercise and no one has to spend literally hours each day to accomplish the things I've accomplished.

Will *stretching exercises have me touching my toes in no time or at least touching my knees?*

Flexibility does not come easily. I told you I stretched at least thirty minutes a day and made only minimal gains in that area. The only thing that touches my toes is my feet. That depressed me until I was told that flexibility by itself probably doesn't do anything for your health. I now stretch about five minutes a day, since stretching muscles may lessen the chance of injury.

What *about warm-up and cool-down?*

Especially if you are over forty or out of shape, warm-up is very important. Start hard exercise without it and you can bring changes in your EKG and maybe worse. Warm-up also reduces injury, lets your oxygen-carrying cells and enzymes work more efficiently, and generally increases blood flow to the muscles you are working.[2] My five-minute stretching, for instance, is a part of my warm-up.

Cool-down is just as important, regardless of your age. After exercise, large amounts of blood build up in the muscles you've been working. The muscles then actually help return the blood to the heart by squeezing the veins. A sudden stop in exercise can cause the blood to pool in the veins, which may reduce blood flow to the brain, which can make you faint or worse.

Both warm-up and cool-down should be for at least five min-

This is the story of a 201-pound man, and let's start it with honesty: My shape on January 1 elicited very few swoons.

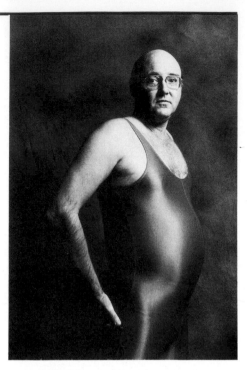

*I wore this to hide reality.
It didn't work.*

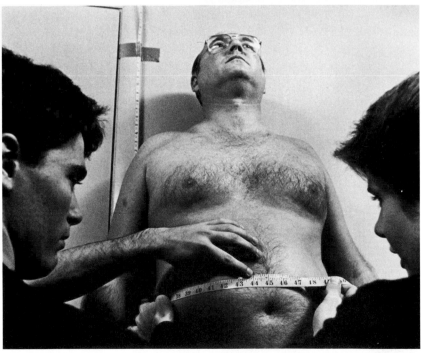

*My trainer Russell Burd and my photographer and friend Deni
McIntyre confront the belly of the beast: forty-three inches on
January 13.*

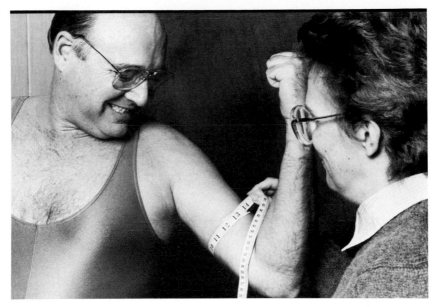

Mary Abbott Waite is my best friend and my editor, a nice combination. She's trying not to laugh as I attempt a flex. How do you like my double chin? January 13.

I am standing on a friend's fieldstone patio. She's smoking, and I'm freezing, since it's thirty-eight degrees. In her eighties, my friend has her own theories about health, and I think she's wondering about mine.

The pictures on the coffee table are color shots of my heart beating. During this meeting, Bob Bell, my nuclear physician, is telling me for the first time about my heart problem.

Jenny Bell, M.D., one of Bob's daughters, joins me in a pose-off. At this point, there's no contest. My jowls are bigger than my biceps.

This machine, a spirometer, told me that 15 percent of my lung capacity was gone—probably due to smoking.

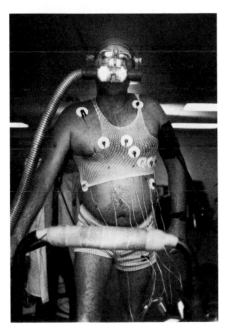

I am trying out for a Godzilla role. The handsome mask directly measures oxygen consumption as I work out on the treadmill.

Members of my aerobic dancing class and a couple of other friends practice lifting maximum weight. John Englander, president of UNEXSO, is the bearded but bald fellow. Doc Clement is to his left. Kathy, the first beautiful woman to sense my emerging hunkiness, is two over from Doc. Kathy is very smart.

In mid-January, I can barely reach past my knee; my weight still hovers around 200 pounds.

I like Russell Burd, my trainer, but I don't like his bicep. He also has far too much hair.

Sunrise on Grand Bahama Island, my home for the remake. Jogging at sunrise is really breathtaking for me, especially during these first weeks.

I jogged a lot at the Lucayan National Park. Did you know that caves and tunnels there run miles out into the sea, where they're called Blue Holes?

UNEXSO has been my main island hangout for years. Here, I'm exercising by hauling up empty scuba tanks. The people who usually hauled scuba tanks endorsed my exercise. They were disappointed when this mode of exercise didn't last more than fifteen minutes.

utes, and should contain a gradual buildup or build down of activity: walking to jogging, then jogging to walking, for instance.

I*f I'm going to do all this work, do I need to stock up on Gatorade and the like to really quench my thirst?*

When you exercise, your body heats up and begins to sweat, depleting your water supply and passing off certain minerals such as salt and potassium. The manufacturers of commercial thirst preparations, looking for an honest way to make a healthy buck, decided to duplicate the ingredients of sweat under the logical assumption that a drink which duplicates sweat does good things.

Unfortunately, all commercial thirst quenchers have something sweat doesn't, unless you're weird: sugar. Sugar definitely isn't good for quenching thirst, either. It actually impairs the passage of water from the stomach to the body, eventually to your individual cells.[3]

Thirst quenchers also contain calcium, potassium, and magnesium in the equally logical assumption that, since these items are depleted to some degree during exercise, we should replace them. Depletion doesn't happen very quickly, though. And a normal diet adequately replaces them. A study of participants in a grueling twenty-day road race showed even these hardy folks didn't need any mineral supplementation.[4]

So what does this tell you commercial thirst quenchers actually replenish? People's pockets, of course. And what's the very best, most healthy drink before and during exercise? Cool water. Faster than commercial preparations, and even faster than warm water, it enters your system quickly and efficiently.[5] The only thing it doesn't do is stimulate further drinking. The commercial thirst quenchers do and in that sense can be good. If you forget to drink, you might want to use them watered down. But remember to use sugared drinks only during exercise, not before.

You may also have caught wind of a new product on the market called "glucose polymers." These things are supposed to increase endurance time by preventing the body's store of glucose from running out.[6] Initial research is promising. For most of us, this product isn't a possibility yet, which leaves us with the commercial preparations and that best of all thirst-quenching fluids, water.

At least thirty minutes before beginning a sustained exercise program, drink two to two-and-a-half cups of water, and try to drink a cup or two every fifteen minutes during your exercise.

Well, *how about a candy bar or something else with a little sugar in it for an energy lift as I exercise?*

When you are fatigued, your body is telling you it needs fuel, energy. What you're physically feeling is the effects in the brain of depleted blood sugar. I used to think M & M's were the perfect energy pick-me-up, which still seems logical to me, and I still do love them as a snack, but they, like all high-sugar-based candies, don't really give you a productive energy boost. After you eat one of those sugary, tasty treats, the level of blood glucose raises quickly in the body. Your brain and nervous system use glucose specifically as a fuel, and are very sensitive to these changes in the glucose levels. They don't like it, and your brain tries to compensate for the extra glucose by having your pancreas secrete extra insulin. Insulin, in effect, tells the body's cells to soak up the extra glucose.

When you take in large amounts of high-sugar things—and large here can be one candy bar—the overproduction of insulin results in drastically lowered blood sugar. Lowered blood sugar, of course, is what makes you feel fatigued.

For most of us, this rebound effect of eating high-sugar sweets doesn't do anything but make us feel weaker and fatter, but for some people it brings on depression of the central nervous system. Excessively high blood sugar can also cause cell dehydration.

Fructose, on the other hand, the sugar found in fruits, has a much more stable effect on blood glucose. It doesn't seem to cause the overproduction of insulin which causes the problem.[7] So, occasionally nibble on a good candy bar just for the hell of it, but plan on getting your energy from fruits.

A*re you saying that refined sugar in itself is bad?*

Refined sugar isn't bad in itself, but the calories it provides aren't very productive. Except in the fat-building area, where they're very productive.

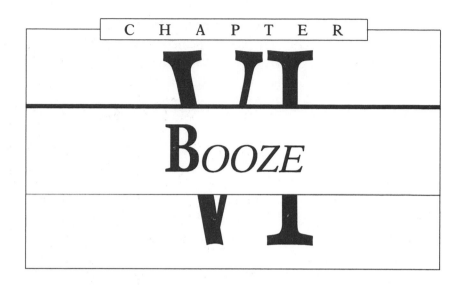

CHAPTER VI

BOOZE

Week 10

Marietta, Georgia

For two-and-a-half months, since I moved to Grand Bahama, my life has been controlled and sheltered. Gluttony and sloth, former friends, haven't seen much of me. Insecurity, an acquaintance, has been pretty much kept at bay, too. I've been safe, others shoring me up and keeping me from all temptation.

Leaving the island without my trainer last night, in the company of strangers who cared only about their hangovers and sunburns, was therefore wonderfully tempting and a little nerve-racking. Airplanes serve *real* food. Junk food. No one told me to avoid butter, or select baked chicken over greasy, tasty stew, and not a soul acted like the dessert was anything but healthy. Even the coffee wanted to seduce me. For two-and-a-half months I have avoided my usual six cups, drinking hot apple juice or bubbling cranberry juice instead. The doctors didn't make me do that, either. Hot juices just sounded a lot healthier and more exotic and they did fill my craving for something hot in the mornings or after a meal.

Until the plane. I decided moderation was just as good as abstinence when it comes to dessert and coffee and consumed them without guilt. Small sins are so nice.

The cart with liquor bottles rattling away rolled by for the last time and my eyes followed it for a moment until I realized how much it tempted me.

I have quietly enjoyed wine and whiskey for over twenty years. I say it like that for no one has accused me of being a drunkard or a problem drinker, and even I didn't realize how much I depended on reasonably moderate amounts of alcohol to help me handle things. Insecurities, worries, pressures, rapid changes in plans, great opportunities, exciting things and terrifying things, boredom, thinking too much, fatigue—I had an encyclopedia of reasons for a glass of wine or beer. The amounts were modest at first, too. But over the years, more and more things seemed to bother me or at least seemed to be a good reason to have another and a stronger drink. And though I never drank alone during the daylight of any of those years, I did like a drink at night to help me sleep. The before-bed drink became the one I really needed. It, of course, only put me to sleep for a few hours and then woke me up.

Now, as I write this, the words look an awful lot like those of an alcoholic, and they scare me as much as my memories of the times I needed *that drink*. They also embarrass me in a way: I may not elicit swoons yet, but I'm quite proud of most of me and don't really like to admit that alcohol was necessary for me to be more comfortable with myself.

"Was" is the operative word here, I hope. I stopped drinking the first night of my remake. Though I was nervous and didn't sleep well for a night or two, I now sleep like I used to sleep back when my biggest worry was going out to feed my horse on a cold morning.

Much more important, I like myself better. People have always seen me as an outgoing, relaxed person with others, especially strangers. Their perception has always been wrong. My heartbeat picks up when I'm alone in an unknown situation. I worry if people will like me and worry if my looks fit the situation and worry about my worry breaking through my well-tended façade. I really thought booze helped me through those moments, too. It probably did loosen my tongue but, on more objective reflection, it brought me a quiet dread of others rather than tranquillity.

I realized that at my first no-booze party two months ago. Though I was nervous at the thought of handling myself without my high-octane friend (still am at times), the gathering was enjoyable and surprisingly nonthreatening. Not a goblin chased me. Even more important, my mood swings don't have peaks and valleys these days. I have spent an awful lot of the past twenty years terrified of things that never happened or happened with no great consequence, and excited about things that would elicit a yawn from most. I thought a drink or two would help me through those moments. When I realized they caused many of them and exacerbated all of them, I felt a nicer high than any drink can bring.

A lot of that old agitation was chemically created, my doctors tell me. The brain acts like a sponge in the presence of alcohol. Though I took my last drink two-and-a-half months ago, portions of it were still having a fun time with my brain cells a month later. I don't want to think about all of the important decisions I've made and foolish things I've done over the past twenty years with the assistance of tipsy gray matter.

But I do like to contemplate this quote from my first blood analysis since the Reformation: in two and a half months, my "triglycerides have dropped precipitously from 355 mg/dl to 174 and the GGT, a liver enzyme study most commonly related to the abuse of alcohol, has dropped from 117 to 51. It is almost back to normal." A liver to elicit swoons.

Heaven, incidentally, did not arrive with abstinence. I still worry about things (like my shoulder, which is better but not well enough for serious lifting), still am nervous at times around others, still have occasional grumpiness and depression. Not a weakness or problem left me permanently, but they all did lose ground to equanimity.

I don't plan to check out an ax from the Carrie Nation Club, either. I don't think drinking per se is bad, and still think the cool bite of a beer when you're hot and thirsty is delightful. I don't even think an occasional convivial high with friends is more than a small, pleasurable sin. But in this year of rebuilding my health and my body, I am more aware than ever of the need to exercise a few gray matter muscles, too. When I drink again, I don't think it will be for the same effect.

I thought about that as the drink cart continued down the airplane aisle. It didn't seem as filled with magic elixirs as it used to. And though I don't like the idea of facing a world of weight lifting, temptations, and pleasures without some support, I am becoming very comfortable facing it without liquid support.

I *have a beer at lunch, a glass of that fancy Gallo wine with Norma's Chef-Boy-Ar-Dee special, and a beer with my Alka-Seltzer before bed. What does that say about me?*

That you are classified a heavy drinker by the National Institute on Alcohol Abuse and Alcoholism and most other research organizations. The institute defines light drinking as under four per week, and moderate as four to thirteen per week.[1] You're talking about *twenty-one drinks per week.*

E*xactly how much booze is "one drink"?*

One and a half ounces of eighty-proof liquor, one five-ounce glass of wine, or one twelve-ounce beer.[2] But most people's idea of "one drink" is more than that. Many researchers say that home drinks mixed without the use of a jigger usually contain two to three ounces of booze and most wine glasses hold more than the five ounces of wine which constitutes "one drink." Some surveys also show that many restaurants and bars may also pour more than one-and-a-half ounce drinks.[3]

I *drink four or five "drinks" a day, but I never feel tipsy. Does this mean I'm doing okay?*

Generally speaking, each "drink" takes about two hours for your body to burn it up, and nothing—not coffee or food or raw eggs or cold showers or pure oxygen or "hair of the dog" can speed your particular body's burning process. If you drink one drink every two hours, your body can pretty much burn off the alcohol as you drink it. If you down two drinks quickly, you begin to overload your system, and that's when you begin to get drunk.[4]

You could theoretically drink four or five drinks, therefore, and never be drunk. But that's not the way we drink. Two drinks with lunch at one, consumed over an hour, put your body in a slightly alcoholic state. It sobers up at five, when you drink two more, and remain under their influence until nine, when your nightcap takes over. Your body, particularly your liver, has been in overtime for about ten hours. A regular pattern like this, not uncommon, can cause health problems.

B*ut I don't feel drunk. So what's wrong?*

As professional drinkers (like I used to be) know, experience covers many sins. Our bodies adjust to the alcoholic state, developing a higher tolerance, requiring more alcohol for that "high." But that doesn't mean we have any lower blood alcohol levels than the amateurs.

N*ow I feel a little depressed. Won't a drink or two give me a lift?*

For most people a cocktail or beer will give you a feeling of relaxation and euphoria at first, why most of us originally like drinking. But alcohol is definitely a depressant. Oddly enough, the first thing it depresses is our inhibitions. That's why Norma took off her bra at your Christmas party last year.

I'm, uh, kind of heroic around the belly. Does that mean I get drunk slower than a runty type?

How fast you get drunk depends on your weight, the speed of the drinking, how much food and what type of food is in your stomach, and the type of beverage you're mixing your booze with. If you are muscular rather than fat, you can handle booze easier, too.[5] But don't think that eating a large meal before a drinking bout prevents you from getting drunk. It simply postpones the drunken state.

Protein, such as milk, incidentally, does a real good job of slowing down alcohol absorption. But that is still "slow down," not "prevent."

When does alcohol consumption begin to affect my liver? Are there any symptoms?

Alcohol, unlike most major sources of calories, can't be stored anywhere in the body for use as future fuel. The body therefore tries to burn it immediately, putting it in the fuel chain before any other fuel. Other fuels, such as fatty acids, have to wait before the body can burn them, and fatty acids in particular seem to favor the liver as a waiting place. This infiltration of the liver by fat is the first abnormality of the liver associated with alcohol over consumption, the first step in a progression of conditions which culminates in cirrhosis.[6] A blood test which measures your liver's levels of two enzymes called SGPT and SGOT can tell you if you're there yet. I was. But in less than three months away from the bottle, my liver was virtually back to normal.

What is cirrhosis, and will it clear up if I'm good?

Cirrhosis of the liver is a progressive disease in which some liver cells are replaced by fibrous, connective tissue. The more cells affected, the more poorly the liver functions, until finally it can't function at all. At that point, you die. Damage from cirrhosis is not reversible, though it may be arrested or slowed.

What about all that publicity about a drink or two being good for your heart?

Please don't lift a sentence or two from this and say it's gospel, for the "drink or two a day is good for you" debate isn't settled yet. But several studies did indicate that moderate drinkers had significantly lower risk of fatal heart attack than either heavy drinkers or nondrinkers. The researchers speculated (didn't state as a fact) that this protection might arise from the seeming ability of alcohol to raise the level of high-density lipoproteins (HDLs) in the blood.[7] A high level of HDLs, as we'll see later, seems to indicate a lower likelihood of coronary heart disease. High levels of HDLs, as we'll also see, are associated also with men who exercise regularly. For example, *Consumer Reports* summarized the findings of one study by saying: "Sedentary men who drank moderately had HDL levels similar to those of moderate drinkers who jogged regularly. When the men who jogged abstained from alcohol for three weeks, their HDL levels remained relatively unchanged. HDL levels in the sedentary men fell significantly, however, when they abstained from drinking."[8]

Now, needless to say, I liked hearing about this study. It seemed to indicate that a slug-type person who didn't exercise or drink could be as well-off cardiovascular-wise as a jock simply by hitting the bottle a little. My type of exercise. Reality is never that nice, though. Like most things in health, these findings are filled with ifs:[9]

1. Many of the most popular studies comparing rates of heart disease and mortality for drinkers and nondrinkers did not separate lifelong abstainers from those who had given up drink, something usually done for health reasons. In the stud-

ies where these types were separated, people who had never drunk (lifelong abstainers) and moderate drinkers usually had about the same risk of heart attack. *Ex-drinkers*, incidentally, had a death rate four times the expected rate.

2. Some studies do correct for never-drinkers/past-drinkers and still show that the moderate drinkers come out slightly ahead. These studies may fail to correct for cigarette smoking. When corrections for smoking take place, never drinkers and moderate drinkers have about the same rate of heart problems.

3. Some researchers say many teetotalers may be type A people, the driven folks already at higher risk of heart attack.

4. Changes in HDLs. Remember that HDLs, high-density lipoprotein, in high numbers, do seem to lower the risk of heart disease. Very moderate amounts of alcohol do seem to raise HDL levels, too. But HDL is not one substance. It's made up of components called subfractions. Very hard research is now showing that HDL_2 is the factor protecting against heart disease. HDL_3, another subfraction, seems to be the HDL raised by alcohol consumption.

5. These studies had to do with heart disease only. Many other conditions, such as high blood pressure or high body fat, can take the wind out of your sails, and these things can be prevented or helped with the proper exercise.

So can Norma and I forget the dancercise classes at the Moose Lodge or not?

If you've read this carefully, you probably feel like I do and like most of the heart experts at this stage in the research. A drink or two isn't going to hurt me, but it's not going to make me healthier, either. Didn't you really know it couldn't be that easy?

But will that drink or two mess up Norma's diet? I don't need to lose weight, of course.

Drinks are filled with those evil "empty calories"—calories which don't do anything but put on weight. But an occasional drink is no worse for your diet than an occasional piece of chocolate cake. If you plan to drink, at least cut down their calorie content. Make your wine 25 percent water and you'll hardly notice the difference. Make your hard drinks with one bottle cap rather than a big pour. Buy mini-cans of beer. So much of drinking is psychological, you'll be surprised how these tricks will help you.

I*'ve been drinking a six-pack a day for years. Am I running any risks?*

Regular heavy drinkers increase their risks of developing a number of health problems. A recently released study, for example, found the risk of stroke to be four times higher.[10] Heavy drinking is also associated with increased risk of cancers of the mouth, throat, stomach, liver, pancreas, and colon; increased risk of heart disease; increased risk of high blood pressure; and increased risk of stomach and intestinal orders.[11] In fact, the National Institute on Alcohol and Alcoholism stated: "Chronic alcohol consumption leads to ubiquitous toxic effects in the body, with medical consequences ranging from slight functional impairment to life-threatening disease states."[12] You decide about the six-pack.

H*ow do you know if someone you know is drinking too much?*

If you and others quietly wonder if someone is drinking too much, they probably are. They may not be an alcoholic by definition, but that doesn't mean they don't need help. Alcohol can begin to control things much faster than most of us (including me) want to recognize. For instance, if reading all this makes you nervous enough to want a drink, you have a reason to be nervous.

Nervous? Who me? I'll just have a little nip or two to make me sleep better.

One one-and-a-half ounce drink consumed leisurely before going to bed probably won't bother you much.[13] But if you, like me, really need a stiff one to fall asleep, you're probably looking at several problems. First, you'll probably wake up a lot needing to take a leak or a drink of water. Most people find that wake-up period like the morning, and find it hard to go back to sleep. Second, needing a drink to "relax" you at any time is a very scary sign of alcohol dependency. And finally, if that drink is gulped, and is a strong one, you're placing extra burdens on your liver.

I don't want to think how many years that drink was important to me, but do know how nice it feels to be able to go to sleep without it.

Some people can be heavy drinkers for their whole lives and probably not have addictive problems associated with their drinking (though most will have health problems). Others become alcoholic quickly. If you see someone you care for developing alcoholic problems or habits (such as keeping booze too readily available at all times or constantly looking for an excuse to have a drink), ask others who care for the person if they, too, are a little worried. If you all agree there's a problem, go to the person's spouse or closest friend and talk honestly about the problems you are seeing. Real alcoholics, virtually all of them, will die prematurely unless someone helps them.

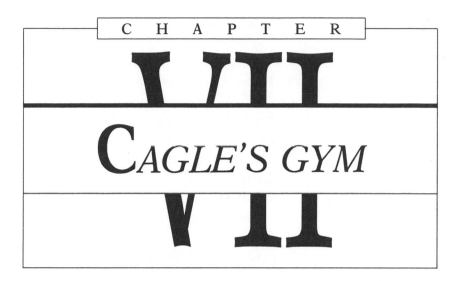

CHAPTER VII

CAGLE'S GYM

Week 11

Marietta, Georgia

Today I lifted weights by myself in a strange gym, my first workout without the prodding and emotional support of my trainer and other gym members who know me. Sounds like a trite accomplishment, doesn't it, like walking down the street? Though I survived with my dignity reasonably intact, it was more like walking through a field of sand spurs with spring feet.

First I had to choose a gym. Though I'm in my hometown, I didn't have the slightest idea how to find a comfortable place. I left the first fancy fitness center when the "hostess" tried to sell me their own brand of cologne before selling me a day membership. I couldn't get through the lobby of the second place. A large group of "Samba Saturday" class members were dancing through there on the way to a seminar entitled "Human Sexuality and Aerobics." Next I drove to a couple of "serious gyms," so-called because everyone in them looks so *intent* and chiseled. The gyms themselves looked like something from an old Brando movie. A person could get beat up in a place like those. I drove on.

Discouraged, I stopped at the Ace Hardware close to my mother's home to collect another bedding tray of bright red salvia for her. Here, chance in the person of a very friendly guy named Jimmy Beasley solved my problem. Jimmy is as serious about weight lifting as he is friendly. Since he had both the body and the personality I admired, I asked where he worked out. Cagle's. That would be the gym for me.

"Friendly" may fit Jimmy perfectly, but when I pulled up in front of Cagle's, I wasn't sure the adjective fit his gym. A low, gray building with one shuttered window squatted in a small gravel lot. The single door faced the world from behind mirrored glass. A big, deep-red Harley-Davidson motorcycle leaned rather arrogantly by the door, its fat wheels digging ruts in the gravel.

Two deserted shanty houses right out of *The Grapes of Wrath* sat across the narrow paved alley. A large, red and white sign on the more run-down of the derelict structures said *THIS PROPERTY NOT FOR SALE OR LEASE BY OWNER*, a nearly laughable sign if you don't know the neighborhood. The gym and the houses are a minute's fast walk from the Cobb County Courthouse and are the last pieces of property not yet gobbled up by law firms whose partners like to walk to work.

I was in my mother's car, a silver Lincoln about the size of my insecurities at that moment. It didn't make the right statement, something which hit me as a truck holding two massive, barrel-shaped, and nonsmiling men parked on my left. You don't just sit in a silver Lincoln in front of a serious gym as barrel-shaped and nonsmiling people look at you, especially if your only companion is a tray of pretty flowers, unless you're doing something. I quickly shifted the tray of salvia, shuffled through my mother's mail and slipped a magazine from its wrapper as the two barrel types walked by my window. We saw the cover at the same time, *Gourmet*. I could have been playing with dolls. I thought briefly of explaining: "Flowers? Hell, I *stomp* gardens, myself." Instead I just forced the car door open and headed to the gym. It was a very long walk.

I think fast when I'm nervous. As the gym door shut behind me, I planned the response which I thought would make me sound calm when greeted, stuck my hand out to the guy standing behind the counter, and without waiting for the question blurted, "I'm fine."

Charlie Thompson, the owner of Cagle's, endeared himself to me by making my gaffe seem normal. "Glad to hear it; I am, too."

As he spoke, the reception area came into focus. An old Spanish-style Naugahyde sofa with the corners gnawed off leaned against the right office wall. Two high school boys sprawled on it, paying more attention to Charlie's two towheaded sons running across the green outdoor carpet than to me. An older man in a Gucci sweatshirt walked from the dressing area and playfully kicked one boy's feet as he walked by, stepping over the other set. Charlie's wife knelt on the floor by several battered black filing cabinets and waved to another young man as she called to her sons. Trophies, some on their sides, some dusty, were everywhere, conveying a pleasant nonchalance about winning.

The place and the people who drifted in and out had the feeling of our old cabin at Lake Sinclair, where the furniture was theft-proof (who would want it?) but perfect and comfortable for our needs, and the company was nonstop and happy.

Charlie Thompson, thirty-three, as wholesome-looking as a glass of milk, has been in the gym business, what he always wanted to do, since he graduated from the University of Georgia nine years ago. He refers to Cagle's as a "heavy weight" gym rather than a health club or fitness center. Charlie looks like a bodybuilder, one of those guys who spend their time sculpting their bodies and are judged in competition on the symmetry of their muscles, on their beauty. In my gym in the Bahamas, virtually everyone is a bodybuilder (me, too). Charlie's background, though, is in power lifting. It's similar to the Olympic weight events you've watched on television in that power lifters are judged solely on their ability to move weight. Those who move the most win.

But power lifting events are different from Olympic events. In the squat, the contestant rests the weights behind his neck on the shoulders and tries to squat then stand up. In the dead lift, the contestant squats, grabs the bar, and tries to lift the most weight from the floor while keeping his arms straight. In the bench press, the contestant reclines on a bench and attempts to press the greatest weight to his chest and then return it to the starting position.

Since power lifters win with strength, not shape, they aren't afraid of fat, and many of them own a good bit of it. Charlie Thompson even says fat adds leverage and cushioning. I don't doubt him, either. Cagle's Gym took first place in eight out of eleven events at the 1986 Georgia Power Lifting Championships. A weight lifting sport that accepts the rotund. Maybe I missed my calling.

I felt real comfortable after talking with Charlie, and entered the weight room rather eagerly, feeling nervous only when I caught the eyes of the two barrel types. They watched me as I walked to a bench, sat a bar on the rack above it, and slid weights on each end. I tried to do all of this very professionally. I lay on the bench. Normally at this point, my trainer would hand me the bar, but my trainer was in the Bahamas. I would have to lift the bar and all that weight from the rack by myself, something I had never done before. A very unnerving thought. Could I lift the weight? I placed my hands carefully on the bar for maximum torque, closed my eyes, prayed the prayer of the insecure, "Oh God, don't let me make a fool of myself," and heaved mightily.

Terror gives great strength. The bar nearly flew from my hands, and a weight from the left side sailed through the air, thumping at the feet of the burly types. The older one, who had glared the most at my mother's *Gourmet*, walked to me. "Hey, buddy, how 'bout someone to spot you?" he said with a grin on his face. "You look kinda eager."

I did not argue with his offer or his observation. But I did explain about the plants and that magazine. You can't have those power lifters thinking we bodybuilders are too effete.

Well, I would never get caught with flowers, but tell me more about the differences between power lifting, Olympic lifting, strength training, and weight lifting.

Power lifters compete in three events: the squat, bench press, and dead lift. In the squat, a barbell is placed on the lifter's upper back. The lifter then squats down until his upper thighs are parallel with the ground and then stands up. The winner can stand up with the most. The record, set by heavyweight Mat Demio is 1,010 pounds. Squats, incidentally, aren't graceful, but they're great for building your legs and your buttocks.

Everyone knows the bench press—you're on your back, you lift the bar from a rack, lower it to the chest, and push it back up—but did you know that the record press is 705 pounds by Ted Arcidi? The bench press is a great exercise for replacing flabby breasts with muscle. Women love chests rebuilt with this exercise. Trust me.

The dead lift involves bending down and lifting a barbell off the floor. The record is 903 pounds by Doyle Kennady. Dead lifts are primarily a leg exercise, but also strengthen the back.

The three power lifting events are part of almost everyone's weight training, but power lifters simply concentrate on them more.

Olympic lifting, the event you watch in the Olympics, has only two lifts: the clean and jerk, and the snatch. And it's a very fast sport, involving dramatic movement. The clean and jerk starts with the bar on the floor. With a few weights on it. Like 500 pounds for the heavy weight champion. The lifter squats down, grabs the bar and in one lightning-fast upward jerk stands up and pulls that 500-pound bar to his chest, where he may pause for a moment. From there, the lifter literally throws the bar up and goes under it, pushing the weight over his head, where he must control it. It's a damn exciting thing to watch, but a damn scary thing to try.

The snatch also starts with the bar on the ground, but instead of pausing with the bar on the chest, the lifter immediately pushes it over his head. The snatch is probably the most difficult and dangerous maneuver any lifter wants to attempt.

Strength trainers and weight lifters are terms used interchangeably by some to describe people who lift weights, but don't call a power or Olympic lifter either name, or they'll turn you into a pancake. Everyone likes specific terms. So don't forget that bodybuilders care more about their looks than their strength or techniques, and power and Olympic lifters care more about their strength than their looks.

P*hysiologically, what are the mechanisms of getting bigger and stronger? Do my muscle cells grow, or what?*

First, increasing your actual muscle measurements is referred to in two ways: hypertrophy is an increase in the size of the muscle cell itself; hyperplasia is an increase in the number of your muscle cells. Scientists don't know for sure which way human muscles grow, but most agree that hypertrophy (increasing the size of your cells) plays a major role in muscle growth.[1]

W*hat is muscle, anyway?*

About 75 percent water, 20 percent protein, and 5 percent minerals, salts, and fuels such as glycogen (a stored sugar). The increase in any of these components will cause increase in muscle size.

W*hat about that theory that you build muscle by "ripping apart" the old muscle tissue?*

That sounds real macho, but isn't really right. Muscle tissue *is* a very dynamic tissue. It is always breaking down and being built back up. But this doesn't happen in stages. For instance, the muscle isn't static and then put in a state of frenzy if you lift weights, it is constantly rebuilding itself.

When you weight train, you increase the buildup phase and *decrease* the breakdown phase, according to most theories.[2] This gives you an increase in the amount of muscle protein actually available to contract your muscle. This contraction, incidentally, is a muscle's sole responsibility. An uncontracted muscle is an unhappy one. It atrophies.

People *seem to toss a lot of fancy adjectives around describing strength-building exercises. What's the difference in isometric, isotonic, and isokinetic exercising?*

Isometric exercises involve an application of force, but no movement. Pushing like Samson against the sides of a door frame is a good example. Isometrics will definitely build strength, but only at the specific angle in which you are working a muscle. Charles Atlas, incidentally, became a rich and famous man when he introduced isometrics to America's wimps. You didn't kick sand in his face. Many people, including Atlas, have believed isometric exercises are an excellent way to build muscle. Even football teams have used them for that. Although it works, muscle building the isometric way takes an awful lot longer than muscle building with weights or machines.

Isotonic exercises involve uniform tension but varying speed. Free weights are isotonic exercises. The weight you are handling does not increase or decrease while you lift, but the speed of your movement will be determined by your strength at different points in your range of movement. There are, incidentally, types of isotonic exercise in which the weight does vary, but these are still classified as isotonic exercise because weight and a varying speed are still involved. These "variable resistance machines," which include Nautilus and some Universal machines, vary the weight according to your strong and weak points, a nice selling feature. People like me who prefer free weights are suspicious of most machines. All of the isotonic exercising methods, including free weights, enable you to work a whole range of motion. They can improve both strength and flexibility in the muscles you are working.

Isokinetic exercise machines, the newest thing in strength and weight training, have the ability to control the speed of the muscle contraction. Regardless of how strong or weak you are, you can't change the speed of your motion. That may not seem very important to you or your muscle, but it is. These machines will only give you as much resistance as you give it. If you can only lift a hundred pounds, it resists a hundred pounds' worth, etc. Because we have different strengths at different places throughout a movement, these machines can work us the hardest at our weakest point and our strongest point.

Nautilus and some other variable resistance machines have tried to duplicate this strength-to-resistance ratio mechanically. To do so, they averaged a group of lifters' strengths at different positions in a particular movement and built their machines to provide different resistances to the different strength levels. Their machines will give you a very good workout. But you must adjust your own strength patterns to these machines, they won't adjust to you. Isokinetic machines will adjust to you.

For professional athletes, isokinetic machines also provide some very special capabilities. The important movement in most athletic events occurs at very fast speeds. A pitcher's arm may be moving at almost a hundred miles per hour when he throws a fastball, for instance. But most strength and power exercises happen at much slower speeds. Isokinetic machines can allow a person to build his strength and power at the speed his body parts move during an actual activity.[3] They can actually control the speed of the muscle contraction, something that's never happened before.

Dr. Gideon Ariel, my biomechanics and strength coach, definitely does have the neatest isokinetic machines out there. They are very expensive (the two machines you'd need to do most things cost over $20,000), but do the work of many machines. You'll find them at some preventive medicine and physical rehabilitation centers, and at the more advanced human performance centers (health clubs)—no self-respecting place with one of these machines would call itself a gym, would it?

Can *I use steroids to speed hunkdom along?*

They'll definitely speed your search, but may kill you along the way. Steroids have anabolic and androgenic qualities. Anabolic refers to the ability of a steroid to convert food into living matter, such as muscle tissue. Androgenic refers to steroid's ability to make the taker more masculine. Side effects include impaired liver function, liver tumors, actual structural changes in the liver itself, lowered HDL cholesterols (the good guys), altered testicular function (a nice way of saying your manhood could shrink away to nothing), acne, baldness, and dramatic and negative changes in your behavior patterns.[4]

Did *you think about using steroids?*

I did, and I would have used them if they had appeared even reasonably safe. But several months of research and a particular fondness for my manhood convinced me to pass on them. Steroids may speed up hunkdom, but hard work eventually brings you the same result.

What's *the difference in strength and power and endurance and tone? And what does all that have to do with big muscles? Norma's been reading all this over my shoulder, and she's gonna become a power lifter, she says.*

Strength is the application of force. It's usually measured by a single repetition, a bench press or leg press. You break strength records when you lift more this week in one repetition than you did last week. Ever had someone take your hand and crush it once in a Texas handshake? That's strength.

Power requires timed movement. Technically, it is your strength multiplied by your speed. If you punch out someone lustfully eyeing Norma, that's power. Be sure the person you punch out isn't more powerful. That's smart.

Endurance is the application of force over a period of time. It's measured by your ability to resist fatigue as you lift the same weight repetitively. When you run from the person you tried to punch out but missed, that's endurance. When he catches you, that's fear.

Tone, as we mentioned earlier, is defined as muscle always in a partial state of contraction. You achieve tone with either strength training or endurance training. Most people's muscles are also in a partial state of contraction when they feel absolute terror, what you'll feel right before the guy who caught you punches you out and doesn't miss.

All of these bad things won't happen to you if you exercise and eat apples and especially if you think before picking on someone bigger than you.

N*orma, that frail thing (she hasn't gained a pound in twenty years, still wears a forty-four), worries about "brittle bones," and is now gulping diet drinks fortified with calcium like I gulp beers to beat the blues. Do men have to worry about brittle bones? Does weight lifting help? Does that calcium in her drinks really help?*

Men's bones can become brittle, too, though usually it happens later in life. But anyone can definitely strengthen his or her bones by lifting weights. The proper lifting program actually increases the mineral content of your bones, the things that make them strong.[5] The best weight program for this is probably high repetitions of low weights.[6] Some people think "circuit training" (remember, that's weight exercises sort of done on the run to get your heart rate up) is very good for this. Start any program under someone's supervision, though. Weight-bearing activity, such as walking or jogging, is also good for strengthening bones.[7]

Making sure you have plenty of calcium in your diet is also important; low-fat milk products, leafy green vegetables, and canned salmon or sardines with bones are good sources. Take your doctor's advice on specific supplements, such as fortified drinks.

Norma *read in the* It's-Startling-But-the-Gospel-Truth News *that all those little weights will really make her workouts more efficient. Now she's wearing hand weights, ankle weights, and a weighted vest, even to bed. She rolled over and flattened my right arm last night. Are those things worth it?*

Wearing them to bed only makes you kinky, not stronger. But miniweights, used properly, can increase your aerobic fitness, burn more calories, and increase your strength.[8] Most people don't use them right, though. Because a half-pound weight looks awfully petite, they buy five-pound ones, then attempt to exercise at their normal pace and intensity, or greater. These people are real popular with doctors. Even a half-pound weight drastically increases the stress on the joint and muscles in the area being worked. Ankle weights, for instance, place considerable strain on the knee joint.

If you want to use light weights, start out below your normal pace. Start with very small weights and work up gradually.

I *don't want to buy anything until I think this thing's for sure. Do I really have to have equipment?*

You don't have to buy out the store to start, but you will need a few things.

Shoes. You need a pair for your particular activity, but you don't need twenty pairs for twenty different things. Did you know there are hundreds of sport shoes on the market now? An active person would need a nubile female servant just to keep up with his shoes if he listened to the manufacturers.

Clothing. If you want to make a fashion statement, fine, but real men don't think about what they wear when they work out. Or at least it looks like they don't think about it. Do wear layers to peel off, though, since exercise heats you up quickly. Of course, many athletes, for instance bikers, take clothing very seriously because it can mean the microsecond difference between winning and losing.[9] But that's not really important for us ordinary types.

Gloves for weight lifting. I list this separately, because you've got to have gloves if you lift—that is, if you're lifting at a real gym versus a spa and if you want to save your hands from a lot of blisters. Weight lifting actually generates enough friction heat to be uncomfortable. But when you get your gloves, for God's sake, don't take them new to the gym. New gloves are a dead giveaway you are a pro or a wimp, nothing in between. Do what I did: rub 'em in the dirt, throw 'em in a gutter, and stomp on 'em a while. This won't add muscles to your frame, but it will make you look more like a great weight lifter who went to seed and is now coming back.

W*ell, I'll never wear a wimpy glove. But what about the real equipment out there, bikes and treadmills and the like? Do I need any of that stuff?*

The only reason to buy equipment is to make your time devoted to exercise either less boring or more efficient. Many devices can help you accomplish both objectives, depending upon your goals. "But," advises Christopher Scott, my exercise physiologist, "never buy on impulse. Try before you buy and pick something you enjoy. If, for instance, you don't like biking outdoors, you'll probably hate stationary cycling. Finally, be prepared to spend some money—most good equipment is expensive." The following notes may help you begin to think about what equipment, if any, is right for you.

Exercise bikes.   They can bore you to death if you don't have something to do while pedaling, but bikes are a practical way to get your aerobic exercise without going outside. Get one that's portable enough to put in front of a television, if possible. Also get one that holds a carrot out in front of you: one that helps you keep your pedaling goal-oriented. For instance, some bikes have a needle which must be kept in one position to maintain your level of activity. Don't buy a bike without something like it.

Some bikes have handle bars that move and add a degree of strength training to your workout; some have TV screens or little maps which let you pretend you're biking through the woods. Some even have motors which move the pedals and, believe it or not, these monsters can give you the hardest workout of all, if they provide a way to gauge your work level. One good bike requires you to keep a needle in the center of a gauge, which requires about as much effort as running up the Empire State Building. What's important is to try whatever bike you seem to like for a while before buying it, and to avoid flimsy bikes sold by mail order or late-night television.

Rowing machines.   Rowing machines are great: they are non-impact, use a lot of muscles, and require a lot of work. But they also require a lot of back work. If you have a bad back, don't think about one of these machines without talking with a sports medicine specialist first. Rowing machines take up a little more room than bikes. Most machines have a sliding seat and two piston "oars." Rowing power comes from the legs, really, so make sure the seat and the rails it moves along not only comfortably support you, but support you in your full range of motion along the track. Some new machines on the market duplicate rowing amazingly well by attaching a wooden grip with a length of cable which usually runs around a flywheel in front of the machine. The thing looks a lot like a spinning wheel, but is probably the best type of rowing machine you can buy.

Treadmills.   They come in electric and manual models and aren't cheap ($500 to $5,000); but if you really plan to be a hard-core jogger, these things can give you relief from traffic and bad weather. If you look at a manual one, definitely try running on it for at least ten minutes. If you can't run that long without dropping dead, ask the salesperson to demonstrate a running effort. Manual machines vary dramatically in quality, and the bad ones are virtually impossible to run on.

Electric treadmills vary in price with their features but not necessarily with their quality. To find a good one, check out what makes local health clubs use.

Generally speaking, don't waste your money on these things until you're really sure you like jogging over other activities.

Cross-country ski machines.   Did you know the highest recorded cardiovascular level reached by any human being was achieved by a cross-country skier?[10] The machines which duplicate this motion are similar to rowing machines in that they use lots of muscles, but they work you standing up rather than sitting. Because they vary so dramatically in quality, try one for a good long time before buying it, or check out the types of machines available in local clubs.

Jump ropes.   I think they were invented by the devil. I tried a jump rope the first day of my remake, and threw my back out on the count of three. Jump ropes do, however, provide fantastic aerobic exercise, take up no room, and work your entire body. But jumping rope also puts lots of strain on your ankles, back, and just about everything else. Jumping can very easily hurt you if you're really out of shape. Don't choose it as a first aerobic exercise, and go slowly when you do choose it.

Minitrampolines.   Great for the professionally coordinated and fit, but dangerous for the klutz. You work out by jogging in place on them; bouncers with poor balance usually fall and crack their crowns.

Late-night television specials in general.   Don't buy any exercise equipment without trying it and looking at it closely. That rule applies doubly to the junk peddled on television. As you know, Norma bought one of those "Tummy Wheels" from late night TV. It's stored under the bed with your "Slide and Slimaway" machine. Most of these gadgets are poorly designed and constructed. Though they may provide some exercise, jumping up and down like a jack-in-the-box provides as much. Don't waste your money. Chris Scott has even invented something as dandy: Gyro Pasties. "The Faster They Twirl, the Fitter the Girl" is his suggested slogan. Chris, a real whiz in advertising, will probably be hired by the people who sell you body wraps.

Weight training equipment.   Whether you want to build endurance or become hunky and muscular, you can use the same equipment, machines or free weights. Strength and bigger muscles come from lifting progressively heavier weights. Endurance—the ability to do something again and again—comes from lifting a relatively lighter weight for more repetitions. In essence, you are training the body to resist fatigue.

Are free weights or machines better for the newly serious lifter?

Free weight or machine, people seem to like what they first lift with, but both have their uses in a balanced program. Free weights definitely teach you balance, and probably work more muscles since the weights are moving three-dimensionally, constantly requiring a tension in all directions. Free weights also look real macho. You don't see machines used in Olympic competitions, and you constantly hear free-weight lifters complaining that "five hundred pounds on a machine doesn't feel like five hundred pounds on a bar." I say that a lot myself around nonlifters. Free weights also instill the essence of weight training: lift anything heavier than normal, and your body responds. When you become used to the movement of dumbbells, you can as easily lift a rock or a heavy log or a chair or, much later, Norma, and receive the same workout. Machines make you dependent.

Machines are safer, however, especially for the newly serious lifter, and machines certainly more easily work some muscle groups such as your lats (latissimus dorsi in formal terms—they give your back a V-shape). In addition, machines let you work out without a partner most of the time. A serious free-weight session always requires two people.

What about those funny spring-type machines I see on TV?

As we said, don't buy something without trying it, and, generally speaking, don't buy machines which provide their resistance with springs. Springs lose their resiliency.

Do you honestly think I'm going to start something like weight lifting at my age? Do you really think I believe my body can change? I mean, you've had all day and tropical beaches and beauties to keep you going. What can a person in the real world accomplish?

I want to tell you about Arno Jensen, a member of my Body Worry Committee, but before doing that, go to the pictures and look at Arno's body.

Wouldn't you like to look like that at fifty-seven? Would you believe he started lifting weights when he was fifty? For those seven years Arno has literally been reversing the most inevitable sign of aging, too. Statistically, everyone loses lean body mass as they age, everyone has more fat. Textbooks accept that fact the way you accept sunrises. But Arno Jensen's lean body mass has *increased* every year for the past seven years. He moves with the grace of a cheetah. He eats 4,000 calories a day. Young women swoon.

He doesn't work out full-time, either, and he didn't even think about being in shape until he was forty. Arnie was a general practitioner then. One night he jumped from bed at 3 A.M. to rush to a maternity patient, made it to the emergency room of the hospital, but had to stop before entering the room because of chest pains. Probably indigestion, he thought. A few hours later he tried to run around the block, and could barely walk around. He started an aerobics program that day.

Arnie's routine includes fifty push-ups every morning, at least thirty minutes on an exercise bicycle virtually every day, and an hour and a half of weight lifting four days a week.

Whenever I wonder what I'm working for, hunkwise and healthwise, I look at pictures of this man.

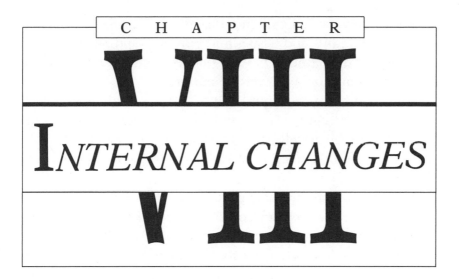

CHAPTER

VIII

INTERNAL CHANGES

Week 14

<u>*The Cooper Clinic, Dallas, Texas*</u>

I hate physical examinations: nakedness, prodding, touching, questions. Everything assaults dignity and pries into places and thoughts that beg to be left alone. Physicals take away our ability to ignore the aging process and to pretend about our health. I, for instance, never felt that any of my bad habits were really catching up with me and secretly believed that there was always time to change things. I was stubborn in those beliefs and steadfast in my ability to ignore any words from my doctors that sounded the least bit threatening to my fantasies of immortality.

You will remember, however, that at the beginning of my remake three-and-a-half months ago, several doctors found the words to get my attention: mild coronary heart disease. Small pulmonary dysfunction. Some abnormal liver function. High risk for heart attack.

I remind you of this because today Dr. Cooper gave me my first complete health evaluation since I took up clean and godly living. And it, in a way, makes the poking and prying worthwhile. In three-and-a-half months my insides have changed. Most of the liquids and tissues and pumping and purifying and growing and dying things have responded quickly to the changes in my consumption and exercise patterns.

I say most because I completely killed some things such as a portion of my lung capacity, and I may have done away with some working liver cells (though I have plenty), and I may not earn back the full function of my heart (though I don't know that yet, either).

But look at what has changed:

My body fat has dropped from 29.7 percent of my total weight to 16.97 percent, a drop of thirty-three pounds of blubber. Aside from the esthetic nicety here, the loss of body fat dramatically cuts down my risk of further heart disease and a dozen other diseases.

My triglycerides have dropped nearly *50* percent. Generally speaking, high triglycerides mean high fat in the blood, which increases the risk of artherosclerosis (more about this in a moment).

My cardiac risk category based on oxygen consumption per kilogram of weight has dropped from very high to low.

My GGT, the liver enzyme which is a nice fingerprint of the steady drinker, dropped more than 50 percent.

My treadmill stress test gave me the most satisfying opinion because I could really savor my progress there immediately. The treadmill gauges many things: aerobic capacity, muscle strength, endurance, cardiovascular fitness, and determination. I added the last category. Three-and-a-half months ago, I collapsed after walking fifteen minutes and achieving a maximum heart rate of 171 beats per minute. Today I walked twenty-three minutes and quit when my heartbeat reached 174. Though that 50 percent improvement may not seem like that much time in minutes, it is. Treadmills increase in angle when you walk on them—the longer you walk, the harder you work. My improvement over the months moved me from a "fair" to an "excellent" aerobic category and literally won me a gold star from Dr.

Cooper. The star is made of foil and probably cost a mil, but I value it immensely.

As I write this, I am sitting in the main waiting room of the Cooper Clinic building itself. Cooper opened this place in 1971, then added an aerobics research center and a very fancy gymnasium and guest lodge. The whole place looks like the campus of a very prosperous small college—stately buildings, old trees, joggers, and sports cars everywhere.

Being examined here isn't actually more comfortable physically (they poke you in more places than a regular doctor does, I think), but it all does feel rather cushy. If, for instance, they served more than water or barium for breakfast and if all the victims, uh, patients, around you had on clothes rather than bathrobes, the setting could be for one of those Texas soap operas.

That's the way it should appear, I guess, since an exam here isn't cheap in the dollar sense. A really complete physical exam like mine, including an upper and lower gastrointestinal series (which has to be the most unpleasant thing next to death itself), costs as of this writing about $1,000, plus travel and lodging.

But as with most of the good preventive medicine/diagnostic clinics around the country (there are quite a few, most for profit), the Cooper Clinic is more thorough than you might want to imagine.

Dr. Cooper took my history.

The blood department analyzed my blood.

A psychologist administered a psychological test. (I "stick to a task until mastery.")

A respiratory specialist evaluated my lung function. (Smoking caused a 15 percent loss.)

An audiologist checked my hearing. ("Outstanding at all frequencies.")

A dentist checked my mouth. (No cavities!)

A technician stripped me naked and weighed me underwater.

Dr. Cooper and Dr. Arno Jensen examined virtually every inch of my exterior and interior.

Finally, Georgia Kostas, the clinic's director of nutrition, met with me to plan my diet more carefully.

After all that, no one can pretend or ignore the realities of his health. And for that reason alone I like these clinics. A good physical can save your life.

I hope the man walking down the hall a little self-consciously in his bathrobe and tennis shoes remembers that, for I know what they are going to do to him in the room on the right. The fellow received his visit to the clinic as a perk for a year's work well done, and though I can't help but wonder if he's planning to slack off a little from now on, I hope he knows how lucky he is.

I do. As you can tell, I am proud of my interior gains because what's inside gives me life. But, after three-and-a-half months, I'm different on the outside, too. Excuse me while I go stand in front of a mirror.

Pardon me, handsome, but getting fit doesn't seem to work all the time. Like Jim Fixx. He had one of those slender, soloflex-type bodies and he ran farther than I can think— the picture of fitness. But he died from a heart attack— while running. Why didn't all that exercise keep him alive?

Jim Fixx was probably the most famous runner in America. When he died at fifty-two of a massive heart attack, thousands of people probably quit jogging from fear of a heart attack and thousands more never started an exercise program because Jim Fixx's death seemed to prove to them that exercise doesn't keep you living longer.

Dr. Cooper knew Fixx well. Several times when the famous runner visited the clinic, Cooper tried to convince Fixx to take a stress treadmill test. Fixx always seemed too busy. Cooper didn't know, of course, that Fixx's father had died at a young age from a massive heart attack. "If we had known that," Cooper says, "we might have finally convinced Jim to have a stress test.

And that test would have very likely shown a major problem. Jim Fixx died primarily of a lack of blood flow to the heart caused by blockage in his coronary arteries, an easy thing to detect with proper testing, and a correctable problem most of the time." Dr. Cooper's book *Running Without Fear* will give you an excellent look at Jim Fixx and his health problems.[1]

But aren't there risk factors none of us can do things about?

As I mentioned earlier, we can't literally change our genetic predispositions to certain things like high blood pressure, high cholesterol levels, or for some of us even the amount of fat on our bodies. But knowing you are in a genetically risky position in any area is the most important reason to fight. If you are from a family of people who die from heart attacks, for instance, you obviously should be concerned about any tests that might show if you have heart disease, and obviously should not do things that already increase your riskier position. If you have genetically high cholesterol, and ignore that as you eat each day, you are simply increasing an already higher probability of trouble.

If you are in high-risk health categories for any reasons—hereditary or simply habit—you have more reason than anyone to have baseline studies done of your engine and its supporting systems. Yearly or at least regular physicals can show changes which can kill you.

Norma and I have spent too many years eating the things we like and living the way we like to really change. We've eaten fried for thirty years, smoked for twenty, carried around our bellies for ten, and we really don't feel that bad. And even though I'm on high blood pressure medicine, our doc *has never acted like we're going to die any minute. Aren't you being a health nut about all of this?*

If you have high blood pressure, eat a lot of fatty foods and therefore have high cholesterol, smoke, and are overweight, you don't need to waste your money to find out if you have heart disease. You do. *Ninety percent of the time* coronary heart disease can be predicted simply by your personal history. And a personal history of excess pounds, cholesterol, smoking, and high blood pressure indicates heart disease.[2] You may not know it yet—they don't call heart disease a silent killer for nothing—but it is definitely there.

Blood *pressure you talked about already, but what is cholesterol, anyway? And if it's so bad, why is it so bad?*

Cholesterol isn't bad, normally. It's a vital chemical substance both manufactured in our bodies and found in animal tissue we eat. It is not really a fat itself, but the body reacts to it as if it were a fat. Cholesterol is manufactured primarily in the liver, but is so important to the functioning of our body that it is a part of and also manufactured by virtually all of our cells at one time or the other.[3]

Cholesterol, for instance, is the main ingredient in bile. Bile, produced in the liver, breaks all fats down into smaller pieces, making it easier for the body to absorb it. These broken-down fats are stored as fuel reserves, used right away as fuel, and used as insulation and protection of our organs. Cholesterol also makes up a portion of our sex hormones.

When some cells need a little more cholesterol, it is sent there in the blood. Cholesterol, since it acts pretty much like a fat, is not water soluble. If it were released directly in the blood, it would clog it in much the same way that fat poured down your sink will clog the sink. So to enable the blood to transport the cholesterol, the liver manufactures a special protein blanket to coat the cholesterol. Together they form LDL, low-density lipoprotein.

The liver also manufactures an element called HDL, high-density lipoprotein. HDLs *return* excess cholesterol to the liver for breakdown and disposal. Your body is normally able to regulate the ratio of LDLs and HDLs available to carry cholesterol. But we complicate their work, especially when we eat animal fats. Eating *some* fats is important. For instance, about 20 percent of our diets should be plant fats and about 10 percent animal fats.[4] When we eat too many saturated (animal) fats, however, our bodies begin to manufacture even more cholesteral at the cellular level.[5] For that cholesterol to travel around, more HDLs and LDLs are produced by the liver.

LDLs, the elements which take cholesterols to our cells, for some reason seem to be attracted to our arteries. And here the real tragedies begin.

Arteries, which take blood away from the heart, are flexible when they're functioning correctly. This flexibility actually helps move blood along, a process called elastic recoil. Arteries have essentially three layers. The inner layer, when its healthy, is smooth. It is also very thin (the thickness of one cell) and fragile. The middle layer is composed of muscle tissue. This layer of muscle normally controls blood flow by contracting the artery when blood flow needs to be decreased and enlarging the artery when blood flow needs to be increased. The elasticity of arteries makes this possible. The outer layer of the artery simply covers the muscular layer.

When LDLs and HDLs are in balance (for a man, 3.5 LDL to 1 HDL), cholesterol travels through our arteries with little impact on the health of the arteries themselves. But when diseases and chemical imbalances in the blood occur, the interior lining of the vessels become damaged. For instance, smoking, high blood pressure, diabetes, and high fats in the blood (like those in the animal fats you eat) virtually always damage vessels.

The most common damage to that fragile inner lining of vessels is a simple rupture. Much like a hernia, the next layer of tissue protrudes. In this case, the thin layer of muscle. As with any injury, the body reacts to this by sending platelets to the damaged area to attempt a repair. The platelets congregate around the damaged area, causing the beginning of a traffic jam in very fast-moving blood. For some reason yet unknown, the platelets seem to actually draw more muscle tissue through the rupture point, causing an even larger traffic jam.

Floating through the blood, normally without causing any real problems, are the artery-loving LDL cholesterols. As these cholesterols approach the rupture points, they become caught in the traffic jam and attach themselves to the damaged area. The more LDLs in your blood, the more damage. This area is now called a "plaque," and begins to block the flow of blood.

This entire process of damage and plaque formation is called atherosclerosis.[6]

Atherosclerosis? Is that the same as arteriosclerosis?

Atherosclerosis is the buildup of plaques which eventually block arteries. *Arterio*sclerosis, hardening of the arteries, is the replacement of the muscle layer and elastic tissue in the artery with fibrous tissue and certain plaques.

What are the effects of atherosclerosis?

In the arteries surrounding the heart, atherosclerosis is simply referred to as coronary heart disease (CHD), usually a progressive disease. Because of the blockage, blood flow decreases to the heart. The muscle literally begins to suffocate. Chest pains can be an indication of that suffocation. Its ultimate progression is a myocardial infarction, death of an area of the heart. Forty percent of the time, the only symptom of this disease is death. Myocardial infarctions cause over 50 percent of the total deaths from diseases of the heart and vessel systems.[7]

If the arteries supplying the brain have atherosclerosis, strokes may result. A portion of the brain literally dies. Strokes usually paralyze, but they also kill approximately 8 percent of all people who die from diseases of the heart and vessel systems.[8] Atherosclerosis is also a cause of senility. Atherosclerosis in other areas of the body like the legs, for instance, causes the same types of blockages and, in their final progression, kill tissues in those areas.

Can atherosclerosis be treated?

There is no treatment as safe or effective as prevention, but several avenues are available to you:

Subcutaneous transluminal angioplasty.   A catheter is introduced into the artery and pushed to the injured site. A small "balloon" is inflated to compress the plaques and create a larger opening. Though this is a relatively new procedure, it seems to work very well for many people.[9]

Bypass surgery.   The injured area is literally bypassed using a saphenous vein (one near the surface) from some other part of your body, usually the leg. Bypass surgery is effective in most cases, but is a more complicated surgery than angioplasty.

Drug treatments.   May prevent plaques from forming, but none seems to have been developed to actually dissolve plaques. This is a very hot area of research.[10]

How important are cholesterols to all this?

Excess cholesterols cause enormous damage to the arteries. These cholesterols are delivered there by LDLs. When our blood contains large numbers of LDLs—for instance, when we eat too much animal fat—we directly contribute to this process and potentially to all of the terrors mentioned above.

Fighting all this damage are your HDLs. Remember, they *remove* cholesterol from cells and return it to the liver for disposal. Large numbers of HDLs in your blood are a very good, perhaps lifesaving thing.

How *do you lower LDLs?*

Eat less animal fat and more fats from plants. For instance, corn oil, safflower oil, or olive oil—the "polyunsaturates" and "monosaturates." Recent findings indicate that fish oil may be among the most beneficial oils. Certain fibers such as oats and bran are also helpful.[11] Didn't your mama always tell you to eat your oatmeal?

How *do you raise HDLs?*

The one scientifically proven way is aerobic activity.[12]

Are *you telling me I can really lower my risk of all these diseases?*

Without question. Remember the things that begin to damage your arteries and rob them of their elasticity even before cholesterols begin to damage them: high blood pressure, smoking, diabetes, fats in your blood. All of these risk factors can be either reduced or controlled by medication, diet, and exercise.

Why *is it even important that my arteries have elasticity?*

Elastic arteries actually do help move blood through our systems. At the moment the heart beats, vessels near the heart expand to accommodate the increased pressure. As the increased pressure begins to move through the system, the vessel contracts behind this pressure point, helping to push the blood along. The pressure wave, incidentally, is your pulse.

If you should have a heart attack, and if your peripheral arterial system is healthy and elastic, your peripheral vascular system, made up of arteries, veins, and capillaries, may help circulate enough blood to help you lead a more normal life than you might expect with a severely damaged heart. Dr. Robert Bell, one of my advisers, states that he has "seen people whose massive heart attacks have damaged so much of their heart that one might expect they could hardly walk. And yet many of them are able to jog quite well. A relatively healthy peripheral vascular system and good leg muscles probably provide these people with enough assistance to their circulation to allow them to lead nearly normal lives." Research in this area is ongoing, but the results so far make me want to keep my arteries happy and flexible.

Flexible arteries also are less susceptible to wall damage. Remember that blood pumps through your body with constantly changing pressures. Inflexible arteries can rupture easily.

Where do strokes fit in all this? And exactly what is one?

A "stroke" is a general term indicating acutely decreased blood flow to the brain. There are several types:

Aneurysms are weak spots in blood vessels in the brain which burst.

A Thrombosis is a stationary clot which eventually grows large enough to block a blood vessel. Thromboses occur anywhere in your vessel system, but in the brain they often lead to a stroke.

A Cerebral Embolus is a clot which blocks an artery supplying blood to the brain. Emboli often originate as thrombi in other parts of the body (heart and coronary arteries) and migrate to the brain.

Strokes are associated with high blood pressure, high cholesterol levels, and hereditary factors. Many of these risk factors can be managed so the risk of stroke is greatly reduced.[13]

If I cut down on my fats, how quickly will my blood change?

Tests generally measure the two major blood fats, triglycerides and cholesterol. Triglyceride levels in the blood change rapidly, within hours. That's why you are asked to fast for twelve hours before having a blood sample drawn.

Overall cholesterol levels take longer, but most research says modify your diet correctly and expect changes within three to eight weeks.[14]

Are you telling me to quit eating steak? Rare roast beef with that wonderful layer of fat around it? A nice tenderloin smothered in mushrooms and onions?

You probably need to be aware of the foods you eat and modify your eating habits, but that does not require giving up all the things you love. First, be conscious of the problem foods. Because saturated fats are found in all animal products, when you eat meat, eat lean cuts. Eat more chicken, very low in fat *if you skin the chicken*. Eat lots of fish, lowest in fat, and that fat seems to be very good for you.

Carbohydrates are found in fruits, vegetables, grains, and cereals. Eat lots of carbohydrates before you fill up on meats. A smart eating habit is to consider carbohydrates as your main course and meat as a side dish. Believe it or not, that isn't a hard habit to acquire, either.

Norma says I'm a "Type A" personality. I nearly punched her, 'cause I'm not. It just drives me crazy if everthing isn't perfect every second. What the hell's she talking about, and don't be slow with the answer.

In 1974, Doctors Friedman and Rosenman introduced a concept of heart disease risk as it relates to behavior patterns. Their book *Type A Behavior and Your Heart* separated people into two categories: the "Type A" person who is always on edge, always ruled by time, and the "Type B" person who isn't ruffled by the lack of perfection or punctuality. Since then, other research seems to back up their theories pretty much. "Type A" people do seem to suffer more heart attacks; tension and stress do elevate blood pressure and cause changes in the blood hormone and lipid levels.[15] While some scientists argue that the separation of all behavior patterns into two distinct categories is an oversimplification, all agree your emotional profile directly affects your health.

So what do I do if I'm an "A"? I already have my secretary remind me every day at 12:10 to relax.

Very few of us are going to change our emotional compositions any time soon, but we can learn to modify our emotional reactions to things. Exercise definitely can help smooth out your ruffles and give you real thinking time. Simple intake changes can help, too. Less coffee or booze directly affects the depth of your reactions. Though it sounds corny, positive thinking can help, too. Did you know many studies show that simply deciding a particular thing isn't going to bother you, isn't worth anger or frustration, can actually lower your blood pressure?[16] (More on that later.) Because "Type A's" are essentially very competitive in the way they attack problems or opportunities, you might want to pick a sport which requires you to function without competition with others for a while.

107

Will anyone respectable give me their absolute guarantee that all these changes in eating and exercise and all that stuff will make me live longer?

I doubt it, because, as we've mentioned before, it's impossible to say specifically when a person is scheduled to die. Without knowing that, it's impossible to know if they lived longer. But the evidence is overwhelming. Diseased parts of your body, whatever the part, don't function like healthy parts. Partially functioning organs such as your heart or liver or lungs obviously place more stress on you than fully functioning ones. Genetics obviously plays a big role in each individual's normal life span— but, regardless of your particular genetic life span, the functioning of your body can lengthen or shorten the number of days you have to live.

CHAPTER IV

SWOON WALKS

Week 15

Grand Bahama Island

When I look at the pictures of me taken just a few days ago, I am reminded of the first time I painted something on my own, my brother George's new bike. I painted it red, including the chrome. I was eight and not the best painter, and the finished product didn't seem to impress others (Brother cried and Father spanked), but, to me, it seemed beautiful.

The most obvious change is the fat change. In just under four months, thirty-three pounds of fat have retreated, taking with them nine inches of waist. I say "retreated" because fat cells don't go away. They collapse like a balloon and wait for their next opportunity to attack. Fat cells are hungry, ambitious, strong, impatient, and very, very proud. They don't like retreating and jump at the first opportunity to attack again, gaining more territory with less effort the next time around, too, one of the reasons many people lose weight then gain it back quickly while still eating less. This may not be a scientific explanation, but it's just as accurate and a lot more understandable.

My exercise program obviously brought some change, too. In four months, I have weight-lifted 800,000 pounds, biked 500 miles, run 40 hours, and scuba-dived at least 20 times. I ache thinking about it. But, to my horror, my actual muscle growth in weight is virtually nothing. My total lean tissues (organs and muscle) weighed 141 pounds in January and 141.5 pounds two weeks ago. Since organs don't really change weight, that paltry .5 pound was my total muscle gain.

I didn't sleep well the night I found out that simple statistic. My hopes for this year—encouraged by a lot of weight-training experts' predictions—included at least fifteen pounds of new muscle, I assumed with requisite blonds attached. But at .5 pounds per three-and-a-half months, my total gains for the year would be less than two pounds. A wimpish-sounding gain.

I went back and looked at my notes from a meeting with Robert Stauffer. Bob is Director of Research at West Point's Physical Education Department, and a member of the faculty of the American College of Sports Medicine. He's also a member of the Board of Visitors at the United States Sports Academy, where we meet from time to time. Bob isn't an official member of my Body Worry Committee, but he is a friend. He is also one of the few people who, from the beginning of my year, tried to realistically quantify the changes that might take place in my body. He never felt my muscles would be enormous in a year. But he did feel I would look dramatically different.

"Remar," he had said, "if you want to have a good appearance and if you want to have that Soloflex look I keep hearing about all the time, you don't necessarily want to have high bulk. What you want is good, sound definition."

Back in January, I hadn't been satisfied with that answer. "But will I have a bicep? Will I ever have real muscles?"

"You can do that. How much you develop will depend on frequency, endurance, and intensity."

I pressed further. "Well, assuming I am motivated, can I have a dramatic change in the shape of my body? And I'm not just talking about losing blubber, either."

"Absolutely. Basically, from cellular physiology, every cell in your body will change. Good-looking bodies don't have to be bulky bodies. The Soloflex look isn't a bulky look." I re-read those comments and decided to call Bob at home that night. After just enough small talk to make it sound like I wasn't worried about a thing, I brought up the thing that was worrying me. "Bob, you know back at the Sports Academy when we were talking about my body shape? That Soloflex look I think I mentioned to you?"

"You mean that Soloflex look you mentioned about ten times?"

"Uh-huh."

"Well, I've decided that I do want that look rather than the bulky look I was kind of toying with."

"Oh, is that right? What brought that on?"

"Just common sense, you know. But there was one thing I was wondering. If I ever do want that bulkier look, can I actually achieve it?"

"Well, maybe. It's just going to take you a lot longer. Didn't I say that around Christmas?"

"Maybe, but I'm forgetful, you know. How much is 'longer'?" I said rather quickly.

"Remar, are you growing slowly or something?"

I was really ashamed to tell him how little muscle had appeared, but I did anyway. He snorted.

"*Remar*. That's an *excellent* growth. Especially considering all that weight you've lost. You're not going to be a Schwarzenegger, but you're not going to be a worm, either. Remember: *definition makes the Soloflex look*, not big muscles."

We chatted on for a few minutes, but my mind fixed on those words. I repeated them to myself silently, like a mantra.

I was feeling better the next morning. Even looking in the mirror was kind of nice. My body did look pretty good, and I decided my frame would look much better with that lean, well-defined look than it would with Arnold's hulking look. Hunkdom meant lean. I rushed through an oatmeal breakfast, looked at my latest pictures once more, and decided this day was going to be just right for a swoon walk, after all.

Swoon walks are simple. I put on the smallest bathing suit

111

my nerves can stand, don a large-brimmed hat, then stroll the mile of beach stretching from the end of my street, Seagrape Lane, to the Bell Channel jetty. The hat, angled jauntily above the eyes, allows me to stealthily observe the dozens of ladies along the strand without being noticed. Any look from the gallery accompanied by a smile or any expression approaching come-hitherness counts as a swoon.

Four months ago, I didn't have too much luck out there on the beach. My swoon walk put the lie to the idea that women like minds over bodies. I had enough body for several, but the only female who acknowledged me was about four, thought I was her daddy, realized her mistake, kicked sand in my direction, then ran away. Two months ago, things weren't much better. A mean, stevedorish woman eyed me for a few seconds, then went back to her book on karate. It's real hard being rejected for a book on breaking bricks, especially since the lady herself pretty much resembled one.

My third attempt needed to be more successful, particularly since the "Today" show wanted to film it. Bob Berkowitz, "Today's" men's correspondent, smiled at me each time he mentioned that possibility. Bob is a rather debonair and handsome fellow. He had already laughed long and hard at my expense earlier in the day when, with the cameras rolling, I had fallen from my bike in the most inelegant way. The cameraman had laughed, too, but not enough to prevent the show from using the footage, I feared. Lying entangled with the pedals, I had thought for a moment of using reverse psychology on the guys ("Boy, any good producer would *die* for that footage!") but dropped the idea when I remembered that briar patches were invented by the Fourth Estate. Redemption would have to come on the swoon walk.

And to the surprise of Bob Berkowitz and the crew, it did, in triplicate, in the form of the Smith sisters of New Jersey and their mother. Attractive, perceptive, obviously appreciative of a well-turned swoon walk and the man behind it, the Smith sisters and their mother "ravished me with their eyes," as someone in a juicy pulp story might characterize the feeling.

Well, after so many failures and so little muscle, this was heady stuff, indeed. My hunk factor rose. And then the "Today" crew began to treat me with the deference hunks think they deserve, and it rose again.

"What did you open with, Remar?" the young soundman said, "I didn't pick it up over my earphones."

All of my life I've wanted to be an expert on openers powerful enough to conquer the most forbidding beauty. Only experts know such lines. But right then, on the beach, with the heady power of hunkdom still on my mind, I could not tell him the terribly powerful words. I only confess them here to protect my conscience and the reputation of the Smith sisters and their mother: "Hi. There's a microphone in my hat and a camera behind that palm tree. Swoon and you're on national TV." The truth works every time.

N*orma is big on spot reducing. She has jars of fat-burning cream to melt fat away, two vibrating machines to shake it loose, a rolling barrel to exercise it, an electrical doodad to scare the hell out of it, and three rubber suits to squash it to death and sweat it off. Our bedroom looks like a sex club. Why does her tummy look porkish rather than petite?*

Because spot reducing does not work. Norma cannot just reduce the fat on her stomach or the "cellulite" on her legs, or even her "love handles," which in her case should be referred to as hams. People who sell you creams, clothes, equipment, or doodads as spot reducing miracles are scam artists, all of them.

First, fat can only be used up at the cellular level in the *presence of oxygen*. Doing spot exercises—for instance, sit-ups— normally does virtually nothing to provide oxygen to the area you are working, and therefore does not burn fat. The energy for all those grunts and puffs generally comes from carbohydrates. All of your work can build muscles to hold your fat in somewhat, but it will not help you lose fat in any appreciable way whatsoever.[1]

But Norma says her minister, who sells her those large buckets of "Descending Dove Secret Fat-Reducing Cream," knows for a fact that fat is burned first from where it was put on easiest. Is he right? Isn't that spot reducing?

He probably is right. Norma will most likely lose weight first from where she gained it first. But that is not spot reducing.

Norma is just as big on every new fad diet that comes out as she is on spot reducing. She really eats up the ones that promise she can eat what she likes or take a magic supplement and still lose weight. Are any of these worthwhile?

Diets that promise you don't have to eat less, diets that make you radically restrict your food intake or restrict the types of food you can eat, and *every single* diet not associated with a sound exercise program *will not work* in the long run. *The only thing that works in the long run is a lifetime change in eating habits combined with exercise.* Diets books aren't needed for that, either; sound books on nutrition are. Please have Norma read that again.

But Norma does lose weight for a while, even though she gains it back. And she has fun reading all those funny diet books. What's wrong with a little off-and-on weight loss?

Any diet, including the worthless ones, can bring temporary weight loss, but, temporary weight loss is *worse for you than being overweight.* "If you stay on a very restricted diet, the metabolic rate goes down, and you burn less and less [calories], you are more likely to store fat rather than burn it because you're burning it at a lower level," says Dr. C. Wayne Callaway, director of George Washington University's Center for Clinical Nutrition.[2]

That's bad, but not the worse news. Continually gaining and losing weight can cause your body to "lay down arterial plaque at an accelerated rate," according to Dr. Gabe B. Mirkin at Georgetown University.[3] Have Norma read that statement again, too. Plaque causes atherosclerosis, probably everyone's main enemy in the fight for a good life.

THE GODLY EATING PLAN

Week 17

<u>Grand Bahama Island</u>

I have never been a good dieter. I love food, had long-standing eating habits which made health buffs choke, needed to eat to handle my nerves and anxieties, couldn't stand the tediousness of counting calories, loved fried foods especially, tired quickly of weird diets, and (most important) couldn't stand the thought of giving up forever all of the things that taste good.

To me, "health," whatever that is, and however important it is, was not worth a lifetime of deprivation simply to add an indefinite amount of time to my life for more deprivation.

I, therefore, did not look forward to the dietary aspects of my year, especially after talking with some of my friends who are very serious about their eating habits. One new friend, in her thirties, healthy, robust, and cocky in her beliefs, raised her eyebrows rather condescendingly at me when she saw me drink a cup of coffee. "*My God*, Remar, you *drink* that stuff?" I was going to ask her what she wanted me to do with it, but she answered my question in a way before I could ask it, taking my coffee cup from my hands, walking out the porch door, and dumping my good brew on the grass. She then wanted me to go to her house for a reading of Tarot cards. "Tarot cards can help us," she said. Uh-huh. When she left, I had another cup of coffee.

Paul, in his forties, was more concerned about the foods I liked to eat. He did not approve of any commercially prepared food whatsover ("Absolutely *filled* with artificial preservatives and unpronounceable things that will kill you"). Paul was a vegetarian, too, and thought I should avoid anything that's been alive, including fish ("Fish are absolutely *filled* with lead. As deadly as a bullet").

I played Russian Roulette with a grouper fillet that night anyway, but got real depressed at what these people and others were confirming to me: to be really slim and healthy, it seemed you had to like pain and probably be a little kooky in other ways, too.

I was curious about all this stuff, but, quite frankly, never thought for a minute that any weirdo or highly restrictive eating plan would work for me, even if it meant my new body wouldn't work.

So I simply started modifying my eating habits as I increased my exercise. (I said this earlier, but repeat it here because it has worked so well for me.) Here on the island, before I began to modify things, my normal food intake for a week would include fried conch (an enormous mollusk, something like lobster meat) at least twice, steak at least once, barbecue always on Tuesday nights at The Tide's Inn at UNEXSO, lobster with nearly a cup of freshly melted butter (butter is cheap here), more fried conch fritters than there are sands on our beach, a thick slice of ham bordered in delicious fat, baked chicken with the skin on it, lots of native peas and rice flavored with fatback, four slices of hot chocolate cake with vanilla ice cream on it, and rum to make it all go down good, as we say here.

I love all those foods (and rum). And there was no way I would give them all up for good, or even for a year. My modifications were therefore planned to shock me as little as possible. I only prepared fried conch twice a month rather than twice a week, and I changed the way I prepared it. Rather than coating it in beaten eggs, I coated it in a mixture of three egg whites and one egg yolk. That cut down my cholesterol from the eggs 66 percent and the difference in taste was nonexistent. I fried the conch in very, very hot vegetable oil rather than animal fat, the native favorite, and before I ate each piece, I pulled off about half the fried batter. The taste was the same, but the calories were much fewer.

I kept eating steak each week, but bought leaner cuts of meat, trimmed them more carefully, and cut my portion in half. Because I eat so many more vegetables, that half portion seems to satisfy me. On Tuesdays at the barbecue, I pull barbecued skin off the chicken and dip the skinless (and virtually fatless) meat in the sauce.

Lobster is on my menu twice each week.[1] Now I melt soft margarine for my dip (better than hard margarine and certainly better than butter), and dip the tip of the meat rather than drown it. The taste is the same. I no longer bury my bread in butter, either. A small bit of soft margarine still enchances the flavor.

I still eat ham sandwiches, too, but I buy ham with the least amount of fat possible, put on about half a thin slice rather than a whole thick one, trim off all the excess fat, use mustard and a touch of diet mayonnaise rather than a thick coating of fat-rich mayonnaise, and munch. Taste buds are funny things. They recognize the taste of the ham, and seem to be happy.

Conch fritters can't really be modified, so I just eat fewer of them. Ditto for my hot chocolate cake and ice cream. Now I have a half piece and one scoop of ice cream on the weekends, and a quarter piece of cake perhaps one other day. The taste is the same, and since I'm always full on things with better value before touching my dessert, my chocolate and ice cream emergency bells haven't set off any alarms. And my rum? I really haven't missed booze much at all.

All of this modificational thinking began to be rather pleasant. Rather than picking up a chocolate cookie without thinking, for instance, I would look at that cookie as an extra one-mile jog of calories that needed to be burned. Walking past the cookie was easier. Rather than drinking a Coke, I drank diet drinks. That 150 calories saved one-and-a-half more miles of jogging. Rather than a sweet roll in the morning, I had a quarter sweet roll with my wheat toast or oatmeal. Four miles saved. Hell, pretty soon I was saving myself a marathon each week.

Modifying, rather than dropping, is becoming a habit now, probably the most important thing to happen to me this year, including the changes in my exercise habits. I think it can become a way of life.

A*re you really saying Norma and I don't have to give up all the foods we love to be healthy?*

If your diet is loaded with fried foods, fats, red meats, eggs, and whole milk products, you must modify your eating habits but you do not have to give up anything. Giving up things, as I've said, is virtually impossible because simply living longer just isn't worth being miserable, particularly since most of us have trouble accepting the idea that we will be vulnerable to this damage.

But *modifying* your habits will not make you miserable. In the beginning, it may. Most of us eat more than we want anyway, and breaking that habit can hurt. But try it like this: develop a plan with Norma and the kids. Buzbo and Binki, if you haven't noticed, are beginning to look an awful like you two, blimpish. Most kids' bodies mimic their parents' bodies. But Buzbo and Binki are still young enough to learn good lifetime habits now. Can you think of a better thing to teach them?

Developing a plan.   Learn to evaluate your eating habits now. Then write out the modifications to improve them. For instance, eat fried foods one time rather than five times, and always on the same day. Make your red meats the side dish and vegetables the main course. Start skinning your chickens and other fowl.

With seasonings, skinned birds actually taste good, maybe even better, since the seasonings flavor the meat, not the skin. Keep skim milk in the fridge. If you hate the taste of skim, try two percent; it tastes almost like whole. Then work your way down to skim. Keep fruit around for snacks. Try alternating your daily eggs for breakfast with such things as hot cereals, and when you eat eggs, don't eat all the yolks. Scrambled eggs with the whites of six eggs and the yolks of three tastes nearly the same. (Or four with two, two with one.)

For your plan to work, everyone's got to participate, but try it, stick with it for a month, and soon the new plan will become the habit.

But *will this make me live longer?*

It probably will, but, more important, it will make you feel better. The right eating plan, combined with a modest exercise program, will also help prevent some things more terrible than death. Strokes, loss of limbs due to blood clots, and maybe worse, losing your mind, can all be traced to less-than-healthy eating habits and lifestyle patterns.[2]

N*orma's preacher, the one who sold her the "Descending Dove Secret Fat-Reducing Cream," says his "Vita-Blasta-Sin" Vitamin Pack will make up for her bad eating habits. And we've got a year's supply under the sink. Won't that do?*

Most people, probably including you two, don't need vitamin supplements. Even if you eat fast foods a lot, that's probably still true. We spend hundreds of millions on vitamins each year anyway because most of us don't have the slightest idea how to judge our vitamin needs. Vitamins are not used as food. They do not supply energy. They aren't depleted by stress.[3] As of yet the only diseases they can cure are deficiency diseases (such as scurvy from lack of vitamin C or rickets from lack of vitamin D), and our country's major nutrition problem is overeating, not malnutrition.

But all of us, including kids, are bombarded with messages implying that vitamin supplements should be part of daily living. In one interesting study of schoolchildren, all of the kids knew about the importance of vitamins, but none of them could name what foods provided them. However, they *all* named several commercial vitamin preparations without any problem.[4]

So how do you know if you need supplements or not?

Generally speaking, if you eat a variety of food types—for instance, eat a salad and fruit juice with your hamburger at Fast Eddie's Burger Barn or choose whole wheat bread for your sandwich and add a salad or vegetable and skim milk—you don't need vitamin supplements.[5] If Norma gets pregnant again (exciting thought, huh), she might need a supplement. Other specific populations may need them, too; for instance, older women and some older men may need calcium, women may need extra iron, and fad dieters consuming fewer than 1,200 calories per day probably need a One-a-Day.[6]

But for most of us, remember: it's hard to be vitamin-deficient and it's impossible to clear up your really bad eating habits with any pill. Magic doesn't work.

What about megadoses of vitamins to just chase away colds and diseases and the like?

Most vitamins already contain more than 100 percent of the Recommended Daily Allowances. Some, in their prescribed dosage, contain over 1000% percent. Because the fat-soluble vitamins are stored for long periods of time, you don't need to overload like this. These vitamins (A, D, E, and K) can build up in your body and literally kill you.[7] Excessive water-soluble vitamins simply run through the system, making expensive urine. In spite of various claims for various vitamins by various enthusiasts, there is little to support the claim that megadoses of vitamins ward off illness or hasten its cure.[8]

Well, *I've got all those vitamins anyway, so I'm going to take them. Will it hurt me?*

Taken at the proper dosage, no. And the "Vitamins Are Good for You" Foundation, holding their annual meeting in Tahiti, asks me to thank you for taking them.

If *I'm actually going to start exercising and all that jazz, don't I need my red meat just to get my protein?*

What your body needs is "complete" protein, one that contains all the necessary amino acids. (Amino acids are what proteins and a lot of your body are composed of.) Complete proteins are found in fish, chicken, dairy products, eggs, and red meats. Fish and chicken provide you the protein without as much fat. Low-fat dairy products and eggs are also good sources of protein, but remember that egg yolks are high in cholesterol. To compare, a four-ounce T-bone steak (about half to a third of the size most folks eat) has 30 grams fat and 80 mg cholesterol, one cup of whole milk has 9 grams fat, 34 mg cholesterol; one cup skim milk, a trace of fat, 5 mg cholesterol; one egg, 6 grams fat, 250 mg cholesterol.[9]

You *say this, the people who want to sell you products say the opposite. How does anyone know what to believe?*

You don't need to be a health expert to judge most claims in the health field. These tips, adapted from American Medical

Association guidelines, can help you sort out claims about diets, products, machines, and doodads.

• ***Is "proof" offered in the form of testimonials or newspaper reports?*** Testimonials are not based on statistical evidence, the only accurate evidence, and mean absolutely nothing. Testimonials sound great, but don't ever buy a product based on them. Do you really think a movie star can make a better judgment than you? Think some individual, probably the seller's mother, is scientific proof? Testimonals are often used when real proof is nonexistent. Quoting newspaper reports as proof is just as meaningless. Stories are easy to place. (Since when did you believe what you read in the papers, anyway?)

• ***Do the sellers attack recognized medical authorities? Simply renounce scientifically accepted theories as wrong without saying why? Do they claim the establishment is "holding back" their wonderful discovery or product? Claim their discovery or product is a "secret" from the past or from some lost civilization?*** Attacking medical authorities is the oldest ploy. People who use it are trying to establish their own credibility by destroying that of others. These are usually the same people who claim "persecution" from the establishment and simply denounce scientifically accepted information as wrong. Claiming that the establishment is trying to "prevent" a true breakthrough product or treatment is not only old, it's cynical as hell in the way it preys on our normal paranoia of big business and government. Breakthroughs, when they really happen, are welcomed by the scientific and business community because they bring fame and great wealth to many people.

"Secrets of lost civilizations" and other "secret" claims are nearly funny enough to accept, anyway, but don't. These things may do harm.

• ***Do they promise "quick" cures or results, fast and easy results?*** Clichés are sometimes so nice, and here the cliché "If it sounds too good to be true . . ." fits. If it does, it isn't.

• **Do they use scare tactics to encourage you to buy?** Don't buy anything or accept anything because of emotion. Rational evaluation always works best.

• **Are degrees of the pitchmen from funny-sounding places?** We all feel more comfortable with nice initials around the people we listen to, but don't automatically assume degrees are meaningful. Too often such degrees come from unaccredited and/or mail-order schools. In other cases, the degree may be in a field totally unrelated to health or nutrition, say, nuclear physics. So check. Also, if someone claims a "doctorate," for instance, then doesn't name the institution but uses high-sounding terms such as "internationally recognized university," take this as a given: you are dealing with a person who is trying to mislead you.

• **Are they trying to sell you something?** Free enterprise is a wonderful thing, but it's based in part on the right of people to make claims for their products or services. The job of the seller is to convince you of need, whether you have a need or not. Authors like me are just as guilty here as anyone, incidentally. Your job is to evaluate before you spend money.

Can I trust my doctor to answer nutritional questions?

The whole concept of preventive medicine is new. Since proper eating is a preventive medicine itself, many doctors who've been in practice more than ten years don't have nutritional training because their medical school either didn't teach nutrition or only taught it minimally. Find out like this: ask your doctor, casually, if he's been to many clinics or study groups on nutritional science. If he looks surprised at the question and says no, get your nutritional advice somewhere else, for instance from your local government health services division. Lots of good free pamphlets are available.

Some doctors' offices these days have nutritionists on staff.

A phone call will help you here. All libraries have hundreds of books on the subject, but look for a book authored by a sound source. Libraries don't (and shouldn't) make judgments on the merits of a book's advice. Major hospitals always have nutritional staffs, and many of these people consult privately. The American Dietetic Association also has a professional subgroup called SCAN, whose members specialize in exercise and sport nutritional needs. The association's toll-free number (800-621-6469) can help you find the right registered dietician for your particular needs.

What's the difference between a nutritionist and a registered dietician?

Anyone can set up shop (or write a book) and call himself a nutritionist. Quacks do it all the time. But a registered dietician has formal training, has passed a national examination, and (obviously) is registered. Ignore "nutritionists." Find a registered dietician.

What are proteins? Why do we need them?

Proteins are substances composed entirely of amino acids. The body requires twenty different amino acids to survive. Eleven of them are produced by our bodies. Nine of them, called the "essential" amino acids, can't be produced, and have to be consumed. These nine are found in all animal products.

We need about 1 gram of protein for each 2.2 pounds of our weight, the Recommended Daily Allowance. RDAs are determined by a group of nutritionists and other scientists, and are published by the government. They're updated about every five years, and are recommendations, not requirements. Some people might need more, some less. Safety margins are built into RDAs and, generally speaking, they are more than adequate for the general population.[10] Athletes, for instance, aren't consid-

Notice the size of the weight. This is my first day in the gym, January 16. Our gym at the Grand Bahama YMCA is managed by Bill and Marilynn Carle. Both of them are hunks. Russ, my trainer, is already a hunk. I am still a chunk.

Russ observes my technique with shrugs. He was a little depressed afterwards.

The fat from one piece of chicken. Look at this picture carefully and then read about cholesterol in Chapter 8.

We normally bike to the store, about six miles. A gallon of skim milk is $4.25 here, a small can of tomatoes is $1.09 on sale, so it's easy to eat lightly.

One of the first shots of the new body. Since I'm not a hunk yet, it's possible the camera had a lot to do with the interest of these maidens. I choose to deny that thought, though.

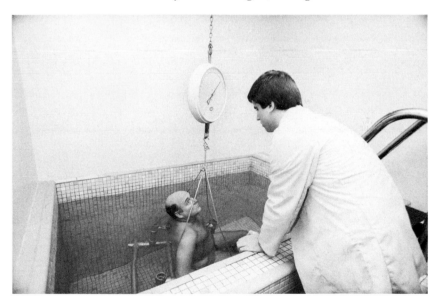

Weighing my fat at the Cooper Clinic in Dallas. Since fat floats, underwater weighing is the best way to determine percentage of body fat. I'm at the clinic for my three-month progress testing in April.

I am making progress. The guy with me is Will McIntyre, my other photographer. Will is married to Deni and thinks he's hunky.

I always dress like this in Texas. The car belongs to the Cooper Clinic.

On the balcony of the Aerobics Activity Center at the clinic, Dr. Arno Jensen coaches me while Will McIntyre shoots. Arnie is fifty-nine, and bikes rather than jogs for his aerobic exercise.

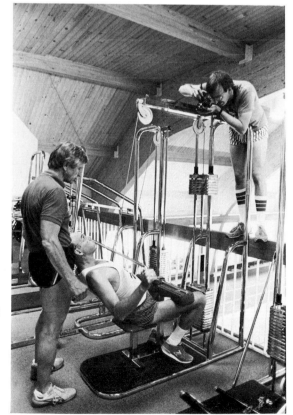

Arnie shows me pictures of my right shoulder. It remained injured for most of the year.

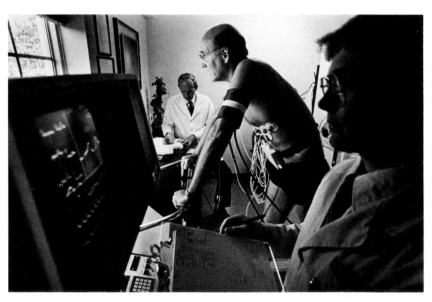

That's Ken Cooper in the background. Ken is my aerobics coach and chief tester. He coined the word "aerobics." My three-month stress treadmill test showed a 50 percent improvement, and moved me from a "fair" to "excellent" category of aerobic fitness.

The main gym at the Activity Center. It's here that I watched the young couple playing basketball with their children.

Who has the best push-up form, Arnie, Ken, or me? Push-ups, incidentally, are still one of the best strength exercises you can do.

I was hoping a young maiden would stop and admire me. Instead, ducks tried to chase me from their pond. The Cooper Clinic.

Wheat toast with diet jelly tastes awfully good after barium, let me tell you.

ered part of the general population. The normal American diet, you will be happy to know, includes nearly twice the RDA of protein.[12]

If you are a 180-pound office worker, a day's RDA of protein could look like this: one glass of skim milk, two slices of toast, two slices of pizza, three chicken legs, and a lettuce and tomato salad.

How do vegetarians get their protein? Is a total vegetarian lifestyle safe?

The nine essential amino acids are found in plants, but all nine aren't found in one vegetable. That's why vegetarians have to be very careful eaters, being sure to include vegetables which complement each other to provide all nine amino acids. But careful vegetarians receive all the protein they need. For instance, a day's supply of food (1,900–2,000 calories) for a 180-pound strict veggie (no eggs or milk products) would be:

1	cup oatmeal
6	slices of whole grain bread
4	wheat crackers
3	Tbs peanut butter
5–6	cups of vegetables composed of such dishes and combinations as pinto beans with tomatoes and onions over rice, lentil soup, potatoes, carrots, tofu, and rice
½	grapefruit
1	banana
1	peach
4	Tbs raisins
2–3	tsp margarine

What are carbohydrates?

Compounds made up of carbon and water. They come in three chemical forms: monosaccharides, disaccharides, and polysaccharides. In their most basic form, carbohydrates are sugars. Simple carbohydrates (the mono and di's) include the carbohydrates in sweeteners: corn syrup, and honey, and table sugars, for instance, the things we flavor with.

Glucose, the simplest sugar in our bloodstream, is a monosaccharide. All carbohydrates are eventually broken down into it. Glucose is the primary usable form of sugar for our bodies. That's why hospitals administer it intravenously.

Disaccharides, the other "simple" carbohydrate, occur naturally in most foods such as honey, cane sugars, and maple syrup. They are composed of two monosaccharides, logically enough. Table sugar is a disaccharide.

The third form of carbohydrate is called a polysaccharide or "complex" carbohydrate. Complex carbohydrates are formed from long chains of the simple version, and are found in things like fruits and vegetables, grains and cereals.

Why are carbohydrates important?

Carbohydrates in their simplest form, glucose, are the only fuel the brain and nervous system can use. If carbohydrates aren't available, proteins must be broken down to provide glucose. Protein is a precious commodity in the body. It is the most important ingredient of cells, and is seldom used as a fuel. When it is, your body must literally cannibalize itself to feed the brain.[12]

Norma boils everything. Does cooking really make a difference in the nutrient content of food?

Definitely. The nutrient value of vegetables, for instance, can vary dramatically with their method of preparation. Raw is best; steamed or microwaved (easy ways to fix things) is second best, and boiled is a distant third.

What *is the nutritional value of frozen or canned vegetables compared to freshly cooked ones?*

Vitamin and mineral content in virtually all frozen or canned foods is good, very close to freshly cooked ones. Frozen is equal to fresh, but if you use a canned product, you must use the water it was canned in to get all the vitamins. Unfortunately, this water probably carries sodium with it.

How *important is fiber in all this?*

Fiber is an indigestible carbohydrate. It's not manufacured by our bodies. It offers us no nutritional value, but adds bulk and water to the solids in our intestinal track, helping to move those things along quicker. Some researchers believe that the quicker waste products move through our systems, the less chance we have to be injured by them. Because we eat cancer-causing things at times, they reason, fiber probably cuts down on our chances of getting cancer by moving those left-over cancer-causing things out of our bodies.[13] You already know some of that reasoning from the televison commercials for high-fiber cereals.

There are also indications that some types of fiber may lower cholesterol in the blood—oatmeal, beans, and apples, for instance.[14] *How* isn't known yet, but many researchers think it may be because the cholesterol binds with the fiber rather than the intestinal wall, where it enters the bloodstream.

As of this writing, there is no absolute scientific proof that high-fiber diets lower our risks of either some types of cancer or our cholesterols, but there is definitely enough epidemiological support to make it worth your while to eat enough.[15]

Is there any RDA for fiber? Do I need extra through cereals and the like?

There are no RDAs for fiber, but the Cooper Clinic recommends a minimum of 20 to 35 grams of fiber per day. 35 grams would be roughly equivalent to eating two apples, two servings of vegetables (such as celery, cabbage, or carrots), two slices of multigrain bread, and two other starches such as potatoes or rice. Eating extra fiber in a high-fiber cereal probably won't hurt you and it may help you to obtain dietary fiber more easily.

Does everyone's body react to salt in a negative way?

Probably some of the U.S. population is salt-sensitive.[16] The remainder don't appear to be. But, by age sixty-five, 75 percent of us (salt-sensitive or not) end up with high blood pressure.[17] Researchers don't know if that very high percentage is due to the cumulative effects of salt or not, but assume that may be the case. It's probably worth your while, therefore, to be moderate with your salt intake even if you're not sensitive.

How do I know if I'm salt-sensitive?

The only definitive way is a test which requires several days in a hospital and constant attention. It will probably cost you over $1500. Doctors have a simpler solution, especially since we all may be salt-sensitive as we get older: they recommend that all people moderate their salt intake and that persons with high blood pressure or a history of it in their family cut down dramatically on their use of salt.[18]

What type of foods contain salt?

Sodium (the water retaining element in salt) appears naturally in foods such as eggs, meats, milk, and vegetables. Sodium content is lower when it's found naturally like this. A cup of milk has only 120 milligrams, an egg around 61 milligrams. Three ounces of any meat cooked without salt, 60 to 75 milligrams.

Sodium, unfortunately, is much, much higher in prepared foods. A can of tuna has about 800 milligrams, a McDonald's Big Mac around 1,000 milligrams. Sodium content isn't easy to know at times, and certainly isn't easy to find on labels of packaged foods at times, either, because manufacturers use its more specific names like sodium bicarbonate, monosodium glutamate (MSG, so popular in Oriental cooking), and disodium phosphate. If you are watching for salt in prepared foods, look for any word, however long, with the word "sodium" attached to it.

Is there an RDA for sodium?

The RDA is between 1,100 and 3,300 milligrams per day. Most salt-restricted diets call for under 2,000 milligrams per day, so even salt-restricted diets allow you salt, incidentally. But remember, a teaspoon of salt has 2,300 milligrams.

I am afraid to ask, but what is the general concensus on the effects of caffeine? And what is it, anyway?

It is a drug that acts as a stimulant to the body. In some people it can be an irritant to the digestive system, and some studies seem to indicate that it may be linked to birth defects and cancer of the pancreas.[19] All those indications are for very high dosages of caffeine, over 600 milligrams per day. One cup of regular coffee contains from 100 to 200 milligrams of caffeine, a cup of decaffeinated coffee, about 3 milligrams. Sodas have from none to 65 grams. Since as little as 300 milligrams per day has been linked to elevated total cholesterol, Dr. Cooper recommends no more than 200 per day.

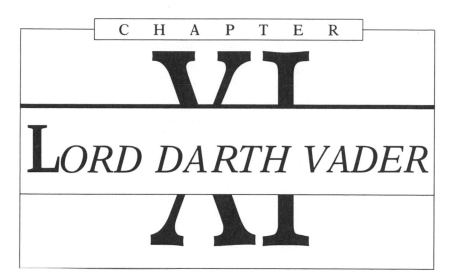

CHAPTER VI

LORD DARTH VADER

Week 20

<u>London, Marshalsea Road</u>

When I was very young and innocent, Superman and his comic books provided me many moments of fanciful safety from real and imagined bullies. At night, after a hard day of feeling picked on or of simply feeling very insecure, I could crawl in those flimsy pages and find more pleasant realities. I could fly in there.

Much later I became a lighthearted fan of Lord Darth Vader, my type of monster because he wasn't really that bad. Even when Vader did away with someone, you couldn't help but like him just a little bit. At least he didn't use bad language or torture people physically. Children understood this. They never felt terror when they saw him, but their skin probably tingled when he swept into a room, the very essence of storybook evil.

My own skin tingled from such memories and thoughts this morning when I first met David Prowse, the man who both played Darth Vader in the three *Star Wars* movies and weight-trained three-time Superman Christopher Reeve. David is my new hunk coach. I flew to London yesterday, after a couple of months of planning, and will spend the next ten days here learning the routines that supposedly make mortals into god types. I think he knows those secrets, too.

David Prowse is the type of person, larger than life in the flesh, we all yearn for when a dark and forbidding alley looms in front of us. He is as manly and rugged as you would expect for one who mingles with mythical characters. His voice, a deep rumble even when he speaks conversationally, fits his frame. He is six-foot-seven, 266 pounds, all muscle. His chest measures 52 inches, the height of many ten-year-olds. He can dead lift nearly 700 pounds. His jaw juts mightily and his brow furrows deeply over thick, expressive, Groucho Marx eyebrows. David does not shake hands, he envelops them, smothers them gingerly so as not to crush them. When I first felt that sensation, I remembered a scene from another mythic classic, when Kong gently sheltered the damsel in his palm.

At fifty, David is very well known in the U.K. in his own right: former British Heavyweight Lifting Champion, an author (*Fitness Is Fun*), an actor in some memorable productions (the bodyguard in *A Clockwork Orange* and the executioner in the BBC's production of *The Balcony*), and an actor in some less weighty productions, too (Frankenstein in *The Revenge of Frankenstein* and Baron Grunwald de Grunt in *Up the Chastity Belt*, a popular spoof movie).

However, David is most recognized in Great Britain as the Green Cross Code Man, a government-sponsored Superman-type character in green tights who appears constantly on British television and in person at hundreds of British grammar schools teaching roadside safety to school children. He travels to these speaking engagements at times in a yellow '69 Camaro with VADERMOBILE emblazoned on the side and a droid just like R2D2 riding shotgun. The droid is green and talks about road safety.

Prowse is a happy man in that car and in the role of Green Cross Code Man, a hero to hundreds of thousands of British schoolchildren and their parents. The children love him because he is as large and strong as children imagine heroes should be, but still very gentle (they run to him without the least hesitation) and not the least bit condescending. Parents thank God for him because, in a country where most children walk to school along roads without sidewalks or traffic lights, his presence as the Green Cross Code Man has helped lower roadside accidents involving children by nearly 50 percent.

We first met in the office of his London gym on Marshalsea Road, not far from the London Bridge. The gym occupies the first three floors of a terrace house. The narrow building looks modest from the outside, and the gym itself is low-key—lots of pine paneling like my gym in the islands, exposed pipes, and different types of free-weight equipment, which looks as if it was picked up here and there (it was).

The basement houses the "heavy" room, all knotty pine and blue carpet, where serious lifters and competitors work out. This room is really the picture gallery. David with *Star Wars* characters, weight lifting characters, and British sports figures; David talking in New York with a group of ladies who watched him film three episodes of "The Edge of Night." Standing behind him in that picture is a then unknown actor named Tom Selleck. There are ninety dumbbells in the heavy room, including a set of eighty-year-old lead-filled dumbbells, and dozens of other free weights and machines.

Upstairs is the "light" room. Sixty by thirty, the walls here are pine, too. Three windows make the room bright and six square columns support the ceiling. Eight mirrors are positioned around the walls. David says this room is for beginners and those who want to work light.

The gym office is equally old shoe. Two Vader statues, one dime-store bought, the other a porcelain mask, sit on a small filing cabinet behind a large Naugahyde chair. Both items are obscured by a toaster oven and electric tea kettle. Piles of folders and books cover a small sofa, several shelves, another filing cabinet, and most of the floor. The wall to the left of the chair is nearly wallpapered with a black-and-white picture of David in medieval costume, javelin in hand, astride a horse. Baron

Grunwald de Grunt. On the wall to the left is a charcoal nude of David poised to throw a javelin. A discrete smudge renders the picture "PG."

All of this very low-key exotica—just being with this guy— was fascinating. But as David walked me through the building and finally settled with me in the office, I had only one thing on my mind.

"David, what can you do to my body?"

David was sitting in the large Naugahyde chair in front of the Vader statues. He eyed me very slowly.

"Would you mind taking off your clothes down to your skivvies?"

It is very hard for a person to undress in front of a nearly mythical person, but I did, self-consciously, crossing my arms in front of my chest. He took a tape measure and gauged my wrists and chest and biceps and calf muscles, and though I had been lifting weights for nearly four months, I blushed at the thought of my muscle size. I needed to get my mind off this.

"David, did you measure Superman, I mean Christopher Reeve, like this? Nearly naked?"

"Oh sure."

"How big was he?"

"Very stringy." Good.

"And what about you? Were you ever a weakling?"

"Oh sure. My goal used to be to have fourteen-inch biceps. Mine were twelve." Good. My biceps were at least bigger than David's used to be. It didn't matter that David at that size was sixteen and recovering from four years in a hospital. In moments of great insecurity, everything is relative.

He put down the tape measure, told me to dress, and sat down. I asked the question again.

"Well, what can you do to my body?"

I told you his voice is deep, but it sounded even deeper and nearly spiritual this time. "Remar, I will personally guarantee that by the end of the year you will have a physique you'll have never dreamed of."

I blushed. And then I quickly rumbled through my gym bag

and pulled out my tape recorder, shoving it toward him in a quick, jerky motion, as if speed would catch the echo of the words and make them reality.

"Would you mind saying that again?"

David Prowse wrapped his hands, the hands that held *the* light saber and helped sculpt the slender body of Christopher Reeve, around the recorder. He pulled it to him and repeated the promise.

When I replayed the tape afterward in my hotel room, the sound was a little muffled. Those big hands were a bit over the mike, accidentally, I'm sure, but that's okay. Everybody knows heroes don't lie.

Two days later, I lay on the floor of the gym's "light" room, legs painfully suspended in the air, in pursuit of the promised end. David was trying to take my mind off the pain by overloading it with juicy gossip about the *Star Wars* movies.

"What d'ya mean, 'Darth Vader wore white suspenders'?"

From my position on the floor, between grunts, I could see out the three tall windows on the western wall and focused my eyes on the SCAFFOLDING BY SGB signs hung in several places. The whole building is covered in scaffolding. "But no one uses it," David says. "Been there for three of my sixteen years here." His feet dropped lightly to the blue carpet. Mine dropped like a bag of sand. He still hadn't told me about the suspenders. David answers things when he wants to.

"Delightful!"

We rested a minute before starting the third of five sets of stomach exercises. Five sets each of twenty leg lifts, twenty sit-ups, and one hundred scissors, all done without resting and all done s-l-o-w-l-y. A total of seven hundred repetitions—if I lived through them. David wanted me to do this every morning. As a warm-up to our regular stomach work. Oh Lord.

I stalled for time between sets by asking again about the suspenders. "Did you really wear braces?"

David's eyebrows went up, far up. I've never seen eyebrows that could talk like his. "I did. Had to hold my blooming pants up. The blooming things kept trying to fall down."

Darth Vader shuffling around with his pants around his knees. I liked the image.

"But why white?"

"They didn't show. And they were store-bought. Most things were custom, though."

"Like what?"

"Well," he said as he lifted his legs for the third stomach set, "there were fifteen pieces to the outfit. The briefs were regular. And the T-shirt was my regular extra-extra-large. It soaked up the sweat. I wore a jacket and waistcoat, custom. A jacket with no front, a front with no arms, and a breastplate, all custom-made. And the face and helmet, of course. Custom-made. I wore a codpiece, too. A boxer's codpiece." I did not ask him if the codpiece was custom-made.

"What about the mask?"

"Two pieces. The face was fitted on with straps which tied behind my head. I had a special circular piece at the top on which the helmet fitted." During all this time, David's legs had been suspended above the floor at about a forty-five degree angle, as if they were frozen there. He looked at my legs, resting on the floor.

"Remar, shall we start? Only four hundred and twenty to go." We began set three. "The most vexing problem," he continued, "was the eyes. The camera could see my eyes in the mask, and they didn't want that. So they put dark lenses over the eyes. So I started viewing things through that triangular mouthpiece, down to the floor. And then they decided they could see through that, so they covered the inside with black gauze. I was essentially blind."

A blind Darth Vader with his pants around his knees. I liked that image even better, and desperately fixed on it as my scissor count approached twenty of one hundred in the third set. Oh Lord.

"David, did you ever want to be Darth Vader's voice, too?"

I told you about David's eyebrows. As I spoke, they recast his face to a more somber look. "I thought I *was*. In the first movie, I learned all the lines, said all the lines. I didn't know they had dubbed over my voice until a friend in California who saw the movie sent me a cable. I mean, I knew nothing about it *at all*." He stopped talking just long enough to watch my leg lifts for a second. *"Slow down, Remar."* David's emphasis on these few words left no doubt in my mind that his voice, when a little irritated, would have been just right for Darth Vader, though perhaps a little British. I promptly told him so. He nodded and continued.

"Then, do you remember in the second movie when Vader and Luke Skywalker were on the gantry and he chopped Skywalker's hand off? My dialogue had me saying, 'Come join me and we will rule the Empire together,' but when I saw the film, Vader said, 'Luke, I am your father.' I knew *nothing* about this at all; it was a huge surprise."

David Prowse is not bitter about his involvement with *Star Wars*, though he was kept in the dark about things like his voice. He is the first person to tell you the movies changed his life and made him one of the most well-known anonymous people on earth, the perfect American Express "Do You Know Me?" commercial.

Now, you may think anyone could have played the part of Darth Vader, maybe a stuntman (even though David had his own stuntman). But, in reality, *David* is the only person on the earth who did play Darth Vader, and he did it magnificently. He deserves his adulation for those things as much as an astronaut who walks on the moon deserves awe simply for walking on the moon—because the act is so exclusive. I personally think my body designer deserved at least an Academy Award for swagger. And I'm not biased at all. There.

Well, I thought such thoughts as we finished the third set of stomach work and started the fourth set. Only 240 reps to go. Oh Lord. The thought of simply counting to 240 hurt. By now my stomach and legs felt as if they had been sliced by a light saber, though I knew those things never really existed. Darth Vader and Luke Skywalker fought with *sticks like curtain rods*, a shocking revelation.

David, however, made even that revelation seem unimportant. "Remar, how much exercise have you been doing?" he asked on about count number sixty.

"Well, I bike ten miles a day, run about five, walk for miles along the beach acknowledging the glances of beautiful women, swim a mile or two, bike to the Underwater Explorers Society, and scuba dive a couple of times." (I exaggerated just a little on everything, but that seemed okay at the moment).

"Oh," he said. "And how much do you eat?"

"Only the best, healthiest foods in very sensible quantities. And I don't snack much and stay away from large quantities and, of course, too much steak and the like."

"Oh," he said again. "I think that's the problem."

"Huh?"

"You exercise too much. And you don't eat enough. You need to be eating at least five times a day, lots and lots of carbohydrates and protein. That's the only way you're going to put on muscles."

I blinked. "But won't I get fat? I mean, David, it scares me to death to think about eating a lot and exercising less. I'm nearly handsome now, you know." I said it half in jest and half defensively. For months I had eaten like a monk and driven myself like a beaver and the thought of facing flab again filled me with angst.

"Remar, you can't do that much aerobic activity and gain muscle mass at the same time. Cut out your jogging and leave in your biking. And do my weight lifting program. And you can eat all you want without getting fat, if you eat the right foods, of course. You've *got to eat* if you want muscles."

My grandmother had a wonderful way of describing heaven: "You can eat everything you want, *and it will be good for you.*" I thought about that as I happily finished my fifth set of David Prowse stomach exercises. I wasn't in heaven yet, but I was getting closer. A bigger thrill than any old *Star Wars* movie. Oh Lord.

I *don't have a coach like Prowse, and don't really want to go through all this exercise just for looks. Will exercise do anything for me that's really important? Particularly at my age?*

As we pass early adulthood, many physiological changes begin to take place in our bodies. Earlier I told you about Arno Jensen's success at literally stopping the visible signs of aging with weight lifting. But there are many things which can be reversed or stopped with exercise. Here are fourteen physiological changes that have definitely been proven to benefit:[1]

Muscle size	Decreases with age, but can be increased or held steady.
Muscle strength	Decreases with age, but can be increased.
Lean body mass	Decreases with age, but can be increased.
Body fat	Increases with age, but can be decreased.
Your heart's pumping ability	Decreases with age, but can be increased.
Your heart's stroke volume	Decreases with age, but can be increased.
The elasticity of your blood vessels	Decreases with age, but can be increased.
Blood pressure	Increases with age, but can be decreased.
Oxygen consumption	Decreases with age, but can be increased.
Lung functions	Decrease with age, but can be increased.
Reflexes	Decrease with age, but can be increased.
Bone density	Decreases with age, but can be increased.
Blood fats	Increase with age, but can be decreased.
Resting energy consumption	Decreases with age, but can be increased.

Our bodies, without disease and the unnecessary complications we place on it, could probably keep us going until we are 115 to 130 years old.[2] Though we can't control many diseases, we can control just about everything else that ages and eventually kills us.

What is the best exercising diet?

The same diet anyone should eat: high in carbohydrates, low in fat. An ideal breakdown for most people would be 55–60 percent carbohydrates, 15 percent protein, and 25–30 percent fat.

Will extra protein help me build extra muscle?

People who make protein supplements certainly say so, but their proof is always less than impressive. Some physiologists and nutritionists are beginning to think extra protein can speed along muscle growth, when it's combined with the right weight lifting program.[3] But Chris Scott notes, "These researchers, myself included, also believe that protein should come from an increase in your protein food, not pills or powers or liquid protein drinks. So called 'free-form' amino acids don't appear to be absorbed through the intestinal wall [where all protein-amino acids are absorbed] as readily as animal protein. Protein supplements are also extremely expensive, and may put a strain on your liver and kidneys."

Well, does intense physical activity increase my nutritional requirements?

When you increase your energy expenditure forty percent, you generally need to increase your fuel intake 40 percent, if you want to maintain your weight and energy reserves. Professional athletes, for instance, obviously need more fuel than Norma at the moment. Manufacturers of supplements have twisted this basic principle a little, however. They like to tell you increased activity makes extra amounts of proteins and other supplements, all handily manufacturered by them, necessary. That is generally not the case. Simply increasing the amounts of food you eat (if you're eating a balanced diet) provides you with the nutrients you need.[4]

Because so many people are pushing supplements, think through the following facts and you'll see why there are probably better ways to spend your money: the RDA of protein for the average nonathlete was established at .57 grams of protein for each 2.2 pounds of body weight. To give us all a big safety margin, that figure was increased to about a gram, nearly twice the amount an average person needs. And the average person already eats twice that, nearly four times the real minimum amount. Because athletes eat so much more (and probably eat so much more healthily), their protein intake is huge.

But what if you're dieting and exercising or weight lifting really hard? Don't you need supplements then?

Virtually all good diets always meet your RDAs. Eat more carefully when you're dieting, and you won't need supplements.

What about Norma's iron-poor blood?

Some people do have iron-poor blood, an easy thing to know with a normal blood analysis. Highly trained athletes who compete in triathalons and iron man competitions can develop anemia (the loss of red blood cells), but this anemia appears to be short-lived. Average athletes don't have to worry about it, but might have to worry about too much iron via supplements.

How important is sleep to our physical health?

It is important for the function of your central nervous system, but the lack of sleep, oddly enough, doesn't seem to cause significant damage to your organs or cause them to function less efficiently.[5]

Norma *says exercise will be good for our, uh, nesting rites. Is she right?*

Some people think high-intensity exercises like weight lifting temporarily raise the testosterone levels in men; others think less-than-maximal exercise temporarily lowers them.[6] No one knows if either of these things is true or important, but everyone knows exercise gives you more strength and energy, and many happy nests have been built on those two qualities.

CHAPTER VII

WELSH GOATS

Week 22

<u>London</u>

During the past weeks I have worked out in more odd, beautiful, and ancient places in Great Britain than I knew existed—with my trainer, my friend Mary Abbott Waite, my mother, and my gym in tow. I have also come to respect Welsh goats.

The gym, a double set of blue solid-rubber Russian weights loaned to me by David Prowse, fitted neatly in the very back of our silver-blue seven passenger Volkswagen maxi-van. Luggage fitted on top of the weights. At first. As we traveled, our luggage seemed to multiply and eventually filled our siesta seat, the long bench seat just in front of our weights. We learned to nap on top of luggage.

Russell Burd, my trainer and the assistant navigator for our trip, usually sat in the captain's chair in front of the siesta seat. Mother, our trip historian, sat to his right in another captain's chair, piles of books at her feet and a leather-bound log book in her lap, pen at the ready. A red ice chest filled with fresh cherries, plums, sandwiches, and juices served as her footstool.

Mary Abbott, trip navigator, rode shotgun. M.A. is the perfect person to have along if you, like us, much prefer obscure paths to well-traveled roads. She used ordnance maps and walking maps rather than tourist maps. Mary Abbott is also the person who helps me keep my sensibilities about muscles. She is not impressed with large ones. "Remar, if you ever look like Mr. Universe, I'll throw up," she said at the beginning of this year. "Don't worry," I said, "they all have hair." I like Mary Abbott a lot, and think of her words when setbacks happen. I don't really think she has to worry about me having muscles in the extreme. I would *like* to have the problem, but right now would be satisfied with as many muscles as those guys have in their eyebrows.

I think Mother feels the same about muscles in extremus. Mom is seventy-six and proud of it. Her hair is still naturally jet-black, and her glasses are the thickness required to compensate for cataract surgery. She has a steel hip, leukemia, a heart problem, and, more importantly, an attitude that none of these things are significant enough to slow her down. I once coaxed Mom onto a frisky pony when I was about ten, talked her into a hike miles longer than she wanted when I was about twelve, and thought it normal when she and my father let me roam around Europe at age sixteen.

None of this seemed special then. Even when my father bought my twelve-year-old brother and me (at eleven) an old truck to drive around our property, that didn't seem unusual. Now, when I am the age my parents were then, these things and my parents seem pretty unique. A fact I never got to tell my father and have had trouble showing my mother. But true hunks eventually deal with things like that. This trip was, therefore, both a thank-you and a chance for our longest visit in some time, and I did not want my twice-daily workout requirements to interfere with more interesting things like talking and history and beauty and shopping. Early mornings and late nights became my muscle time.

In Salisbury, Russ and I worked out at 5:45 A.M. in the Winston Churchill Room of the Red Lion Inn, a hostelry since the thirteenth century. Winston, in oils, larger-than-life, glances rather demurely across that large, vaulted room at an equally large portrait of the late proprietor of sixty years, a Mrs. Thomas. Mrs. Thomas seems to glance back equally demurely. Some people might construe a liaison from these two glances, but I know better. According to a plaque in the Thomas Suite, Mrs. Thomas "neither smoked nor drank" during her sixty-year tenure as an innkeeper. Winston wouldn't have put up with that.

At Ruthin Castle in northeast Wales, we worked out before an enormous fire in a room built in 1210. The logs were nearly as long as I am tall, and still looked small.

In Windemere, the heart of England's mountainous, unearthly Lake Country, we worked out in a mountainside hotel's billiards room before a full-length lake-view window and an occasional couple who wandered in simply to watch us grunt. "Hear, Hear," one older lady volunteered as she tipped her sherry to us and plopped down into a red overstuffed leather sofa by the window. A retired teacher, she liked to take long walks to restore her energy, she said. The next morning at first light, in the driving rain, Russ and I jogged around Lake Windemere for twenty minutes, mists rolling around us, then retreated to a gazebo above the lake for our stomach work. We shared the space with several drier and more intelligent tame mallard ducks.

On another morning as the sun rose, we lifted weights on the actual battlements of Airth Castle near Stirling, Scotland. The portion we lifted on was over 650 years old, built by the second son of Robert the Bruce. The proprietors here have recently turned the castle stables (only 280 years old) into an elaborate health club, an oddity in Great Britain.

As you can tell, we stayed away from large hotels and cities and spent most of our evenings in imposing old castles, manor homes, or converted mills—like the Arrow Mill near Stratford-upon-Avon, which dates back to at least 1086 when it was valued at six shillings and eight pence. It is now run by the Woodham family, who between puffs and sips actually lifted a few weights with us.

In Ely, close to Cambridge, we worked out *over* the Cam River on a nearly deserted public footbridge. Four students from Cambridge, walking the bridge to reach a favorite picnic spot, stopped to chat with us as we lifted, and as they talked, sculls from their college raced by under the bridge. "Muscles! That's what you bloody need!" the picnickers, champagne in hand, yelled to their puffing colleagues.

It was all delightful, except for the Welsh goats. Mary Abbott, incidentally, says they were sheep, but sheep aren't this mean. We met the first pack in a dew-covered field near Llanwenarth House, a grand, four-bedroom, sixteenth-century manor house in Abergavenny, Wales. The goats here fraternize with Welsh ponies. As we quietly and unobtrusively attempted to enter their field, the goats gave one bleat, which promptly unleashed the ponies in our direction. We chose another field.

Several days later, we had a more serious incident. We were staying at Ardsheal House in Kentallen of Appin, Scotland. Once home of the laird of the Stewarts of Appin, this place sits on a tall cliff overlooking Ben Nevis (the tallest mountain in Great Britain), the hills of Movern, and Loch Linnhe. Russ and I were at the bottom of that cliff, minding our own business, taking in that magnificent view, doing leg lifts on our portable carpets at sunrise, when a single baby goat ambled over to watch us. Though we were in Scotland, I knew a Welsh goat when I saw it, but did not show my nervousness as it eyed us between chews of grass. Goats are like horses in that regard—clairvoyant.

The goat bleated and instantly a protector was at its side, head down, hooves testing the turf. This was a very large beast and its bleat was not a friendly one. As we rose and retreated in slow motion, it moved with us. As we began to trot, it trotted, the thick wool on its body bouncing like springs. When we broke out into a run, it bleated ominously, twice, and ran after us, the brush of wool against our backsides. Russ, young and fast, quickly outdistanced the danger and climbed up the cliff. I leaped up the cliff rocks, gasping for air, just a breath ahead of it.

Later, I dutifully reported our narrow escape to Mary Abbott and Mom. Russ's recollection was somewhat different; as a matter of fact, he even said the animal wasn't really chasing us and wasn't really a goat. "That mother sheep was sort of trotting along with us." I, however, know better. Russ may be my trainer and Mary Abbott may be my friend, but Mom agreed it sounded like a goat to her, and I listen to my mother a lot more these days.

S*ince Norma and I don't travel with our own gym any more these days, what can we do to help stay fit on the road?*

First, think a little more about your eating. Most of us don't think we have much control over our meals when we're not at home, a nice way to eat things like fried grease balls without guilt. But thinking about what you eat and drink away from home is especially important. Many commercial establishments, including the fancy ones, drown food in fats, butters, salts, and God knows what. Here are some tips that will improve your chances of eating a healthier meal.

• If you must have a fried food fix, pull most of the crust or batter from the food before eating it, and eat smaller quantities. Just a taste of crust will add flavor to the food.

• Eat broiled, baked, and roasted things and season with pepper rather than salt. If you have a blood pressure problem, ask that your food be prepared without salt, and take along your own bottle of salt substitute or one of the other good no-salt seasonings. Years ago, a man who brought out his own bottle at a table would be laughed at by other diners, but now, the feat has a certain *cachet* attached to it.

• If you're in a restaurant that cooks to order, tell your waiter you would like your dishes prepared without butters and sauces. Request soft margarine as the flavorer. Soft margarine is better for you than either butter or hard margarine.

• If you're ordering eggs, ask that half the yolks be removed. Most restaurants are used to requests like this these days. If you normally eat your eggs fried, try poached.

• Eat whole wheat breads and buns, and use soft margarines here, too, rather than butter.

• When you order soups, choose clear ones rather than cream-based ones. Cream soups generally contain more fat.

• Eat more salads and fresh vegetables, and eat them, as I said earlier, as more of a main course than a side dish. If possible, ask that your vegetables be lightly steamed rather than boiled to death. Lightly steamed vegetables tend to fill you up more, since they're crunchy and contain more nutrients than boiled or oversteamed ones.

• When dessert time comes, wait a few minutes before ordering. Give yourself a chance to feel full, since that sensation is a delayed one. When you order, eat fresh fruit or smaller portions of other desserts. Three bites of chocolate cake, if you're already full, are just as satisfying as a whole piece, and might save you 200 to 300 calories and a lot of fat, too.

A*nd how do we exercise on the road? Especially if we don't have time to find a gym?*

Even if you are not a regular exerciser, there are things you can do on the road to keep you fitter. First, ask your hotel if they have a printed jogging map. Even motels are beginning to provide these. A walk will ease those travel jitters, quell your appetite, take away travel cramps, and give you a chance to laugh at all the funny joggers.

Second, try some of these simple exercises. These work as well at the office or at home, too, and will build your strength and endurance, and tone you up if done regularly.

• Squeezing a tennis ball will build your forearm muscle and grip strength, and work out frustrations, too. Keep an old ball with you when you travel.

• Push-ups against a wall will work your chest and tricep muscles. Place your feet as far from the wall as possible for more shoulder work, closer to the wall for chest and triceps. Do a set of 10–20 repetitions four times.

• Leg lifts in a straight chair will build abdominal and hip flexor strength. Sit up straight, grip the chair, extend your legs straight in front of you, and bring your knees to your chest. Straighten them. Do a set of 10–20 repetitions four times.

• For flexibility and toning, place a towel behind your back; use it as if you were drying. Keep the towel as taut as possible, using your own body to create resistance.

If you travel alone on the road, boredom and loneliness can affect you as much as anything. Don't sit in your room or, worse, at a bar. Ask the front desk for the location of the closest gym, and go for a steam bath or sauna even if you don't want to work out. Go bowling. Even go to a play or a show. Keep moving, be active, and think before you eat.

Your mother sounds like an active person for any age. But Norma's mother hasn't moved from her special Norman Rockwell rocking chair, except to get her copy of Soap Opera News, in ten years. Isn't it too late for her to start exercising now?

The most dramatic changes in strength and energy and aerobic fitness take place in sedentary older people. According to Dr. Herbert deVries, a noted authority on exercise and aging, a sedentary person's "maximal aerobic power can be improved; the ability of the lungs to function as a bellows improves; the ability of the blood to transport oxygen improves."

But how much can an older person improve? Enough to make life better?

Dr. deVries says that sedentary people over seventy who exercise properly may have a *25–30 percent increase in their aerobic power* within eight to ten weeks!

But how much exercise?

Again, I quote the authority. "Evidence is growing rapidly that we can achieve close to optimal aerobic performance just with walking." The key here, Dr. deVries says, is a program and progress tailored to the capacity of the individual. Before they begin an exercise program, it is especially important that older people undergo testing to determine precisely what they can and cannot do safely. Dr. deVries, incidentally, is a very fit man. His main exercise is surfing ("when the surf's up," he says— just like Troy Donahue) or walking "up and down a hill with my dog Amigo for a couple of hours. Or I run three miles." Dr. deVries is sixty-nine.

Getting really old should not mean a life of inactivity. For most people, it should be the time to get in their best shape. "You may have the body of a seventy-year-old," deVries says, "but you may be able to function like a person twenty or thirty years younger." His book *Fitness After Fifty* is an excellent guide for people over fifty.

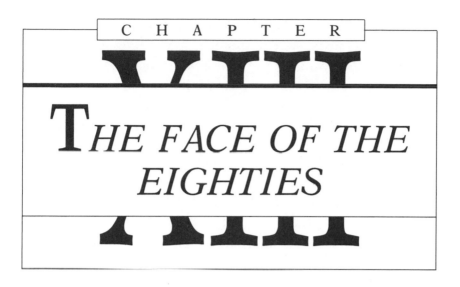

THE FACE OF THE EIGHTIES

Week 26

<u>Grand Bahama Island</u>

I returned from England with a back problem, a reinjured shoulder, and a telephone message from the "Donahue" show.

My shoulder continues to react poorly to the amount and intensity of stress our workouts inflict on it. When I first tore my right rotator cuff muscle (one of the three muscles which hold the ball and socket of the shoulder joint in place), that tear healed and scar tissue, zipper-shaped, formed. Scar tissue is abrasive, and as I continued to work out, especially movements which required me to raise my arms over my head, scar tissue rubbed against bone, causing more swelling which eventually affected my shoulder tendons.

If you play baseball or racket sports much, you may be familiar with the pain. It runs along the top of the shoulder when you raise your arm. You cure it by stopping the movements which make it hurt, and the more severe the pain, the longer the rest. If you continue to injure it, you can lose movement in your arm and eventually need surgery.

153

I'm giving you all these details because injuries are beginning to jeopardize my year. The shoulder injury has nearly stopped my upper-body work for the time being. We have not been able to find a way to work around it, to work muscles from different angles of attack. My back injury is much more painful and has stopped all our gym work. I hurt it on my last day in England, during my last workout with David Prowse. David is such an enthusiastic person about my quest for muscles (and I want so desperately to perform for people who see muscles on me) that I insisted on trying a far heavier dead lift than I have ever attempted, 150 pounds.

A dead lift, as you may remember, is really a leg movement when it's done right. You squat down, grasp the bar, keep your arms and back absolutely straight, and stand up. Because your arms are simply holding the bar, the pressure is on your legs. Do it right, and your legs and your back get stronger eventually. Do it wrong—either try to use your arms to lift the weight, or try to shift the weight away from a hurting shoulder, for instance—and you get hurt. I did both things, bending my arms slightly in the excitement of the moment, then quickly trying to shift the pressure away from my bad shoulder. The pain from the torn muscles in my back was instant and vicious.

Though my back gives me the most discomfort, it will heal faster than my shoulder, within three to four weeks, if I leave it alone. We don't know what will happen with my right shoulder yet. If I have to, I'll just build up my left arm and become a one-sided hunk.

I got to check out the current accuracy of my hunk factor recently on "Donahue." Donahue's staff is all women, it seems, and all bright. They wanted to do a show on the Face of the Eighties, "and we think you would be *perfect* for the show," Marlaine Selip said cheerily when she called.

The Face of the Eighties. Well, that sounded pretty good to me. The phrase wasn't quite as strong as "hunk," but if Phil Donahue himself said it, I could put it on my business cards, like a title.

"Who else are you going to have on?" I asked, masking my excitement.

"The editor of *Gentlemen's Quarterly*. We even want him to dress you in a tuxedo from Saks, if that's okay . . ."

The Face of the Eighties strolling out in a custom tuxedo to the applause of a largely female studio audience and an enormous television audience, all thinking, "If Phil says he's good-looking, he is." As Marlaine spoke and as I imagined my reception, I was talking on the phone right next to my word processor, leaning slightly over the keys. Probably the only reason I didn't drool.

Marlaine then mentioned that the show would borrow me an expensive human hairpiece to wear just for the end of the show, if I didn't mind trying it on for the audience. The Face of the Eighties asking his fans to vote for his best face, so to speak. Rather than simply saying yes, I let my mind wander out loud. "Yeah, maybe I could ask for thumbs-up for bald and thumbs-down for hair, you know what I mean?" I always wanted to be a director.

Well, after all of this, I arrived several nights later in New York with great hope and confidence. The next morning Lilian Smith from the "Donahue" show picked me up in a car for my toupee fitting. Lilian is pretty, bright, and perceptive. ("You look pretty hunky to me," she said when I asked her my standard opening question, "How 'm I looking today?")

We then headed to Saks Fifth Avenue, and it was there my dream began to fall apart a little. Some of the most handsome, manly men I had ever seen (my age and half my age), literally off the covers of magazines, were already trying on tuxedos in the changing room set aside for "Donahue." I casually asked Lilian who these people were.

"Oh, that's Rich Popejoy, the winner of *Gentlemen's Quarterly*'s The Face of the Eighties contest, and that's Kevin Luke, runner-up, and over there is David Belafonte, Harry's son. They're on the show with you." Lilian mentioned some other names, but I didn't hear her. For a moment I tried to convince myself these guys wouldn't detract from my own hour of glory. Maybe they were going to be my honor guard or something. I (casually, of course) asked Lilian their function.

"Oh, they open the show. And close it. And Rich Popejoy, The Face of the Eighties, is on the panel with you along with the plastic surgeon and the man who had his face lifted and the lady who gives facials and the two men we picked from yesterday's audience to redo, and Bob Beauchamp from *Gentlemen's Quarterly*, of course."

A person could get trampled to death in that group. I forced a smile and made small talk while my tuxedo was fitted. I then introduced myself to Beauchamp, an important and busy man in men's fashion who still had time to walk me through the men's department at Saks for fifteen minutes until he found the right tie and shirt for my blazer. I even laughed a little as I said good-bye to my competition and the rest of the "Donahue" crew. My smile wasn't very cocky, though. I walked back to the hotel feeling subdued and slightly plump.

The next morning at the studio my spirits picked back up a lot. If you have any ham in you, and I do, a live television appearance in front of hundreds of laughing and clapping people is a thrill. I, of course, tried to look cool. But when the audience seemed to appreciate my physical progress (Donahue showed them "before" and "after" pictures) and then laughed at my request for a brain transplant with the Face of the Eighties, and then clapped even harder when a person in the audience said they admired my determination, I grinned an awful lot.

And at the very end of the show, after the other guys had made their final entrance, marching one at a time up and down the very short runway, Phil Donahue brought me back out. Most of the audience hadn't noticed my momentary absence from the stage, but they all noticed the mop on my head when I returned. I marched up and down the runway just like the pros (I had watched them from offstage, quickly practicing their gait) and, for good measure, even struck a weightlifter's pose in my new hair and tux. I didn't feel the least bit plump. When I asked the audience for their opinion on my borrowed mop and the verdict was for bald, I felt quite muscular.

And do you know who impressed me the most in all of this? After the television cameras were off, when most personalities seem to disappear, Phil Donahue asked his audience to stay seated until he could make it back to their exit. He shook hands with all 250 of them, chatted with them. Hunkiness isn't in the dictionary yet, but that quality should be part of the definition.

R*emar, you're not the only one with back pain and the rest of us don't have a public triumph to help us forget that pain. Will exercise help?*

Lots of people have back pain. Most studies say 80 percent of us suffer from it at some point in our lives. About 80 percent of those who do suffer probably do so unnecessarily, too, for their pain is related to lack of proper exercise, poor posture, obesity, or injury caused by improper movement.[1]

Most back pain is caused by muscle inadequacies. "As we become inactive, our abdominal muscles become weaker, and our hamstrings, the muscles in the back of the thighs, become tighter," says Christopher Scott, the exercise physiologist on my Body Worry Committee. "A tight hamstring tilts the hips and causes stress on the lower back, the most common area of back pain."

If your back pain is caused by inactivity, "The Y's Way to a Healthy Back" program at many YMCAs probably can help you. The program teaches flexibility and abdominal strengthening, and you don't need to be an athlete to participate.[2]

Two exercises to help you right now, if you're too busy to visit the Y, are:

Stomach crunches. Lie on the floor on your back with your knees bent at a right angle, legs resting on a chair. Cross your hands on your chest. Do not put them behind your head, you can hurt your neck. Try to sit up at a count of one-one-thousand, two-one-thousand, etc., as you do them, but only raise off the floor six inches or so. Do three sets of ten each day.

Hamstring stretches.   Many exercises stretch your hamstrings, but this one is easy and safe: lie face-up on the floor with your back flat and your knees bent. Place both hands on the back of one thigh, close to the knee, and slowly pull your leg toward your chest until you feel a slight strain on the back of your thigh. Hold it for five to ten seconds. Do this three times on each leg, daily, gradually extending the leg as you become more flexible. When you can do the exercise with your leg nearly fully extended, loop a towel behind your leg on the calf and use the towel to pull your extended leg to you. These exercises can prevent back pain as well as decrease it. As with any pain, if it won't go away, see a doctor.

N*orma likes the idea of you with hair. How did you go bald?*

Like most men: in the vast majority of cases, baldness is caused by genetics. It's called "male pattern baldness" because it can't occur except in the presence of the male hormones. Just as hormones trigger puberty, they trigger baldness, if that is your particular genetic makeup.

I*s there any definite way to prevent it from happening?*

Absolutely, without question. Castration before hair loss begins prevents baldness nearly every time. It's not recommended by the AMA, however, as a cure.

From Dallas to Govilon, near Abergavenny, Wales. Russ and I had been running, or, rather, being chased by a few of those famous Welsh goats, when Mr. Alfred Davis of Govilon stopped by to watch. Running here, even with goats after you, is exhilarating.

These are some of the famous goats themselves. We are staying at Llanwenarth House in Govilon, a sixteenth-century Welsh manor house, home of Bruce and Amanda Weatherill. If you like lovely manor homes but few guests, you will love this place. But watch out for the goats.

Robert Sengstack (courtesy of Donahue)

Walking the runway on the "Donahue" show. Rich Popejoy, the Face of the Eighties, is the guy with the black hair, the one clapping. Some people think we look like twins.

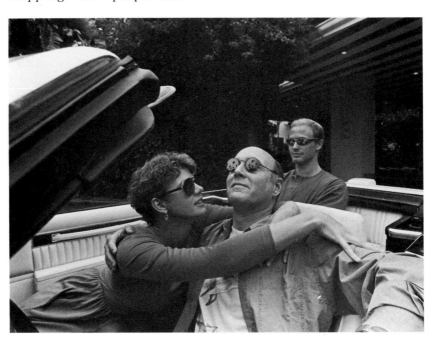

Beverly Hills did not affect me at all, but this mysterious Hollywood starlet could not keep her hands off me at the Beverly Hills Hotel. Chris is in the back seat to protect me from myself.

Muscle Beach, California. One hundred-and-one, one hundred-and-two. . . . I always do lots of chin-ups before strutting along with the other hunks.

This is a Beverly Hills garbage can. They can be rented for summer homes.

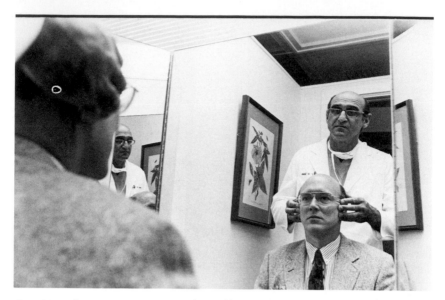

Dr. Frank M. Kamer, Beverly Hills surgeon to the stars, gives me an idea of what my new face would look like if I had a lift. An honest man, he didn't encourage any surgery at this time. I like his hairline.

At Gold's Gym in Venice. Tony Pearson takes a lesson from me. Tony is a former Mr. Universe.

The Plimptons: George, Freddy, Medora, and Taylor. Everyone's impressed with my muscles but George. I think he's jealous. George encouraged this book, and took a particular interest in the size of my stomach.

Taylor is a special friend of mine. In the islands, I take him diving. In New York, he coaches me on my hockey skills.

September in New York. I am still not a hunk, but small muscles lurk. I really don't have posing down yet, as the position of my left wrist indicates.

Matjaz Bren

It's really hard to look happy when you've been biking over terrain like this. Near the Devil's Punchbowl in Oregon, with Bret Anderson, Anne Knabe, Martin Engel, Steve Buettner, and Dan Buettner. I biked about forty miles of their 18,000-mile trip.

Mike Sahlen, the Bahamas

September, back on the island. I've gained weight as I've tried to put on muscle. David Prowse, the man who played Darth Vader and weight-trained Christopher Reeve, checks his air before a dive. David is one of my hunk coaches, and has come to the island to check my progress since May. Christopher Scott, my exercise physiologist, watches.

Scuba diving on the shallow reef. I tried to dive at least once each week.

Many days at sunrise, Chris and I would head out to spear lunch. We're both pretty good shots now. And how do you like the way my body is coming along? Late October, and a lot of my extra weight is off again.

What actually produces hair?

Each hair is produced by a follicle. There are about 100,000 on the average head. An individual hair grows for about three to five years, about an inch every two or three months. After all that growing, the hair actually rests for another three months, then falls out. If your follicle is healthy, a new hair begins growing in the same place immediately.

So what happens in male pattern baldness?

Most of us would say the follicle "dies." Actually, it's still there but your particular genetic code turns it off. The man who discovers "the switch" to reactivate these retired follicles will make billions.

Does hair ever fall out from "lack of circulation"? That's what the man said who sold Norma the full-head massager.

Baldness isn't caused by lack of circulation, or lack of "follicle food," or vitamins. Healthy hair follicles transplanted into a bald spot grow very well, for example, until their programmed time to die. If you transplant hair from the back fringe which never dies to your balding hairline, for instance, those follicles will produce till you die.

Do you mean individual hairs seem to have a predetermined life span?

Yes. If you transplant a hair follicle from an area that is already balding to an even balder spot, you'll probably lose that transplanted hair, too. Hair seems to have a mind of its own when it comes to life span.

How *ow much hair loss is normal?*

The normal person will lose thirty to sixty hairs a day. At any one time, about 90 percent of your hairs are growing, and 10 percent are resting and thinking about falling out.

Can't *an't sickness and the like cause baldness, too?*

High fever, childbirth, major illness, some surgical procedures, and severe emotional distress seem to affect hair production and loss. Very low diets (under 800 calories) can affect it, too. A very, very few men suffer baldness caused by treatable medical problems; only a knowledgeable physician, usually a dermatologist, can make these diagnoses.

What *hat about all those things to rub on the scalp and encourage growth? Aren't they real?*

There is absolutely no scientific evidence to support the value of vitamin rub-ons, biotin, inositol, and virtually all other "miracle" applications. (More about the possible exception, minoxidil, in a moment.) Applying a male hormone to the scalp may help a dying follicle to recycle one last time, but it will then die.[2] A few other preparations may get those follicles which produce little one-sixteenth-inch fuzz to grow to one-fourth-inch fuzz, but this makes you look like a peach, not a man.

Doesn't *oesn't washing hair too much encourage faster fallout?*

No. You don't lose hair if you overwash, but you do lose friends if you underwash.

Is it worth using very expensive shampoos?

It's worth it to the manufacturers only. Washing it with virtually anything this side of acid will not speed your rate of hair loss. Some conditioners and hair sprays or even a perm can help you achieve a fuller look with what you've got, if you want to spend as much time as Norma in front of the mirror.

Are there really a lot of quacks in the hair business, or am I just being overly suspicious?

It's hard to be overly cautious with your money in the hair field. Like other quack areas, the quack remedies for baldness prey on false hope. They try to build their claims on "scientific fact," or at least scientific-sounding fact. For example, some quacks claim they have products "formulated by specialists" or, at times, doctors. Others offer testimonials (as worthless in this area as they are in weight loss) and "money-back" guarantees. There are two problems with "money-back" guarantees from quacks: the words alone make many trusting people assume the sellers must be honest, which most of them aren't, and the guarantees themselves are worthless. Most simply don't refund money. Trusting people, therefore, buy because they take advertisers at their word. They are taken because the word of quack advertisers is worthless. In the hair area, incidentally, many of the people taken aren't simpletons. Every man with a bald spot will try a funny product at least once, and most of those guys are too embarrassed to seek their money back when the spot grows rather than shrinks.

Quack remedies seem to fall into four categories. You might want to see which one you like the best:

Remedies taken orally. Absolutely none of these over-the-counter things work at all, but they may have side effects which can jeopardize your health.

Remedies applied to the scalp. All of these seem to be based on feeding your hair follicles. Hair follicles don't eat. Such topical products don't work.

Appliances. Things to help massage your scalp, or "wake up" your follicles. A scalp massage feels great without a special follicle enhancer, so save your money.

Clinics. All manner of places offer themselves as specialists in the treatment of hair loss. Some claim they are "doctor supervised," but most have little to do with science. Virtually all clinics recommend an extended series of expensive treatments or visits which not only won't put hair on your head but will also scalp your wallet.[3]

W*hat about hairpieces? Are there any that really look natural?*

Nothing is sadder than a man who makes a fool of himself with a hairpiece without knowing it, and so many of us do that. But there are hairpieces that make you look like the man you so richly think you deserve to be. They are expensive, however, and, since they can't rejuvenate themselves, take constant maintenance and must eventually be replaced.

W*hat's the difference between a natural one and a funny one?*

No off-the-rack pieces really look natural. The shape of an individual's head and hairline is so personal that wigs (full-head covers, essentially) and hairpieces (partial covers) need to have that hairline individually designed. The hair itself makes a difference, too. Real hair is virtually the only thing that really looks natural.

Where do I find a good designer?

You need an artist, not a mass-produced hair center. Use your Yellow Pages for the first selection. Visit each center, and then ask for clear pictures of their products installed. Look at the hairline. If all the pictures have hair dropping over the hairline, the pictures are probably covering something unrealistic.

I have a hairpiece in my closet, from my appearance on the "Donahue" show. I planned to bring it out for special occasions, but haven't used it yet. Yes, it looks real and, yes, I feel great with it on for a while, but eventually tire of looking like something other than the genuine thing. Hairpieces are probably the best-looking, certainly the safest, and maybe the least troublesome artificial hair procedure out there. The best are virtually undetectable. But all of them still are somewhat like an actor wearing a mask, and I'm not personally comfortable with that yet. I show my vanity in my search for muscles.

What about hair weaving?

From the pictures in the paper, this looks good. The "before" and "after" pictures are a seemingly honest visual testimonal, and draw folks to hair weaving centers in droves. The reality isn't always quite that nice, however.

From the pictures and accompanying words, hair weavers seem to imply they weave artificial hair in with your remaining hair. A concept which sounds morally nicer to those of us who worry about pretending about hair. I am one of those people. And phony hairs among the real does sound a little more straightforward than totally dishonest hair.

Hair weavers don't do that at all, of course. Hair weaving is simply a method of attaching a semipermanent hairpiece to your head. In most cases, the "clinician" or "trichologist" (fancy words with absolutely no medical/scientific/training basis) makes a plait of the client's remaining hair, usually with a reinforcing string woven in. A hairpiece is then permanently secured to the plait.

There are several problems with the hair weave approach. Because the bases of these hairpieces are loosely woven, hairlines are poorer than with traditional hairpieces. Much more importantly, it's hard to clean the scalp under the hairpiece. Skin infections are fairly common. Even if you don't contract an infection, hairpieces take attention. Since the plait of natural hair which serves as your anchor grows, you have to return to your hair weaving center for adjustments regularly.[4]

Hair weaving clinics list the pluses as being able to wear their pieces at all times—in bed, shower, pool—and without fear when a damsel runs her hands through it. Nearly all the TV commericals for these things use the "damsel's hands in my hair" ploy to hook us, a smart but cruel thing, since the greatest fear of any toupee wearer is having the wig discovered at the moment of erotic potential. Even this image isn't really accurate. Since woven pieces are anchored around the sides but not at the hairline, they don't fly off, they simply rise up like the vinyl roofs of old cars moving down the highway.

Or worse. We all got a big laugh not long ago watching a scuba class in the UNEXSO pool. One poor, unsuspecting soul had no idea his perma-weave headpiece was serving as a catch basin for his exhaled breaths. At each exhalation, ole perma-weave would rise and fall like a fast-talking clam shell. So much for this man's swimming guarantee.

How *about hair implants?*

"Hair implants" is another term which misleads us. It is generally used by sellers who plan to anchor your hairpiece with actual sutures in the scalp.

In a hair implant, a number of suture loops (made of nylon-type material) are fixed permanently in the scalp. The hairpiece is then attached to these suture loops. The drawbacks here are the same as with weaving, but with the very big additional drawback of foreign bodies sticking through your scalp. Infections are always an eventual danger. All those openings in the scalp receive daily stress from the tugging of the hairpiece, and are perfect little doors for bacteria.[5] Add to that the difficulty of keeping the scalp under the hairpiece clean, and you begin to wonder if users of this procedure are stupid rather than vain like the rest of us.

Some practitioners attach locks of hair to an individual suture, supposedly a more natural-looking approach that's easier to keep clean. But this procedure still requires placing foreign matter through the scalp, and the scalp treats all foreign matter as an irritant. There are usually more infections here, too.

But don't these procedures require a doctor? Doesn't that mean the procedures are safe?

A doctor is required to put in the sutures. The "clinic" staff does the rest. You normally see your regular doctor when and if the infection problems begin.[6] If this procedure interests you, check with an AMA office close to you and the Better Business Bureau about the reputation of the clinic.

What about the procedures that use skin to hold a mop on?

The technique is called "tunnel grafting." Two skin loops are constructed on the front and back of your head and serve as anchors. This replaces things like plastic sutures to hold the mop, but the skin loops themselves are as vulnerable to injury as the artificial sutures themselves. Tunnel grafting also provides only two anchors for the hairpiece, which can make it shift a good bit more.

What about actual artificial hair implants?

These things are being done in Rio. Thousands of actual artificial hairs are implanted in your scalp, over 10,000 for a full head of hair. That's 10,000 potential infection spots.

But that's not the worst of it. These hairs fall out on a regular basis, and have to be surgically replaced. Since each hair costs a dollar, keeping hair like this can cost you $15,000 a year. Plus airfare and hotels and lots of doctors bills. But that's not the worst of it. Most of these hairs don't seem to like the heat too much. In the wrong conditions, they melt. Oh God.

The medical horror stories about artificial implants would make Stephen King blanch. Go to Rio for the girls, instead.

How about hair transplants? Those things really do work, don't they?

This seems to work extremely well for many patients, but picking the right surgeon is very important. Just as a number of balding men aren't good candidates for transplants, a number of doctors who practice the procedure aren't good candidates for your trust.

In the most common type of hair transplant, a small plug containing four or five follicles is punched out of the donor area (usually down low on the back of the head) and placed in a punched out place in the site to be filled in. It takes about 200–300 plugs to fill in a normal receding hairline, a two- or three-step procedure over time.[7]

Does this work if you are really bald?

If you're really bald, with only a horseshoe fringe of hair, say, you probably are not a good candidate because you have few of the right trees available to cover a lot of desert. Donor hairs must come from a relatively permanent place, usually the nape of the neck.

How do I find a good doctor? Norma's preacher says he knows one who also communes with the spirits.

Since doctors are just people, there are doctors who practice scams and/or sloppy medicine. Since poor results will always be highly visible, think before you plant. If possible, talk to people you know who've had transplants. If possible, look carefully at hairlines of these folks and make a judgment on how natural their new hair really looks. Trust your judgment on the esthetic issue; don't trust the newly planted person's judgment. We all tend to see through those rose-colored glasses when our own looks are involved.

If you can't find some transplant patients themselves to talk to, call up your regular doctor and a good local dermatologist for recommendations. Find at least two potentials, if possible. If you'd like, ask your barber for some ideas. Barbers are the priests of hair lore, so you may listen to what they've learned from any confessionals, but don't automatically take their word as correct. Some less-than-scrupulous hair doctors pay barbers for referrals.

Actually interview the doctors, if possible. Look at pictures of their work. Try to talk to some of their patients in the waiting room, or over the phone. Successful patients are nearly evangelical in their loyalty to a good doctor; victims of failed plantings are equally as vehement in their disappointment.

What is "scalp reduction"?

A doctor, using a balloon-type device inserted under the skin, stretches the scalp. He then cuts out as much of the bald spot as possible and sews the new edges together to provide as much hair cover as possible. Not everyone is a candidate for this, including me. Stretch my scalp enough to cover my bald spot and my ears would be on top of my head.

W*hat about minoxidil?*

Many are touting it, and since minoxidil is expected to receive the approval of the FDA, a blessing the Upjohn Company, its producers, are very optimistic about, millions will probably buy it. Something, at last, from other than quacks. Upjohn has applied for the name Regaine Topical Solution.

Upjohn sponsored studies at twenty-seven centers around the country. The research there was certainly objective and scientific, the good news; but the results so far haven't been that promising, the bad news. Safety is also a question you might want to think about.

Minoxidil did grow hair, usually in men just beginning to go bald (mostly men in their early twenties). Seventy-six percent of the men using the product showed hair growth. But only 40 percent of those felt their new hair growth was moderate, and only 10 percent felt it was dense. Placebos, incidentally, in some instances, were just as effective as the drug.[8]

Dr. Arthur P. Bertolino at New York University Medical Center, using a formula parallel to Regaine, found only 10 percent of the patients have a "cosmetically significant improvement." He also found the solution works best if a bald patch is no larger than four inches across and at the back rather than the front of the head.[9]

H*ow safe is it?*

Minoxidil is a very powerful blood pressure medicine, which has various side effects, including impotence, in some users taking it to treat high blood pressure. Even though the solution applied for hair growth is only 1–2 percent as strong as the blood pressure medicine itself, the solution must be applied as long as the user wants hair growth. The long term effects of the solution can't be known yet.

Why can't I just get some minoxidil from my doctor and apply it myself? Won't that be cheaper than waiting for the real stuff?

Regaine will probably cost about a thousand dollars for a year's prescription.[10] It really isn't that expensive to make (and has been around in blood pressure form for quite some time), but Upjohn is no fool when it comes to the price balding people will pay.

Doing it yourself isn't the way to go, however. Because oral medications like minoxidil are suspended in other solutions, and since self-medication isn't easy to control strengthwise, mixing up home remedies could do you harm.

What are you going to do, Remar?

No one would like to have a real head of hair more than I would. During the year, I've looked for it a lot, but real hair just doesn't exist for most of us (yet) unless we were born with it.

If you are determined to have something close, anyway, find the simplest, easiest-to-maintain substitute. If you decide to have a transplant, virtually the only reasonably successful and safe procedure other than mops, don't expect perfection. Regardless of what you do, don't be discouraged. Lots of new surveys show that bald is becoming sexier in the eyes of women (Foxy and smart women, I like to think) every day.

Norma says my teeth are yellow and cracked and crooked. And I'm afraid the gap in the front nearly reminds me of

the width of her hips. Other than that, they look fine. But, what can I do with them?

A lot of interesting things are happening in people's mouths these days, and most of them are pretty good.

Bonding. It isn't related to modern sex, but it is one of the most popular and relatively inexpensive procedures for fixing chips, discolorations, cracks, and even gaps between teeth. In the procedure plastic resins are applied directly to the surface of teeth already treated with a mild acid solution. The coatings are hardened with chemicals or ultraviolent light, and then polished.

Bonding normally costs only a third to a half as much as having teeth crowned, but there are a few disadvantages. The procedure is usually only good for five to seven years. And the bonded surfaces themselves are vulnerable to hard wear and staining. Smoking, coffee, tea, nail-biting, ice-chewing, raw carrots, and corn on the cob can all be hard on the process, for instance.

Capping/Crowning. These procedures involve grinding down teeth and then seating a crown or cap on the stub. For years, these have been the best methods for fixing broken or badly damaged teeth, and are still the most durable. The cost, of course, is higher.

Implants. These are certainly the hot thing in dentistry, but the long-term durability and effectiveness of the procedure are not known yet, regardless of what your dentist says. In implants, a titanium screw is implanted in the jawbone and allowed to heal. Then a gold-and-porcelain tooth is attached to this support.

Implants are usually done only when other procedures such as root canals are not feasible.[11] Before you rush in here, ask your dentist for the names of patients who have been sporting implants for a year or so.

Adults Wearing Braces.   Orthodontics involves the movement of teeth which are fixed in bone, and it's become a popular and nearly trendy thing with many adults. The process has a few drawbacks, though, so think about them before opting for a metallic or plastic smile: adult jaws are full-grown and their bones denser than children's. Adults' bones don't respond as fast as children's bones, therefore, in terms of healing or recontouring. Because of that, adults have to have more overcrowded teeth removed and more supplemental jaw surgery than most children.[12] Both procedures cost and both can lead to the chance of infection.

Adults also have a higher incidence of gum disease even before orthodontic appliances are added to the mouth. The appliances make it harder to keep teeth free from plaque and gums healthy.

W*hat can I do to make Norma's eyes alluring?*

Medical science hasn't progressed that far yet, but here's a rundown on the things that may help.

Eyeglasses.   The greatest advance is those glasses that don't show that you are wearing bifocals and trifocals. I got my first pair four years ago and only my ophthalmologist knows.

Hard Contact Lenses.   These things are durable, long-lasting, easy to clean and care for, and can correct all types of vision including astigmatism. They take your eyes quite some time to adjust to, however, and have to be taken out nightly. Some people never adjust.

Soft Contacts.   Your eyes usually adjust easily to them, so they can be worn quickly with little discomfort. Although they don't fit all eye problems, the newest lenses reportedly work with very nearsighted people or people with astigmatism, problems older soft contacts couldn't help. However, soft contacts must

be carefully cleaned in special cleaning equipment and are fragile. Improper cleaning can result in eye infections. Soft lenses
can rip or tear, and have to be replaced more frequently than
hard contacts, perhaps every year.

Extended-Wear Lenses.   When the FDA gave its blessing to
extended-wear lenses, both the manufacturers and the cus-
tomers alike began to drool. Thirty days without fooling with
your vision sounded like a miracle to virtually all of us who
need help to see.

The real world of extended-wear lenses hasn't been that perfect. These lenses are very, very thin, as little as .002 inch in
the center, and are extremely susceptible to tearing. Most people
go through several pair a year, an expensive habit.

Most doctors don't even recommend that the lenses be worn
for thirty days (two weeks seems to be the limit), but wearing
them even for two weeks can lead to the deposit of eye protein,
clouding the lenses and causing eye irritation and at times infection.

Extended lenses also seem to be more difficult to fit for the
best vision. Before choosing an eye center for these, try to talk
to several people who've been dealing with the center for a year
or two.

W*hy don't I just forget glasses and have my eyes operated
on? Aren't those radial keratomies the best thing?*

Since radial keratomy is essentially cosmetic surgery on the
most precious thing you've got next to life, your eyes, please
read this carefully before letting a scalpel touch them.

This surgery to correct nearsightedness (myopia) involves
making eight to sixteen slashes in a pinwheel on the cornea. It
remains very controversial surgery, with its proponents arguing
that it is perfectly safe while many opthamologists (doctors with
advanced training in eye disease and surgery) maintain a wait-
and-see attitude. These ophthalmologists argue that it is the long-

term results that matter, not the short-term results—particularly on something as valuable as your eyes.[13]

Isn't it safe if the government lets them do it?

Surprise. The government has no regulatory authority over the testing and approval of any new surgical procedures, unlike its authority over the approval of new drugs and medical devices. Deciding whether a new surgical procedure is effective and safe enough to use is left to the surgeons who perform the operation and the various peer review processes under which they operate (hospital boards, professional societies, etc.)

Radial keratomy, however, was so controversial that, in a rare move, the government funded a five-year study on the safety of this procedure. Called PERK (Prospective Evaluation of Radial Keratomy), the study was conducted at nine medical centers around the country, most university-related.

A number of independent doctors already performing this surgery didn't like at all the intrusion on their business of the PERK study and the accompanying keratomy moratorium recommended by the American Academy of Ophthalmology. They claimed doctors at universities and institutions were curtailing their rights to practice medicine. They sued. As in many lawsuits, the persons conducting the study decided it was cheaper to settle than fight, agreed to pay a quarter of a million dollars in damages to the plaintiffs, and also agreed to release a statement suggesting that radial keratomy was an acceptible treatment, based on the results of the first year of the study.[14] That statement was released to the press and, of course, the public took it as a blanket endorsement.

The results released after four years of the PERK study, however, are not very encouraging. In fact, they'll probably come as a surprise to many prospective patients who are familiar with the glowing reports in the popular press and the newspaper advertising claims of some radial keratomy clinics. The Harvard Medical School *Health Letter* summarized the four-year results as follows: "Between one and four years after the operation, only 6 percent of the treated eyes retained the correction achieved by the operation. About 20 percent had shifted back toward nearsightedness, and over 70 percent had tended to become more farsighted. The drift away from normal vision was regarded as significant [enough to require correction with lenses] in about one-third of the patients."[15] Even though the surgical techniques have changed since these operations were done and the studies of these techniques are not finished yet, the Harvard folks feel that the message is that "good results after one year won't necessarily last a lifetime."[16] They recommend caution until the long-term results of these new techniques are in.

Remember that physicians performing this surgery can claim the procedure is safe, and they may be splendid surgeons, but if you are among those whose improved vision doesn't last or those who have problems, no lawsuit can correct your vision.

Week 29

<u>Grand Bahama Island</u>

On our island, the heat begins to leave about thirty minutes before sunset, taking with it the color of most things, depositing it in the clouds, it seems, which turn from threatening and dark to the colors favored by hip designers. I'm sure this happens many places, but it seems special here. This time of day is my favorite for pleasure biking.

My bike is a Royal Enfield ten-speed, bright red, with a Sears speedometer which read 897 miles this morning. That's five and one half months' riding. My pedals have toe clips with leather straps. Clips, I was told, make your legs work on the upswing, increasing your pedaling efficiency by about 30 percent. They make you look very serious, too. But toe clips grip very tightly, and at stop signs, when I needed to drop my foot to the ground to keep from falling over, my toes would stick, and I would fall, in slow motion, to the ground. My clips are now for show.

I usually ride for about forty-five minutes. Grand Bahama's infrastructure—broad, four-lane avenues and hundreds of miles of other roads and canals—was designed to support half a million people. Only 40,000 live here permanently, so the biking along most major roads is pleasant and the biking along the smaller roads, many running close to the beach and through stands of casuarinas, banyans, and palms, is dreamlike at this hour.

Along what I call my "A" route, the most handsome route, cocoa plum bushes are now being staked out by all of us regular bikers and walkers. Cocoa plums produce only twice each year. The fruit, about the size of a Ping-Pong ball, has an enormous seed and only the smallest bit of flesh, but when the flesh turns soft and the skin reddish-pink, the taste is exotic and sweet, like cotton candy in its sugary elusiveness.

All this good taste dooms cocoa plums to a short but purposeful life, and quarrels over plucking rights at a particular plum bush can become vegetarian versions of California Gold Rush disputes. Some people avoid this with stakeouts, usually grandmothers, who sit during the day near favored harvesting areas to chase away birds and people.

My method of collecting is called hit-and-run. I pick just a few plums from each bush, dropping them down my shirt, then move on before any alleged proprietor can catch me. If my strategy works, I look pregnant before the ride is over.

Much later in the season, when the easy pickings are over, we all go much farther on the unpaved real backroads of Grand Bahama, really the prettiest parts of the island, and bring out large bags of plums. Going toward the East End, the best plum areas are along the deserted beach road to Old Freetown. Bushes here are jungle-thick, the plums seem meatier, and the flesh tastes unusually sweet, especially if you're lying on your back under a palm on a isolated beach. Bikes will only get you to the beginning of this road, incidentally, for it quickly turns to very fine and deep sand. At that point, we hide our wheels in the brush and start walking or, if the tide is low and the moon right, speed along the waved-packed beach.

Whether I'm pleasure biking at twilight or on a serious plum expedition, I usually end my days at the Tide's Inn, our island's scuba-diving hangout. I start my days there lots of time, too. The Tide's is upstairs at UNEXSO and is the type of place that likes people in bathing suits and T-shirts, even at night. Chairs here are blue canvas directors' chairs, the decor fishy (including two stuffed sharks, the standard gallows humor prop at every dive spot I've seen in the world), and the food very informal. One large wall is virtually covered with the names of The Underwater Explorers Society's members. At night, videos related to diving play constantly on a wide-screen television.

At least once each week, I bike to UNEXSO about an hour before sunset, grill a couple of hamburgers with friends or eat a couple of spicy Bahamian beef patties, and then grab my diving gear for a night scuba dive.

To many people, scuba seems like an awfully exotic and dangerous sport, like I think of skydiving. In truth, it's a peaceful, easy sport, very good for nonathletes like me. It also has great brag potential with nondivers. ("Sharks? Oh sure, I see a lot of them." The diver then yawns.)

But even good shark stories don't have as much brag potential as night dives. Look at ocean water at night and it looks *solid black*. God knows what lives down there, big, grouchy, and hungry, just waiting for a juicy human. Most experienced night divers, including me, encourage those thoughts in the uninitiated, supposedly for good-natured amusement. I really think we're venting our own embarrassment at the memory of the fear we felt the first time and might still feel. After hundreds of night dives, I still wonder about the things down there just before jumping in that cool blackness. Sharks do feed at night, you know.

But in my hundreds of nights dives (note the casual brag), I've only found beauty down there. Leave your diving light off as we do most of the time, and night diving is like swimming into the early evening sky, when you can still see but stars are out. Many of the smallest undersea creatures create their own light. Simply move your hand through the water and that movement creates bioluminescence, like the sparks of sparklers coming from your hands. Look in the distance and see a small chain of lanterns floating by, salps. Turn on your light and look for sleeping fish. Some of them, like parrot fish, sleep so soundly you can actually pick them up and swim around with them under your arm.

Lobsters and crabs carouse at night. Bahamian lobsters don't have claws, but they do have long tentacles. They roam the ocean floor and coral heads freely, occasionally side by side, brushing against each other gently, using their tentacles like blind men's canes, moving with the jerkiness of a happy old couple trying to make it home after their first night on the town in years.

After about forty-five minutes of gliding around with carousing lobsters and the like, most of us, excited, return to the balcony at the Tide's. We talk loudly if any nondivers are around, soaking up their looks of admiration at our bravery, and we invariably fall prey to the lore magnification syndrome, a syndrome fisherman in particular know very well. With each repetition of a good story, things grow. If a person was lucky enough to see something unusual by himself, the thing *really* grows. I personally grew a nurse shark, about as dangerous as bad breath, from two feet to seven feet in three conversations, probably a record.

A good deal of drinking goes on during this time, especially if the dive has been blessed with at least one dramatic moment: riding a large turtle, or spotting a school of large eagle rays, for instance. I'll even have one beer myself, now. But around eleven, I wander back through the Tide's, past the backgammon games, then past the table where Fritz and Dave and Jack, my friends who live on sailboats in the harbor, are solving world problems, then out the back gate. I bike home in less than five minutes.

I usually have a juice at the house and stretch out on the softest sofa on my porch. My house isn't fancy here, but it's spread out and islandy. The porch, about twenty-seven by twelve, is really a part of the living room, since I seldom pull the glass wall shut which separates them. Large, leafy plants fill both rooms. Ceiling fans turn most of the time. From my position on the softest sofa, I can watch curly-tail lizards, the terror of tourists, scurry around my deck, just outside the porch and under a large banyan tree.

My island lifestyle, while it doesn't yet include a hammock on the beach and tropical maidens at my beck and call, would fulfill most people's island fantasy. But life here is very down-to-earth, too. Things stay in perspective. A nice definition of what "normal" should be. I've thought about that a lot in the last few days, for I soon leave for the land of the "abnormal"— Hollywood.

A*re biking and diving both aerobic exercises?*

Diving really isn't exercise at all. Moving under the water in a weight-free environment doesn't provide enough resistance to do you good aerobically. But it's a great activity, aside from the fact most of the women wear bikinis. Biking, on the other hand, is one of the very best aerobic exercises. It's nonimpact (unless you wear toe clips and fall, like some bald people I know), can be performed as well in your home with a stationary bike, and is fun since it brings back lots of childhood memories.

Y*ou eat all that natural island food, that's why you're healthier, isn't it? Norma and I should go out and buy those "free-range" eggs and organically raised vegetables, shouldn't we?*

The people who usually benefit from the "natural" phenomenon are the people who sell the products. The health food industry takes in billions each year, and with all that money comes the power to advertise and create even more false awareness of the supposed benefits of health foods.

First, there is no legal definition for most of the terms used by this industry. The sellers can therefore use virtually any terms at will. Second, "natural" businesses use down-home labels and nature scenes to imply their products are simply better because of this down-home quality. But foods raised on animal fertilizers don't have any more nutrients than ones raised on chemical fertilizers. And "natural" vitamins have exactly the same chemical composition as laboratory-produced vitamins.[1] The one real difference between "natural" products and regular products is the price: health foods cost approximately 50 percent more.

What *hat about food preservatives? Are they all bad?*

Preservatives are added to our foods for many reasons, including improvement of food quality (to fortify and enrich), maintaining freshness (which can preserve the nutritional value), and simply adding consumer appeal (such as color, flavor, or sweeteners). Preservatives at times may cause problems because they are biologically active. They go through extensive testing before being used commercially, but the pressures from manufacturers and potential users is so great that some preservatives are probably approved before they should be.[2]

D *oes reading labels help here?*

The nutritional information on packaging can be an enormous help to you, if you get in the habit of reading labels. The habit can scare the hell out of you, though, if you really learn what some of the ingredients do. Unfortunately, manufacturers also make it hard at times even to know what the real ingredients are. For instance, they can add ingredients which are compounds themselves, but they are not required to list the ingredients in the compound. Say your quick-fix macaroni and cheese box dinner lists cheese as one of the ingredients. It need not say what went into the cheese.

At least you don't have to worry about additives and preservatives with things like fruit, right?

Oranges, bananas, even nuts have been altered with gasses, colorings, and other "enhancers." If you really don't want anything unnatural, take the coverings off. If you want to eat the coverings, wash and scrub the fruit well.

Norma says it's okay to eat lots of sugar, since the sugar manufacturers are advertising how "natural" it is. And I saw that beef is really "natural," too. Are you telling me we can't accept those nice folks' claims?

Sugar does contain "only" sixteen calories in a very level teaspoon, and it is "natural" in some sense, too, I guess. What the ads don't tell you, of course, is the fact there's no nutritional value in sugar, and that one soda contains nine teaspoons of this nutritionally useless, natural thing. The sugar isn't bad, as we noted earlier (I love it), but the calories won't help you.

The beef people are taking the same approach. Since cattle roam free and happy (from the way it looks on TV), their natural state alone must make it better for you. All beef contains saturated fat, such a close friend of coronary heart disease. When you eat beef, eat the leanest cuts possible.

Milk cows are being promoted for their naturalness, too. The "realness" of their milk is supposed to make it better for us. Unfortunately, whole milk has 4 percent fat. Stick with 2 percent or, even better, skim milk, which has all the nutritional value and virtually none of the fat.

Even honey bees are being abused. Honey does taste great as a sweetener, but its sugar has virtually the same chemical makeup as regular sugar, and it contains more calories per measure since honey takes up less space than sugar granules.

Norma's preacher sold her some special herbal rejuvenating juice, which she can drink or put on her hair. Is all this herbal stuff okay?

Herbal remedies are not regulated by any government agency, so no standards exist. They contain natural chemicals that can very definitely affect the body. The *Journal of the American Medical Association* warns doctors the products may be the culprit in signs of food poisoning. Herbal products are sold many times by "pyramid" or "multilevel" type companies; the sales meeting and person-to-person selling style of such companies allows many questionable claims to be made orally by salespeople while shielding the company from responsibility. The head office can claim, "Oh, we didn't authorize them to say that," though in staff or distributor sales meetings they may have done just that. Although the products are required by law to carry a label indicating that they do not replace the services of a doctor, such face-to-face selling techniques keep these outrageous claims flowing.[3]

And unfortunately, the products sell as if they did you some good. They don't, and may do you real harm.

Well, why doesn't the government prosecute the sellers?

Government agencies don't have the time or money to prosecute many false claims. As William Jarvis, president of the National Council Against Health Fraud, has observed, "You've got a line of quacks 3,000 deep and taking them one at a time, some of them are going to die of old age before [the FDA] gets to their cases."[4] Further, in this particular area it is often hard to document the false claim since, as we've noted, so many claims are made orally, usually at sales meetings where potential sellers are whipped into emotional frenzies that would make Elmer Gantry smile. Truth is very seldom a part of these meetings, and the message spread there is passed on by the individual sellers to innocent (and usually older and less-educated) victims. Listen to what one reporter heard said at such a meeting, and decide for yourself how much fact and how much hyperbole is present:

> What this product does is *awesome*. This will normalize blood pressure, reduce the plasma and cholesterol level in the blood, reduce the buildup of plaque inside the arteries, stabilize blood pressure. If it's high, brings it down; if it's low, brings it up. *Incredible*. Nothing else like it in the world.[5]

Scumbags like the people who say such things make fortunes, and obviously couldn't care less who they hurt. Stay away from herbal remedies, and stay far away from the people who try to sell them to you with a smile. They are not your friends.

Now before you sling a cup of Red Zinger at me, let me say that many herb teas are indeed tasty. But beware of teas which are supposed to have "medicinal" properties and are said to treat several conditions. If overused, even such common herbs as chamomile, ginseng, or sassafras (often used in teas) are toxic.[6] You need to know what you're really drinking in an herb tea, and an herbal enthusiast is not the person to get your information from.

What are some other favorite quacktics out there?

Here are a few fun techniques and gimmicks in the world of food and/or supplement quackdom:
• Assertions that food from supermarkets is unhealthy.
• Instant, computerized nutritional evaluations where supplements are sold. Sounds like a nice idea, but remember the purpose of the evaluation is to promote the supplements.
• Claims of effortless dieting through starch blockers or fat melters. Though some of these products have been banned; similar new ones are always popping up.

If a product quotes an article, isn't that a sign of an upright seller?

A number of magazines will publish anything if the author buys an ad. In quackdom, articles are written constantly for public consumption, and then quoted as if they were scientific papers. A generally good rule for judging the integrity of a magazine is this: if all of the articles in a particular issue are positive about products, services, and treatments advertised in that magazine, you are probably dealing with a sleazebag publication. If the magazines also rail against conventional products, treatments, and services—and rail against established authorities—you can bet your flea powder you are dealing with people who put your dollar above your health.

Norma read about a neat way to really check your nutritional needs by psychic testing and hair analysis. You mean the article might not be scientific?

Psychic testing and hair analysis aren't the only bizarre "tests" out there. "Pulse" tests for nutritional needs are popular. Certain blood tests, which claim to spot food allergies and which go under names like "cytotoxic testing," "leukocyte antigen sensitivity testing," and "food sensitivity testing," are even more popular and in clinical trials have been found just as worthless.[7]

I bet you don't like bee pollen, either.

Bees are nice, and honey is nice, but promoting bee pollen as the world's "most perfect food," as some sellers do, is about like promoting Norma as the world's most perfect woman.

But there are worse things out there. For instance:

Spirulina. Sold in pills or powder, spirulina is a blue-green algae that grows in brackish ponds and lakes. In its pure form, it's a source of protein with many minerals and vitamins. But quacks claim more power for it. They claim that phenylalanine, an amino acid found in it, can switch off hunger pangs in the brain. Un-huh. Some nutritionists feel that large amounts of spirulina can be dangerous, and that the excess uric acid in the product may cause kidney stones or gout.[8]

Glucomannan.   That wonderful "secret" of the Orient. This stuff comes from the konjac root, and is supposed to speed the food through your digestive tract. Ergo, eat more without gaining weight. Buy it and, ergo, you are taken again. Since the konjac root has been eaten for many years in Japan, glucomannan is marketed as a food, incidentally, though the FDA has tried to change that.[9]

HCG.   This product comes from the urine of pregnant women, and is approved by the FDA for treatment of "certain problems of the male reproductive systems and in stimulating ovulation in women who have difficulty conceiving." That's not why some diet clinics use it, though. They claim that injections of this hormone will help you lose weight. Both the FDA and the AMA say the product is useless for that purpose.[10]

Q*uack products and quack remedies must cost plenty in money and suffering. Why can't we put an end to it?*

Though we Americans are an educated people, quackery and health fraud do thrive. The practices presented in this chapter are only a few of the hundreds of scams, schemes, and false hopes sold every day. Some device sold as the "latest breakthrough" is often just a new twist on a practice which may be hundreds of years old. Quackery has always been with us and probably always will be, as long as disease and suffering exist. When our current scientific knowledge cannot help or treatment seems too slow, our instinct is to do something. As I was working on this, serendipity led me to a passage from Tolstoy's *War and*

Peace, which states reasons for quackery's continued existence that are as valid today and tomorrow as when they were written in 1869. One of the young heroines has fallen ill and her concerned family brings in practitioner after practitioner and doses her with various useless nostrums in an effort to help. Tolstoy writes of these practitioners:

> Their usefulness did not consist in making the patient swallow substances for the most part harmful (the harm being scarcely perceptible as they were administered in small doses), but they were useful, necessary, indispensable, because they satisfied a moral need of the patient and those who loved her, which is why there will always be pseudohealers, wise women, homeopaths, and allopaths. They satisfied that eternal human need for hope of relief, for sympathy, for taking action, which is felt in times of suffering. They satisfied the eternal human need that is seen in its most elementary form in children—the need to have the hurt place rubbed. A child hurts himself and at once runs to the arms of his mother or nurse to have the hurt place kissed or rubbed. He cannot believe that the strongest and wisest of his people have no remedy for his pain. And the hope of relief and the mother's expression of sympathy while she rubs the bump comforts him.[11]

Today we often cannot believe that our scientists and physicians, the "strongest and wisest of our people," have no answers. So we listen eagerly to anyone who promises hope—the charlatans, the quacks, the pseudohealers.

SMOKING

Week 32

Grand Bahama Island

I was rummaging through the library at UNEXSO and found a copy of John Fowles's *The Magus*, a great book which brought back an unusual memory.

Except for a rabbit tobacco cigarette or two when I was learning about adult things at twelve (rabbit tobacco grows wild in many parts of Georgia, and we would pick, dry, and roll our own), I had never smoked a cigarette until reading *The Magus* in August 1971. Thirty and balding, I was visiting friends in Bermuda—islands held a special attraction for me even then— and on the day I smoked my first real cigarette, I was sitting in a fighting chair of a forty-two-foot sport fisherman, my feet propped up, a pipe in my mouth.

I had not smoked the pipe long. A friend had given me two in New York several months earlier because she felt they made me look "distinguished," and since I just loved that thought, I had learned to hang one constantly from my lips with the most practiced casualness. The damned thing would never stay lit, though.

Anchored near a wreck several miles from shore, I had been able to keep my pipe lit as I read *The Magus*, however, and found myself puffing more than ever as the novel drew me in. A mystical, byzantine tale, *The Magus* also took place on an island, and as the plot became even more complex, my pipe tobacco ran out. Right by my feet, on the rail, was a pack of Kool menthol. I remember the pack had only two or three cigarettes in it (even a slight breeze would have blown it seaward), and I remember thinking what a stupid place the rail was to place something so light. So I picked it up, looked at the word "Kool" for a minute, and pulled out one cigarette. Until that moment, I had not smoked cigarettes because I did not want to do what all my friends seemed to be doing and also wasn't quite sure how to keep the cigarette from looking "funny" in my mouth. Some people looked very laid-back when they smoked. My image, I feared, would probably be more like Mr. Peepers sucking a straw. Until that moment I had also hated the smell of cigarette smoke. It reminded me of claustrophobic meeting rooms and miserable colds.

I put the Kool in my mouth anyway, lit it tentatively, turned my eyes back to the book, and inhaled, deeply. And saw stars. That Kool was the most powerful, and oddly wonderful, drug I'd ever taken. I tried to read, but could not for an instant. And then I began to read and puff. The few cigarettes in the pack were gone within the hour. I rummaged through the galley and found a full pack.

That night, when we returned to shore, I bought my own. Benson and Hedges menthol. And through that pack and the next, I pretty much smoked for the instant high the cigarettes gave me, savoring each puff for another charge.

At first, the rush was the only reason I smoked. A nice, legal drug trip. Then the immediate pleasure seemed to diminish, and something for a while as nice replaced it: Cigarettes gave me something to do when I was nervous or restless or insecure or frustrated, and at that time in my life, I was many of those things a lot. I did not think of my new friends as addictive, however, and enjoyed them fully.

I didn't think of them as too unhealthy, either; though, at times, logic made me wonder. During the early seventies, there was a lot of press about pollution in the air and its deleterious effect on health. Oil or coal power plants in particular were damned in the polution debate. It did cross my mind a few times that directly inhaling smoke from a cigarette had to be something like sticking your head in a power plant smokestack, but the thought went away. I smoked rather happily for five years.

And then I started paying attention to press about smoking and health. The articles made me think, but I needed the habit then, and I sided more with the tobacco industry spokesmen than alarmists. I mean, could responsible businesses like tobacco companies really sell things they knew would kill? Because my smoking habit was such a short-term thing (What was five years? All the press talked about "long-term" dangers), I didn't worry too much but did start telling myself that one day I would quit. Especially on the mornings my throat tasted like the muck from a horse stall. I switched to lower-tar-and-nicotine brands.

By 1978, during regular physicals, doctors started telling me rather casually that I should quit smoking. None of them seemed to make it life-or-death, but all seemed to say if smoking was bad, it would get you with cancer. No one mentioned heart disease at that time.

But as I read more on smoking, as my cough developed, as cigarettes became a necessity even when my mouth and throat burned, my real problem with cigarettes started to bother me. In 1979, visiting my friend Jerry Preston, a nonsmoker, I for the first time got out of bed at three A.M. and drove around a strange town until I could find someone to sell me a fix. The next day, I deliberately ran out of cigarettes again to prove my willpower, but the cigarettes won again. I drove to a corner market, didn't open the cigarettes as I drove back (self-control), then sat on Jerry's wonderfully open and green Florida porch (the only place in the house he allowed smoking) and slowly drew in the first deep breath. It tasted so damn good, but was followed by the bitter aftertaste the mind can deposit when it loses an important battle. The damn things were stronger than my will. Self-esteem went down a little, then.

The quitting attempts started. I went to a hypnotist. She was expensive. "That's part of the therapy," she said, a really great line, as she took my money and tucked it in her cleavage. I made it about an hour and kicked myself for being such a weak-ass. I bought some of those graduated filters. Aside from the fact some people thought the filters made me look like a bald FDR, they did nothing to help me. My self-esteem notched down.

And then, while I was again visiting Jerry in Florida three years later, my mother called and asked me to fly home, a problem with my father's health. Mom isn't nervous or dependent, and the tone in her voice scared me. Dad had developed a blind spot, and simply did not want to move or talk.

We knew Dad had emphysema. His doctors had forced him to give up cigarettes for pipes twenty years before. We knew it had slowed his activities down, too. But we didn't really think he was too sick. I walked out of the house with my mother and father the next morning, pausing for a moment because he wanted to look at the yard, and drove to the hospital. By three that day we knew he was dying of a lung cancer that had spread and formed an inoperable tumor in his brain. He died in two weeks. I smoked a lot the day of his funeral.

My habit became more self-destructive then. I smoked more when I was worried the most. I smoked more when I sat down at the typewriter, and a lot of my time is spent at typewriters. The thing really won, and even on the mornings when my cough sounded an awful lot like my father's, I lit up. For me, the most destructive thing about cigarettes (I thought) was their ability to quietly take away your self-respect.

I tried dozens of times to quit. In mid-1983, a low-stress time, I actually made it three months without smoking, but never once quit thinking about cigarettes. The first puff was more sensual than an orgasm. In December 1984, my continual throat problems sent me back to a doctor for about the twentieth time in four years. This fellow had given up trying to convince me to quit smoking. But on his office wall was a recent article about the dramatic health changes even in very old people who quit smoking. I liked that. I had pretty much decided that thirteen years of smoking—how did that many years go by?—had already done its damage. But if the article was right, even people who had smoked *fifty* years could change physiologically by stopping.

Without much thought I asked the doctor for a nicotine gum prescription, and without any resolve I chewed the first piece as I drove home. Out of curiosity. The gum tasted absolutely terrible, and it burned nearly as much as smoke down a raw throat. But for the first time in years I did not smoke for two hours. I didn't want to. That scared the hell out of me, so I instantly lit up a cigarette and thought about really trying to quit one more time.

My plan was very cautious. Rather than swearing off, I'd simply go hour by hour and see what it felt like. Each time the urge came for a cigarette (and they came very frequently. I was smoking over three packs a day), I chewed and the urge went away. The first full day I chewed twenty pieces. For the rest of December I chewed nearly that many every day. But I went through the Christmas holidays without smoking once. Several members of my family smoke a lot, but I even made it through the holidays without preaching at them. I wasn't at all sure my smoking habit was ended. There is no hunger like the hunger for nicotine, and I didn't believe gum could really take that away.

And then a favorite aunt was taken to the hospital with pneumonia. Edna, seventy-one, had quit smoking five years before. Her pneumonia wasn't that bad. It only prevented her from using around 30 percent of her lungs, a loss anyone can stand with healthy lungs. But my aunt had already lost 40 percent of her useful capacity because of emphysema. And she could not live very well on the remaining 30 percent.

Edna, her eyes bulging from the strain, was gasping for air

191

when I first saw her in the hospital. Her daughter was trying to hold her hands down, trying to prevent flailing hands from jerking out tubes. My aunt was suffocating. Down the hall, three other people were dying the same way, tubes down their throats, respirators replacing lungs, all of them smokers at one time in their lives. And during the time it took for my aunt to die, two of those people died also.

I used my gum a lot that week, too. But I also decided not to smoke again. And though I kept gum in my pocket for nearly a year, using it for about six months until my physical and emotional dependency habits left me, I haven't smoked yet.

Now, finally, two significant things have happened. *I don't miss cigarettes any more*, even in down moments or moments of stress. The emotional addiction has left. And, more important, I feel pretty damn good for finally taking control of my life when it comes to at least one vice. Quitting smoking was really the beginning of my remake. Anyone who can do that can do anything.

Norma *quit smoking with the help of something she calls her tantric yoga research partner. She says quitting makes food taste better. Is that why she gained 40 pounds? I don't like her at 310.*

Smoking over long periods does dull your taste buds, and quitting does seem to bring some of them back to life. Don't forget, I started my blimp imitation after quitting. But many psychologists think emotional cravings rather than physical ones are the reason people gain weight when they quit. Whatever the cause, smart smokers have always used that as an excuse not to quit. I certainly did. Smoking certainly couldn't be as bad for you as being overweight, right?

Wrong. Smoking is *always worse for you than being overweight, if you have a choice of the two*.[1] And you don't have to gain weight, either, if you substitute other things for that part of your life. Starting an exercise program at the time you quit, for instance, can usually control your weight problem.

Who smokes, anyway? Haven't most people quit?

According to the American Cancer Society, 33 percent of all American males over twenty are cigarette smokers. 28 percent of women smoke.[2]

What is cigarette smoke, anyway?

It is a mixture of the air around you and the various gasses, liquids, and solid particles produced or given off when tobacco burns. The solid matter is collectively called "tar." Cigarette manufacturers love to put the word "tar" in quotes, because they like to imply no such things exist, (and therefore can't hurt you) and, in part, they are right. "Tar" isn't the stuff you pave with. It's composed of thousands of compounds, including hydrocarbons, organic acids, alcohols, nicotines, and, to a lesser degree, radioactive lead and polonium. Virtually all of these things are toxic,[3] and this is where the cigarette manufacturers' cute use of quotes around the word "tar" is misleading. "Tar," as we've defined it, is a lot worse for you than the tar your foot may pick up on the beach.

The gasses in smoke include carbon monoxide, carbon dioxide, and significant amounts of cyanides, acrolein, nitrogen oxides, and ammonia.[4]

How specifically does smoke damage the lungs, if it does?

Think of your lungs as a big tree. The major airway, the trachea, is the trunk. It branches into smaller and smaller branches and twigs, the bronchi and bronchioles, and finally into leaves, small airsacks called alveoli. Much as the leaves of a tree present a surface area for carbon dioxides in the air to be absorbed, the alveoli, loaded with oxygen, present their surface area to oxygen-starved blood. As blood cells absorb the new oxygen, they cast off an equal amount of carbon dioxide, which is carried out through the branches of our lungs and expelled.

Alveoli are hard-working, rather single-minded, and very, very fragile. So fragile our bodies produce special cell linings just to protect them. One type of these special cells secretes a mucus to prevent alveoli injury or irritation. Another type cell grows fine hairlike structures called cilia. The cilia are like an efficient flypaper-coated conveyor belt. They trap anything that lands on them, irritants and germs and the like, and move them along until they reach your mouth. When you cough sometimes, you're finishing their work.

Unfortunately, cilia cannot handle the toxins in smoke *at all*. Inhale some for just thirty seconds and your cilia become paralyzed for at least fifteen minutes. They cannot trap and repel other irritants, germs, and particularly the particles in the smoke itself. Continue to expose them to smoke, and they die. They literally fall off and are replaced with cells which cannot protect your alveoli from foreign matter.[5]

While your lung tissue is losing these defenses, it builds another defense by producing special fighter cells (alveolar macrophage) which battle the tars and also attract white blood cells to fight off the smoke attack. But the enzymes and chemicals produced by these cells to help fight off the smoke attack are not very selective in their battles. They accidentally traumatize lung tissue, weakening the alveoli and robbing the small airways of the elasticity vital to proper expansion and contraction. Ultimately, the alveoli collapse and die. As with any traumatic injury like this, your body forms scar tissue to cover the injured area. This thick tissue begins to block the tiny passages in your lung. Those portions are now dead. Your body labors to operate with less surface area for feeding your blood.[6]

At that point, you have emphysema. And it was at that point that my aunt Edna lost her chance to live. She died of one of the chronic obstructive pulmonary diseases, COPD, as the doctors refer to them: uncomplicated bronchitis, chronic bronchitis, and emphysema. Studies indicate that 80 to 90 percent of all COPD is caused by smoking.[7] COPD is also known as COLD, chronic obstructive lung disease.

I *don't like scare tactics, and I don't like alarmists, either. So what diseases does smoking definitely cause or contribute to?*

What I present here is cold fact: cigarette smoking is the most important preventable cause of disease and death in the United States.[8]

Smoking is the major cause of lung cancer. It is a major cause of coronary heart disease; diseases of the arteries (there are many); bronchitis; emphysema; cancers of the larynx, oral cavity, esophagus, pancreas, and bladder. Smoking, combined with things like alcohol, certain oral contraceptives, and other inhaled elements like asbestos, also dramatically increases the risk of certain other diseases.[9]

Has *anyone actually tracked how many people die each year from illness and disease directly related to smoking?*

Yes. According to the U.S. Office on Smoking and Health, three hundred and fifty thousand Americans die *prematurely* each year from diseases directly related to smoking.[10] These deaths account for one in six of all deaths in the United States each year.[11] Smokers are ten times as likely as nonsmokers to die of lung cancer.[12] *At the same time,* smoking increases the risk of cancer of the larynx by five times, cancer of the mouth by three times, cancer of the esophagus by four times, and doubles your risk of cancer of the bladder and cancer of the pancreas. Your chances of getting emphysema as a smoker are thirteen times higher, and your chances of getting heart disease are doubled.[13]

The U.S. Surgeon General, in a report based on comprehensive study of all research in the field, says more than three-fourths of deaths from diseases of the heart and blood vessels are positively associated with cigarette smoking. These deaths represent almost half of all deaths from *all* causes.[14]

And, if all this isn't enough to make you squeamish, let me continue: smokers experience a coronary heart disease death rate 70 percent greater than nonsmokers. Heavy smokers—over two packs a day—have a 200 percent greater chance of dying. For men under fifty-four, smokers experience a coronary heart disease death rate three times that of nonsmokers of the same age.[15]

How *does smoking bring about damages other than lung damage?*

Those "tars" seem to be the major cancer-causing elements. Nicotine, an oily alkaloid in tobacco, actually affects the cardiovascular system. It literally raises your systolic blood pressure and cardiac output, increases the levels of free fatty acids (which leads to diseases of the arteries), and probably increases the stickiness of "platelets," the things that stick to your artery walls, eventually blocking them.[16]

The carbon monoxide gas in your smoke (about 4 percent) does something more interesting. Your blood has an almost suicidal love of this poisonous gas. If your body needs 200 units of oxygen, the blood will accept 1 unit of oxygen and 199 units of carbon monoxide, it it's available. Your heart, among other things, does not react well to that type of treatment.

But isn't there a point of no return when it comes to quitting? If someone's smoked all his life, isn't it cruel to make him try to stop when the damage must already be done?

Even if you have been a two or three pack-a-day smoker for fifty years, your body will respond dramatically to a smoke-free existence. Specifically:

• Your risk of dying from heart disease drops the day you quit smoking and in the majority of cases eventually becomes no greater than people who have never smoked.

• If your lungs haven't already been damaged, you are unlikely to have more lung-related diseases than nonsmokers. If your lungs have been damaged substantially, the damage will not increase.

• Blood circulation in the brain will probably increase.

• Even people over seventy have dramatic increases in the amount of blood and oxygen reaching the brain, which reduces their chances of stroke. Smokers over seventy also reduce their chances of things like Alzheimer's disease.

• The skin doesn't age as fast.

• Ulcers heal faster.[17]

Does smoking lower-tar-and-nicotine cigarettes help at all?

Probably not. Studies indicate that smokers keep the supply of nicotine in their blood reasonably constant.[18] When they switch to lower-tar-and-nicotine cigarettes, they subconsciously take bigger puffs more often. Some people actually take in *more* tar and nicotine, because they take bigger and more puffs, and smoke extra cigarettes, to boot. Thank your cigarette manufacturers for this nice marketing ploy.

What about smoking cigars or pipes instead of cigarettes?

A recent study found that smoking four or more pipe bowls or
cigars exposed the smoker to smoke equivalent to smoking ten
cigarettes.[19] Research also shows that pipe and cigar smokers
are at higher risk than nonsmokers for cancers of the mouth
and throat.

Some other things you don't want to know:
• Nicotine is so deadly that one drop in the eye of a rabbit will
kill it instantly. Keep your cigarettes away from your rabbits.
• When you smoke, changes instantly take place in heart rate,
skin temperature, blood pressure, peripheral blood circulation,
brain waves, and hormones affecting the central nervous
system.
• Nicotine qualifies as an addictive drug, just like heroin: it
affects brain waves, alters moods, and serves "as a biological
reward that elicits certain behavior from both laboratory animals and human volunteers."[20]

If all this is true, how can cigarette companies stay in
business without the hell being sued out of them?

First, people are starting to sue them. I wish we had a central
place to send money to support more suits, too. Second, cigarette companies are defending themselves with the most cynical
defense. As they continue to present cigarettes as manly, just
great for the outdoorsmen, and oh, so right, they tell the court,
"Smokers should know smoking will kill. Don't those fools read
the warning labels?" Doesn't that legal strategy make you respect those guys?

How *ow do you know if you already have lung damage?*

A test of lung function called spirometry can measure the capacity of your lungs as well as their efficiency and flow rates. By comparing your results to a "population" of the same age, sex, height, and percentile rank on performance, physicians can tell if you have lost part of your lung function and how much. This is the test that told me I had lost some lung function. You can have one as part of most physicals these days. If your doctor can't help you here, call the respiratory therapist at your local hospital.

W *ill I actually feel better the minute I quit?*

No. As a matter of fact, you'll probably feel awful, and if you were a heavy smoker, you'll feel really awful. Withdrawal symptoms associated with smoking can be nearly as traumatic as symptoms from heroin for some people. But the pains do go away.[21]

W *hat works?*

Many things really do work, but they're all based upon the following understandings and, most important, upon a person's real desire to quit.

1. Understand specifically what cigarette smoking does to you. Reading these pages may make you light up, for instance, which is okay. But if it doesn't also make you want to really try to break the habit, go visit any hospital's respiratory unit.

2. Be objective with yourself. How much do you really smoke a day? Mark down each cigarette, and the number itself may scare the hell out of you. Write down the number and the reason you're smoking (wake-up smoke, cup of coffee, nervous energy, etc.) and you may better understand your particular physical and psychological dependencies.

Different analysts may use different names, but all of them break down the types of smokers like this:

• Smoking for stimulation: to pick you up, keep you going, wake you up.

• Smoking for physical pastime: you like to doodle, play with pencils, like the ritual of lighting up.

• Smoking for pleasurable relaxation: because you enjoy it.

• Smoking to reduce tension: when you are angry, uncomfortable, or upset about something; when you are blue or depressed.

• Smoking to satisfy craving: having a real, openly addictive, desperate need for a cigarette when without one.

• Smoking from habit: lighting up without even being aware of it; you let the cigarette burn up in the ashtray or light another without realizing you've already got one going. You light up like clockwork.[22]

Knowing what factors influence your smoking may help you select the best methods of breaking the habit. For instance, if you have addictive cravings, quitting cold turkey is apparently more successful than trying to taper off.

What's available to help someone quit?

Whatever the method, all of these are based upon cold turkey or tapering off.

Help Groups. There are two kinds, nonprofit and for-profit. Most have some success (remember, it's really up to you in the end), but watch out for rip-offs in the for-profit outfits. Some of these guys charge as much for one group session as a good shrink would charge for an individual visit. Some don't like to tell you how they work without signing you up first, and some put a really high-pressure sales job on you. Before choosing a group, call your local office of the American Cancer Society, the Heart Association, or the Lung Association for some recommendations.[23] Check any for-profit outfits with your Better Business Bureau and local medical association, and don't pay a lot of money in advance, though some outfits will tell you that's part of the therapy (just what my hypnotist said). Generally speaking, group support really helps a lot of people.

Hypnosis.   I've personally had a bad experience here, but some people swear by it. There's no accurate scientific data to support either case. Some reports suggest a high initial quitting for a short time before backsliding. If you are the type of person who responds well to biofeedback and other meditation-type techniques, this might work well for you.

Aversion therapy.   There are lots of these, and they all make me a little queasy. Aversion therapies supposedly make the smoker associate unpleasantness or pain or discomfort with smoking. Therapies range from electric shock therapies at clinics to self-aversion tactics such as rapid smoking to the point of nausea or sticking yourself with a pin when you want a cigarette. If you are big on things like this, I know where you can get a great catalog of whips.

Acupuncture.   Acupuncture itself works for many things, and it seems to work for some people here. Acustaple—that's right, staple—is touted by some people, too, but traditional acupuncture fans don't think much of it.

Exercise.   You can't smoke when you're exercising. Cigarettes don't taste as good when you smoke after exercising. And exercising does take people's minds off their habit. A regular, moderate exercise program can help you quit. Jog each time you want a cigarette, for instance, and you'll probably be running marathons soon.

Gadgets.   Filters and other over-the-counter toys don't seem to have an identifiable track record.

Nicotine gum.   It does not work for everyone, but it does work for some. In the usual prescription, each piece of gum contains

2 mg of nicotine, about as much as in two regular cigarettes or three to four "light" cigarettes. The directions tell you to chew each piece for at least twenty minutes when you feel the urge for a cigarette.

This product is in gum form so that it can be absorbed through the linings of the mouth. Because it doesn't give the immediate "hit" to the brain smoking provides, the manufacturer claims it does not seem to create addiction since the "hit" is missing.[24]

The gum certainly seemed addictive to me, however, but it was an easier addiction to break.

People seem to have better luck with gum when it is used with a support group and counseling. In two studies, 47 percent and 30 percent of those who had taken the gum as part of a larger plan were still not smoking after one year. (Those numbers are very good, but in the same study, 20 percent of the people given placebos rather than real nicotine gum had also quit for a year.[25] Does that tell you anything?)

In that same study, only 10 percent of those people given nicotine gum independent of a support group quit for a year; 10 percent of those given a placebo quit, too.

Well, *after all this, if I quit smoking, will I have fun kicking people who still are weak?*

The most rabid evangelists seem to be reformed smokers, but please don't be like that. Smoking is probably the hardest and most important battle anyone can fight for their health—ever.

CHAPTER XVI

HOLLYWOOD

Week 36

Grand Bahama Island

I leave the island tomorrow for the month, a tour for a consumer book of mine. In between radio and TV shows (about eighty), I'll work out at a lot of different gyms, try to eat right, exercise some, and fly a lot.

My last trip off-island wasn't fast but it was weird. To Hollywood. Beverly Hills. Right by the Yoga Tantra Center and the Bowser Boutique, which share the same building, and Jaxon's Dogramat, where the dogs are really clean. This place is Garrison Keillor's Lake Wobegon gone wrong, I am afraid.

I flew to California for something I thought only happened to people in movies, to meet the folks who have bought the movie rights to my life. What they're really interested in, of course, is my search for hunkdom, but I prefer to think they actually care about some other important events, too, such as the time I won the state championship for playing solo tuba. I played "Till Eulenspiegel."

Now, I know a movie isn't an important thing, and know I

203

probably won't recognize even myself in the finished product, if, indeed it makes it to the silver screen or television tube (most things don't). I also know Robert Redford, my choice for the hunkified me, may not be available for the part. I think he's going to be busy that week. But I was still excited. Though a film doesn't make you good or happy or important or even rich, it does make you immortal in some way, like a good granite monument, and it does impress all the people you grew up with, which is worth something.

Christopher Scott went to Hollywood with me. I finally stole Chris full-time from the Ariel Human Performance Center in Miami. Gideon Ariel, of course, is one of my advisers. Gideon's place, a combination gym, health club, and preventive medicine center, is very fancy and impressive.

The center's star physiologist, Chris is bright, decent, enthusiastic, and very down-to-earth. As we pulled up the long, limousine-lined driveway of the Beverly Hills Hotel, to the Hollywood community as Buckingham Palace is to Royalists, I started getting a little excited at the thought of the movie stars strolling around, the deals being made as producers "took" lunch in the Polo Lounge or "did" meetings in one of the poolside cabanas. Chris didn't sense any of this. He got out of the white convertible I had rented to make the right theatrically understated statement, walked right past Harvey Korman without a double take, and absentmindedly turned to me and said, "Remar, can I get on over to the library at UCLA? I've got to get that article on free fatty acids and plasma."

I nodded yes and walked up to the reception desk, slightly nervous but masking it well. As I said, very powerful things happen at this hotel, and normally only very powerful people stay here, and you don't just walk up and say "Hi" at the registration desk, you say something that quietly indicates you're a part of the show business power structure. I had asked a friend for tips.

"Yes, Sutton. Checking in. Any telephone calls?"

You don't say your first name and always ask for phone messages, in a low key voice, my friend had said. For a minute, I didn't think it would work. The very distinguished-looking man behind the counter made a quick glance to check out my famous quotient, obviously failed me there, smiled a practiced smile, then signaled to an assistant with one hand as he searched for the "S" telephone messages with the other. He found nineteen messages there with my name on them.

Nineteen messages at the Beverly Hills Hotel, before you check in especially, means something. The distinguished-looking man stepped in front of the assistant he'd summoned and smiled genuinely, placing the messages before me carefully, as if rough handling would show disrespect to the callers.

"Oh *yes, Mr.* Sutton! Welcome back!"

I did not remind him this was my first visit, obviously did not tell him how many of those calls were plants. I simply smiled. Low-key, of course. That afternoon I bought some reflecting sunglasses.

The next morning, at about seven, Chris picked me up for an hour's aerobic work in hilly Beverly Hills. When I'm in a new city, especially one with a different terrain or climate, I try to scale back my exercise program. Lots of walking to allow for in-depth sight-seeing seemed right for here, so I give you a quick sight-seer's review:

• Some of the houses are pretentious to the point of tackiness, but all of the yards are lush, beautiful, and better-tended than most people's children. I'll bet there are more gardeners in Beverly Hills than there are commercials in a year of made-for-TV movies.

• Virtually all of the gardens have lots of small but serious signs announcing the name and threat level of that particular garden's security service. Where I come from, a nice sign saying SECURITY PATROLLED is considered pretty neat, a definite status sign. Here, they don't fool around. ARMED RESPONSE is the favorite wording, ARMED GUARD ON PREMISES was the most prestigious, and I honestly became a little nervous when I absentmindedly picked a leaf from a tree next to one of those signs. We decided to jog a little after that.

• People here have a lot of garbage, as evidenced by the size of their garbage cans, about 5 by 4 feet. One of these rather handsome things, embossed with the name of the city, is provided free to each residence. Some residences have several. I wanted to lift a lid or two, see if these people's garbage actually had odor, as they say, but thought it best not to tempt those signs again.

There must be many moral lessons in all of these things, but, because I hope to visit Beverly Hills again (a reporter's curiosity, you understand) I would appreciate it if you would draw your own conclusions.

After our walk, I did a hundred leg lifts and a hundred stomach crunches in my room, then quickly showered and slowly dressed for my big meeting. I had to look just right. The "Today" show had decided to film it. Will and Deni McIntyre (you see their pictures all the time in *People*) had decided to shoot it. And the first part of the meeting was to take place in the Polo Lounge itself, the sanctum sanctorum of Hollywood dreams. After about six changes of clothes, I decided on a look of studied insouciance, that look so prevalent in men's fashion magazines. My pants were wrinkled. I wore a tie, but pulled loose at the neck. My shirt was striped and my coat an understated silk tweed. No socks, of course. I don't even think the bellmen wear socks at this hotel.

I then practiced some deep breathing to help me relax, and, at about ten after eight, entered the Polo Lounge. Aware that these people were buying the story of a man who said he cared about health as well as hunkiness, I ordered the most wholesome breakfast: one skinned, roasted chicken breast ($7.50) and a quarter piece of melon ($3.50) and a glass of fresh orange juice (a bargain at $2).

During breakfast and the subsequent ceremonial filming in the gardens with TriStar Pictures and Green-Epstein Productions, and a final meeting at ABC Television (filmed by "Today's" NBC crew, a funny twist), I did my best to be myself and at the same time not visibly affected by the strange conversations going on. I understood it when my injuries were talked about as "good" for the story. ("Do you think you might have some more?" one of the guys cheerfully asked.) In an odd way, I even understood it when my heart disease was presented as a positive thing. "We're talking about a guy who could die here," one man said to the ABC bigwig—a show-business-sized dose of exaggeration (I hope). That might improve the story, but I won't like the ending, let me tell you.

I enjoyed most of my Hollywood adventure probably more than I want to admit. There is something disturbingly tasty about so much attention, so much glamour, so many powerful illusions. I do not think, however, any of it will change the underlying me. Though these days I do have an overpowering desire to put on my sunglasses before shaving.

Remar, you were in the land of hot tubs, exotic massages, and "meditation." What about those things?

All of the "hot" things—saunas, steam rooms, hot tubs, and whirlpools—can be fun, especially if you're with the right person. Except for whirlpool-type machines used in treating some injuries, they really don't have any proven health benefits other than the relaxing (or stimulating) feeling that may arise from your presence in one. There are some potential problems with them, though. First, don't use one if you suffer from heart disease, diabetes, or high or low blood pressure. You shouldn't use one if you're under the influence of drugs, including alcohol, anticoagulants, antihistamines, stimulants, vasoconstrictors, vasodilators, tranquilizers, or narcotics. Pregnant women should be extremely careful, but then, they shouldn't be in a hot and sultry place anyway. All of these things apply, unless you have an opportunity to take a famous Hollywood starlet in one of these things to be wicked.

The problem with hot tubs, saunas, whirlpools and the like is the heat that's associated with them, logically enough. When the body heats up, it sends extra blood to the peripheral regions, which requires extra pumping, which places a strain on the heart. The blood is sent to the skin to help dissipate body heat, which doesn't happen, incidentally, when you're sitting in 104 degrees of steaming water with a Hollywood starlet at the Beverly Hills Hotel, for instance.

Getting out of these situations can be tricky, too. If you should feel a need to stand up quickly and exit (for instance, if the Hollywood starlet's boyfriend, the stuntman stand-in for King Kong, should arrive) you could faint. That's because much of your blood has been pumped to the body surface to help cool it. More blood to the surface means less blood to the brain.

On second thought, using these things can be damned dangerous. But if you're going to use them anyway, make sure the water is changed daily (chemical reactions can happen quickly there), and/or the thermostat in your tub or steam room is operating properly.

W*hat about massages?*

These, too, are wonderful when administered by Hollywood starlets, if the door is locked. Massages actually have health benefits, too, including improved circulation, elimination of waste products, stretching of muscles and tendons, and rehabilitation of soft-tissue injuries.[1]

Massages aren't a cure-all, though. Never massage a severe injury, or a site where there is hemorrhage or infection.

W*hat about biofeedback and other weird stuff like that?*

Biofeedback is one of several relaxation techniques that actually do help some people. All the techniques help to identify what being relaxed really is and assist gravitation toward that state. Mind-over-matter. And since so many health problems can be brought on by mental problems, like the high blood pressure that comes from the tension that arises when a Hollywood starlet's boyfriend finds out your room number and is beating on your door at 2 A.M., think about giving one or more of these things a try sometime:

Biofeedback.   This is the term used to describe a way in which information is being received from the body. Practicing it initially requires equipment to determine heart rate changes, skin temperature, muscular activity, brain wave activity, and skin conductance. Now, believe it or not, we can control some of those processes with our mind.

Biofeedback can be thought of as a three-stage process: information, such as your heartbeat, is measured. That information is converted into something you can understand, such as your heart rate. You are trained to literally think your heartbeat down, something you can actually see happen.

Biofeedback has served many uses: it's worked to relieve some headaches, high blood pressure, asthma, and ulcers.[2] It is not a cure, but it's not a snake oil salesman-type thing, either. If you'd like more information, call the Biofeedback Society of America, or a local university psychology department.

Meditation.   It isn't only for monks or weirdos, and it's free—rare when it comes to anything having to do with health. Meditation is simply a mental exercise which helps you focus your attention on what you want to acknowledge rather than the things that demand to be acknowledged. It teaches you to use the mind to relax the body. Beware, though, of meditating groups or organizations which resemble religions and charge you gobs of money.

Autogenic Training.   This uses the body to relax the mind, the opposite of meditation. It teaches you a type of self-hypnosis that induces a feeling of heaviness and warmth in the body. Now, look deeply into my eyes. That's what I said to you-know-who at the Beverly Hills Hotel.

Progressive Relaxation.   This teaches you to tense up a specific body part and then relax it. What you're trying to do here is get the feel of yourself in both the tense and relaxed state. You can progress from body part to body part, and the tension phase can be especially fun if you've escaped from the Hollywood starlet's boyfriend and rendezvoused again with your meditational object in a hot tub, where the temperature is always rising.

All of these types of self-help mind disciplines are interesting to know about, even if you aren't particularly into mind games. Your local library can provide you some good information on each.

I *travel a lot to places as strange as Hollywood, and I feel more strung-out on those trips. What can I do to lessen the strain?*

Dr. Eric Goldstein, Ph.D., a stress management specialist in Miami who works with me at times, and Chris Scott have some good advice on stress and travel-related stress.

Changing time zones.   Three nights prior to flying, begin to switch your body's timing. If you are flying eastward, go to bed an hour earlier each night, and rise earlier, too. If you are flying westward, go to bed (and get up) later. Try to also move your meals to coincide with the new time zone.

Handling long trips by plane.   Sleep as much as possible on a plane, but when you're awake, make your time productive. Take a book or work with you. Take your own tape recorder and tapes, and create you own "space."

Handling strange environments.   Make them as familiar as possible. Take along a picture or a familiar object. Dr. Goldstein has worked with well-known athletes who take along stuffed animals. When you're away, also keep your concentration and focus on the present, on things you can do right then.

Here are some good exercises for managing stress:

Diaphragmatic breathing (a fancy word for breathing deeply) can relax you. Breathing usually becomes shallow and rapid during stress. Deep breathing counters this reaction and better oxygenates the blood. Place your hand on your stomach, above the navel. Breathe in slowly and very deeply, holding your breath for one or two seconds. Breath slowly out through your mouth— the slower the better. If you're breathing correctly, your stomach will *rise* when you breath in and fall when you breathe out.

Try the Progressive Relaxation technique I mentioned a minute ago. It works any place, in any position, with the exception of what is commonly known as the the starlet reflex syndrome I also mentioned earlier. Tense a muscle group (for instance, your shoulder muscles) for several seconds. Then relax them. Be conscious of the different sensations. Recognizing muscle tension will make it easier for you to tell your body to relax.

"We can't change many stressful situations," Dr. Goldstein says, "but we can change our reactions to those situations in ways that will help us." For instance, at all times walk, don't run, from the Hollywood starlet's boyfriend.

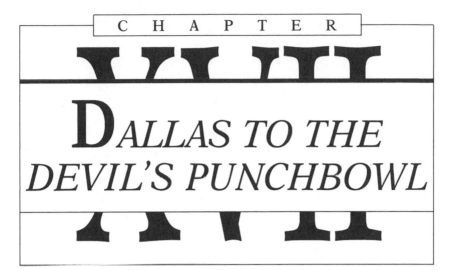

CHAPTER XVIII

DALLAS *TO THE* DEVIL'S PUNCHBOWL

Week 38

Dallas, Texas

I am in Dallas, one of the last cities of my month-long book tour. This is an especially busy tour, too. My weekdays usually start at 4:00 or 4:30 A.M., when twenty-four-hour room service brings me decaffeinated coffee, wheat toast, and oatmeal. Invariably, whatever city I'm in, my toast is accompanied by three mini jars of "gourmet" preserves, which aren't on my eating schedule right now and therefore go instantly in my goody bag before they tempt me.

This trip's goody bag already contains twenty-seven mini jars, and lots of other things nice hotels give you, too. The bag probably weighs fifteen pounds, a good weight for morning exercise, but instead I drop to the floor before pouring a coffee and do very disciplined push-ups. Right now I can do fifteen perfect ones before my shoulder begins to hurt. My feet then go on the bed and I do hundred crunches in four sets. These two exercises, which take less than five minutes, can help keep your body physically toned.

After exercise and breakfast, I work at my portable computer. My most productive writing hours have always been before sunrise, and these hours on tour seem to be especially good ones. But by seven I'm usually showered and dressed. If my day calls for only radio or newspaper interviews, I wear very informal clothes. For TV, I put on the blazer and slacks that comprise my dress wardrobe.

Invariably by seven, a car picks me up for the day's interviews. A writer can always tell how his publisher likes him by the way he gets around for interviews. Four years ago, I had to catch cabs. Two years ago, ladies in very small cars picked me up, sometimes with their kids in the backseat. This year, the ladies are driving Mercedes and Cadillacs, have fruit waiting in the car for me, and drop their kids off at private schools. I don't know if I'm doing better or the ladies are doing better.

By nightfall, after five to seven shows, my escort drops me back at my hotel. This tour, I am staying in hotels with some type of health facilities. Though at times I don't want to, each day I make myself change and head to that facility. At first, I felt a little uncomfortable walking in elevators and through lobbies dressed so skimpily. But after looking at the bellies and tired faces of many men checking into nice hotels these days, I feel nearly smug. It is not easy to work out when you're tired and strung-out, but invariably those are the most satisfying workouts.

Before this year, my hotel routine while on book tour wasn't quite that satisfying. Tours are lonely things, in a way. People, cities, and shows become a blur; it's hard to sleep with time changes and all that adrenaline pumping through you from having to be "up" constantly; hotels, even nice ones, lose their charm quickly. I spent my free time by the television with a beer in my hand. No more.

Here in Dallas, it's especially easy to be good healthwise. I'm staying and exercising at the Cooper Clinic, where all my testing this year takes place. Everyone walks or jogs between buildings, the only alcohol within sight is rubbing alcohol, and food is so wholesome-looking it probably blushes at the thought of cholesterol.

A couple of thousand families belong to the clinic Activity Center, a handsome place. The gym itself is vaulted wood, glass-walled, and large enough to host several activities at once. A balcony filled with free weights and machines overlooks the gym floor. Fast-paced, pleasant music plays constantly. One wall is lined with the total distances logged by many center members in their particular sport. I don't want to make you feel wimpish, but Louis Patrick Neeb, forty-five, has jogged over 50,635 miles. Marcia Goldenfeld has swum 3,246.66 miles.

Last evening from the balcony I watched people in their seventies doing aerobics with people in their twenties. At the other end of the gym, a couple about twenty-five and their two children, no more than two years old, were playing basketball together. The father held his daughter high and threw the ball with her, then the mother, blond, tanned, and athletically fit, chased it with their son. "Good! Nice catch!" The parents seemed to be having as much fun as the kids, and I could not help but think how lucky those two children were.

This morning, between interviews, I went back to the clinic for my ninth-month physical. My doctor this trip was Arno Jensen. I told you in Chapter 7 some things about Arnie (you will remember him as the fifty-seven-year-old hunk), but I'll tell you more here. Arno personally doesn't like to jog. Since the Cooper Clinic was founded and is run by the man who started the world jogging, that's pretty much like being a Cardinal who doesn't support the Pope.

Arnie, however, definitely believes in fitness (including jogging for some). He trains on his stationary bike hard enough to beat out every single jogger his age ever tested on the stress treadmill at the clinic—enduring thirty-two minutes! Until the last test, that is, when a man beat him by ten seconds.

Arnie told me this trip his lean body mass has increased again. At forty-one, Arnie was 18 percent fat. At fifty-seven, he is now 9.6 percent fat. He eats like that proverbial horse, too. And he really does draw the looks (unrequited—he's happily married) of twenty-year-old beauties when he works out on the balcony overlooking the gym area. I had heard of this from others, but experienced it myself this trip. I like Arnie, but I don't like to stand by him in the gym when the ladies are around.

My own physical state continues slowly to improve in most areas, however. Since my last exam in May, I've added 2.7 pounds of muscle. Though I would like more muscle, Bob Stauffer's words of many months ago are true: good definition makes for a great look. And working with my body is doing more for me emotionally and stamina wise than I had ever imagined. Arnie Jensen made me feel pretty good about my growth, too. Arnie has added only fifteen pounds of muscle in seven years, which maybe makes me hunkier than him in the muscle-gaining area, right?

The fats in my blood continue to decrease, too. My "good" cholesterols are rising and my bad ones falling. At the Cooper Clinic, the ratio of good to bad cholesterols is the most important measure of interior health, and my ratio has dropped from 7.2 to 6. To be really healthy, mine needs to be below 5. My triglycerides, another fat, have also dropped marginally. My count is now 173, getting closer to my recommended maximum of 124.

The one really disappointing test result was my percentage of body fat. In May, when I was still restricting my calories to lose weight, that percentage had dropped from 30 percent to 15 percent, a point under my "ideal" percentage of fat, according to the docs. This time, after eating five special meals a day to help feed my muscle growth, it's up to 21.5 percent. I am not fat, but the new ripples on my stomach are looking a little smothered. I'm therefore going on a diet which weight lifters use to "rip down" for contests.

Just a few moments ago, I received a phone call from some friends near the Devil's Punchbowl along the Oregon coast. They're completing 3,000 miles of an 18,000 mile bike trip, and I, with the thought of excess fat creeping back on my nearly healthy and beautiful body, have decided to spend my weekend biking with them a little bit. How spontaneous have you been lately?

Depoe Bay, Oregon, three days later: is anyone interested in taking over an Alaskan gold claim? It's a pretty piece of land, I'm sure, a big claim right on Canyon Creek—1,320-by-1,320 potentially gold-rich feet in the midst of Fairbanks Township itself, and dutifully registered on Page 240 of Book 490 at the Fairbanks office of the Alaskan Department of Natural Resources.

The claim is owned by my young friends from Minnesota, Spain, and Yugoslavia. They don't have time to mine it right now, since they're still fifteen thousand miles away from their final destination, Terra del Fuego (the "Land of Fire") at the very tip of South America. Their trip is an extraordinary athletic endeavor and has interested me since I heard about it many months ago. No one has ever biked from Alaska to the tip of South America before. If fortune is with them, they will cross a hundred miles of roadless jungle at the Darien Gap (bikes on their backs), pedal across the driest desert on earth, the Atacama in Chile (where it hasn't rained since the sixteenth century), and bike the length of every troubled South American country you've seen on television.

On this very misty, fog-shrouded day, however, the eight of us are spending the weekend at a cliffside cabin on the Oregon Coast, and as the others go about individual chores, I can watch sea lions climbing rocks with some effort, then beating their flippers together enthusiastically, occasionally using a flipper to wipe a brow, it seems. A small deep-V-hulled boat keeps circling about a thousand feet beyond the shoreline, six well-wrapped people on its bow, watching for a whale to surface and blow again. The whale likes this particular cove, for he's been in the vicinity most of the morning. The music as I watch and the seven others work is Simon and Garfunkel's "Bridge Over Troubled Waters," much more my music, you would think, than my young friends'.

Dan Buettner, twenty-six, of Roseville, Minnesota, chased me down at the Cooper Clinic with this biking invitation. I have known the four Buettner boys and their parents for five years, and have often wondered how Roger and Dolly keep their sanity with such an independent crew. Dan studies and bikes throughout Europe, honing his writing skills, for months on end, on virtually no money, with the casualness of a person walking down a street. His knapsack usually includes several classical books, and his first stop in any city is at a newstand to buy some newspaper with American stocks listed in it.

Tony, twenty-seven, runs a ski-related business in Colorado. Nicky, seventeen, is still at home, but planning his first solo hiking trip of Europe. Nicky just told his parents he feels "confined" by normal life. And Steve—right now downstairs in the garage working on the group's bikes—plans to return to Spain after this little biking diversion to continue his international studies. All of the boys are black-haired, rugged, tall, and handsome. Roger and Dolly are proud of their kids and their independence (they taught them to love being active in the outdoors) and at the same time are scared by it.

Dan thought up and largely organized this particular bicycle trek to first promote friendship among nations and secondarily to set a Guinness record. To those ends, many municipalities and governments here and south of the border are helping the seven along, and the group meets lots of people (and has even saved the life of a seriously injured kid in an automobile accident), and each bicycling mile is logged.

But because I know Dan and have now met the group, I don't for a minute think these five guys and two women are doing this primarily for nobility or records alone. Above everything else, they are doing it for sheer adventure, the *energy* of it, about the best reasons in the world to do anything, I'm coming to believe.

I had intended to spend this weekend working off a few pounds, escaping from the pressure of touring, and listening to the exciting experiences 3,000 miles of biking must have already generated. I thought I might pick up a few tricks real jocks use to keep in shape as they bike halfway around the world, too. But as I watched and became a part of this weekend, I was more fascinated by these people themselves, not just their adventure.

Martin Engel, twenty-seven, and Anne Knabe, twenty-four, are both second year medical students. Anne, slender and quiet-natured, is the only woman biker, but she was accepted by the others with a natural assumption of equality which would make Gloria Steinem proud. She appears to be the group philosopher.

Martin is tall, broad-shouldered, and equally quiet. From a family of mountaineers, Martin is an encyclopedia of outdoor facts and a beaver when it comes to storing things. The one pot used to cook virtually all the group's meals since their cooking utensils were stolen in Seattle is a five-quart Boy Scout pot Martin received when he was thirteen.

Bret Anderson, twenty-four, is probably sick of hearing it, but is all-American looking, the type of young man you expect to say "sir," which he did until I told him to knock it off. Bret is studying international business, but I enjoyed his knowledge of the guitar more.

Last night, after a dinner of fresh crab and salmon, and chanterelle mushrooms picked less than a mile from the cabin, Bret sat with his feet propped up and played classical guitar as we ate freshly picked grapes for dessert. He then joined Matjaz Bren, the group photographer, in a chess game. A Yugoslavian, Matjaz, twenty-four, taught English at a school in Morocco before immigrating to the States, and plans to join the foreign service here eventually.

At about nine last night, Rafaela Salido came upstairs from helping Steve Buettner work on the bicycles. Raffi, an attorney from Spain, has dark eyes and hair, freckled cheeks, and one of those smiles which seems to make her look at once shy and very naturally happy. She and Steve are the support crew for the trip. They joined Dan and me in Scrabble. Anne and Martin were lost in books, occasionally coming back to the world to kibbitz our game.

This quiet time seemed to be important to the group. After 3,000 miles of sleeping together in a ten-foot camper and eating breakfast, lunch, and dinner from a community pot, privacy becomes a discipline if you plan to keep your sanity. This weekend in a borrowed cabin was the last planned break before South America.

But then Bret pulled a tango tape from the group's music case and placed it in the recorder and for the next hour the men from Minnesota and Yugoslavia and the Bahamas took turns dancing tangos with the medical student from Minneapolis and the attorney from Spain. I didn't know how to tango, felt awkward with these wonderfully relaxed young people who danced dances from my generation's dreams, but eventually felt like the eighth person on their team. I must tell you it was a totally unexpected and enchanting evening.

We biked together this morning for about forty miles along the Oregon coast. My biking on Grand Bahama is flat and easy, not at all like the hills here, and I had never biked so far before without a break. At the start of my year, the thought of biking four miles to Freeport scared me. But today, even though it nearly killed me at times, I kept up with the group, even taking the lead twice. And when it occasionally crossed my mind that these nice folks might be going easy for my sake, I pushed the thought away faster than my wheels could spin. Appearances, I decided, were as exciting as reality.

I fly out in the morning for a day in Seattle and then an overnight flight to Grand Bahama. My friends continue south for another 15,000 miles. I worry some for their safety, but I envy and admire them, don't you? And I think their resourcefulness will get them through. It's like that gold mine claim that's now for sale. When my friends were told only miners have access to the first 500 miles of rutted road from Prudhoe Bay, Alaska south, they simply went and filed a mining claim. The claim's good forever—as long as someone works on it 200 hours a year. And I have calculated that 200 hours of work on a gold claim will work off about ten pounds of fat and put on about three pounds of muscle and, you know, that's worth about as much as a good strike.

After eight months, my interests and friends in life are changing somewhat. Active people interest me a lot more, and more important, I think I interest them. I am reminded of much new research which states that being active and involved in life has as much to do with longevity as simply exercising. If that's the case, I'm going to live a very long time, I've decided.

Before Norma lets me dig for gold, she wants me to have a physical. Should I have one? And what should they do to me?

In the opinion of many, the best preventive medicine specialist in the country is Dr. Cooper, so my answers here are based on his recommendations.

If you consider yourself healthy and are under thirty, physicals every two or three years are fine. Between thirty and thirty-five, have one every two years. During these years, have at least one resting electrocardiogram simply as a reference point for the cardiac changes that come later in life.

If you are over forty, have a thorough physical, including a maximum performance stress test, every year or eighteen months. After fifty, definitely have a physical every year.

This may be a dumb question, but what's the big deal about physicals, other than the doctor making money?

As Dr. Cooper says, virtually all our major health problems start out small. That's the reason regular physicals can be important. And if you are in some of the high-risk categories we talk about in this book, physicals can definitely be life saving.

Okay. So what constitutes a good physical?

Obviously, if you have definite things wrong with you, or if you know you're in some high-risk groups, your physical should deal with those areas. Obviously, you should be honest and non-blushing when you talk to the doctor, too, though most people lie and blush. Don't worry about sounding like a hypochondriac and don't leave out a detail.

Now, with that said, here's a rundown on a good, comprehensive physical.

A complete health and medical history. How you feel about yourself, your health history, your family history, social history (your interaction with people, not those fancy clubs you and Norma belong to). Histories lead the doctor to potential problems, and make you an individual rather than some type of health statistic.

Standard measurements allow comparisons to statistical groups and are the basis for measuring changes in you. For instance, blood pressure, weight (or, more important, body fat), heart rate, pulse, circumferences (is your stomach larger than your chest?).

Examination of your head, eyes, ears, nose, throat, neck, and lymph nodes. And on down toward the toes. Part of this isn't bad (like checking your chest) and part of this is godawful. The prostate exam and a sigmoidoscopic exam (something the size of a telephone pole is inserted in your rear end) are terribly important, the only ways to determine prostate and colon cancer. Because those cancers are brutal ones if left untreated, put up with the pain and embarrassment of these tests, and make sure your doctor administers them if you are over forty.

Central nervous system tests, like when the doctor hits you with that little hammer. Your reflex (or lack of it) might be a sign of things like multiple sclerosis, spinal cord damage due to disease, and, believe it or not, syphilis.

Blood and urine tests. Probably the best windows to the function of many organs.

Henry Charlton has been the guest poser at many world body-building events. The most famous Bahamian bodybuilder, Henry works out regularly with us at the YMCA.

We were supposed to have our tongues out for this shot, but only the dog Sai and Marilynn listened. Bill and Marilynn Carle are the managers of my gym, and both hold bodybuilding titles. Her most recent one is "Miss Southern States 1986."

Ollie and Pam Ferguson join us for breakfast. That's a conch shell on the table, and one of my seven bikes in the background. Ollie is a supervisor at UNEXSO, and Pam a member of my exercise class.

November. Marva Monroe, administrative director of the Grand Bahama Promotion Board, works out and jogs with me. In the brains and looks department, she's the female equivalent of what I want to be.

Banzai! I can't tell you how my energy level improved during this year. I jump off boats all the time now. Ollie Ferguson, Mike Sahlen, Chris, and Ben Rose (of Ben's Caves at the Lucayan National Park) join me as we calmly step off the boat.

Called "Burfing," this sport requires a strong arm, a fast boat and a tight bathing suit. We don't tell women the last requirement.

Mary Abbott and I won't reveal the name of this road, for it's on the way to our secret cocoa plum patch.

The proper way to transport cocoa plums. They taste best in pancakes on Sunday morning.

I really do like Arnie Jensen, but I hate it when he steals all the maidens' stares.

Arnie and Chris. These two could be brothers, though they're thirty-four years apart in age.

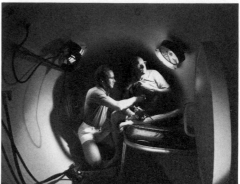

(Left) Notice the size of the weights, and the smile on my face. A November picture.

(Right) Kurt Alcorn and I spent six hours pretty much like this in the recompression chamber. Mortality isn't an abstract idea in a chamber.

Charles Atlas, eat your heart out.

Day 1

Day 300

X rays may not be necessary, depending on your age and physical condition. They are important in judging the condition of your organs, lungs, and skeletal system.

Treadmill stress tests. They can help detect the presence of heart disease and determine your system's physical limits. You can't fool a treadmill.

A meeting with the doctor. Detailed written reports and letters are good, but a consultation with the doctor is a must.

Physicals are a hassle. They're expensive. But they are the linchpin of preventive medicine.

Looking into the future. Would you like a preview of what the doctor will say to you? If you're gutsy and really honest with yourself, this test may tell you a lot. Run your answers down the right margin, or use a sheet of paper.

1. In the course of your normal activities such as getting in and out of chairs, mowing the lawn, doing chores around the house, do you become winded or fatigued?
2. Do you frequently wake up fatigued?
3. We talked earlier about ways to judge the amount of fat on your body: the pinch test, looking at yourself naked in the mirror without trying to suck it in, remembering your shape in high school if you were lean, and thinking about the sizes of clothes you wear now. Lock yourself away, release the stomach, and give yourself an accurate blubber reading. If you're close to high school size already, you shouldn't be reading this book anyway, so give it to a real person. Or go on to Question 4.
   • Are your stomach and chest about the same size?
   • Is your stomach larger than your chest?
   • Are you much more "filled-out" than you were in high school?
4. Do you eat fried foods, gravies, dishes prepared with a lot of butter, creams, or sauces more than once each week?

5. Generally speaking, are your breakfasts composed of eggs and bacons and/or sausages and hams?
6. Are your lunches usually fast foods or foods fried and/or breaded?
7. Generally speaking, are your favorite dinners composed of red meats, fried foods, foods with sauces?
8. If you eat red meats, do you leave on a portion of the fat?
9. For dessert do you choose cakes, pies, and other baked/sweet items over fresh fruits?
10. Do you smoke?
11. Do you smoke over two packs a day?
12. Do you drink more than two drinks a day?
13. Do you drink every day?
14. Do you think of your work situation as stressful?
15. Do you have high blood pressure? (If you don't know, stop here and find out).
16. Has your doctor ever told you to "watch" your blood pressure?
17. Do you take any prescribed or over-the-counter medication for "nerves"?
18. Do you ever experience tightness in your chest, usually associated with pain?
19. Are you over forty?
20. In your perception, are any of your parents, grandparents, aunts, or uncles seriously overweight?
21. Do any of your parents, grandparents, aunts, or uncles have "adult-onset" diabetes?
22. Have any died from diabetes-related complications?
23. Have any of your parents, grandparents, aunts, or uncles had a heart attack or coronary heart disease?.
24. Have any of your parents, grandparents, aunts, or uncles had a stroke?
25. Have any had cancer?
26. In your personal time, do you seek inactivity rather than activity and interchange with others?
27. Do you seem too busy to exercise, or avoid actual exercise?

The only crystal balls in medicine, the only things that in any way help doctors predict your future well-being, are the patterns of your past and present life—your genetic inclinations, your intakes, your activities and attitudes toward your own body and mind.

If you answered yes to many of these questions, most doctors and health specialists would rate your future prospects for health and general well-being as less than optimal. If you answered yes to virtually all of them—for instance, if the questions show you're overweight, eating wrong, inactive, smoking, drinking too much, and from a family with a history of health problems— virtually all doctors and health specialists would fear for your health and perhaps your life. Your chances of serious premature health problems and an earlier death are astronomical.

I do not mean to be melodramatic about this, but in reality serious disease and death *are* pretty melodramatic, aren't they?

But if you decide to make a change for the better, you can. That decision never seems very dramatic or exciting, which may be the problem. Arnie Jensen says, "It takes ten minutes to convince someone to have his stomach removed, but ten years to convince him to change his lifestyle." It has taken me more than ten years to make that decision, but I have made it. And, I promise you, if I have, you can.

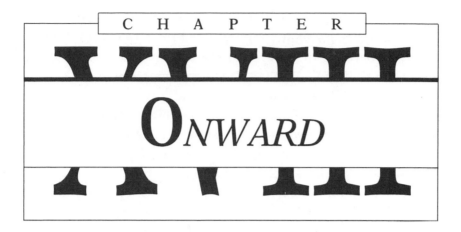

C H A P T E R

ONWARD

Week 42

Grand Bahama Island

As I started my remake nine months ago, my intentions (and my dreams) were of a final book chapter which would detail the end result of hunkification. I envisioned the chapter as rather X-rated. Perhaps a racy excerpt or two would appear in *Penthouse*, and the last words on the final page would be a quote from some beauty who had shunned my old, blimpish body but, on a subsequent swoon walk, caught a vision of the new me (so muscular even the biggest hulk would shudder a bit) and fell prey to my animal magnetism. I expected she would say something like, "Remar makes every beautiful girl a fallen woman."

Of course, the months didn't quite go like that. They did bring changes in my body and more notoriety than I had thought possible. I am very proud of the new, leaner, tighter me, too. I worked for every damn change, and, by God, I plan to keep working. And I'm finding that a little notoriety is worth about two inches on your biceps. But I still am somewhat insecure about my looks and, at times, feel as fat as I ever looked. Probably always will. I haven't fallen in love with exercise itself, either, whether for vanity (sit-ups) or health (jogging). I do it, however, because the end results are now believable for me, and the activities themselves are becoming habit.

As the body has changed, my mind has undergone some changes, too. I knew that would happen, but did not anticipate all the changes. For you to understand that, I need to tell you about a few incidents during this final month.

First, people who knew me fat seem to have grown accustomed to a slender me. For a while there, everyone commented on the changes in my body shape. But after the dramatic weight loss of the first months, very few people commented on my shape. One very young and popular lady on the island made a passing reference to my looks, but in the same breath said minds always impressed her more than bodies. Though I took a good deal of pleasure in her thinking, an affirmation of things deeper than flesh, I was a little disappointed she hadn't made some comment like, "Boy, I wish my dad looked like you." Or at least wanted to feel my stomach muscles. You know, tentative fingers on the firmness there, as she looked deeply in my eyes. I mean, I did lose nine inches on my belly. I went from pear-shaped to slender, from forty-two to thirty-three.

I went from nervous to confident in the gym, too. The biggest, hulkiest lifters were saying things like, "Hey, brother, you're whipping that devil, aren't ya!!!?" And my muscles did seem to reshape themselves though they haven't yet grown enough. People use the word "tight" to describe my body now. My back, which used to look like a slab of bacon, is lean, slightly V-shaped, and ripply with small muscles when I flex, which I do a lot if anyone is looking. My chest really developed. Nine months ago, my breasts sagged so much they embarrassed me even when I was alone, but now, by God, I look pretty good there. My stomach is just beginning to have the washboard effect so highly prized, I am told, by young maidens.

My shoulders are coming along, too. Nine months ago, they were nonexistent. Now, as I type, I can see a pleasant curve on both arms. And probably most interesting of all, my new tight state has really affected my face. Several people assume I've had a face-lift. An older man on the island asked me at a party for the name of my plastic surgeon. I did think about a face-lift, and some hair, too. I'm not dead set against either procedure, but I've decided they're not right at this time. I have worked for all my changes this year, and even though some of them may be minimal, they are all mine, a part of my body.

I'm not trying to say foreign hair and surgical procedures are more vain than my own pursuits, either. As my looks have improved, I have discovered mirrors. For so much of my life, I've avoided the truth of those things with the determination of a vampire avoiding a wooden stake. But now I kind of like them. I've found a way to flex my right bicep as I shave, and after a shower I dry off in front of the full-length mirror rather than a blank wall. I even decided Paul Harvey's headline, written at the beginning of my new year, was going to be at least a little prophetic rather than simply funny because of its impossibility: FAT MAN INVITES US TO WATCH AS HE TRANSFORMS HIMSELF INTO BRONZE GOD. I worked on my tan a lot.

And then, on a very beautiful blue-skied Bahamian day two weeks ago, an incident happened which made me confront the real substance of this year—and my life, too.

Scuba diving has always been my very best tranquilizer. A diver doesn't need to worry under normal circumstances, and after the thousands of dives I've made in fifteen years, normal circumstances make breathing underwater as natural as breathing on the surface. Therefore, when Chris Scott and I went on a seventy-five-foot dive a couple of weeks ago, a last-minute decision to pass the time while my friend and editor Mary Abbott Waite hooked up my new laser printer, my mind was on fish and coral canyons and caves.

At the end of every dive with the Underwater Explorers Society, all divers, including the most experienced, normally come back to what is called the ascent line. It's a large rope with a forty pound weight on the end dangling from the stern of the boat. The rope, which hangs within ten feet of the ocean floor, is used by divers to carefully control their ascent rate. This ascent from the dive holds the only potential danger for sensible divers.

As you rise, the pressure on your body is lessened, since less water is over you. At seventy-five feet, for instance, the average depth I was diving, your body experiences close to four "atmospheres" of pressure—this means that the pressure of the water is four times as heavy as the pressure at sea level of air on your body. The water above you is as heavy as the distance from the edge of space to the surface of the water times four. You don't feel this pressure because liquids and solid matter don't compress.

But gasses are affected by pressure; they compress under heavier pressure and expand under lighter pressure. My problem began here. Rather than rising very slowly, hand-over-hand on the ascent line, I decided at the very last minute to practice what is known as an emergency free ascent (EFA). In an emergency ascent, a diver forgets the first two basic rules of diving—(1) breathe all the time and (2) rise no faster than your slowest bubble—and rushes to the surface, blowing out continuously on one breath. EFAs in a way serve a real purpose: they let a diver know he can have an out-of-air emergency at great depths, even 120 feet or so, and still make it to the surface in one breath.

But statistically, EFAs are dangerous. Because the very rapid ascent forces gasses such as oxygen and nitrogen to expand very rapidly in the body, the pressure of that sudden expansion can very occasionally force air through the lung tissues themselves into cavities around the lung, the tissue area around the neck, or the tissue around joints. These particular types of problems may cause a lot of pain, but normally don't kill you. If the air enters the bloodstream itself, it may kill you. When an air bubble enters your bloodstream, it travels along the interior walls of your arteries without incident for a millisecond or perhaps even a number of seconds or minutes, until the bubble, traveling in progressively smaller blood vessels, is larger than the vessel.

At that point, the bubble sticks, usually in an artery in the brain, blocking the circulation of further oxygen-laden blood to the precious tissues there, much like a clot. Brain tissue is most intolerant of oxygen starvation. Within four or five minutes, if the blocked area, now a clot, is not cleared, the affected brain tissue dies.

Because of these dangers, no scuba organizations actually teach EFAs any more. Diving students practice swimming horizontally for long distances on one breath rather than vertically.

They taught EFAs when I learned to dive, however. And on this day, I decided it was time to practice it. Quite honestly, before starting to rise, I looked to make sure none of the instructors from the Explorers Society were watching me, for any of them would have lectured me for the foolishnesss of it.

But no one was watching me, and I had broken this rule, gone against these odds so many times before without any consequences. I dropped my regulator to my side, raced to the surface nearly eight stories above me, my head tilted back to allow expanding air to flow freely from my mouth, and broke through the surface with the practiced aplomb of a dolphin rising for air. At some point during the ascent, an air bubble entered my bloodstream.

Because I do dive so much and have very low air consumption, my dive was longer than most of the divers, and the boat was nearly rigged to pull anchor as I climbed aboard. I felt great, and chatted with the ten other divers around me. For about a minute.

And then the pain began. It started in my back, directly under my right scapula, a pain so hot I began to sweat. For several minutes I attributed it to a muscle pull. But as *The Explorer I* entered the Bell Channel near port, the pain began to move. I remember feeling very alone at that moment. Muscle pulls don't move. I also did not want to tell anyone. Very experienced divers are at times foolishly proud, and I did not want to alert people with a false alarm if my pain was a muscle pull, and, even more foolishly, did not want to face the worse alternative: that I was in the midst of a diving accident, especially one caused by my mistake. I went to the bow of the boat, away from people, and began to breathe deeply and slowly.

As the boat pulled up to the dock, my symptoms were beginning to resemble a heart attack. Pain under my rib cage. A lightheadedness. Very spotty vision. I walked from the boat quickly, up a ten-foot gangplank, and stood alone by a bank of scuba tanks, confused, and for the first time really afraid. For, as I stood there, and as the pain made it hard to breathe, an overwhelming feeling of doom settled on me, as heavy and suffocating as any I want to experience before I die. And then I had the oddest thought. It seems so very funny now, but it did not then. I was going to die and would never see my new laser printer at work.

Mike Sahlen walked by me with two empty scuba tanks. Mike is the Explorers Society's underwater photography expert, and on this very unusual day, he walked by at the right moment. "Mike, don't say anything yet, please, but something's really wrong with me," I said.

"What, Remar?" He stopped walking, as if an invisible wall had stopped him. I told him about the pain. He sat me in a nearby chair, then walked away, very calmly but very quickly, I remember. I could not see very well by then, and the pain was moving up my back toward my shoulder and neck, and I suppose my head and brain. It was a grudging pain. It stuck in one place, and then it moved.

I don't think I had sat for more than thirty seconds when Mike returned with Steve Watson, one of UNEXSO's diving supervisors. Even as Mike and Steve walked to me quickly, other diving instructors were beginning to initiate a diving emergency plan. Diving accidents are not time-forgiving accidents. Any problem is considered the most serious problem until the actual accident is diagnosed. People moved quickly, therefore.

Steve talked to me first, asking questions which sounded as casual as the briefing airline stewardesses give before a flight, but as important to me as that stewardess's orientation toward an escape door in a crash. John Englander joined us. John is the president of UNEXSO, a special friend, and as he, too, asked me the most innocent questions, another instructor placed an oxygen mask over my face. Pure oxygen is critical in diving accidents, since it helps to get more oxygen to oxygen-starved areas, such as the brain, and helps to reduce swelling. We walked to John's office, an instructor carrying my oxygen bottle, another walking by me, watching me closely. I did not know it then, but they all were prepared for me to pass out.

John already had Dick Clark, one of the world's authorities on diving accidents, on the phone. As I breathed oxygen, John described my symptoms. I could not hear Dick. But when John looked up at me and the instructors watching me and said, "Okay, we need to take him down," I was so very glad Dick was at home Saturday. And when John said, "Bubs, we need to take you down to 165 feet," I was especially glad he was home. That depth in treating diving accidents is normally only used for embolisms, air in the blood, blockages of the brain, things that can kill you.

In diving accidents, the most important, and at times only lifesaving, treatment, is called a recompression chamber. A chamber recompresses the air around you, taking your body and its gasses back to pressures similar to the depths of the ocean, the great pressure recreated there squashing things like air bubbles traveling in the bloodstream until they disappear. Because diving is such a statistically safe sport, and because chambers and the treatments are so expensive, chambers are scarce.

But there is a chamber at UNEXSO less than twenty feet from the docks. Four of us walked from John's office toward the chamber room. As we walked, others were cutting off the supply of air used to fill the scuba tanks and redirecting it to the chamber. Marian Wilson grabbed a gallon of orange juice from the Tide's Inn restaurant, while two others checked oxygen bottles and attempted to locate Doc Clement, the chamber's official doctor.

Kurt Alcorn, a new instructor in his twenties, red-haired, freckled, and quiet, volunteered to enter the chamber with me. Kurt's job was to watch me, take my pulse, listen to my lungs, take my blood pressure, administer resuscitation if I should pass out from either the embolism or oxygen toxicity.

The chamber looks like an iron lung. Made of steel, its interior is four feet ten inches by eight-and-a-half feet. It has two locks, one bed like an ambulance stretcher, a sound-powered telephone, and two small portholes. There is nothing electric inside it. Nothing flammable. No paper, no loose metals. Because of the great pressures created in chambers, the oxygen in the air is concentrated, and can flame up. No one has ever survived a recompression chamber fire.

Kurt and I spent six hours in that very close space. I was wearing an oxygen mask most of the time and could not talk. But I thought a lot. I had no control over my life whatsoever in that chamber. The four people just inches away, turning levers and controlling oxygen and air flow, ruled my life more completely than any jail tender ruled a prisoner's life.

A foolish, thoughtless decision had put my life in jeopardy. Because of that decision, my life was literally taken out of my control, and though I trusted the people running that chamber, I could not help but wonder what would happen to us if they turned a lever the wrong way. Or if an exhaust valve should rupture. Explosive decompressions turn people into spaghetti. And then I thought about people who've had strokes. An embolism is really like a stroke. What if the chamber hadn't been there? If I had died, that would have been the end of it, I guess. But what if I had been paralyzed? Left with a mind that couldn't will a body to do things? Any debilitating illness is probably like being isolated in that chamber, only worse. The thought reminded me of the red-and-white land crabs prized as a delicacy by most of us on the island. The crabs have powerful claws which give them mobility and protection. But when land crabs are caught, all of their appendages are broken off before the crabs are carried to local markets. The crab bodies sit on market shelves and the only way to know they are alive is to watch the jerky movement of their eyes.

And then, as the pain left me, as the air bubble in my bloodstream was crushed by the great pressure in the chamber, my mind went back to the sense of doom which had overcome me only minutes before as I stood on the dock. That moment defined "regret" for me in a way I cannot define for you. What was happening to me had been in my control and I had botched it. How many times had I made emergency ascents, ignoring the fact they were dangerous? Why did I think the rules didn't apply to me? Because of the chamber I was a very lucky person, was given a second chance to correct a needless risk. From that day on, Remar Sutton would rise to the surface at the lazy pace of a sea slug.

At five-thirty that afternoon, I crawled out of the chamber tired, somewhat sore, and feeling very mortal. Mary Abbott and Chris drove me home, and though it still sounds stupid, I went directly to my office to watch my new laser printer work.

My diving incident—I won't call it an accident, because it wasn't—gave me an opportunity to think about the elements of risk I confront in my own life, particularly concerning my health, and reminded me more forcefully than I wanted to know how many of those elements are under my control. Until this year my concerns about health were as immediate as my concern about an embolism. Rules of cause and effect didn't apply to me. Let me assure you that a confrontation with death reminds you they do.

Well, after this experience, I needed some reaffirmation of things less serious than mortality. The next morning I decided to take my final swoon walk before closing out this book. Because my swoon walks have been the subject of a good deal of press interest, and because I have openly confessed to cheating on my last swoon walk, I decided *this* one had to be judged as objectively as a Miss America beauty contest. (Those things are objective, aren't they?) I therefore asked Chris Scott to be the official judge.

I wore my newest and scantiest bikini. Before walking to the beach, I pumped up with some dumbells and a Z-bar loaded with eighty pounds of weight. Then I rubbed oil all over me. Oil-based suntan lotions burn the hell out of me, but they also make a hunk look even hunkier. Vanity always rules sense in swoon walks. Chris wanted to pump up, too, incidentally, but I stopped him. Swoon walk strategy always says, "Do away with competition."

We walked for about two miles on the beach, Chris slightly behind me, his eyes on other people rather than me. I had asked Chris to confirm each "hit" as it happened. A hit, in the vernacular of swoon walks, is a definite look of interest, appraisal of flesh. Looks at your face don't count. Ugly bodies can have handsome faces attached to them.

We had not walked by three people when Chris muttered under his breath, "By God, Remar there's your first hit!" My chest started to pump up even more until I saw the swooner. A guy. Thanks a lot. We walked on. I saw a middle-aged lady really stare at me. "Chris! Do you see it? Do you see it?" I muttered, trying my best to look disinterested. He had. That was number one. The lady virtually raped me with her eyes. It did take away a little of the effect as I saw her reach down and put on her glasses *after* she had raped me, but I think she needed them for reading, not swooning.

During the course of the walk, according to Chris Scott's account—and Chris wouldn't lie—two people actually swooned, one lady couldn't take her eyes off my crotch, the aforementioned guy looked at me again on the walk back, and one young maiden-type stared me down. There was some discussion about whether she was looking at Chris or me, but I'm sure she was choosing the maturity of a real man.

As I sent a knowing nod in her direction (it seemed to go right past her, for some reason), I remembered the one truly erotic night these months had brought to me, and leave you with this fond memory and true story as a hope for all less-than-perfect men who want a little lust thrust upon them.

I was sitting in the Tide's Inn talking with a group of college students from Georgetown University in Washington. The group had been drinking a lot, perhaps a mitigating circumstance in the incident that follows, but I like to think not. I had just regaled the group with juicy details about appearing on the "Donahue" show.

As I started to pick up my soda water, one girl, perhaps twenty, beautiful and rather wild-looking, without any encouragement on my part, lurched from her chair to mine, threw her arms around me, grabbed my head with both hands, and planted a french kiss on me with the passion I only remember experiencing in excellent pornographic movies in college. I think she was a weight lifter too, for her grip was so strong I couldn't push her off.

She did this in front of at least ten people (I have their names, if you need proof), and she then said several vulgar things to me I will cherish forever.

The suddenness of her attack, of course, took me off guard. But do you know what? I wasn't *that* surprised. I mean, my body looked better than it had in forty-five years. And then one of the girl's friends (the one taking her feet as they lugged her down the stairs) said, "She likes older men. Especially famous older men."

Well. Being attacked by a young beauty and called famous all in the span of ten minutes weren't exactly the things I had in mind when this year started. But they are close enough to my dreams to send me back to the beach right now for an impromptu stroll before the beauties. This hunkdom thing does have some serious responsibilities attached to it.

Muscles and Health,

GLOSSARY OF TERMS

aerobic—living in air, or utilizing oxygen

aerobic dance—an organized form of rhythmic movement set to music, which meets the requirements of aerobic or cardiovascular exercise. Two major forms of aerobic dance exist: a) high impact, which involves running in place, jumps, and leaps; and b) a new low-impact form, which utilizes marching, lunges, and side steps to keep one foot on the ground at all times and reduce trauma to the lower joints.

aerobics—a term used to describe an activity that uses oxygen as a method of obtaining energy. Such activities are usually continuous (at least twenty minutes), rhythmical (repetitive movements), and use large muscle masses such as the legs. This form of exercise places demands on, and improves, the cardiovascular and muscular endurance systems. Such activities include running, walking, swimming, biking, etc.

aging—the process of growing older; gradual decline in physical and mental health naturally occur during this process. This term can also be used in a more technical sense to refer to the genetic biology of the aging process.

alveoli—the smallest functional part of the lung. These tiny air sacs make contact with the capillaries, the smallest part of the circulatory system, where the exchange of oxygen and carbon dioxide take place.

amino acids—the building blocks of protein, twenty amino acids have been found to exist. Of these, eleven can be created in our bodies from the food we eat, nine others must be taken in through the diet. The best, most complete source of amino acids is animal protein.

anaerobic—without oxygen; this term usually describes brief, intense activity that does not require the immediate use of oxygen. For example, you can run fifty yards while holding your breath.

angioplasty—(percutaneous transluminal coronary) An operation which enlarges a narrowed coronary artery by inserting a catheter tipped with a small balloon. The balloon is inflated at the narrowing to enlarge the inside of the vessel.

aneurysm—A thinning, stretched out blood vessel wall. This weakened area can eventually burst and lead to internal bleeding and/or death of the tissue the vessel was feeding.

arteriosclerosis—a hardening of the arteries. Occurs mainly in old age, but heredity can cause it in younger people. If we live long enough, it will occur in all of us. It is characterized by the replacement of muscle and elastic tissue in the artery with fibrous tissue and calcified plaques.

arteries—the vessels responsible for carrying blood away from the heart. Arteries are composed of three layers, a smooth inside layer, a muscular middle layer, and an outside covering.

atherosclerosis—a term used to describe damage to the inside of the arterial wall, and the subsequent buildup of fat deposits and calcification in this damaged area. These circumstances narrow the artery and cause decreased blood flow to the area which they supply.

atrophy—the wasting away of tissue. If a weight lifter were to stop lifting all together, the muscle tissue he did not require for everyday use would be broken down by the body. The body will not support that which it does not need; in a sense, if you don't use it you'll lose it.

BAL (blood alcohol level)—the concentration of alcohol in the blood after drinking. the first consistent, sizable changes in behavior occur when BAL reaches .05 percent; a level of .10 percent is legally drunk, a state in which voluntary movements are seriously impaired; at .20 percent one is "falling down" drunk; past .40 percent or .50 percent the drinker is unconscious.

blood fat profile—the analysis of the fats which can be found in the bloodstream and which contribute to your overall state of health. This profile consists of triglycerides, total cholesterol, and the transporting form of this cholesterol and fat, HDL and LDL.

blood pressure—the measure of the force of blood against the arterial walls. There are two numbers in the blood pressure reading, 120 over 80 is usually considered to be a textbook normal. The top number, the systolic, indicates the pressure of the blood in the arteries as the heart contracts. The bottom number, the diastolic, indicates the pressure in the arteries between beats, when the heart is at rest. For high blood pressure, see hypertension.

body fat—the amount of fat that a person carries within the body. It is usually expressed as a percentage of the total body weight, so that a person weighing 100 pounds and having 20 percent body fat would have 20 pounds of fat. There are two forms of fat, essential and storage. Essential fat is that amount of fat which is necessary for survival (about 3 percent in males; 12 percent in females), while storage fat is the excess fat we carry in storage form. Body fat is best determined by percentage and not by body weight.

bomb calorimeter—a hollow steel container in which food is placed for measuring its caloric content. After the container is filled with oxygen, the contents are ignited and the amount of heat given off is collected by a pool of water surrounding the calorimeter. One calorie equals the amount of energy it takes to raise one liter of water one degree celsius.

bronchioles— small tubes in the lungs which carry air to the the alveoli.

bronchitis—an inflammation of the mucous membrane of the bronchial tubes which lead to the lungs. Chronic bronchitis usually consists of a cough and increased mucous secretion over a long period of time.

bypass surgery—a surgical procedure where a vessel (usually the saphenous vein from a leg) is put in place over an obstructed artery so that blood flow may be diverted away from the obstruction and continue to supply the heart.

calorie—a measurement of the energy content of food and physical work. One calorie is the amount of energy it takes to raise the temperature of one liter of water one degree celsius. If a food contained 100 calories, then it contains enough energy to raise the temperature of 100 liters of water one degree celsius. You will sometimes see this food calorie referred to as a kilocalorie (kcal), its more precise technical designation.

carbohydrates—a substance found in many foods, especially plants, which plays a major role in body functioning. Carbohydrates are usually termed "simple" or "complex." Simple carbohydrates are usually sugars that may contain no nutritional value (empty calories). Complex carbohydrates are found in plant products which contain vitamin and minerals for the diet.

cardiology—the study of the heart and its diseases.

cardiovascular—a term used to describe the heart, lungs, and blood transporting systems. The terms aerobic and cardiovascular are sometimes used synonymously, as the cardiovascular system transports oxygen to the working muscles.

catheter—a small, thin tube for entering into a body cavity.

cerebral hemorrhage—blood flow, usually from a burst vessel, into the brain.

chronic—long term; most often refers to a disease that progesses slowly and proceeds for a long period of time.

cholesterol—a fat-like substance found in all animal tissue, that is manufactured in many body cells, especially the liver. It is a constituent of body cells, an ingredient in certain hormones, and important for the formation of bile acids which aid digestion. Research has shown that a high level of blood cholesterol is associated with an increased risk of coronary heart disease.

circuit weight training—a form of weight training that involves a selected group of exercises performed in a sequential manner with predetermined exercise/rest periods.

cirrhosis—a progressive disease of the liver which causes damage to the liver cells.

COLD (COPD)—chronic obstructive lung (pulmonary) disease.

coronary heart disease—a term used to describe the excessive formation of atherosclerotic plaques in the coronary arteries which supply blood to the heart.

dysfunction—lack of regular function; abnormal function.

EKG—electrocardiogram; a measurement of the electrical activity of the heart.

EKG stress test—a physical exertion test usually performed on a treadmill or bicycle while the subject is hooked to an electrocardiogram. The heart's response to exercise can then be evaluated.

embolism—a floating clot in the bloodstream; This clot can lodge in a vessel, preventing blood flow. The result is death to the tissue being supplied.

embolus—a plug or stopper of clotted mass which clogs a vessel (plural- emboli).

emphysema—a lung condition characterized by destructive changes in, and a reduction in, the number of alveoli. This results in a considerable decrease in lung function.

endurance—the ability to resist fatigue. The term can be used in a weight lifting or aerobic sense.

enzyme—a chemical substance that acts like a catalyst (speeds up a reaction) in the body.

epidemiologist—a person who studies the occurence and spread of a disease in a population (a particular group of people).

exercise—a structured form of activity involving physical exertion. The term can be applied to almost any form of physical activity. Exercise is task specific. This means you will only obtain improvement in those areas that you work; aerobics improve the cardiovascular system, weight lifting gives you strength, stretching improves flexibility, etc.

fat—a term used to describe adipose tissue, the cells which store fat. Fat is not only stored as energy but serves many other important roles, including protecting and insulating internal organs, transporting and storing the fat soluble vitamins A,D,E,K, and depressing hunger. Dietary fats differ in their chemical structure. Saturated fats are associated with heart disease and are found in animal products. They are usually solid at room temperature. Unsaturated and polyunsaturated fats are of plant origin. They are usually liquid at room temperature.

fatty acid—a linkage of available energy substances (fats, carbohydrates, or proteins) which can be stored as fat, used as fuel, or used in a number of other bodily processes.

fitness—a state or condition of optimal performance.

free weights—barbells, dumbbells or any other form of nonrestricted weight.

fructose—a simple sugar found in fruit.

GGT—a liver function test.

glucose—the most common sugar found in the body. It is the only fuel our brain and central nervous system use.

glycogen—the storage form of glucose in the human body. Plants store glucose as starch.

hair implant—this term may be used to designate either the injection of individual artificial hairs into the scalp (a process discovered to be dangerous and rarely performed in the U.S. anymore) or the use of suture implants in the scalp to secure an artificial hairpiece.

hair transplant—a surgical procedure in which small plugs of hair-growing scalp are transferred to a bald area.

HDL cholesterol—high density lipoprotein cholesterol. Frequently called the "good" cholesterol, it may be responsible for removal of cholesterol from the body's periphery and returning it to the liver for breakdown and removal. HDL seems to be more affected by exercise than diet.

health—the absence of disease, a properly functioning organism.

heart attack—a general term used to describe a sudden affliction of the heart. Heart attacks can occur from a variety of circumstances including lack of blood flow, sudden trauma, irregularities of the heartbeat, etc.

hernia—the protrusion of a tissue through the structure that normally contains it.

hyperplasia—an increase in the number of cells of an organ or tissue.

hypertension—high blood pressure. This condition forces the heart to pump harder and can lead to heart failure and other problems over the years. Hypertension usually carries no symptoms. Blood pressure screening should be performed on a regular basis, at least every six months.

hypertrophy—an increase in the size of a cell or tissue.

ketosis—an acidic state of the body caused by the incomplete breakdown of fats. This may be caused by a high-fat diet, an absence of carbohydrates in the diet, and/or starvation diets. This condition may lead to depression of the brain and nervous system.

LDL cholesterol—low density lipoprotein cholesterol. Termed the "bad" cholesterol, LDL is responsible for the transport of cholesterol to the body's cells. LDLs are affected by the diet.

maximal workout range—performing an exercise movement throughout the greatest range of motion that the involved joint will allow.

metabolism—the total of all energy processes which occur in an organism. In the laboratory it can be measured by the amount of heat produced or the amount of oxygen consumed.

muscle tone—a condition in which the muscle is in a partial state of contraction. This gives it firmness and rigidity.

myocardial infarction—a lack of blood supply to the heart muscle which results in death to the tissue that was being supplied. This is one of the afflictions we generally term "heart attack."

Nautilus machine—a popular variable-resistance weight lifting machine that uses kidney shaped pulleys to vary the weight load.

obesity—a condition of excessive body fat.

ophthalmology—the branch of medical science dealing with the structure, functions, and diseases of the eye.

overweight—weighing more then the population average for your age and height. This is usually based on insurance tables.

plaque—a small, differentiated area on a body tissue. An atherosclerotic plaque is located on the inside of an artery and looks quite different from normal arterial tissue.

power—strength multiplied by speed; strength that has the element of time involved. If two people lift a 100-pound weight and one does it in two seconds, the other in one second, then the quicker individual is said to be more powerful. Almost all athletic events require power.

preventive medicine—the practice of intervention before the onset of disease. In the medical setting this usually involves questioning the individual for current lifestyle habits, testing present health and physical condition, a review of the test results, and a counseling session to bring about improvements.

protein—a vital substance needed by the body. Almost three quarters of the dry weight of a cell is made up of protein. Protein is valuable for the roles it plays in structure, enzymes, hormones, muscles, the immune system, acid-base system, and other important functions.

skinfold test—a "pinch" test where predetermined folds of skin are measured for determining the underlying fat content. A total body fat content is then extrapolated from these figures.

stamina—the ability to endure.

strength—the application of force, usually measured by a maximal single repetition in any form of weight lifting.

stroke—a general term used to describe a lack of blood flow to the brain tissue. This results in death to the region where blood supply has been cut off.

tar—the collective particle matter in tobacco smoke.

thrombosis—the formation of a clot in a blood vessel.

thrombus—a clot in the blood vessel formed during life from the normal "ingredients" that make up blood (plural- thrombi).

type A personality—a behavioral pattern typified by excess aggressiveness, time restraint, and competitive urgency.

underwater weighing—a means of determining body fat. It is considered the most accurate of body fat tests.

varicose veins—enlarged or dilated veins usually caused by malfunction of the valves in the veins which only permit blood to flow in one direction. Some known contributors to this condition are prolonged periods of standing, and pregnancy.

vascular—relating to the blood vessels, arteries, veins, capillaries.

veins—the vessels responsible for returning blood to the heart from the body's tissues.

GLOSSARY OF TERMS

WEIGHT LIFTING TERMS

bodybuilder—one who lifts weights for aesthetic purposes.

free weight—any form of free moving weight. Barbells and dumb-bells serve as the typical example, although anything from Heavy Hands to soup cans will qualify.

Nautilus machine—a weight lifting machine that uses a kidney shaped cam to vary the resistance you're lifting.

Olympic lifting—the competitive form of weight lifting involving strength and technique, found in the Olympic Games. It consists of two lifts, the clean and jerk, where the weight is hoisted to the chest and then lifted overhead, and the snatch, where the weight is taken from the floor and lifted directly overhead as the lifter squats under it and then stands.

overload principle—the concept that in order for gains or progress to occur, you must stress the body in that particular area at a greater rate than what is usually encountered.

periodization (or cycle training)—this training incorporates a time table made up of specific periods of different forms of training. For example, in weight training a power lifter cannot lift maximal weights all year round or he/she will experience overtraining and eventual fatigue or injury. The training may instead revolve around six-week periods; a light weight-high repetition (20+) phase to build endurance, a medium weight-medium repetition (10–12) phase to build size and gradual strength, and heavy weights-low reps (1–6) for strength gains. This cycle can be repeated throughout the year.

power lifting—a strength competition consisting of three lifts: the bench press, the squat, and the deadlift. The bench press is performed while lying on the back and consists of lifting a weight from the chest to arm's length. The squat places the barbell on the upper back, across the shoulder blades. The lifter then squats down until the thighs are parallel with the floor and stands up. The deadlift involves simply lifting a weight off the floor until the lifter is in the standing position.

strength training—a form of weight lifting in which primary emphasis is placed on the development of strength of the individual.

Universal machine—a variable-resistance machine that uses a lever system to vary the weight.

weight lifting—any form of resistance training. The goal can be strength, endurance, tone, or muscle size.

quarters—slang term for a twenty-five-pound weight plate.

Z-bar—a crooked bar that is usually used for bicep curling. It puts the hands in a more natural position.

N O T E S

Chapter 1

1.
Although conclusive evidence is not yet available, research currently in progress supports the relationship of fat distribution and a variety of disorders including diabetes, hyperlipidemia, coronary heart disease, etc. See, for example, A.H. Kissebah, et al., "Relation of Body Fat Distribution to Metabolic Complications of Obesity," *Journal Of Clinical Endocrinology and Metabolism*, 54:254–259, 1982. and B. Larsson, K. Svardsudd, L. Welin, et al., "Abdominal Adipose Tissue Distribution, Obesity, and Risk of Cardiovascular Disease and Death: Thirteen-year Follow-up of Participants in the Study of Men Born in 1913," *British Medical Journal* 288: 1401–4, 1984. Dr. Kenneth H. Cooper also discusses this phenomenon in *The Aerobics Program for Total Well Being*, (New York: Bantam, 1982) p. 221.

2.
You can read more about the relationship of health and fitness in G. Legwold, "Are We Running from the Truth About the Risks and Benefits of Exercise?", *The Physician and Sportsmedicine*, 13:136–148, 1985, and P. Raber, "Aerobic Exercise in Perspective . . .", *Rx Being Well*, Nov/Dec 1985.

3.
a) Y. Friedlander, J.D. Kark, Y. Stein, "Family History of Myocardial Infarction As An Independent Risk Factor for Coronary Heart Disease," *British Heart Journal*, 53:382–387, 1985.
b) A. Rissanen, "Premature Coronary Heart Disease: Ask About the Family," *Acta Medica Scandinavia*, 218:353–354, 1985.
c) K-T. Khaw, E. Barrett-Conner, "Family History of Stroke As an Independent Predictor of Ischemic Heart Disease in Men and Stroke in Women," *American Journal of Epidemiology*, 123:59–66, 1986.

4.
A.J. Stunkard, T.T. Foch, Z. Hrubec, "Twin Study of Human Obesity," *Journal of the American Medical Association*, 256:51–54, 1986.

5.
T.B. Van Itallie, "The Overweight Patient," *Clinical Implications of Nutrition*, 1(2):1–7, 1985.

6.

F.I. Katch, W.D. McArdle, *Nutrition, Weight Control, and Exercise* (Philadelphia: Lea & Febiger, 1983), pp. 134–135.

7.

K.H. Cooper, *The Aerobics Program for Total Well-Being*, p. 221.

8.

American College of Sports Medicine, "Position Stand on the Recommended Quality and Quantity of Exercise for Maintaining Fitness in Healthy Adults," *Medicine and Science in Sports and Exercise*, 10:vii–x, 1978.

9.

For more in-depth discussion of the factors associated with increased risk of heart disease, see the following articles:

a) S.M. Fox, J.P. Naughton, W.L. Haskell, "Physical Activity and the Prevention of Coronary Heart Disease," *Annals of Clinical Research*, 3:404–432, 1971.

b) L. Wilhelmsen, H. Wedel, G. Tibblin, "Multivariate Analysis of Risk Factors for Coronary Heart Disease," *Circulation*, XLVIII:950–958, 1983.

c) W.B. Kannel, D. McGee, T. Gordon, "A General Cardiovascular Risk Profile: The Framingham Study," *American Journal of Cardiology*, 38:46–51 1976.

d) "Lowering Blood Cholesterol to Prevent Heart Disease," *Nutrition Reviews*, 43:283–285, 1985.

e) R.A. Bruce, L.D. Fisher, K.H. Hossack, "Validation of Exercise-Enhanced Risk Assessment of Coronary Heart Disease Events: Longitudinal Changes in Incidence in Seattle Community Practise," *Journal of the American College of Cardiology*, 5:875–881, 1985.

Chapter 2

1.

The following articles give an overview of ongoing research on the relationship of activity to longevity. Your attention is particularly directed to the articles by Paffenbarger, who pioneered research in the field. The Monahan article provides a good, easily accessible summary.

a) T. Monahan, "From Activity to Eternity," *The Physician and Sportsmedicine*, 14:156–164, 1986.

b) R.S. Paffenbarger, R.T. Hyde, A.L. Wing, C. Hsieh, "Physical Activity, All-Cause Mortality, and Longevity of College Alumni," *New England Journal of Medicine*, 314:605–613 1986.

c) I. Holme, et al., "Physical Activity at Work and at Leisure in Relation to Coronary Risk Factors and Social Class," *Acta Medica Scandinavia*, 209:277–283, 1983.

d) R.S. Paffenbarger, et al., "Physical Activity as an Index of Heart Attack Risk in College Alumni," *American Journal of Epidemiology*, 8:161–175, 1978.

e) R.E. LaPorte, et al., "Physical Activity or Cardiovascular Fitness: Which Is More Important for Health?," *The Physician and Sportsmedicine* 13:145–149, 1985.

2.

a) American College of Sports Medicine, "Position Stand on the Recommended Quantity and Quality of Exercise for Maintaining Fitness in Healthy Adults," *Medicine and Science in Sports and Exercise*, 10:vii–x, 1978.

b) S.B. Gibson, S.G. Gerberich, A.S. Leon, "Writing the Exercise Prescription: An Individualized Approach," *The Physician and Sportsmedicine*, 11:87–110, 1983.

3.

R.S. Paffenbarger, R.T. Hyde, A.L. Wing, C. Hsieh, "Physical Activity, All-Cause Mortality, and Longevity of College Alumni," *New England Journal of Medicine*, 314:605–613, 1986.

4.

W.D. McArdle, F.I. Katch, V.L. Katch, *Exercise Physiology: Energy, Nutrition, and Human Performance* (Philadelphia: Lea & Febiger, 1986), pp. 157–158.

5.

G.L. Blackburn, K. Pavlou, "Fad Reducing Diets: Separating Fads from Facts," *Contemporary Nutrition*, vol.8(7), 1983, pp. 1–2.

6.

a) E.J. Drenick, H.F. Dennin, "Energy Expenditure in Fasting Obese Men," *Journal of Laboratory and Clinical Medicine*, 81:421–430, 1973.

b) G.A. Bray, "Effect of Caloric Restriction on Energy Expenditure in Obese Patients," *Lancet*, 2:397–398, 1969.

c) A.J. Stunkard, "Anorectic Agents and Body Weight Set Point,", *Life Sciences*, 30:2043–2055, 1982.

7.

R.H. Colvin, S.B. Olson, "A Descriptive Analysis of Men and Women Who Have Lost Significant Weight and Are Highly Successful at Maintaining the Loss," *Addictive Behaviors*, 8 (1983), p. 294.

8.

For a full discussion of the methods used by quacks and faddists to sell their ideas and wares, see Stephen Barrett, M.D., "Diet Facts and Fads"; and William T. Jarvis, Ph.D., and Stephen Barrett, M.D., "How Quackery Is Sold," in *The Health Robbers: How to Protect Your Money and Your Life*, edited by Stephen Barrett (Philadelphia: George F. Stickley, 1980), pp. 173–183 and 12–25, respectively.

Chapter 3

1.

Though many physicians report changes beginning as early as these time frames, remember that this may not be true for everyone. Changes may take longer to begin for some individuals. Also remember that these times represent the *beginning* of changes, not the end; change for the better continues over a much longer time if you follow the proper intake and exercise regimen. The following resources support the point made in the text and here.

a) W.R. Frontera, R.P. Adams, "Endurance Exercise: Normal Physiology and Limitations Imposed by Pathological Processes (Part 1)," *The Physician and Sportsmedicine*, 14:95–106, 1986. (cardiovascular changes)

b) P.A. Farrell, J. Barboriak, "The Time Course of Alterations in Plasma Lipid and Lipoprotein Concentrations During Eight Weeks of Endurance Training," *Atherosclerosis*, 37:231–238, 1980. (cholesterol changes)

c) Unpublished Cooper Clinic observations support changes beginning as early as these time frames.

d) G.H. Hartung, "Diet and Exercise in the Regulation of Plasma Lipids and Lipoproteins in Patients at Risk of Coronary Disease," *Sports Medicine*, 1:413–418, 1984. (an overview)

2.

The first article discusses fat-burning efficiency; articles (b) and (c) discuss the increase of pumping power, and articles (d) and (e) the increase of blood vessels.

a) P.D. Gollnick, B. Saltin, "Hypothesis: Significance of Skeletal Muscle Oxidation Enzyme Enhancement with Endurance Training," *Clinical Physiology*, 2:1–12, 1983.

b) B. Ekblom, et al., "Effect of Training on Circulatory Response to Exercise," *Journal of Applied Physiology*, 24:518–528, 1968.

c) M.H. Frick, A. Konttinen, H.S. Samuli Sarajas, "Effects of Physical Training on Circulation at Rest and During Exercise," *The American Journal of Cardiology*, 12:142–147, 1963.

d) P. Anderson, J., Henriksson, "Capillary Supply of the Quadriceps Femoris Muscle of Man: Adaptive Response to Exercise," *Journal of Physiology*, 270:677–699, 1977.

e) P. Brodal, F. Ingjer, L. Hermanscn, "Capillary Supply of Skeletal Muscle Fibers in Untrained and Endurance Trained Men," *Acta Physiologica Scandinavia*, supp.440:179(abs 296), 1976.

3.

a) F.I. Katch, W.D. McArdle, *Nutrition, Weight Control, and Exercise*, (Philadelphia: Lea & Febiger, 1983), pp. 162–164.

b) K.D. Brownell, A.J. Stunkard, "Physical Activity in the Development and Control of Obesity," in *Obesity*, edited by A.J. Stunkard (Philadelphia: W.B. Saunders Co., 1980), pp. 300–324.

4.

In "Diet Facts and Fads," in *The Health Robbers: How to Protect Your Money and Your Life* (Philadelphia: George F. Stickly, 1980), pp. 174–176, Dr. Stephen Barrett discusses how fasting was developed by Dr. George L. Blackburn as a strictly controlled, medically supervised last resort and how (as Dr. Blackburn had feared) the concept was seized upon by the popular press and radically distorted, misleading the public.

5.

F.I. Katch, W.D. McArdle, *Nutrition, Weight Control, and Exercise*, p. 258.

6.

For an excellent discussion of most available methods and the importance of body composition for different people, see J.H. Wilmore, "Body Composition in Sport and Exercise: Directions for Future Research," *Medicine and Science in Sports and Exercise*, 15:21–31, 1983.

7.

A.S. Jackson, M.L. Pollock, "Practical Assessment of Body Composition," *The Physician and Sportsmedicine*, 13:76–90, 1985.

8.

a) F.I. Katch, B. Keller, R. Solomon, "Validity of BIA for Estimating Body Fat in Cardiac and Pulmonary Patients, and Black and White Men and Women Matched for Age and Body Fat," *Medicine and Science in Sports and Exercise*, 18(2):S80, 1986.

b) H.L. Nash, "Body Fat Measurement: Weighing the Pros and Cons of Electrical Impedance," *Physician and Sportsmedicine*, 13:124–128, 1985.

9.

a) American Heart Association, *Heart Facts 1983*, (Dallas: American Heart Association, 1982).

b) American Heart Association, *Risk Factors and Coronary Disease: A Statement for Physicians 1980* (Dallas: American Heart Association, 1980).

c) J.T. Lampman, et al., "Effect of Exercise Training on Glucose Tolerance, in Vivo Insulin Sensitivity, Lipid and Lipoprotein Concentrations in Middle-Aged Men with Mild Hypertriglyceridemia," *Metabolism*, 34:205–211, 1985.

10.

W.B. Kannel, D. McGee, and T. Gordon, "A General Cardiovascular Risk Profile: The Framingham Study," *American Journal of Cardiology*, 38:46–51, 1980.

11.

H.A. Solomon, *The Exercise Myth*. (San Diego: Harcourt Brace Jovanovich, 1984), p. 37.

12.

If you'd like to immerse yourself in the subject, the following text for administrators is recommended: M.H. Ellestad, *Stress Testing: Principles and Practise* (Philadelphia: F.A. Davis Co., 1986).

For a shorter discussion of the same issues see the following:

a) N. Goldschlager, A. Selzer, K. Cohn, "Treadmill Stress Tests As Indicators of Presence and Severity of Coronary Heart Disease," *Annals of Internal Medicine*, 85:277–286, 1976.

b) J.B. Barlow, "The False Positive Exercise Electrocardiogram: Value of Time Course Patterns in Assessment of Depressed ST Segments and Inverted T Waves," *American Heart Journal*, 110:1328–1336, 1985.

c) A.F. Calvert, "True Sensitivity of Cardiac Exercise Testing," *The Medical Journal of Australia*, 140:131–135, 1984.

13.

a) American College of Sports Medicine, *Guidelines for Exercise Testing and Prescription* (Philadelphia: Lea & Febiger, 1986), pp. 1–8.

b) American Heart Association, *The Exercise Standards Book*, 1979; see pp. 31–39. You may find the same information in *Circulation*, 59:421A, 1979.

14.
Unpublished data from the Cooper Clinic.
15.
P.L. McHenry, "Risks of Graded Exercise Testing," *The American Journal of Cardiology*, 39:935–937, 1977.
16.
For further discussion of the type risks see, M.H. Ellestad, *Stress Testing: Principles and Practise* (Philadelphia: F.A. Davis Co.), 1986, pp. 119–126. In addition, B.F. Walker, "Cardiac Emergency—Sudden Death in Midlife," *Cardiovascular Medicine*, Jan:55–59, 1985, found that most people who died during exercise suffered from over 50 percent blockage of the coronary arteries.
17.
a) *The Merck Manual* 14th Ed., ed. R. Berkow (Rahway, N.J.: Merck Sharpe & Dohme Research Laboratorics, 1982), p. 381. The Merck Manual is a comprehensive diagnostic reference for physicians.
18.
a) See the section on "hypertension" in American Heart Association, *Heart Book: A Guide to and Treatment of Cardiovascular Disease* (New York: E.P. Dutton), 1980.
b) *The Merck Manual* 14th Ed., p. 393.
19.
National Center for Health Statistics, *Health USA 1985*, DHHS Publication Number (PHS)86–1232, 1985, pp. 16–17.
20.
These articles offer an overview of the treatment of high blood pressure with exercise:
a) M. McMahon, R.M. Palmer, "Exercise and Hypertension," *Medical Clinics of North America*, 69:57–70, 1985.
b) R. Fagard, "Habitual Physical Activity, Training, and Blood Pressure in Normo- and Hypertension," *International Journal of Sports Medicine*, 6:57–67, 1985.
c) J.J. Duncan, et al., "The Effects of Aerobic Exercise on Plasma Catecholamines and Blood Pressure in Patients with Mild Essential Hypertension," *Journal of the American Medical Association*, 254:2609–2613, 1985.
21.
For a more extensive discussion of this subject see the following:
a) R.J. McCunney, "The Role of Fitness in Preventing Heart Disease," *Cardiovascular Reviews and Reports*, 6:776–791, 1985.

b) K.H. Cooper, "Physical Training Programs for Mass Scale Use: Effects on Cardiovascular Disease—Facts and Theories," *Annals of Clinical Research*, 34:25–32, 1982.

c) G. Jennings, et al., "The Effects of Changes in Physical Activity on Major Cardiovascular Risk Factors, Hemodynamics, Sympathetic Function, and Glucose Utilization in Man: A Controlled Study of Four Levels of Activity," *Circulation*, 73:30–40, 1986.

d) R.D. Hagan, M.G. Smith, L.R. Gettman, "High Density Lipoprotein Cholesterol in Relation to Food Consumption and Running Distance," *Preventive Medicine*, 12:287–295, 1983.

e) A.S. Leon, "Physical Activity Levels and Coronary Heart Disease," *Medical Clinics of North America*, 69:3–19, 1985.

22.

American Heart Association, *Textbook for Advanced Cardiac Life Support*, 1983, p. 25.

23.

a) S.P. Van Camp, R.A. Peterson, "Cardiovascular Complications of Outpatient Cardiac Rehabilitation Programs," *Journal of the American Medical Association*, 256:1160–1163, 1986.

For further reading see:

b) L.W. Gibbons, et al., "The Acute Cardiac Risk of Strenuous Exercise," *Journal of the American Medical Association*, 244:1799–1801, 1980.

c) D.S. Siscovick, W.S. Weiss, R.H. Fletcher, et al., "The Incidence of Primary Arrest During Vigorous Exercise," *New England Journal of Medicine*, 311:874–7, 1984.

24.

a) K.H. Cooper, et al., "Physical Fitness vs. Selected Coronary Risk Factors: A Cross Sectional Study," *Journal of the American Medical Association*, 12:166–169, 1976.

b) H. Blackburn, "Concepts and Controversies About Prevention of CHD," *Postgraduate Medical Journal*, 52:464–469, 1976.

25.

a) R.S. Paffenbarger, et al., "Physical Activity, All-Cause Mortality, and Longevity of College Alumni," *The New England Journal of Medicine*, 314:605–613, 1986.

26.

The first article gives an overview of the issue. If you are interested in a more technical discussion, any one of the books [(b)–(f)] will offer this.

a) "The Physician and Sportsmedicine, Exercise and the Cardiovascular System," *The Physician and Sportsmedicine*, 7(9):54–74, 1979.

b) P. Astrand, K. Rodahl, *Textbook of Work Physiology* (New York: McGraw-Hill Book Co., 1977).

c) W.D. McArdle, F.I. Katch, V.L. Katch, *Exercise Physiology: Energy, Nutrition, and Human Performance* (Philadelphia: Lea & Febiger, 1986).

d) G.A. Brooks, T.D. Fahey, *Exercise Physiology: Human Bioenergetics and Its Applications* (John Wiley & Sons: New York, 1984).

e) M.L. Pollock, J.H. Wilmore, S.M. Fox, *Exercise in Health and Disease: Evaluation and Prescription for Prevention and Rehabilitation* (Philadelphia: W.B. Saunders Co., 1984).

f) P.S. Fardy, J.L. Bennett, N.L. Reitz, M.A. Williams, *Cardiac Rehabilitation: Implications for the Nurse and Other Health Professionals* (St. Louis: C.V. Mosby Co., 1980).

Chapter 4

1.
This figure is based on data found in American Heart Association, *Risk Factors and Coronary Disease: A Statement for Physicians*, 1980. Readers may also find this statement printed in *Circulation*, 62(1980):445A.

2.
Any one of these references provides an excellent discussion of what cardiovascular fitness entails:

a) P. Astrand, K. Rodahl, *Textbook of Work Physiology: Physiological Bases of Exercise* (McGraw-Hill, 1977).

b) American College of Sports Medicine, position stand on "The Recommended Quantity and Quality of Exercise for Maintaining Fitness in Healthy Adults," *Medicine and Science in Sports and Exercise*, 10:vii–x, 1978.

c) American College of Sports Medicine, *Guidelines for Exercise Testing and Prescription* (Philadelphia, Lea & Febiger, 1986).

d) P.B. Hultgren, E.J. Burke, "Issues and Methodology in the Prescription of Exercise for Healthy Adults," in *Exercise, Science, and Fitness* ed. E.J. Burke (Ithaca, NY: Mouvement Publications, 1980).

3.
Readers desiring an in-depth look at lactic acid metabolism will find an excellent presentation in G.A. Brooks, T.D. Fahey, *Exercise Physiology: Human Bioenergetics and Its Applications* (New York: John Wiley and Sons, 1984).

4.

D. Costill, *A Scientific Approach to Distance Running* (Los Altos, CA: Tafnews Press, 1979), p. 60.

5.

a) L.R. Gettman, M.L. Pollock, "Circuit Weight Training: A Critical Review of Its Physiological Benefits," *The Physician and Sportsmedicine*, 9:45–60, 1981.

b) L.R. Gettman, P. Ward, R.D. Hagan, "A Comparison of Combined Running and Weight Training with Circuit Weight Training," *Medicine and Science in Sports and Exercise*, 14:229–234, 1982.

c) J.H. Wilmore, R.B. Parr, et al., "Physiological Alterations Consequent to Circuit Weight Training," *National Strength and Conditioning Association Journal*, 4:17, 1982.

6.

P.F. Freedson, et al., "Intra-Arterial Blood Pressure During Free Weight and Hydraulic Resistance Exercise," *Medicine and Science in Sports and Exercise*, 16:131, 1984. Since, as this article shows, blood pressure is raised during lifting, it follows that persons suffering from high blood pressure should not pursue an activity that could place them at even greater risk.

7.

M.H. Kelemen, et al., "Circuit Weight Training in Cardiac Patients," *Journal of the American College of Cardiology*, 7:384–2, 1986.

8.

Flexibility is the range of motion around a joint. Flexibility need not be lost as a consequence of strength training, if it's done properly. While lifting weights, make sure that you are lifting throughout the full range of motion that the exercise will allow, and you may even gain flexibility. Of course, the best way to improve flexibility is through stretching and flexibility exercises. The loss of flexibility with weight training is an old myth that doesn't seem to want to die.

9.

The following articles present research on the impact of weight training on the cardiovascular system and on factors related to that system's health:

a) P.A. Farrnell, M.G. Maksud, M.T. Pollock, et al., "A Comparison of Plasma Cholesterol, Triglycerides, and High Density Lipoprotein-Cholesterol in Speed Skaters, Weightlifters, and Non-Athletes," *European Journal of Applied Physiology*, 48:77–82, 1982.

b) B.F. Hurley, D.R. Seals, J.M. Hagberg, et al., "High Density Lipoprotein Cholesterol in Body Builders vs. Power Lifters: Negative Effects of Androgen Use," *The Journal of the American Medical Association* 252:507–513, 1984.

c) R.C. Hickson, et al., "Strength Training Effects on Aerobic Power and Short Term Endurance," *Medicine and Science in Sports and Exercise*, 12:336–339, 1980.

d) B.F. Hurley, et al., "Effects of High Intensity Strength Training on Cardiovascular Function," *Medicine and Science in Sports and Exercise*, 16: 483–488, 1984.

Chapter 5

1.

For a more complete explanation of the causes of muscle soreness, see:

a) W.D. McArdle, F.I. Katch, V.L. Katch, *Exercise Physiology: Energy, Nutrition, and Human Performance* (Philadelphia: Lea & Febiger, 1986), pp. 392–396.

b) M.F. Bobbert, A.P. Hollander, P.A. Huijing, "Factors in Delayed Onset Muscular Soreness of Man," *Medicine and Science in Sports and Exercise*, 18(1):75–81, 1986.

2.

You'll find a full discussion of the reasons for warming up, and some of the consequences of not doing so, in the following:

a) R.J. Barnard, et al., "Ischemic Response to Sudden Strenuous Exercise in Healthy Men," *Circulation*, XLVIII:936–942, 1973.

b) B.D. Franks, "Physical Warmup" in *Ergogenic Aids and Muscular Performance*, ed. W.P. Morgan (New York: Academic Press, 1972).

c) U. Bergh, B. Ekblom, "Physical Performance and Peak Aerobic Power at Different Body Temperatures," *Journal of Applied Physiology*, 46:885–889, 1979.

3.

D.L. Costill, B. Saltin, "Factors Limiting Gastric Emptying During Rest and Exercise," *Journal of Applied Physiology*, 37:679–683, 1974.

4.

R.H. Dressendorfer, et al., "Plasma Mineral Levels in Marathon Runners During a 20-Day Road Race," *The Physician and Sportsmedicine*, 10:113–118, 1982.

5.

For a thorough discussion of what's best to drink during exercise, see the following:

a) American College of Sports Medicine, position stand on "The Prevention of Thermal Injuries During Distance Running," Indianapolis, 1985.

b) D.L. Costill, B. Saltin, "Factors Limiting Gastric Emptying During Rest and Exercise," *Journal of Applied Physiology*, 37:679–683, 1974.

c) D.L. Costill, "Fluids for Athletic Performance: Why and What Should You Drink During Prolonged Exercise," in *Toward an Understanding of Human Performance*, ed. E.J. Burke (Ithaca N.Y.: Mouvement Publications, 1980).

d) D.L. Costill, et al., "Effects of Elevated Plasma FFA and Insulin on Muscle Glycogen Usage During Exercise," *Journal of Applied Physiology*, 43:695–699 1977.

e) L. Levine, et al., "Fructose and Glucose Ingestion and Muscle Glycogen Use During Submaximal Exercise," *Journal of Applied Physiology*, 55:1767–1771, 1983.

6.

Two preliminary studies are:

a) P.B. Leatt, I. Jacobs, "Effects of Glucose Polymer Ingestion on Muscle Glycogen Utilization During a Soccer Match," *Medicine and Science in Sports and Exercise*, 18(2):S6, 1986.

b) M. Millard, K. Cureton, C. Ray, "Effect of a Glucose-Polymer Dietary Supplement on Physiological Responses During a Simulated Triathlon," *Medicine and Science in Sports and Exercise*, 18(2):S6, 1986.

See also, Bonnie F. Liebman, "Sports Drinks Slug It Out," *Nutrition Action Health Letter*, July/Aug. 1986, p. 11.

7.

a) S. Akgun, N.H. Ertel, "A Comparison of Carbohydrate Metabolism After Sucrose, Sorbitol, and Fructose Meals in Normal and Diabetic Subjects," *Diabetes Care*, 3:582–585, 1980.

b) P.A. Crapo, O.G. Kolterman, J.M. Olefsky, "Effects of Oral Fructose in Normal, Diabetic, and Impaired Glucose Tolerance Subjects," *Diabetes Care*, 3:575–582, 1980.

Chapter 6

1.

Position of the National Institute on Alcohol Abuse and Alcoholism cited in B. Liebman, "Drink for Your Health?," *Nutrition Action* (March, 1984), p. 12.

2.

Facts About Alcohol. U.S. Department of Health and Human Services, National Institute on Alcohol Abuse and Alcoholism, Publication Mc 81–1574, 1980, p. 8.

3.

For an interesting, informative discussion of how much social drinkers drink, when, and how, see Leonard Gross, *How Much Is Too Much: The Effects of Social Drinking* (New York: Random House, 1983). Mr. Gross's book provides a thorough, excellent presentation of the effects on health and behavior of social drinking and the questions surrounding the various issues.

4.

For a brief description of how alcohol is handled by the body, see *Facts About Alcohol & Alcoholism*, pp. 7–14, or "Alcohol in Perspective," *Consumer Reports*, July 1983, pp. 351–354. If you are interested in alcohol's effect at the cellular level, see Dora B. Goldstein, M.D., "Drunk and Disorderly: How Cell Membranes Are Affected by Alcohol," *Nutrition Today*, March/April 1985:4–9.

5.

a) *Facts About Alcohol & Alcoholism*, pp. 7–8.

b) "Alcohol in Perspective," p. 351–352.

6.

National Institute on Alcohol Abuse and Alcoholism, "The Fifth Special Report to Congress on Alcohol and Health," in *Alcohol Health and Research World 9* (Fall, 1984), pp. 20–21. See also, John R. Senior, M.D., "Alcoholic Hepatitis," *Alcohol Health and Research World 10* (Winter 85/86):40 43.

7.

If you would like to read some of the studies themselves, here are several of the most often cited. Though the popular media leapt on the findings, please note the caution with which all the researchers present their findings. See also, note 9 below.

a) C.H. Hennekens, et al., "Daily Alcohol Consumption and Fatal Coronary Disease," *American Journal of Epidemiology*, 107:196–200, 1978.

b) C.H. Hennekens, et al., "Effects of Beer, Wine, and Liquor in Coronary Deaths," *Journal of the American Medical Association*, 242:1973–1974, 1979.

c) W.D. Castelli, "How Many Drinks a Day?" (editorial), *Journal of the American Medical Association*, 242:2000, 1979.

d) K. Yano, et al., "Coffee, Alcohol, and Risk of Coronary Heart Disease Among Japanese Men Living in Hawaii," *New England Journal of Medicine*, 297:405–409, 1977.

e) M.G. Marmot, G. Rose, et al., "Alcohol Mortality: A U-shaped Curve," *Lancet*, 1:580–583, 1981.

8.

"Alcohol in Perspective," p. 352.

9.

Though various of these arguments are mentioned by other sources, you will find succinct, comprehensive presentations in Bonnie Liebman, "Drink for Your Health?," *Nutrition Action*, March 1984, pp. 10–13; and in "Beer or Skittles?," *Harvard Medical School Health Letter*, 11(Jan. 1986):1–2.

10.

"Study Links Heavy Drinking to Increased Risk of Stroke," *New York Times*, Oct. 23, 1986, p. A22. Drinking thirty or more drinks a week was associated with increased risk of stroke, even with smoking and high blood pressure taken into account.

11.

a) "Medical Consequences of Alcohol," from *The Fifth Special Report to Congress on Alcohol and Health*. pp. 19–25.

b) The Spring 1986 issue (Vol. 10, no. 3) of *Alcohol Health and Research World*, a journal produced by the National Institute on Alcohol Abuse and Alcoholism, focuses on the relationship of alcohol and cancer. "Overview: Alcohol and Cancer," by D.M. Podolsky, gives an excellent summary of current research findings, pp. 3–9.

c) Esteban Mezey, M.D., "Alcohol Abuse and Digestive Diseases," *Alcohol Health and Diseases World* 10 (Winter 85/86):6–9.

12.

"Medical Consequences of Alcohol," p. 67.

13.

Though the study of the effect of alcohol on sleep is complicated by such factors as the amount of alcohol consumed, the alcohol tolerance of an individual, the sleep and drinking history of an individual, the difficulty of testing a sleeping subject, etc., there is evidence that even a single drink before bed affects Rapid Eye Movement sleep during the first half of the night in many subjects. More restlessness has also been observed in some studies. There is little research on the effect on nonalcoholics of several drinks (such as one might consume during a party).

Heavy drinking and long-term alcohol abuse are associated with sleep disturbance. For a review of the subject, see Alex D. Pokorny, M.D., "Sleep Disturbances, Alcohol and Alcoholism: A review," in R. L. Williams, M.D. and Ismet Karcan, M.D., eds., *Sleep Disorders: Diagnoses & Treatment* (New York: John Wiley & Sons, 1978), pp. 233–260.

Chapter 7

1.

If you'd like to read more about the mechanisms of muscular growth, see:
a) N.A.S. Taylor, J.G. Wilkinson, "Exercise-Induced Skeletal Muscle Growth Hypertrophy Or Hyperplasia," *Sports Medicine*, 3:190–200, 1986.
b) W.J. Gonyea, D. Sale, "Physiology of Weight-Lifting Exercise," *Archives of Physical Medicine and Rehabilitation*, 63:235–237, 1982.
c) L.G. Shaver, *Essentials of Exercise Physiology* (Minneapolis: Burgess Publishing, 1981), pp. 259–264.
d) S. Salmons, J. Henriksson, "The Adaptive Response of Skeletal Muscle to Increased Use," *Muscle and Nerve*, 4:94–105, 1981.
e) P.D. Gollnick, et al., "Muscle Enlargement and Number of Fibers in Skeletal Muscles of Rats," *Journal of Applied Physiology*, 50:936–943, 1981.

2.
a) A.L. Goldberg, et al., "Mechanism of Work-Induced Hypertrophy of Skeletal Muscle," *Medicine and Science in Sports and Exercise*, 7:185–198, 1975.
b) R. Zak, "Nitrogen Metabolism and Mechanics of Protein Synthesis and Degradation," *Circulation* 72(suppl IV):IV-13—IV-17, 1985.

3.
a) T.V. Pipes, J.H. Wilmore, "Isokinetic vs. Isotonic Strength Training in Adult Men," *Medicine and Science in Sports and Exercise*, 7:262–274, 1975.
b) E.F. Coyle, et al., "Specificity of Power Improvements Through Slow and Fast Isokinetic Training," *Journal of Applied Physiology*, 51:1437–1442, 1981.

4.

The following position papers reflect the collective reasoning on steroids by two of the largest and most respected professional organizations in their fields.

a) American College of Sports Medicine, "The Use Of Anabolic-Androgenic Steroids in Sports," *American College of Sports Medicine Position Stands and Opinion Statements* (Indianapolis: 3rd Ed. 1985).

b) National Strength and Conditioning Association, "Position Statement: Use and Abuse of Anabolic Steroids," *The National Strength and Conditioning Association Journal*, 7:27, 1985.

5.

See E.L. Smith, "Exercise for Prevention of Osteoporosis: A Review," *The Physician and Sportsmedicine*, 10(3):74, 1982. Although there is evidence that stress placed on a bone will increase its mineral content, and though studies are underway on the possible effect of weight lifting on osteoporosis, the experts advise that there is as yet no conclusive scientific evidence that weight lifting will *reverse* the effects of osteoporosis. Since there is evidence that weightbearing activities such as walking or aerobic dance increase bone mass (see note 7 below), there is a good probability that lifting will be shown to be useful, particularly as a preventive measure. See note 6.

6.

Although studies are not yet complete, exercise physiologists speculate that since activities such as walking, jogging, or aerobic dance increase bone mass on the weightbearing bones, then weight lifting, which can place beneficial stress on other areas, *may* prove helpful in preventing or retarding bone mass. However, no one should rush into a program without consulting his or her physician. Remember, safety must always be a prime consideration. Using low weights and many repetitions is safer, and the exercise more closely resembles those weightbearing activities which have been shown to be helpful.

7.

The following articles discuss the kinds of benefits weightbearing exercise offers.

a) E.L. Smith, "Exercise for Prevention of Osteoporosis: A Review," *The Physician and Sportsmedicine*, 10(3):72–83, 1982.

b) C.E. Goodman, "Osteoporosis: Protective Measures of Nutrition and Exercise," *Geriatrics*, 40:59–70, 1985.

c) P.L. Fitzgerald, "Exercise for the Elderly," *Medical Clinics of North America*, 69:189–196, 1985.

d) R.J. Stillman, et al., "Physical Activity and Bone Mineral Content in Women Aged 30 to 85 Years," *Medicine and Science in Sports and Exercise*, 18:576–580, 1986.

8.

a) T.E. Auble, L. Schwartz, R.J. Robertson, "Cardiorespiratory Responses to Heavy Hands Exercise," *Medicine and Science in Sports and Exercise*, 18(2):s29 #140, 1986.

b) J.E. Zarandona, "Physiological Responses to Hand Carried Weights," *"The Physician and Sportsmedicine*, 14:113–120, 1986.

9.

a) C.R. Kyle, "Athletic Clothing," *Scientific American*, March:104–110, 1986.

b) C.R. Kyle, V.J. Caiozzo, "The Effect of Athletic Clothing Aerodynamics upon Running Speed," *Medicine and Science in Sports and Exercise*, 18:509–515, 1986.

10.

a) P.O. Astrand, "Human Physical Fitness with Special Reference to Sex and Age," *Physiological Review*, 36:307–335, 1956.

Chapter 8

1.

Kenneth H. Cooper, M.D., Ph.D., *"Running Without Fear: How to Reduce the Risk of Heart Attack and Sudden Death During Aerobic Exercise* (New York: M. Evans and Company, Inc., 1985).

2.

V.F. Froelicher, "Exercise Testing-Screening: Positive Tests in Asymptomatic Patients. Estimation of Severity of Coronary Heart Disease," cited in *The Exercise Myth*, Harold A. Solomon (San Diego: Harcourt Brace Jovanovich, 1984), pp. 37–38.

3.

You may find a good description of what cholesterol is and how the body uses it in A.C. Guyton, *Textbook of Medical Physiology*, 7th Ed. (Philadelphia: W.B. Saunders Co., 1986), pp. 825–826.

4.

Reported in Marion Burros, "Diet Guidelines Revised by Heart Association," *New York Times*, Aug. 27, 1986, p. C4.

5.

A.C. Guyton, *Textbook of Medical Physiology*, pp. 825–826.

6.

a) R. Ross, et al., "Endothelial Injury: Blood-Vessel Wall Interactions," *Annals New York Academy of Sciences*, 401:260–264, 1982.

b) S.M. Schwartz, "Disturbances in Endothelial Integrity," *Annals New York Academy of Sciences*, 401:228–233, 1982.

The physical processes in the development of atherosclerosis have not yet been conclusively determined. I have picked the explanation by Ross and colleagues because it gives a very clear picture of the total process which may be occurring, and the role the risk factors (which you can control) play in its development. Other noted authorities also excel in this area of study. The Nobel Prize was recently won by two Texas scientists (cited in reference [c]) who have devoted their work to the mechanisms of LDL cholesterol and its receptors in the body. Their work supports the idea that injury does not have to occur for the atherosclerotic plaque to develop (although injury surely helps). You may read about their work in:

c) M.S. Brown, J.L. Goldstein, "How LDL Receptors Influence Cholesterol and Atherosclerosis," *Scientific American*, 251:58–66, 1984.

7. and 8.

a) Information from the National Center for Health Statistics, U.S. Public Health Service, Department of Health and Human Services, 1980, cited in M.L. Pollack, J.H. Wilmore, S.M. Fox, *Exercise in Health and Disease* (Philadelphia: W.B. Saunders Co., 1984), pp. 3–4.

b) American Heart Association, *Heart Facts 1983*, Dallas, 1982.

9.

T. Corcos, et al., "Percutaneous Transluminal Coronary Angioplasty for the Treatment of Variant Angina," *Journal of the American College of Cardiology*, 5:1046–1056, 1985.

10.

You may read about some of the ongoing research on drug treatment for atherosclerosis in the following:

a) H. Engelberg, "Heparin, Heparin Fractions, and the Atherosclerotic Process," *Seminars in Thrombosis and Hemostasis*, II(1):48–54, 1985.

b) D.H. Blankenhorn, "Drugs to Produce Atherosclerosis Regression," *Atherosclerosis Reviews*, 12:1–8, 1984.

c) C. Nakazima, et al., "Roles of Smooth Muscle Cell in the Atherosclerotic Model and Effects of Drugs on the Atherosclerosis," *The Japanese Journal of Pharmocology*, 39:133, 1985.

11.

There has been a lot of publicity about the benefits of fish oil lately; a good summary of research findings can be found in reference (a). For more technical information in the area, see references (b) and (c). The remaining references discuss the effect of fiber on cholesterol and other blood factors.

a) J. Dusheck, "Fish, Fatty Acids and Physiology," *Science News*, 128:252–254 1985.

b) W.S. Harris, W.E. Conner, M.P. McMurry, "The Comparative Reductions of the Plasma Lipids and Lipoproteins by Dietary Polyunsaturated Fats: Salmon Oil Versus Vegetable Oils," *Metabolism*, 32:179–184 1983.

c) J.Z. Mortensen, et al., "The Effect of N-6 and N-3 Polyunsaturated Fatty Acids on Hemostasis, Blood Lipids and Blood Pressure," *Thromb Heamostas* (Stuttgart), 50:543–546, 1983.

d) "Dietary Fiber, Exercise and Selected Blood Lipid Constituents," *Nutrition Reviews*, 38:207–209, 1980.

e) J.W. Anderson, et al., "Hypocholesterolemic Effects of Oat-Bran or Bean Intake for Hyphercholesterolemic Men," *American Journal of Clinical Nutrition*, 40:1146–55, 1984.

12.

Here's only a sample of the extensive research which supports this statement.

a) R.J. McCunney, "The Role of Fitness in Preventing Heart Disease," *Cardiovascular Reviews & Reports*, 6:776–781, 1985.

b) S.M. Grundy, "Dietary Intervention—Diet and Hypercholesterolemia," *Cardiovascular Medicine*, Jan. 1985, pp. 39–52.

c) K.H. Cooper, "Physical Training Programs for Mass Scale Use: Effects on Cardiovascular Disease—Facts and Theories," *Annals of Clinical Research*, 14 suppl.34:25–32, 1982.

d) R.D. Hagan, M.G. Smith, L.R. Gettman, "High Density Lipoprotein Cholesterol in Relation to Food Consumption and Running Distance," *Preventive Medicine*, 12:287–295, 1983.

e) Z.V. Tran, et al., "The Effects of Exercise on Blood Lipids and Lipoproteins: a Meta-analysis of Studies," *Medicine and Science in Sports and Exercise*, 15:393–402, 1983.

f) P.D. Wood, W.L. Haskell, "The Effect of Exercise on Plasma High Density Lipoproteins," *Lipids*, 14:417–425, 1979.

g) P.A. Farrell, J. Barboriak, "The Time Course of Alterations in Plasma Lipid and Lipoprotein Concentrations During Eight Weeks of Endurance Training," *Atherosclerosis*, 37:231–238, 1980.

13.

a) P.A. Wolfe, "Risk Factors for Stroke," *Stroke*, 16:359–360, 1985.

b) P. Mustacchi, "Risk Factors in Stroke," *The Western Journal of Medicine*, 143:186–192, 1985.

14.

See the discussion in note 1, Chapter 3.

15.

M. Friedman, R.H. Rosenman, *"Type A Behavior and Your Heart* (Greenwich, Conn: Fawcett Publications Inc., 1974).

16.

J.S. Greenberg, *Comprehensive Stress Management* (Dubuque, Iowa: Wm. C. Brown Co., 1983). This book covers in depth the psychological aspects of handling stress.

Chapter 9

1.

If you are still a doubter, the following studies will convince you of the futility of spot reduction.

a) M. Noland, J.T. Kearney, "Anthropometric and Densitometric Responses of Women to Specific and General Exercise," *The Research Quarterly*, 49:322–328, 1978.

b) F.I. Katch, et al., "Effects of Sit-Up Exercise Training on Adipose Cell Size and Adiposity," *Research Quarterly for Exercise and Sport*, 55:242–247, 1984.

c) G. Gwinup, R. Chelvam, T. Steinberg, "Thickness of Subcutaneous Fat and Activity of Underlying Muscles," *Annals of Internal Medicine*, 74:408–411, 1971.

2.

Quoted in Richard Trubo, "Fad Diets: Unqualified Hunger for Miracles," *Medical World News*, Aug. 11, 1986, p. 46. Also, see Chapter 3, note 6.

3.

Quoted in Trubo, p. 46.

Chapter 10

1.

The old figures for cholesterol in shellfish included cholesterol and other sterols (chemical compounds resembling fat). Now we know that there is a distinction between the two, and that actual levels of cholesterol in shellfish are much lower than originally thought, so the cautions against eating shellfish have been dropped.

2.

Since many of the risk factors for stroke can be modified through proper eating habits, then it stands to reason that reducing your risk factors can reduce your chances of a stroke. Recommended reading: *Stroke: A Guide for the Family* (Dallas: American Heart Association, 1981).

3.

For an overview of the facts and controversies about vitamin supplementation see the following:

a) "Vitamin Supplements," in E.M. Hamilton, E.N. Whitney, *Nutrition: Concepts and Controversies*, (St. Paul: West Publishing Co., 1982), pp. 45–49.

b) "Some Facts and Myths of Vitamins," *FDA Consumer*, HHS publication No. (FDA) 79-2117.

c) D.A. Roe, J. Levinson, "Vitamin Facts & Fallacies," *Rx Being Well*, March/April 1985.

d) "The Vitamin Pushers," *Consumer Reports*, March 1986, pp. 170–175.

4.

"Nutrition: Food Nutrient Interactions," *Journal of Dentistry for Children*, May–June 1985, p. 206.

5.

Many food faddists hoping to make a quick buck often argue the opposite. But this opinion that people eating a varied and balanced diet from the four food groups don't need vitamin supplementation reflects the overwhelming and scientifically established opinion of trained professionals in the field of nutrition. For a fuller discussion, see:

a) E.M. Hamilton, E.N. Whitney, *Nutrition: Concepts and Controversies* (St. Paul: West Publishing Co., 1982).

b) F.I. Katch, W.D. McArdle, *Nutrition, Weight Control, and Exercise* (Philadelphia: Lea & Febiger, 1983).

c) "American Dietetic Association Statement: Nutrition and Physical Fitness," *Journal of the American Dietetic Association*, 76:437–443, 1980.

6.

"Vitamin Supplements," *The Medical Letter*, 27:66–68, 1985.

7.

a) F.R. Sinatra, "Food Faddism in Pediatrics," *Journal of the American College of Nutrition*, 3:169–175, 1984.

b) "Toxic Effects of Vitamin Overdosage," *Medical Letter*, 26:73–74, 1984.

c) R.M. Issenman, et al., "Children's Multiple Vitamins: Overuse Leads to Overdose," *Canadian Medical Association Journal*, 12032:781–784, 1985.

8.
a) R.M. Hanning, S.H. Zlotkin, "Unconventional Eating Practises and Their Health Implications," *Pediatric Clinics of North America*, 32(2):429–445, 1985.
b) V. Herbert, "Facts and Fictions about Megavitamin Therapy," *Journal of the Florida Medical Association*, 66:475–481, 1979.

9.
You can find tables of comparison for these and other foods in E.M. Hamilton, E.N. Whitney, *Nutrition: Concepts and Controversies*, pp. 573–609. Other good nutrition textbooks also have tables; ask your librarian for help.

10.
Food and Nutrition Board, *Committee on Recommended Allowances, Recommended Daily Allowances*, 9th ed. (Washington, D.C.: National Academy of Sciences, 1980).

11.
a) D.L. Elliot, L. Goldberg, "Nutrition and Exercise," *Medical Clinics of North America*, 69(1):71–82, 1985.
b) V. Aronson, "Protein and Miscellaneous Ergogenic Aids," *The Physician and Sportsmedicine*, 14:199–202, 1986.

12.
For a clear description of the process, see:
a) W.D. McArdle, F.I. Katch, V.L. Katch, *Exercise Physiology: Energy, Nutrition, and Human Performance*, (Philadelphia: Lea & Febiger, 1986), p. 8.
b) A.C. Guyton, *Textbook of Medical Physiology*, 7th ed. (Philadelphia: W.B. Saunders Co., 1986), pp. 816–817.

13.
a) "Dietary Fiber," *Harvard Medical School Health Letter*, 11(10):1–4, 1986.
b) R.M. Kay, "Dietary Fiber," *Journal of Lipid Research*, 23:221–236, 1982.
c) D. Kritchevsky, "The Role of Dietary Fiber in Health and Disease," *Journal of Environmental Pathology, Toxicology and Oncology*, 6:273–284, 1986.

14.
J.W. Anderson, et al., "Hypocholesterolemic Effects of Oat-bran or Bean Intake for Hypercholesterolemic Men," *American Journal of Clinical Nutrition*, 40:1146–1155, 1984.

15.

G.R. Newell, "Cancer Prevention: Update for Physicians, Four Years Later," *The Cancer Bulletin*, 37(3):103–107, 1985.

16.

F.C. Luft, M.H. Weinberger, "Sodium Intake and Essential Hypertension," *Hypertension*, 4(supp III):III-14—III-19, 1982.

17. and 18.

a) M. Jacobson, B.F. Leibman, "Dietary Sodium and the Risk of Hyvpertension," *The New England Journal of Medicine*, 303(14):817–818.

19.

a) P.C. Pozinak, "The Carcinogenicity of Caffeine and Coffee: A Review," *Journal of the American Dietetic Association*, 85:1127–1133, 1985.

b) T.L. Whitsett, C.V. Manion, "Cardiovascular Effects of Coffee and Caffeine," *American Journal of Cardiology*, 53:918–922, 1984.

Chapter 11

1.

This list of physiological factors affected by age was derived primarily from resources (c) and (d). Additional supporting data is found in the other two.

a) H.A. deVries, "Tips on Prescribing Exercise Regimens for Your Older Patient," *Geriatrics*, 35:75–81, 1979.

b) P.L. Fitzgerald, "Exercise for the Elderly," *Medical Clinics of North America*, 69:189–196, 1985.

c) G.A. Brooks, T.D. Fahey, *Exercise Physiology: Human Bioenergetics and Its Applications* (New York: John Wiley and Sons, 1984), pp. 683–700.

d) W.D. McArdle, F.I. Katch, V.L. Katch, *Exercise Physiology: Energy, Nutrition, and Human Performance*, 2nd ed. (Philadelphia: Lea & Febiger, 1986), pp. 563–570.

2.

Sharon Begley, "Why Do We Grow Old?," *Newsweek*, June 16, 1986, p. 61.

3.

a) P. Lemon, K.E. Yarasheski, D.G. Dolny, "The Importance of Protein for Athletes," *Sports Medicine*, 1:474–484, 1984.

b) I. Gontzea, R. Sutzescu, S. Dumitrache, "The Influence of Adap-

tation to Physical Effort on Nitrogen Balance in Man," *Nutrition Reports International*, 11:231–236, 1975.
4.
American Dietetic Association Statement, "Nutrition and Physical Fitness," *Journal of the American Dietetic Association*, 76:437–443, 1980.
5.
A.C. Guyton, *Textbook of Medical Physiology*, 7th ed. (Philadelphia: W.B. Saunders Co., 1986), p. 670.
6.
D.C. Cumming, et al., "Reproductive Hormone Increases in Response to Acute Exercise in Men," *Medicine and Science in Sports and Exercise*, 18:369–373, 1986.

Chapter 12
1.
a) H.A. deVries with Dianne Hales, *Fitness After Fifty* (New York: Scribner & Sons, 1982).
b) H.A. deVries, "Tips on Prescribing Exercise Regimens for Your Older Patient," *Geriatrics*, 35:75–81, 1979.

Chapter 13
1.
H. Kraus, *Clinical Treatment of Back and Neck Pain* (New York: McGraw-Hill, 1970).
2.
A. Melleby, *The Y's Way to a Healthy Back* (Piscataway, N.J.: New Century Publishers, 1982).
3.
a) G. Timothy Johnson, M.D., and Stephen E. Goldfinger, M.D., eds. *The Harvard Medical School Health Letter Book* (Cambridge, Mass.: Harvard University Press, 1981), p. 43.
b) T. Gerard Aldhizer, M.D., Thomas M. Krop, M.D., and Joseph Dunn, *The Doctor's Book on Hair Loss* (Englewood Cliffs, N.J.: Prentice Hall, 1983), pp. 55, 65, 80–88.
4.
You'll find an interesting presentation of the types of hair quackery in *The Doctor's Book on Hair Loss*, pp. 80–88, and in Herbert S. Feinberg, M.D., *All About Hair: Avoiding the Ripoffs, Making It Better, Replacing It If It Is Gone* (New York: Simon & Schuster, 1979), pp. 3–29.

5.

If you'd like to read more about hair weaving, you can do so in *All About Hair*, pp. 108–111. An interview with a cosmetologist who performs hair weaving is offered in John Mayhew, *Hair Techniques And Alternatives to Baldness*, (Owerri: Trado-Medic Books, 1983).

6 and 7.

For a good discussion of the pros and cons of these suture implants, see *All About Hair*, pp. 113–114, or *The Doctor's Book on Hair Loss*, pp. 103–105.

8.

If you are contemplating a hair transplant, you may want to read about it in several sources. The following books have clear, illustrated discussions and arc available in many libraries.

a) *The Doctor's Book on Hair Loss*, pp. 109–122.

b) *All About Hair*, pp. 117–166.

c) James J. Reardon, M.D., and Judi McMahon, *Plastic Surgery for Men: The Complete Illustrated Guide* (New York: Everest House, 1981), pp. 67–85.

d) Dr. Walter P. Unger & Sidney Katz, *The Intelligent Man's Guide to Transplants and Other Methods of Hair Replacement* (Chicago: Contemporary Books, Inc., 1979).

9. Anastasia Toufexis, "Some Bald Facts About Minoxidil," *Time*, July 14, 1986, p. 43.

10.

"Going Bald? 'Miracles' May Be Costly—and Risky," *Business Week*, July 28, 1986 p X.

11.

Toufexis, *Time*, p. 43.

12.

"Dental Implants," an interview with Dr. Paul Schnitman, head of the Department of Implant Dentistry at the Harvard School of Dental Medicine, in *The Harvard Medical School Health Letter* 11 (Oct. 1986): 5–8.

13.

Marilyn Linton, The new price of a smile, *MacLeans*, Jan. 28, 1985, p. 48.

14.

a) Marshal F. Goldsmith, "*Caveat Emptor* tops the eyechart for radial keratotomy candidates," *Journal of the American Medical Association* 254 (Dec. 27, 1985):3,401–3,403.

b) Maureen K. Lundergan, M.D., George L. White, Jr., M.S.P.H., and Richard T. Murdock, "What Patients Should Know About Radial Keratotomy," *American Family Physician* 33 (May 1986):169–172.

c) "The Nearsighted Operation," *The Health Letter* 27 (Jan. 1986):2–3.

d) "Radial Keratotomy: an Unkind Cut?," *Science News* 128 (Oct. 12, 1985):229.

15.

For an excellent summary of the issues and events in the case, see Colin Norman, "Clincial Trial Stirs Legal Battles," *Science* 227 (March 15, 1985):1,316–1,318. See also Karen Freifeld, "Myopic Haste?," *Forbes* (May 6, 1985): 95–98.

16. and 17.

"Follow-up and Feedback: Surgery for Nearsightedness," *Harvard Medical School Health Letter*, 10 (Oct. 1985):8.

Chapter 14

1.

"Vitamin Supplements," in Eva May Nunnelley Hamilton and Eleanor Noss Whitney, *Nutrition, Concepts and Controversies*, 2nd Edition, (St. Paul: West Publishing Company, 1982), pp. 45–49, includes an excellent discussion of this and other points.

For a longer look at the issues related to vitamins and "natural" foods, see Victor Herbert, M.D., J.D., and Stephen Barrett, M.D., *Vitamins and "Health" foods: The Great American Hustle* (Philadelphia: George F. Stickley Company, 1982).

2.

W.H.B. Denner, "Colourings and Preservatives in Food," *Human Nutrition: Applied Nutrition* 38A:435-449, 1984.

3.

a) James DeBrosse, "Some Patients Lose Only Money: Some Pay with Their Lives," *St. Petersburg Times*, Sunday, July 29, 1984.

b) James DeBrosse, "FDA Has Strict Rules on Health Product Claims," *St. Petersburg Times*, July 30, 1984.

c) James DeBrosse, "FDA, Industry Dispute Value of Herb Use," and "Herbalife Rally," in *St. Petersburg Times*, July 31, 1984.

   The above articles are part of a series written by James DeBrosse, who holds master's degrees in public health as well as journalism. The FDA Press Office and many FDAers encouraged the series, publication of which was delayed because of threats of prepublication suits against the *Times*. Readers who wish to read the whole series will find it reprinted in the *Health* volumes of the *Social Issues Resources Series* (*SIRS*) in most libraries.

d) William T. Jarvis, Ph.D. and Stephen Barrett, M.D., "How Quackery Is Sold," in *The Health Robbers*. Stephen Barrett,M.D. ed., Second Ed. (Philadephia: George F. Stickly Company, 1980), pp. 12–25.

e) William T. Jarvis, "Food Faddism, Cultism, and Quackery," *Annual Review of Nutrition*, 3:35–52, 1983.

4.

William Jarvis, quoted in "Quick Hits," in *50 Plus*, July 1986, p. 12. Also in personal phone interview.

5.

Quoted in James DeBrosse, "Some People Lose Only Money. . . ."

6.

a) Eva May Nunnelley Hamilton and Eleanor Noss Whitney, *Nutrition, Concepts and Controversies*, p. 19.

b) Michael A. Dubick, "Dietary Supplements and Health Aids—A Critical Evaluation, Part 3—Natural and Miscellaneous Products," *Journal of Nutrition Education*, 15(1983): 123–129.

7.

a) "Cytotoxic Testing Advertised As Money Maker," *National Council Against Health Fraud Newsletter* 8 (March/April 1985):3.

b) "Cytotoxic Testing," *Nutrition and the M. D.* 11(1985):1.

c) "Pennsylvania Prohibits Cytotoxic Testing for Food Allergies," *National Council Against Health Fraud Newsletter*, 8(Nov./Dec. 1985): 1.

d) "Hair Analysis," *Harvard Medical School Health Letter* 11(June 1986), p. 8.

e) S. Barrett, "Commercial Hair Analysis: Science or Scam?," *Journal of American Medical Association* 254:1041, 1985.

8.

a) Dubick, p. 125.

b) Judith Willis, "About Body Wraps, Pills and Other Magic Wands," *FDA Consumer*, Nov. 1982. pp. 18–19.

9.

a) "What's This Glucomman?," *FDA Consumer*, Feb. 1984, p. 31.

b) Willis, p. 19.

10.

a) Stephen Barrett, M.D., "Diet Facts and Fads," in *The Health Robbers*, p. 181.

b) Willis, p. 19.

11.

Leo Tolstoy, *War and Peace*, trans. Ann Dunnigan (New York: New American Library), p. 790.

Chapter 15

1.

The Health Consequences of Smoking: Chronic Obstructive Lung Disease, report of the surgeon general. U.S. Department of Health and Human Services, DHHS Publication No. (PHS) 84-50205, 1984, p. 417. The urban dweller breathes in an average of two milligrams of particulate matter from the air per day; the smoker of two packs of cigarettes a day at twenty milligrams tar, about 800 mg.

2.

As reported in "Number of Adult Smokers Down by 7 Percent Since 1976, Study Shows," The Miami Herald, Oct. 19, 1986, p. 12A.

3. and 4.

a) *The Health Consequences of Smoking: Chronic Obstructive Lung Disease*, p. 417.

b) *The Health Consequences of Smoking: Cardiovascular Disease*, report of the surgeon general. U.S. Department of Health and Human Services, DHHS Publication No. (PHS) 84-50204., 1984, pp. 206–208.

5.

You can find this information in many places, but a very clear description may be found in Doctors Myra B. Shayevitz and Berton R. Shayevitz, *Living Well with Emphysema and Bronchitis* (New York: Doubleday, 1985), which is available in many public libraries. For a much more technical discussion, see Chapter 5, "Mechanisms by Which Cigarette Smoke Alters the Structure and Function of the Lung," in *The Health Consequences of Smoking: Chronic Obstructive Lung Disease*, pp. 251–328.

6.

For a review of the research on the various ways in which smoke damages the lung, see "Cigarette Smoke Toxicology," in *The Health Consequences of Smoking: Chronic Obstructive Lung Disease*, pp. 426–450.

7.

Health Consequences of Smoking: Chronic Obstructive Lung Disease, p. viii.

8.

National Center for Health Statistics, *Health USA 1985*, DHHS Publication No. (PHS) 86-1232, Dec. 1985, p. 16.

9.

Health USA 1985, p. 16.

10.

The figure was given to us in a phone interview with the office. Earlier printed sources put the figure at 340,000, but at least one authority, Dr. Elizabeth Whelan, writing as executive director of the American Council on Science and Health, put the estimate of premature deaths associated with smoking at 400,000 ("Big Business vs. Public Health: The Cigarette Dilemma," *USA Today* [magazine], May 1984, p. 62).

11.

U.S. Department of Health and Human Services, Public Health Services, Office on Smoking and Health, *A Physician Talks About Smoking: A Slide Presentation* (Title document No. A14700), p. 27.

12.

a) *A Physician Talks About Smoking*, p. 7.

b) See also, *The Health Consequences of Smoking: Cancer*, a report of the Surgeon General, U.S. Department of Health and Human Services, DHHS Publication No. (PHS) 82-50179, 1982.

c) *Smoking, Tobacco, & Health: A Fact Book*, U.S. Department of Health and Human Services. DHHS Publication No. (PHS) 80-50150.

13.

a) Whelan, "Big Business vs. Public Health: The Cigarette Dilemma," p. 63.

b) *The Health Consequences of Smoking: Cancer*, pp. vi–vii, 5–8.

14.

Facts About Smoking and Your Health, U.S. Department of Health and Human Services. This pamphlet is excerpted from the text of Dr. Koop's Nov. 17, 1983 press conference announcing the release of the 1983 *Report on the Health Consequences of Smoking: Cardiovascular Disease*. For further information consult this volume, pp. iii–vii.

15.

Facts About Smoking and Your Heart.

16.

The following articles will give you an overview of the relationship of smoking and heart disease.

a) David W. Kaufman, Constituents of Cigarette Smoke and Cardiovascular Disease, in *The Cigarette Underworld*, ed. Alan Blum, M.D., a publication of the Medical Society of New York (Secaucus, N.J.: Lyle Stuart, Inc., 1985), p. 27.

b) Lloyd W. Klein, M.D., "Effects of Cigarette Smoking on Systemic and Coronary Hemodynamics," in *The Cigarette Underworld*, pp. 24–26.

c) See also, *Health Consequences of Smoking: Cardiovascular Disease*, pp. 209–219 for a discussion of the effects of nicotine, and pp. 219–224 for those of carbon dioxide.

17.

a) "Older People and Smoking," *From the Surgeon General*, a newsletter published by U.S. Department of Health and Human Services, Public Health Service, 1986.

b) Robert Lee Holtz, "It's Never Too Late to Stop Smoking," *Atlanta Constitution*, June 4, 1985, p. 4A.

18.

David Kaufman, "Constituents of Cigarette Smoke and Cardiovascular Disease," *The Cigarette Underworld*, p. 27.

19.

T.F. Pechacek, A.R. Folsom, R. de Gaudermaris, et al., "Smoke Exposure in Pipe and Cigar Smokers Serum Thiocyanite Measures," *Journal of American Medical Association*, 254:3330–3332, 1985.

20.

Jack Henningfield of the Addiction Research Center of the National Institute of Drug Abuse, quoted in Diane E. Edwards, "Nicotine: A Drug of Choice," *Science News*, 129 (Jan. 18, 1986):44.

21.

For a further description of the addictive qualities of nicotine see:

a) Edwards, "Nicotine: A Drug of Choice," pp. 44–45.

b) William Pollin, M.D., "Why People Smoke Cigarettes," a statement developed from testimony before Congress by the director of the National Institute on Drug Abuse, March 16, 1982. PHS Publication No. (PHS) 83-50195.

22.

I have drawn these types from the National Institute of Health pamphlet, "Why Do You Smoke?," NIH Publication No. 84-1822, 1984. It includes a short self test.

23.

The U.S. Office on Smoking and Health has free materials to help you quit; write and ask them.

24.
"What RPH's [Registered Pharmacists] Should Know Re New Smoking Cessation Drug," *American Druggist*, March 1984, pp. 108–110.
25.
"Gum to Help You Stop Smoking," *Consumer Reports*, Aug., 1984, pp. 434–435.

Chapter 16

1.
B. Stamford, "Massage for Athletes," *The Physician and Sportsmedicine*, 13:178, 1985.
2.
For a complete guide to biofeedback applications, see G.E. Schwartz and J. Beatty, eds., *Biofeedback: Theory and Research* (New York: Academic Press, 1977).

R E S O U R C E   O R G A N I Z A T I O N S

National Council Against
Health Fraud
P.O. Box 1276
Loma Linda, CA 92354
*You may receive a bimonthly
newsletter at $15 per year.*

Lehigh Valley Committee
Against Health Fraud
P.O. Box 1602
Allentown, PA 18105
*Information on consumer health,
quackery, and health frauds.*

U.S. Department of Agriculture
Food and Nutrition Information Center
10301 Baltimore Blvd.
Beltsville, MD 20705
*Provides information on nutri-
tion and diet.*

Food and Drug Administration
5600 Fishers Lane
Rockville, MD 20857

The American Dietetic Association
430 North Michigan Ave.
Chicago, IL 60611

American Heart Association
7320 Greenville Ave.
Dallas, TX 75231

American Medical Association
535 North Dearborn St.
Chicago, IL 60610

American Cancer Society
777 Third Ave.
New York, NY 10017

American Lung Association
1740 Broadway
New York, NY 10019

Office on Smoking and Health
U.S. Department of Health,
Education, and Welfare
5600 Fishers Lane
Park Building, Room 110
Rockville, MD 20857

The National Strength and
Conditioning Association
Journal
P.O. Box 81410
Lincoln, NE 68501
*A great place to get a compre-
hensive view on weight train-
ing; used by many strength
coaches.*

I N D E X